THE
CASTLE

The Sean Rooney Psychosleuth Series

Tom O. Keenan

MᶜNIDDER | *&*
GRACE
CRIME

Published by McNidder & Grace
21 Bridge Street
Carmarthen SA31 3JS
Wales, UK
www.mcnidderandgrace.com

Original paperback first published 2023
© Tom O. Keenan

A catalogue record for this work is available from the British Library.

ISBN: 9780857162427
Ebook: 9780857162434

Designed by JS Typesetting Ltd, Porthcawl
Cover design: Tabitha Palmer

PART ONE

CHAPTER 1

Stephenson rubs his eyes and squints at his watch. It's three in the morning. He's a nurse, but he's the same as the rest, a keeper not a carer. On the night shift, he'll do his walk-through, and be back in ten to resume his nap. Stretching his arms above his head he peers down the ward, pushes himself up on the arms of the chair, set strategically at the top of the ward, and gets to his feet. Making his way down through the dormitory, he passes rows of beds on each side, identifying the patients by their snores, coughs, cries, and the things they mutter in their sleep.

Reaching the middle of the ward, he taps the glass on a large tank to stir the terrapins. Comparing them with the patients under his care, he'll watch them, feed them, keep them safe and secure: the feeble safe and those detained on long-term hospital orders secure. Most are a risk to themselves, others pose risk to others. The inadequates and the demented are easy, he thinks, but the psychotics and the psychopaths are hard work, they need watching and the occasional jag. Knocked out, strapped to the bed, they'll be off to the secure ward if they don't settle. Care in the community is a long way off for these men, as are patients' rights. He doesn't care for rights.

He'll wake them at six thirty, get them to the bathroom, showered and clothed for the procession to the cavern-like dining room for breakfast, along with the other fourteen hundred or so patients. Most in this ward have been there for more than ten years, some thirty, a few for most of their lives. Some are in their sixties and seventies. These patients are going nowhere, except in a box to the hospital cemetery.

Though it's just past three and dark, the light from the glazed corridor gives an eerie glow through the internal windows of the ward. It silhouettes the human mounds, fifteen to each side. Provided they're all quiet, he likes the night shift. After they're put to bed, he'll get a few hours kip, do the walk-through and return to his cosy armchair.

Stephenson moves closer to the toilet at the end of the dormitory and notices the last bed to the right is empty. This is Oliver Turnbull's bed. Oliver is known to need the toilet numerous times through the night due to a prostate problem, why he is allocated the nearest bed. He shakes his head and moves into the toilet. Oliver is nowhere to be seen, but a closed cubicle confirms he'll be in there.

He knocks on the door.

"Oliver, you in there? Time you were back in your bed." There's no answer. "Oliver, I hope you're no' masturbating again." He shakes his head again. "Bloody man has no shame."

He leans on the door.

It swings open and the sight makes him recoil. Before him hangs Oliver's body, his neck held by a plastic rope entangled around the hinge on the window. His bleary, poking, dead eyes stare out at him. He recoils once more as the eyes appear to gaze accusingly at him, as if to punish him for his constant haranguing and denigration. He suddenly feels guilty for being horrible to him. He lifts the body to release the neck from the window hinge. It comes away easily. He was frail, old, weak.

He lets Oliver slip to the floor. He's well dead. Another suicide, another report for the physician superintendent and the management group. A new policy on ligatures, another bed to offer another man going nowhere. Another referral to the social work department to go out and tell relatives he doesn't have. Another interment into the graveyard with or without a funeral.

Although suicides are common in the hospital, few are on the ward, most are in the grounds by hangings from the trees, drownings in the loch, sometimes on the railway track.

He hates the formality of the process which will occur next.

He makes his way back through the ward to get to the nurses' office. He'll call the porters to move the body to the mortuary and have the toilet area cleaned and returned to normality for the patients to use three hours later. There'll be some explaining to do, especially to those friends with Oliver. Some will be upset. He takes a mental note to ensure he has adequate Midazolam should others go off it or react aggressively.

CHAPTER 2

My feet crunch through glass-sheet frost as I walk from the car park to the front door of the hospital. This one door entry into a world of the bizarre fascinates and scares me in equal measure. I always wondered what lay behind this door separating the world of the sane with the insane.

It's Monday, the 25th of January 1982, and, as a student psychologist three quarters through my course, I'm embarking on my placement at Hillwood Psychiatric Hospital. I requested this placement. On the surface I need to develop my understanding of mental illness and of asylums, but, personally and stupidly, I need to know what goes on in here.

The Castle, as it's called locally, has intrigued me my whole life. I know passing through these doors will change my life. This is before opinions alter about these large institutions warehousing people. This place is notorious; those who come here seldom leave. This is an in-door without an out, a step into Victorian care, a portal to the underworld of the mad, a personal introduction to Hades.

I stop at the step, indented from multitudes of feet, and recall how my mother once had an old red Bakelite phone in our hall. She'd lift it occasionally should she need it and call into the mouthpiece.

"Yes, is that Hillwood, I can't control him anymore, could you come and get him?"

This usually worked and I would spend the rest of the day peering through my bedroom window, waiting for the white van to come around the corner to take me away. That the phone had never been connected since the last occupier of the house was lost on me, the effect was absolute and successful. I would remain quiet until the next time it was needed.

I look up to the twin clock towers which resemble the battlements and turrets of many Scottish castles, square with gaps. They stand like sentinels in each side of the main hospital administration building,

5

ready to reach for me, grab me in a stone vice grip, and fire me off into Hillwood Loch with other unwelcome visitors. The Castle keeps people out and holds those inside in. Built in Baronial style, this lunatic asylum, as it was called in the late nineteenth century, was to house five hundred patients. It grew, however, to accommodate over fifteen hundred souls, with additional wards constructed to cope with the large influx of damaged minds.

I approach the doors with all the courage of a cat approaching a hedgehog. I hesitate before going through this entrance to the netherworld. I'm early as usual, but this isn't the reason for my hesitation. I'm shit scared. I retreat to the bench in the car park for a few minutes to summon some bottle.

The local bus that travels through the hospital grounds dropping off and picking up staff and relatives stays a bit longer than necessary at the stop.

I hear the driver say, "You one of the woodentops?" I ignore it on the basis he's an arse. "I'm saying, are you one of they woodentops?"

I look along the side of the bus. I see some folk. Some older women heading into town to shop, children going to school, those hiding behind newspapers trying not to engage with the driver's laughter, others enjoying the entertainment. The driver grows impatient at my lack of response. Is he looking for a Bonnie Prince Charlie or a Jesus Christ? He gets neither, he gets me, Sean Rooney, a raw recruit into the redoubtable ranks of the head shrinks. No entertainment this day, he moves away.

It's time for me to enter. I approach the door with the courage of the hedgehog approaching the cat, quills poised. I wonder how many poor folks had travelled through this never-to-return-home door. It looks impenetrable, massive, solid. I stand looking at it, from bottom to the top, from side to side. The doors are old, battered, and worn around the handle.

If I turn around now and walk away I could be back to my own world unchanged, none the worse, and none the wiser for being at this door to the unknown.

A large lady pushes past me.

"You no' going in?" she says. "It's no' loaked."

No' loaked? But they'll escape!

She holds the door open for me as I creep across this entry from everywhere to nowhere. Of course there'll be a burly guard on the inside to frisk me and spit me back out. He'll ask my business in being there, tell me I have a few hours sightseeing before the door is bolted from the inside, then no one will get out or in, ever again. Then, magically, I'm in and the door gently returns back to keep the wind and normal folks out.

Although this's a one door entry, most wards have their own locked access. This door is seldom locked, but it doesn't matter; when closed, it's as impenetrable as a lowered portcullis. I move farther in and approach a half-closed window with a sign above it.

"Re-cept-tion," I say, peering up at it.

"Aye," comes from behind a large typewriter. "What do you want?"

Shit, I have to talk to it.

"I've to go to the Psychology Department."

"Up the east corridor, just past the Social Work Department and the Patient's Shop. You'll see the sign." The words emanate upwards from a head unwilling to reveal a face. "You could have gone up the west corridor, that's because most departments have doors into both corridors to allow the same access for the men and the women patients."

"Oh, equal opportunity?"

The head turns upwards to reveal piercing bespectacled eyes that have all the emotions of a dead dog.

"The west corridor leads to the female wards and the east corridor to the men's," she says. "But some of the departments lock one of the doors so you have to go in the other door, from one of the corridors. The psychologists' door is open to the east corridor, but not to the west. I know it's mad, but so's everything in this place."

"Aw right, thanks."

She studies me for a few seconds.

"And what are you?"

These are the days before the plastic ID card clipped to a lapel. I rely on my non patient ID being evidenced by my everyday attire and presentation. I remove my coat to reveal a suit, collar and tie. I need to look like an outsider, not a patient.

"I'm a professional."

"Aye, that's what they all say. Right, off you go. Mind, up the east corridor."

I grin nervously and move out of the gloom of the reception area and the offices for everything keeping this mad machine working. The structure includes the head man himself, the Physician Superintendent, who is up the stairs in a large Victorian chamber overlooking the grounds to the south. I'll be introduced to him one day, but not today.

I stop at the large sign outside the admin offices, in the short central corridor, which leads left to the west corridor and right to the east corridor. I'm to find out later this area is also known colloquially as The Pass, as most people in the hospital go past this pivotal point in the hospital at least once a day. A map shows where certain departments are located. The Psychology Department is marked by a penned arrow located on the east, my destination today, as is Occupational Therapy, Recreational Therapy and Physiotherapy. The Mortuary, Chapel and Dentist are accessed from the west. I smile at the thought of dying while having root treatment, then being given the choice of being laid out in the Chapel or the Mortuary. From the sign, the east male corridor appears more therapeutic, I think, inciting a thought around equality I'll consider later.

Through the windows, I see these departments and wards are linked by glazed enclosed external walkways. I presume they're to control the movement of the patients around the site. Surrounded by faded and decaying woodwork, the half walls of the corridor are of sandstone, leading up to ornate iron wrought window framing. The peeling paint shows their age. Big stone blocks taper off their width to meet multitudes of single window panes.

The Pass is the mid-point crossroads with signs pointing left to west-female and right to east-male wards, odd numbers in the west for the female wards, from ward 1 to ward 49, and even numbers in the east for males, leading from ward 2 to ward 50. Fifty wards in total, twenty-five in each corridor. The wards are also sub-divided into distinct wards, starting in the low numbered wards with acute, sub-acute, then the high numbered wards with long stay chronic, and then demented patients, at the higher ends or the deeper ends of each corridor.

I look at the map and scratch my head at my first lesson in patient administration.

There, at this apex of the male and female divide, I encounter my first 'woodentop'. I skirt around her as she sits at the side of the wall of the central corridor, her back to it, her legs flat out on the floor, her urine emanating in equal puddles to her sides. Later I find out this is her spot at the Pass, where she gets the most attention, any response, but mostly none. In the ward, although mute, she's known to approach nurses in her ward and urinate in front of them to get a response. People walk by. Had she been on a street in Glasgow, someone would have stopped to ask if she was OK or to drop some change in her lap. She's there in her spot ignored by all except me and my glaikit look down upon her. She doesn't engage my eyes. Hers are fixated horizontally parallel one yard above the floor. She's as much a fixture as the stands for missing pot plants breaking up the corridors.

I go to the left briefly, more out of curiosity to look up the west corridor into a decreasing level of light. The dark recesses contain old wards which had been closed due to the declining numbers of patients in the hospital from its heady days as the largest Asylum, as it was called back then, in Europe. As patients died or were discharged, the hospital's numbers had decreased over the years, but it still remains one of the most populated psychiatric hospitals in the country.

The corridor is reminiscent of a TB hospital I remember from my youth, minus the smell of disinfectant. This is a long tunnel going off to the distant reaches of the long stay or back wards, as they are called. The back wards are in the depths of these long tunnels into the underworld.

The female and male demarcation exists also in the hospital cemetery, found in a secluded enclosure within the grounds. There, over a thousand patients never left the hospital grounds, progressively being joined by a good proportion of the patient population. The graveyard includes staff, in particular nurses from places so far afield it was difficult to repatriate them, so that no one ever tried. The overwhelming majority are recorded as 'pauper lunatics', which makes me wonder why others would pay to be there. Males and females are never interred in the same lair, each lair is five feet deep and holds two bodies.

I walk back to the Pass and the woman sitting there and then into the east corridor, and creep past the departments mentioned. The door of the Occupational Therapy department is open. In there, patients while away hours, days, years, fashioning crafts to ease boredom, supposedly to prepare for the outside world.

I reach the Patient Affairs Department, where every Thursday patients collect their meagre social security pocket money. There they queue for a measly ten pounds, then attend the Patient Shop, to purchase ginger (soft drinks), crisps, sweets, and fags; all to be finished that day, leaving a six-day gap to the next pay out.

I pass the Social Work Department, where patients are referred for a home assessment to establish the possibility of them returning to a more homely environment, not home; most had lost home a long time ago. The social workers assess for return to the community and try also to make contact with a long-lost family in the hope they'd take their relative home.

I see the sign for the Psychology Department sticking out ahead into the corridor. I approach it slowly and open the outer door from the corridor. I go inside to find another reception window. It becomes clear to me most departments have reception windows, their own access control.

There's another woman, again behind a massive typewriter.

"Hello, I'm Sean Rooney, the trainee."

She looks up, another look from another receptionist, but this time a friendly one with a wide smile. She pushes out her hand.

"Hello, I'm Agnes Connolly, and I'm the dogsbody."

Her eyes drill into mine. She gets up from her seat only enough for me to see she's sexy in a cuddly way. I smile nervously and shake her hand.

"You're right on time, Archie's expecting you. You've just to go in, second door on the right."

She smiles again. It settles me. She takes my coat and hangs it on a hook on the door.

"You won't need that. I'll look after it for you."

"Thanks."

I pass the first door, the waiting room. It's filling with a procession of patients asking to be assessed for going home or going anywhere. The sign on the second door confirms: Archibald MacDonald, Principal Psychologist, Head of Department.

Archie, a big man, greets me warmly and puts a large hand on my shoulder. He removes the other, which has a mouse in it, from his pocket. He says he uses the mouse for aversion therapy for patients with irrational fears. My fears are almost always irrational, but can also be a motivator, a stimulant, getting me to do things I wouldn't normally do. I feel the fear, but I'm here anyway. We talk about my hopes for the placement. He explains I'll get my own referrals at the referral meeting every Monday morning and I'll be allocated to Donna Watling, senior psychologist, who'll be my supervisor and ultimately write my placement report. I dearly hope it'll say I have fulfilled all the placement objectives. If I need advice, Donna will be there, as would he, and the rest of the team.

Archie takes me around the psychologists and leaves me with Donna. I'll share her room and see patients in the wards or in the meeting room, which also acts as an interview room.

Donna is a feisty American who settled in Glasgow and lives in one of the cottages by the gates of the hospital. She explains to me she has a pragmatic approach to working with patients and particularly enjoys manic depressive patients. They're the most entertaining, she says. She explains the rules of the office, the priorities, the paying of the weekly tea money, how to use and submit audio tapes of interviews for typing, the writing of records, the psychology reports for psychiatrists, the courts, and the social work department.

She tells me I should develop an innate sense of safety—there are dangerous patients there. She explains psychologists in psychiatric hospitals had been killed in the course of their work. I've not to interview any patients on my own if I feel uncomfortable. She explains the referral meeting is always first thing each Monday and I'll be expected to attend every time.

CHAPTER 3

I go into the referral meeting with trepidation.

I wonder how I would cope, do I know enough to get by, will I get on with the team, these experienced professionals? Archie presents each referral and a psychologist will offer to take it, or not as the case may be. I wait, but I want to impress. He mentions a referral that has been raised with the team for the previous few meetings and no one has taken it. I accept it eagerly. Archie explains the woman, Joan Trainor, from ward 29, prefers to see people in the dining room.

"She's there most of every day," he explains. "She'll be there just now. Endogenous depression, nothing touches it. Not even ECT, but letting her talk might give her a bit of relief."

I nod and take the file. I hope my psychoanalytic training will be up to the mark.

I return to my desk in Donna's room. She goes off to a meeting which gives me a chance to look around the room. It's well stocked with a variety of books, predominately antipsychiatry like Thomas Szasz and Goffman's *Asylums*. Szasz posed the view mental illness is a myth. Goffman's *Asylums* described the total institution where inmates live in frightful exile. I'll read both of them.

I read some background information in the Joan Trainor file. She struggled with depression, intractable, or endogenous as described in the file. She's been a patient for over thirty years and has a particular pattern of arriving in the massive recreation hall each day at nine a.m. to stay there all day, returning to the ward each evening twelve hours later.

I go to see Joan. I feel I have arrived. Within three hours I'm going to interview an actual patient.

As advised by Archie, she's to be found sitting almost in the middle of the dining room and she'll be wearing a big hat. There she observes every person, patient or staff, entering and leaving. That the room is used for dining and feeding, and is capable of seating

12

a thousand people, allows her a unique opportunity to observe the totality of the patient group in the hospital.

I identify her by the hat, the kind you would see at Ascot or a wedding. I approach cautiously as I don't want to scare her. She studies my every step towards her.

"Are you Joan Trainor?" She holds her gaze down through the hall. "I'm Mr Rooney, the trainee psychologist. Just call me Sean."

She doesn't respond, but continually looks behind me. I look around her to see an older man sitting on a bench behind. I look back at her, she appears interested in him. Then, when I look around quickly at one point, I see why. The man has his trousers at his knees ready to whip them back up should he be rumbled, but it is not for me to interfere with his game. This is my first incursion into the world of the confused, as they are called now, and it isn't an unhappy experience.

It's approaching lunchtime and the dining room will soon fill with patients arriving for lunch, the main meal of the day. This's Monday, though it's the same on Tuesday, Wednesday, and Thursday: it's soup, followed by meat, potatoes and veg. The hospital is a self-sustaining community. The meat comes from the cattle in the fields and the potatoes and the veg are grown in its own farm. The only produce brought in are the fish on a Friday and the tea leaves in big tins for every meal. The farm colony, as it is known, used to have patients tending both the fields and the animals, but this was thought to be exploitative and now patients are volunteers, or are there as part of occupational or rehabilitation programmes.

The hospital has its own golf course and gardens, again tended by groundsmen and assisted by patients. The railway line cuts right through the hospital grounds, which had also been used occasionally by patients seeking to end their lives. There's a power plant, and a fresh water reservoir, the loch, only another favoured place to commit suicide.

By day, I'll see patients referred to the psychology department. Talking therapies, psychoanalysis, behavioural therapies, and counsel-ling, are all becoming commonplace. I look forward to practising them, now I have human subjects, or guinea pigs? Over the following few weeks I'll set up groups on a variety of subjects, including confidence building and self-esteem, promoting mental health, and self-help.

Most patients are long stay and disinterested, but I'm confident they'll be happy to get off the ward for a couple of hours.

I'm allocated a small garret on the top floor of the nurse's home. The home is a grand red sandstone building, built at the same time as the hospital. Most nurses stay there due to the remote location of the hospital and their shift patterns, and many live away from home. There, the nurses, including students, are carefully segregated in male and female wings, policed by mature nurses, or border guards charged with keeping the sexes apart. Some staff go home at the end of a fourteen-day shift; some don't, however. Coming from afar, like the Highlands or Islands, they live here permanently, some to be buried in the graveyard, their bodies never returning home. Most long stay patients will also remain, to be buried in the same graveyard.

I become aware the hospital is a community, patients and staff together, albeit separated, but with a sense of confinement on both counts.

CHAPTER 4

Tuesday, I arrive for work. Donna is busy doing her notes from the day before.

"Another suicide, in ward 22," she says.

"Oh, dear," I say, sorting my desk.

She lifts her head.

"Oliver Turnbull, found hanging from the toilet window, poor bugger. Another escapee, perhaps?"

"Oh, really." I wonder if I should show I'm shocked. "Does it happen often?"

"Too often." She continues to write her notes. "Team meeting today, we might discuss it there."

"Another meeting?"

"Yeah, you'll get used to them. You've also to attend a couple of ward meetings. A long stay ward meeting in a female ward and an acute ward meeting in a male ward. It'll give a good insight into interdisciplinary working."

I nod, raising my eyes, wondering with all my groups and meetings when I would have time to see patients.

I had attended team meetings in previous placements and know how they work. They allow for some discussion over some common issues, such as where the team would go for Christmas lunch and hospital management issues. She passes me an agenda for the meeting.

I look at the agenda, right enough, hospital management issues, and there I see it.

"Suicides?"

"Yeah, Archie is on the HMT and after the last one ligature policy is to be updated."

"HMT?"

"Hospital Management Team."

"Thanks."

We move into the team meeting. I'm nervous, but eager to

impress. Suicides come up. I had taken a forensic course at university. I know unexplained deaths should prompt an investigation.

"Will there be an inquiry, an unexplained death?"

They all look at me. Archie talks for all of them.

"Perhaps there should be," he says. "But there won't be. Suicides are inevitable in mental hospitals. It comes with the turf."

I shouldn't say any more. I'm surprised just the same at the lack of interest, even policy on suicides, leading to a clearer idea on why people are doing it, involving better risk management, identification of at-risk patients, better ward procedure. I feel if I say anything I'll sound like a smart arse.

"Wouldn't do any harm if you visit the ward," Archie says. "Be good for your understanding of the matter." I purse my lips and nod like a professional. "We have a referral for a psychological assessment of a depressed man in there. He has unresolved grief over the loss of his wife and three children in a car crash. He was left disabled in the crash." He passes me a thick file. "His name is Walter Paterson. I doubt if you'll get anywhere with him, but an assessment may lead to some psychological treatments. It's worth a try."

I guess Archie is testing me, giving me this referral outwith the Monday referral meeting of a depressed guy in a ward where there had just been a suicide, but I accept it eagerly and scan the file briefly in the office before going to see Walter.

I call the ward to say I'll arrive this afternoon.

"Leave it until after three," the nurse says, nonchalantly. "The workmen are in taking the handles off the windows and hangers in the booths in the toilet cubicles, and putting a keypad lock on the door."

Just before three-thirty I make my way across the corridor to the ward. I introduce myself to whom I think to be the charge nurse sitting square at the nurses' office desk.

"Hello, I'm Sean Rooney, trainee psychologist," I say from the door.

"Tommy Stephenson," he says, not lifting his head, "occasional charge nurse here, but also nurse manager across this whole bloody hospital. Come on in, it's safer in here."

"Occasional?" I move in.

"Aye, staffing is so bad here I have to cover five wards. A bugger.

Anyway what do you want?"

"I'm here to see Mr Paterson, he was referred."

"Not by me, must have been his consultant."

I see this could become difficult.

"Yes, I suppose so. Can I see him?"

"If you must."

"Thanks." I look at him. He's wearing a white coat, marked by pen marks above the chest pocket and filthy widened pockets from years of hanging his hands in them. Best to get him on my side, I think.

"Your patient committed suicide."

"It comes with the turf," he says slowly, shrugging his shoulders. "I found him."

"Not nice."

"I was sleeping. Only found him in my walk-through."

I look into his eyes for a hint of emotion, but there's none. I ask if there's a policy of debriefing staff who had been exposed to a major incident. I'm full of the latest research on post-traumatic stress disorder, aware of how emergency agencies, such as the fire service and the ambulance service, refer their staff for debriefing after witnessing horrendous scenes.

He doesn't answer, leaving me with the thought that offering my services might be a bit outwith my remit this day. I explain my purpose in seeing Walter. He gives me some background, such as the fatal crash, his disability, his depression. I had read most of this from the records, but I let him continue.

"He sees things. Talks to himself."

His depression is in the realms of psychotic illness, I wonder.

"Psychotic depression?"

"Away with the fuckin' fairies."

I look at him, momentarily, wondering if I should challenge him on his form of words. I decide not to. He takes me to Walter, introduces me, and leaves. Walter is sitting in a wheelchair in the conservatory looking out over the grounds. He has a book on his lap. It's a cold day and the room is stifling from the large iron radiators lining the walls. No windows are open and the emergency exit to the outside is locked. I pull in a chair close to him.

I reckon Walter sits there most days, staring dispassionately out into space. I see his eyes are trained on a large tree just on the edge of the gardens in the grounds. From his file, he had been tried with all sorts of anti-depression medication, and, even with three courses of ECT, nothing touched him. I explain who I am and why I'm there to see him. He ignores me, never taking his gaze from the tree, which is surrounded by clusters of beech trees.

I sit quietly for a few minutes.

"A tree is always up for a hug."

There's a naturally empty response to my stupid comment.

Not looking my way, he says, "The one who plants trees, knowing he will never sit in their shade, has at least started to understand the meaning of life. Rabindranath Tagore."

I nod and smile like I know what he's talking about.

"Do you like poems?" He doesn't answer. I had seen from the file he does; he had drafted many poems, mainly about trees, animals, nature in general, and continually recites them.

I sit silently for another few minutes or more, then get up to leave.

"They talk to you, you know."

I look down on him, wondering if his illness is coming through.

"Oh, who does, Walter?"

"Not who, *they*." He nods out towards the trees.

"The trees?"

"They take their time, so if you shut up and be still and silent, and listen, they'll talk to you."

We sit silently for a while looking out at the trees. Then I tell him I'll return the following day. I say I hope we could talk about what concerns him, what is in his mind. I expect uppermost for him would be the loss of his wife and three daughters in the car crash. He had been driving. I don't really expect he'll be able to talk about it openly. I just want him to know I'll be there for him if he decides he can.

Maybe I shouldn't have, but I put my hand on his right shoulder as I turn to walk away. Then, as I walk back towards the ward, I hear him say, "Murder."

It's clear. I don't need him to repeat it. I turn back towards him once more and stand over him, if anything to acknowledge what he said, but this is no time or place to quiz him on what he means. I would think about it before I see him again, however.

Stephenson stops me on the way out. "The hanging."

"The gentleman who killed himself?"

"Archie says Psychology would be available to talk about the incident."

"Yes, that's what we do."

"He—"

"Who?"

"Oliver, the guy who topped himself."

"Right."

"Well, he managed to find some plastic twine from the OT department, looped it and passed it over his head. Then, hanging it on the window catch, he slid down the wall until he was hanging, his backside no more than a few inches from the floor, his feet outstretched, until he strangled and died."

It's like he's talking about something he saw on the television. I wonder if I should tell him that this is not what Archie meant. Then he thrusts out an A4 envelope.

"In there, it's the twine."

I wonder why he offers it, it being taken from a dead man. I open it and remove the twine. It's been cleanly severed with scissors or a knife when it was removed from Oliver. It would have been around twelve inches in circumference when around his neck.

"It was just enough for him to link it with the window catch and slide downwards, his weight pulling the twine fast around his neck as he slid down the wall. Quite effective."

It's like he's complementing Oliver on a successful suicide.

I look at the knot. It's a slip-knot, which can act as a noose. I recognise it as I had a small boat once in Loch Sween and used slip-knots to tie up the boat.

"Did Oliver ever have a boat or had been a seaman?"

He looks at me quizzically, like he's wondering why I should be asking questions.

"Not to my knowledge. Oliver never left Garthamlock in his life. More interested in repairing radios."

"Oh right. And don't hesitate to get in touch if any staff want to talk."

"No need, I've told you."

"If you need support."

"We don't need support."

Back in the office, I tell Donna what Stephenson had said about staff not needing support. Then I mention Walter voicing the word 'murder'. She says she isn't surprised Stephenson said this, and regarding Walter, there had been an inquiry into the car crash and the death of his family.

"No blame was attributable to him, the driver," she says.

She explains, on a family day out, the brakes had failed, the car had careered down a steep hill just outside Lanark and plunged into the River Clyde. Walter was unconscious when pulled from the vehicle by a local farmer, but his wife and three daughters could not be saved and had drowned. He blamed himself for the accident, although it had been established the brakes had failed as he hurtled down the hill. The investigation found the pipe from the brake cylinder reservoir had been loose and the brake fluid had leaked from the chamber. My first thought forensically is that pipes from brake reservoirs don't normally become undone on their own.

"Murder," I utter.

"Steady pal," Donna urges. "Walter has gone through enough. To suggest foul play on the basis of him saying one word is not going to help him now."

"Sorry, I shouldn't have."

"It's OK, we're all like that at first."

"Thank you." I counsel myself that I need to control the Rooney-foot-in-mouth disease.

Later, I return to see Joan Trainor in the dining room. This time she catches my eye as I approach her. Progress, I think. I get alongside her on the bench and lean over the long dining table, as she does. I see a Bible open in front of her. I don't mention it in case it embarrasses her; some people don't like drawing attention to their religion, especially in West Central Scotland.

Instead, I say to her, "You'll see most things in here, Joan?"

She frowns and nods. I'm to discover she has a good knowledge of everything that goes on here.

"They are going down."

"Eh?"

"One less in ward 22, with God now."

"Aye." I think she's referring to Oliver.

"Now one thousand, three hundred and fifty-two."

I'm amazed she knows exactly how many patients are in the hospital, now one less with Oliver's death.

"One thousand, three hundred and fifty-eight three weeks ago," she adds. "Then, one in ward 19, two in ward 6, one in ward 26, one in ward 13, and the one in ward 22. That's six in three weeks."

This is clearly her subject and it would be impolite not to engage her.

"People die in hospital, Joan, especially older people and those with illnesses."

"There'll be another one soon. I watch things."

"Right."

I look around to see if the flasher is behind. She looks into her Bible and flicks through the pages. I have to refer to it, she'll expect me to.

"Does the Bible help?"

She nods again.

"Thou shall not murder."

"Right."

For the first time she turns to look me squarely in the eye. I feel uneasy and resist the urge to pursue this line of discussion. I smile and go back to the office to write up my notes.

"A few folk have died in the hospital," I say to Donna, keeping my head in my notes. "In the last weeks."

"So I believe."

"Strikes me as unusual."

She looks at me.

"Must admit it's more than normal."

"What's normal?"

She gets up and goes to the file cabinet.

"Normally around a dozen or so a year, we keep them in a separate file."

"A suicide file?"

"I'm afraid so."

"Not concerning?"

"Well, it's keeping the management group busy. They get a report on all of them. It gets sent to the Mental Welfare Commission. If the Commission think there are lessons to be learned, they do an investigation and make recommendations."

"Right."

"Yeah, there's a procedure."

"A procedure."

I finish my notes and wander back to the nurses' home and my room, where I make myself a sandwich and a mug of tea, and pick up Goffman's *Asylums*.

Goffman posed as a pseudo-employee of a hospital in Washington, D.C. For a year in the late fifties, he and his cohorts gathered data on aspects of patient social life. In his book, the hospital was generally regarded as an authoritarian system forcing patients to define themselves as mentally ill. This changed their thinking and behaviour, suffering humiliations, accepting restrictions, and adjusting to institutional life. The institution changed them.

I think of Hillwood and of these patients separated from the outside world, their reality based in an institution which governs their every move, their every thought. I wonder if taking their lives was the only act whereby they could govern themselves, a complete act of independence.

I open a bottle of Glenfiddich, a present from my girlfriend Jackie Kaminski, up-and-coming Detective Inspector, stationed in Partick in Glasgow. She's also a student in the new forensic ways of crime investigation, some common ground between us. I've one more than I should have as I read Goffman's treatise and fall asleep in my chair. Next thing, the door is being bashed violently.

"You there, Sean, we need you outside now."

This is John Scott, the male nurse who has the room next to mine. He's lived in the nurses' home for years and is very much the boss of the male underworld here. Need some dope, go to John; need some booze, go to John; need a female nurse, go to John. He's also something of a lord protector. Female nurses had been attacked in the grounds of the hospital and John is always on the lookout for women on their own, advising of the dangers of the shadows and creepy and hidden corners of the hospital grounds, where not to go. He's not unsuccessful in making a few acquaintances of the nurses himself, happy to have him as a friend and protector.

I open the door. He's there with two golf clubs. He hands me one.

"Here, take this, you may need it."

Reluctantly, I take it. I see this could be a common occurrence, local guys coming into the grounds to get at the nurses. We make our way along the corridor and out, passing the end of the female side of the building.

The female nurse matriarch is at her station with a primary purpose of keeping the male and female residents apart in their sides. She's really a concierge, so it's cruel to call her a nurse matriarch, but even more to call her the Rottweiler, as she's called by the nurses, including Scott. Her real name is Bella Ross, but I think she suits the Rottweiler title best.

There are a few female nurses outside in housecoats. They are saying 'the guys' are in the grounds and shouting up at their windows. John assures them 'he'll sort it', they should go back to their rooms and 'all will be OK'. When we get outside there's no sign of anyone, but we sit on a low wall looking into the trees, listening for any noises which would indicate intruders. Immediately, I get the feeling we are sentinels, sentries posted to prevent an attack on the nurses' home.

"Did you hear that?" John whispers. "They're in the woods."

I listen. It's not unknown for a Friday night for guys from the local scheme coming out of the pub to make their way over to the nurses' home to see if they could get a woman.

"Over there," John says.

I listen again and he's right, there's a sound of talking from the dark of the woods.

"Get it up ye', darlin', real men here looking for some action if ye're up for it."

John's on his feet, golf club at the ready.

"Aye, just try it and I'll bend this roon yer heid."

I hear more talking, though I'm saying nothing. It's highly likely there are a few of them and the guys in the scheme are well able to look after themselves and some carry chibs themselves. It's a rough place of rough men. Two soft inhabitants of a nurses' home aren't going to deter them.

"Easy, John," I say. "There may be a gang of them."

John will have none of it and starts towards the edge of the woods.

"Right, you fuckers," he screams. "I'm coming for you."

Jesus, I think, this's going to end up a battle with Glasgow kisses dished out liberally on both of our cheeks. But John's tactic appears to work and the sound from the trees abates.

"Right, that scared them," he says. "That'll keep them at bay for another night."

The two heroes return to the nurses' home, passing the ladies who might be willing to show their gratitude, but not this night, most of them are on the early shift in the morning, as is John.

I have some more whisky to calm my nerves and end up finishing the bottle.

Saturday, I recover from the bottle I finished on Friday night, Sunday, I see Jackie in the Horseshoe Bar.

She's late as usual and starts right away about policing the 'thugs of Partick'. Her father, Hubert Kaminski, the Chief Constable of Strathclyde Police, is determined to challenge Glasgow's gang culture. Glasgow has become a territorial battleground for gangs and organised crime is on the rise. Jackie is determined to make it in the police force and be every bit as manly as her father. She'll break through the glass ceiling of the police force and get there; and, as a newly appointed detective inspector, she's quick to challenge those who say her father helped her in her career. A woman in such a position is a rarity, especially in the male-dominated Glasgow force. Not that anyone would say it to her face, nor would I, Jackie is well able to defend herself.

She tells me of crooks trying to buy her off, which she would have no part of. She's proud to be attached to a new crime investigation unit determined to use all the new advances in forensics to solve crimes.

She asks about my new placement.

"Oh, a total asylum with suicide the only way out," I say.

"Sounds a bundle of laughs."

"Only if you're mad."

We drink and talk, and talk and drink. I'd normally catch a train and she'd take a short walk to her flat in Partick. We go to her flat instead and I get the train in the morning back to Hillwood.

I suppose Jackie and I are a bit of an item, though commitment is not a word in my vocabulary. I need to become something, a professional. I need substance, something concrete in my life. In my thirties, I've bounced around in dead end jobs, fixing TVs, and working in bars; not a good idea for someone with more than an amateur liking for booze.

My childhood had not been a happy affair. An alcohol abusing father and an abused mother. I was brought up in a strict Roman Catholic household. I also have certain bad experiences of abuse myself, from a particular man, which I find hard to talk about, possibly why I have an alcohol problem myself, and possibly why I have mental health problems. I wonder if this why I became interested in psychology, in the mind, in mental health, in dangerous men.

I guess psychology is a way to understand myself through others.

I took Highers late in life, got into university, got an Honours degree in Psychology. Then I moved onto postgraduate taught clinical psychology, the DClinPsy. My three-year Doctorate in Clinical Psychology is collaboratively funded through NHS Education for Scotland and the University of Glasgow. I'll be employed by the NHS for the duration of the programme, hopefully to be offered a post somewhere. I'm now over two years into the course, and have had a couple of placements, one in Barlinnie Prison, where I learned about forensics and dangerous men, and where I met Jackie, this proponent of the new criminal science, before she moved to Partick Police Station. I also had a placement with the social work department in Hamilton, where I learned about child abuse, joint working with the police, and more dangerous men.

Hillwood is my last placement and crucially important in my getting through the course and becoming a full-time working clinical psychologist.

I can't mess this up.

CHAPTER 5

Monday, I accept my next referral for Alex Barr, a young man admitted to Hillwood after sleeping rough for weeks in the woods near the hospital. He's extremely delusional, believing himself to be Cobra, a character created by Sylvester Stallone. He has a mission to find and destroy members of the New World gang which he believes are out to kill the weak, the mentally ill, the homeless, the elderly. He threatened to kill a man he thought to be a member of the gang at Bridgeton Cross. He was admitted and detained on a hospital order and was lucky not to have been sent to the State Hospital.

Alex is starting to come down and Archie thinks this's a good time to challenge some of his fixed delusions as part of his treatment plan. I see him in the department's meeting room, with a nurse escort waiting outside. He arrives dressed in a combat jacket and beret. He moves to the window.

I smile at the nurse. He shrugs his shoulders.

"It's what he came in with."

I take a note to mention to Alex's consultant that he needs a new set of clothes. He's still quite high and paces the floor until I tell him to sit down.

"You're wearing out the carpet."

He looks at me as he sits and a smile comes across his face. It doesn't take any prompting for him to start.

"I know you think I am mad, Mr Rooney. But my mission is clear, I must destroy those who pose a risk to the weak and vulnerable."

"Right."

I need to avoid any possibility of reinforcing his delusional beliefs.

"And you'll want to know why." I don't pursue this and I don't need an answer. "There's an underground organisation set up to kill us. They're all around us. In here, on the streets, killing those who can't look after themselves. I'll protect humanity from them."

I look at him, thinking psychological intervention might be too early in his treatment plan. I tell him I'll see him again soon.

He turns to me. "I'll get them for you."

Having no idea what he's referring to, I smile at him and nod to the nurse to take him back to the ward.

Donna and I go to the staff restaurant for lunch. We chat on the way. We pass the woman sloped on the central corridor floor, her back against the wall. I ask Donna about her. She says her name is Myra Higgins and she is there every day and has been for years. She doesn't talk and the ward staff try to get her to do something else with her day, but she insists on going there and staying until late every day.

"Why?" I ask Donna.

"She has a serious anxiety state, very fearful, doesn't like being on her own. Being out here ensures there is always someone around."

"Right."

I'm thinking I would be more scared being out here.

"She was a well-paid statistician in her previous life working for the Scottish Office in Edinburgh. An attractive lady, once." Donna doesn't look at her as she walks by. "She refuses to go to the toilet. Just sits there and wets herself."

"I wish I could help her."

I cast an eye towards Myra, she doesn't respond. I catch a sight of her face though and notice she has thick makeup, garish, high pencilled eye brows.

"At least she isn't subjected to the stigma most mentally ill people suffer outside."

"Stigma."

I recount in my mind some of the things mentioned in Goffman's. At lunch we discuss stigma. I'm full of research on the subject and well up for a discussion.

Over my soup, I say, "They say stigma serves sociobiological functions by categorising and excluding individuals who may threaten a community through the spread of disease or perceived social disorder."

I know immediately the way she looks at me I sound like I have swallowed a text book.

"Give us a break, buddy. We don't use that kind of garbage in the real world."

"Labelling human differences." I am determined to impress her. "Stereotyping difference separates them from us and discriminates those labelled."

"Nimbyism." Nimby aka not in my back yard. "Who wants a Myra in their street," she says, "living next door, sitting in their local shopping mall?"

I look at her. She's American, she says 'shopping mall', rather than 'shopping centre'.

"Once community care comes in, life will be better for her." I am determined to show her I have the kind of values to be a psychologist. "She'll get her own wee house."

"Most end up homeless, Sean." She grips my arm. "In large barren hostels or sleeping in the street. Would you want that for Myra?"

I go back to my soup. Then this elderly gentleman is standing over us holding a tray.

"Do you mind if I sit here?"

"Absolutely not, John, please join us," Donna says.

The man smiles and sits down at the table.

"Thank you." He takes a plate and a glass of milk from the tray. "Are you the new shrink in town?" He puts out a hand towards me. "Well, I'm John Jamieson, the oldest shrink in here."

"I'm Sean, and I'll be here for a few months." I take his hand. It's warm and soft, no power grip.

"To learn?"

"To learn."

He looks me in the eye a bit longer than is comfortable. I look down at my soup. I feel that kind of deference most people feel when talking to a psychiatrist. Is he looking into my head? Donna sees it and engages Jamieson on how the hospital is really showing its age.

"Not unlike myself," he says. Donna laughs. "Think you'll cure some of our incurables, Sean?" He turns to me again. "You know, with the talking therapies."

I wonder if I have the confidence or gall to engage him about the pharmaceutical verses psychoanalytical approach to treating mental illness. I mention the psychiatrist RD Laing instead, assuming he would have a view on the anti-psychiatry movement.

"Oh, Ronnie, a bit misguided in his approach." His response says he probably knows Laing, given they both practised locally. "A sane response to an insane world?"

This's Laing's comment about what going crazy is like. I avoid mentioning my own personal experience of mental illness.

"A double bind leading to madness." I'm relieved I'm able to recall the double bind theory.

"I know, God help them."

He leaves the comment hanging in the air and we discuss it no more. Donna and I finish our lunch and go off back up the corridor, leaving Jamieson there.

I ask Donna, "Does he think he will?"

"Who, what?"

"Do you think God will help them?"

She looks at me, like she's trying to work me out.

"John is a lovely man, Sean." She sounds sincere. "Probably the most caring of all the consultants in here. Well respected, would do anything for his patients."

"Right."

Over the coming days I get to know Doctor Jamieson, or Doctor J as he likes to be called. He's excessively paternalistic; like taking patients to his home to try to rehabilitate them. At seventy-two he is well past retirement, but refuses to consider it. Fit for his age, an avid golfer and small boater, he feels well able to carry on his duties.

"I'll go and see Walter," I say to Donna, going off to ward 22.

CHAPTER 6

Wednesday, I'll work on building my rapport with Walter.

I approach him from behind as I enter the ward's conservatory. "Hello Walter, it's me, Sean." He's unresponsive, focused as usual on the trees in the grounds.

"I know, I saw you coming."

I turn and see, with the half glass windows of the conservatory, he can see into the corridor, also half glass, and anyone moving through it. He can also see, by using the conservatory windows as mirrors, anyone moving through the ward. I pull a chair close and mention the title of the book on his lap.

"Illustrated Guide to Trees. Looks interesting, Walter."

"The appley top'd oak in the old narrow lane, and the hedge row of bramble and thorn will ne'er throw their green on my visions again. The Round Oak by John Clare."

Best to be honest this time. "Sorry, it's lovely, but I don't know it."

"No, I didn't think you would."

"A particular nice tree." I look out to the large tree framed in the window.

"It's an oak, do you know what kind?"

"No, what kind?" There is only one kind, I think.

"There are two main species of oak native to Scotland, the pedunculate oak, known in Latin as Quercus robur, and the sessile oak, called Quercus petraea."

"I am sorry," I say, in my ignorance.

"Oh come on, it's a common oak, a pedunculate oak, European oak or English oak. The sessile oak is the national tree of Ireland."

"Right."

My rapport building isn't going very well, but I persist with my one and only conversational piece on oak trees.

"You'll know about the Victory." He stares at me with blank indignation. I prevail. "It took six thousand trees, of which ninety percent were oak." Again, no response. "They left it to season for three years, lengthening its lifespan."

"Aye, very interesting." Not an eyelid flickers.

"Aye, interesting."

"These oaks were planted about 1895 when this place was built. They've seen everything to happen here, and still do." He pauses to leave it with me. "An oak starts producing acorns at around forty years old and peaks in yield around eighty to one hundred and twenty years. So these are close to full productivity, as by the acorns on the ground around the tree." He takes out a small set of binoculars from his jacket pocket. "Several hundred to a yard. A mast year, acorns galore, too many for the wildlife to eat."

"Right." I look out and make out a carpet of acorns.

"Mast, from the old English word maest. The nuts of trees accumulate on the ground." I try to look interested, relieved at least he's conversing with me. "A lot of animals feed on them. Woodpeckers and crows; squirrels, red now grey. Rabbits, and deer, red, some roe and fallow."

Far from an uninteresting day observing a boring old tree, Walter enjoys observing a rich micro-ecology.

"And what else do you see?" I hope to open up our discussion to include other things, such as people coming and going along the path to the hospital.

"Oh, checking me for hallucinations, like shrinks do?"

Shit, I didn't mean that, but think it would be good if I did.

"No, I'm sorry if I—"

"They are out there. Out there, in the trees. Is that what you want to hear?"

It's clear I need to withdraw from this and work on my communication skills.

"Walter, I just wanted—"

"Aye, you just wanted." He turns to face me. "What do you want, Mr Psychologist?"

I look at him. Could I really engage him in any discussion about why he is in hospital, such as the losses in his life? I can't ignore what he said, however, when I last saw him.

"Last time, Walter, you said 'murder' to me, just as I was leaving you."

He doesn't flinch, but it's necessary to pursue this. He wouldn't have said it to me if he didn't want to leave it with me. It would have been disrespectful not to mention it, but I refuse to jump to any presumptions it's to do with him or something in his life, perhaps the loss of his family.

"What did you mean?" I give him time. Maybe he didn't mean to say it or maybe there really is something paranoid going on.

"What's happening here is murder. The trees know it, they can see." He turns his focus to the window mirror to look into the ward. He doesn't want to be overheard. "The trees see them."

There's chatter from inside. I want to be sure I had heard him properly.

"Could you repeat that, Walter, please?"

He shifts in his seat and this time turns his head to face me.

"You heard me, and that is the last time I'll say it."

"Murder, Walter? Who's been… murdered?"

"Oh, for God's sake," he says, irritated at my ignorance.

Do I press him on this? Do I take a stab at this has something to do with his family? Do I leave it? Maybe I should change the subject. I change the subject.

"Your knowledge of oak trees, has this always been an interest of yours?"

"Oh, shut up," he growls. I have to stay quiet. "They are like this place, roots stretched in the earth, same age as the tree, soon to be one hundred years old, a living organism, same as the hospital."

I look out at the tree. "It doesn't look like a hospital to me."

"Open your bloody mind. The hospital is essential to humans, same as the tree. Each sustains life, provides shelter and safety. They both begin with a single seed, a single brick The seed is put in the ground, the brick the same. As both grow, they are weak. They grow strong as their roots and walls form structure. Branches and the corridors develop, the connections which give them life. The tree fills out from the capillary action, drawing up nutrients and the hospital fills out with people, long-term patients, a growing population."

"Right."

I'm beginning to get it, his metaphors, but I wonder about his state of mind, why he would want to spend his days comparing a tree to a hospital.

"Then they both throw off their residue, abscission, falling off at maturity, leaves on one, dead people on the other."

"Leaves and dead people, Walter?"

"Watch and learn. I have nothing to do all day and night sitting in this damn wheelchair, but watch. Those poor lemmings in there." He nods into the ward where the patients are sat around the walls all gazing in the same direction, to the 26-inch Philips colour TV in the corner. "They are watching Hi-De-Hi and no one is laughing." I look in, he's right. "They are as the leaves in the trees, like bricks in the walls, the birds in the branches, the deer in the woods, the insects in the leaves, the worms in the ground, the mice in the walls, the pigeons in the—"

"All right, Walter, I get the point." I need to keep this reality based. "You said, *they* are out there, Walter; them, out there, in the trees."

He turns to me and gives me a look which goes all the way into the back of my head. It's time to call it a day.

On the way out, I stop in the nurses' office to ask some more about Walter and to access his medical notes. I want to learn a bit more about him before I see him next. Stephenson is briefing a temporary charge nurse.

"Can I ask about Oliver?"

"Talk to him," Stephenson barks as he goes out of the door. "He's acting up."

"Sit down," the charge says, looking up. "Mr Paterson?"

"Yes, do you think he was affected by the suicide?"

"No outward signs. In time it may come out. Oliver was a popular patient."

He explains Walter has been referred to the Social Work Department because it is thought he was 'nursing home material'. He explains the plan is to transfer him and let him live out the rest of his years in a nursing home in Easterhouse, but he doesn't want to go. He tells me, although consenting to this, Doctor J worries it may unsettle him and he may become, as many similar patients who had moved to the community, a source of ridicule, a joke figure for the local neds to pick on.

"The caring community isn't always so caring."

"You're so right."

I return to the Psychology Department, but before I do I take up Donna's suggestion to say hello to the social workers. I have a few social work friends from my placement in Hamilton and appreciate the need for joint working between the disciplines, the multidisciplinary approach, they all foster. No reception window to encounter this time, however. A stressed looking secretary greets me as I enter.

"Do you have an appointment?"

I'm worried I may be taken for a patient, wearing normal clothes, no white coat for me.

"No, I'm from the psychology department. I'm just wondering if any of the social workers are around."

She looks up at the in-out board on the wall. "Sorry, most of them are out, doing visits, interviews, meetings." She stops. "Oh, there's Bill, he's in."

I had heard of Bill Simmons from Donna, an old school social worker, she said, now a senior.

"Only if he isn't busy."

"He's grabbing a sandwich, in the meeting room, never has a minute. I'll check."

"Oh, it's—"

"I'll see him, send him in," comes from behind the meeting room door.

I thank her and go into the meeting room. Similar to Psychology, it's everything rolled into one, tea room, sitting room, meeting room, interview room. He's reading a newspaper as I enter, and takes a large bite from his sandwich. He's thin, wiry, a nervous type; tough looking though, not your usual laid back, bearded, benevolent social worker kind.

"Sit yourself down," he says.

"Don't mind me," I say. "Have your lunch, I'm Sean, from Psychology, just saying hello."

"I heard they were getting a trainee." He puts out his hand. I shake it as he guides me to a corner seat, one of the hospital type chairs I had seen around the wards. "Tea?"

"Thanks."

He makes me a mug of tea and describes the makeup of the team, like who is allocated to which ward and who had a particular interest, who I would likely come across in my work. I explain my interest in forensic work and the link between the criminal justice system and mental illness. He'd been a social worker in the hospital for ten years and would have seen changes with the moves towards care in the community.

"Where are you hoping to practice, when you qualify?" He tucks into his sandwich. "Not here though, you'll not get the big wages here."

He doesn't smile when he says this, making me think he means it.

"Oh, I'm not sure, with the rich clients perhaps." I laugh, showing I am joking.

"Best way of making a living," he says, showing he is not.

I pause, to show I don't support his point of view.

"I have a leaning towards the criminal justice system," I say.

"Aye, a lot to do there for a psychologist." He wipes the crumbs from his hands into his bin. "A lot of mentally ill patients end up in the courts."

I didn't quite mean working with the mentally ill, but I nod anyway.

"Yes, they do."

"What do you want?" He tops up his tea.

I'm not sure I want anything, but he asks me like it was a demand.

"I'm interested in the social work department's role in transferring patients to community-based settings. Are there many patients moving out?"

"Of course." He looks at me as if I have horns on my head. "They want them out, so we facilitate. Hardly any of them have family and none of them could cope in their own place."

"Do you think there is a sympathetic population out there, ready to accept them?"

"No one cares, they prefer them out of sight, out of mind, out of the way." He drums his fingers on the phone receiver, like he's hoping for a call to distract him from my questions.

"But, social work—"

"Straddles the institution and the community, makes the connection, gets them out."

I see I'm treading on slippery ground, time to raise the tempo while I can.

"There have been a number of suicides," I say, then pause. "I wonder if there are any... connections there with patients who would prefer to stay, but it's been decided they should go out to the community, similar to Oliver. It's something I am interested in."

Am I making assumptions some people are unhappy about the prospect of going out?

"Kind of thing a psychologist would be, you'll do well."

"Well, do you think there are?" He doesn't answer and finishes his sandwich. "There appears to be some strange—"

"Strange?"

"You know, suicides."

"Suicides are strange?" He studies my face.

"Sorry, more than normal."

"More than normal, like in other mental hospitals, you mean."

"Yes, any ideas why?"

I wait for the inevitable 'it comes with the turf in mental hospitals', but it doesn't come.

"There are a lot of scared people in here."

"Scared of what?"

He looks at me and smiles a cold smile. "Now if you'll..." He gets up, gathers his mug and newspaper and looks towards the door. "I am very—"

"Yes, busy, sorry I won't keep you. What are they scared about?"

"Look." He gets up and stands over me. "It's sorrowful, tragic, but inevitable." I think the 'inevitable' is inevitable. "One yesterday in ward 17, the ladies' ward, poor sod found in the loch. Another, ward 38, a guy managed to get a pile of pills, swallowed the lot. Both of them referred to us for resettlement."

"This is scary?"

"I try to make it less so."

"And how do you do that?"

"I take them out to places just like here."

"Like here?"

"Nursing homes, mini-institutions, less scary, less threatening."

"Thanks, maybe things'll improve." I'm not sure I want to hear any more about his idea of community care at this point.

"What will be, will be."

His negativity concerns me. I'm hoping he thinks the numbers of suicides would go down. Better procedures, more risk assessments.

"Surely we need better safeguards around the key risk areas, like hangings, drownings, people on the tracks."

"At least we have no gas ovens, no bridges, no tall buildings to jump off, no guns to blow brains out."

It's time to go. I get up.

"Thanks." I go into the corridor. "I hope I haven't spoiled your lunch." I hope I had.

"It comes with the turf." I knew it'd come out. He wishes me well with my placement, but I don't feel it.

I've no doubt I'll be seeing Simmons again on other occasions during my placement; maybe more discussions about the regime in the hospital, the structures, the philosophy of care, the paternal nature which creates institutionalisation, the removal of skills and abilities in patients leaving them unable to function outwith the hospital. I doubt it, though; this man is the opposite of what I think a social worker should be.

CHAPTER 7

Friday, I go down the corridor to the patients' dining room and pop my head inside the door. Joan notices me from her pivotal point in the middle of the room. Although cavern like, her voice booms out like a diva at Covent Garden.

"One thousand, three hundred and forty-nine, and going down."

I move closer to her, aware she's about to tell me of another one before I stop her. "And that was three over the last couple of days."

"You're counting well, Joan."

"Aye, they're with God and there'll be more."

"Three less for lunch today?"

"Aye, more pudding to go around."

I wonder if this is an attempt at humour until I see her eyes moisten and hear her voice deepen.

"Does this upset you, Joan?"

A sorrowful frown develops as she drops her head into her Bible, her flowery hat covering her face. I wonder if she uses it intentionally to hide herself, whenever she wants to have distance between the world she faces every day and the world in her head. As I look at her I notice a lump in her neck, not so noticeable when she keeps her head up. But when down, it seems to accentuate it, pushes it out to the side slightly. I had read a deficient thyroid could play a part in depression, if underactive, and a goitre could be a sign. I'd ask Doctor Jamieson about this.

I leave her there worried about her mood; wondering if the deaths in the hospital could be having an effect on her. Doctor J gets back to me right away and says he's surprised Joan had never been assessed for thyroid problems. He'll get it done and tell me what the result of the assessment is.

The following Monday he gets back to me.

"We got the results of Joan's bloods back from the lab, and yes, an underactive thyroid. Well done you for identifying the goitre, totally missed by the ward staff. I'll prescribe a course of Thyroxin. We'll see if it has any effect on her depression."

Sure enough, within days Joan's mood appears to improve. She smiles, which apparently she had never done for years. So much so there's a thought she could be assessed for a care home. I feel happy I have done something constructive to help a patient.

I decide to see her in the dining room. I look in through the door.

"No Joan," I say.

I go to ward 29 and ask for her.

"You haven't heard?" The charge nurse says, rising to put a file in the cabinet.

"What?"

"Joan committed suicide last night."

Just like that, that's the way he says it, then he sits down again.

"Apparently, we all thought she was much improved in her mood, so we allowed her a pass out into the grounds for a walk. She was found this morning in the Clyde. She had jumped off the Dalmarnock Bridge, not so far from Tollcross where she used to live."

"Jesus, Joan." My words sound weak against the noise of nursey mutters. "How did she get that far?"

I think about Joan's rotund figure and how this might have been the result of being in the dining room all day, the dinner ladies giving her treats of extra scones or sausages, extra pudding, and how she found it difficult to walk any farther than the ward to the dining room. I know immediately she'd have needed help to get to the Dalmarnock Bridge, over five miles from the hospital.

"We don't know. She may have been picked up in a car on the road and driven there. Maybe someone feeling sorry for a solitary figure walking along the road, not thinking she came from a psychiatric hospital."

"A kindly person?"

"The police are investigating the possibility, asking for anyone who saw her or gave her a lift to come forward."

"Right, thanks."

I mutter 'Jesus' under my breath. I wonder if I had a hand in Joan's death. Had I not reported the lump on her neck, she may have still been in the dining room today. I'll question myself over this, but I know patients coming out of a deep depression are at risk, as they gain insight into their predicament and their sorry lives. They need to be watched.

I have to ask. "Was she wearing her hat?"

"No, it's there. Here, if you want it you can have it." He reaches up and takes the hat from a hook and passes it to me. "And there's this too." He hands me a plastic bag. I look inside it and see a cardboard box and her Bible. "The box has your name on it, she obviously wanted you to have it."

I take out the box. I'm not sure I should take the Bible. I do, though, not really sure why she left it for me.

"Thank you."

I put the hat in the bag with the box and the Bible, and walk off down the west corridor.

I talk to her as I walk along. "One thousand, three hundred and forty-eight, Joan. One more pudding for others to share."

I'll miss her. I liked her. She was a character, a personality in a place where personality is repressed. I go to her place in the dining room, vacated as I expect. I sit and look around, the room is empty, too late for lunch and too early for tea. I reach into the bag and take out the hat and place it on the table. It's seen better days, as had Joan. I study it, wondering where she got it. It looks like the kind of hat worn at a wedding; her wedding, perhaps, or a son, a daughter? It was white, though greying, a black hat band with three artificial flowers where the bow was. It's out of shape, fraying with stains, possibly food stains. I'll ensure the hat and the Bible go with Joan into her grave in the hospital graveyard. I put the hat into the bag and take out the Bible and flick through the pages. I see certain pages are marked by turned over corners. I feel something in there, inside the back cover, preventing it from shutting properly. It's a small notebook, four inches by three with a small pencil in the spiral spine. I remove the book with the pencil and put them in my pocket.

Then I open the cardboard box and place it on the table. It's about three inches by six, by five. I open the box and feel something solid inside wrapped in crepe paper. I take it out, there's Sellotape holding the wrapping paper in position. I bite it free and open the paper, carefully folded around the object. I open it out, keeping the weight of it in my hand, until I'm left with a layered series of wrapping sheets.

I look upon a ceramic elephant, just big enough to fit snugly into the box. It stands with its trunk high, like it was a trumpet. There's a small rider on its back. He has a turban and it looks Indian or Malaysian. It's orange with blue markings and gold definitions around the eyes, the trunk and the rug where the rider sits on its back. It's fascinating and I feel honoured Joan would have wanted me to have it. My eyes start to fill and I can't stop serious sniffing, which I muffle with my handkerchief. I look over at the dining ladies preparing the long communal tables for tea. I don't want them to think I am crying. I carefully rewrap the elephant and put it back in the box and into the bag.

CHAPTER 8

There's a palpable drop in the already reduced mood throughout the hospital. Joan was a popular woman, everyone knew her and her seat in the dining room remains vacant.

I want to spend a few minutes with her and to give the Bible back to her. I'll go to the hospital Chapel. I check on the sign in the corridor where the door to the Chapel is and see, contrary to the other departments, it has open doors into both corridors. I decide to approach it from the west corridor, given it's close to Joan's ward. It's right at the end of both corridors and the end of the building, giving access to the outside through main doors, but also providing outside light through the stained-glass windows above the alter. It's farther into the depths of the corridor I have been so far. I heard it was similar to St Christopher's Chapel in Great Ormond Street Children's Hospital, although this chapel is starting to decay like much of the fine architecture of the hospital.

Donna explained the Chapel functions well under the chaplaincy of Reverend James Gordon. "These days it is ecumenical. There's a mass on a Sunday as well as Church of Scotland services."

She explains funeral services are a common occurrence for those who indicate a wish for it, as is with Joan, a constant user of the Chapel. Generally, however, she says it is a place of peace where patients spend some time in quiet contemplation. She explains the Chaplain defends the view, as do the other faiths, that pastoral care has its place in a holistic sense alongside the other range of care and treatment options.

I see the door of the Chapel is open and I move in slowly. I see Joan's coffin in front of the altar. I walk slowly down the aisle and take a seat in a pew. Then I notice a nun sitting on the front pew close to the coffin. From behind I can only see her habit and her tunic.

I get up and move to the coffin and bless myself. I see the coffin is open and there's Joan laid out in her best Sunday frock. She looks serene and it's almost like she has a smile on her face. I reach in and put my hand over hers. Strangely, her cold body doesn't faze me; dead bodies generally don't, but the place feels scary, not warm or inviting, like a chapel should. Maybe the nun disconcerts me.

"Hello Joan," I say, softly.

I really don't know what to say, but I pull out her Bible knowing it should be with her in her coffin. I place it inside, just to the right of her clasped hands. I nearly put her hand over it, but feel this wouldn't be right. However, I smile at her dogged determination to detail all that is going on in the hospital. It's enough.

"Time to leave this with you. I'll leave you with your God."

"That is a nice thing to do," comes from over my shoulder.

I turn to see the Chaplain, fully confirmed by his dog collar.

"I'm James Gordon. I'm Chaplain here."

"I felt it should be with her."

He has a somewhat perplexed look on his face.

"How did you come to have it?

"She left it in a bag on the ward."

"It's a Catholic Bible."

"Oh, I didn't know that," I say, even though I did. I remember the Catholic Bible, my father would spout it at me as often as he could.

"No matter, she is with the Lord," he says.

"Yes, with her God."

I turn to go back down the aisle, catching sight of the nun's face. She's looking intently at me through piercing blue eyes. She's clothed in a long loose habit going all the way to her feet. An elderly woman, frail, with a worn and aged face, she has lines across her forehead and mouth, and wisps of white hair peeping out from the side of her habit. I smile and she smiles back.

Joan's funeral is a barren and sombre affair. No relatives could be traced nor close friends, but there's a small smattering of patients from her ward. Reverend Gordon, Dr Jamieson, and Tommy Stephenson are standing next to each other, and at the back the nun I saw earlier in the Chapel. Then, the top doctor steps forward from behind the group, Professor Donald Owen, physician superintendent. My first thoughts are, this is an elegant, interesting looking man; tall, around six three, thin, long white hair and beard, in his early sixties, wearing a light coloured suit, every bit the eccentric. He moves to the front of the group and says a few words.

"Go to God, my child, your humanly burdens are over," he says, and moves back into the group.

I wondered why he has given something of a religious blessing and not the Chaplain, however, the Chaplain has been given something of a role.

I had read about the lonely funerals in the Netherlands, where a poet would write a tailored poem for those who die anonymously, unclaimed by friends or family. I'm now aware Walter is an amateur poet and I asked him if he could do something for Joan. He didn't answer when I asked, but there he is at the grave in his wheelchair. As Joan's coffin is placed in the grave, the Chaplain reads his poem:

"It's of its nature all things must die, and why we are here and none of us cry. She was a child of a life only we know, from a world outside where none of us go. Her life was not as the bird in the tree, only caged in a place where no one is free. But now she has flown and gone her own way, free as a bird, her soul is away."

Heads are bowed and no more is said. No eulogy, no thanks for coming, no tea and scones served in the dining room in her memory, and no one dropping sand or earth onto the coffin. I take her hat from the bag and drop it into the grave. It lands on the coffin close to the top where the brass plate has her name, as near to her head as I can get it. It'll do. I turn, worrying they would have seen me, but if they did no one says anything. There's no air of sadness in their eyes, no hands shaken warmly, people just move away.

Doctor Jamieson moves to my side. "A lovely poem, it just hit the mark."

"Yes." My head remains bowed. "Walter is a talented poet."

"Yes, he is. Another troubled soul."

I'm not sure if he's talking about Joan or Walter.

"She was your patient, you'll be upset."

"Ah well, she's in a better place, with God."

I look at him. Being with God appears the thing to say, and I suppose being in a better place too, though surely a better place would not have been here, not to have died here, in a hospital. Although I don't say it, I am sure Jamieson sees it in my eyes.

I walk away and find a bench in the grounds to sit, to reflect on the inevitability of this place, they all end up in the ground, in the hospital grounds. I open Joan's notebook and start to move through the pages. It feels voyeuristic to look upon the small precise scribe.

Each page starts with a date, the first almost two years before now. The first page is headed: 13th of January 1980. Then, it says, 'Today we buried Mary Burns, ward 17. I saw her yesterday in the canteen.' I note she uses the word 'canteen', like it is a work or factory canteen. 'They want her to go to a home,' she writes. The next page is headed 6th of February 1980. 'Jimmy Stewart, ward 37, killed today,' it says. 'He was to go to a halfway house next week.' The next is 23rd of March 1980. 'Isobel McGroarty was buried today. I saw her the other day,' she writes. 'She said she has to go to the social workers to talk about a place.'

I turn the pages and find many more the same, sometimes interspersed by other observations such as, 'I saw him today, I know what he's doing, God will be his judge.' I wonder if Joan's mental illness is spilling out into these pages. Delusional material, paranoid thoughts expressed in an occasional diary.

I move through the book reading many more similar statements from patients she names. Then, I reach the last page and read, "He freed me from my chains." There's no name, though naively I hope she is referring to me, but I have no way of knowing this. I open the bag and take out the box and remove the elephant. I study it. It looks like the kind to be purchased in Nepal or India. I feel embarrassed, as if I stupidly could have thought she didn't have a life once. I look back towards her grave than back to the book.

Then there, like a final epitaph, a final entry, which says: "If you are reading this, then I'll have been murdered. I didn't do it. To kill myself is a sin."

"Jesus," I say out loud.

I feel a cloud of sadness descending on me and a shame I didn't know her or her life better than I did, and I didn't do more to help her.

CHAPTER 9

Friday, the 12th of February. I go to work with Joan's notebook tucked in my inside pocket. I'm both humbled and intrigued by it. Were these really ravings from a mentally ill woman or was there something in these statements? I have to find out, for her. I always have to find out, it's in my nature. My mother always said I would have unknitted a sweater to see how it is purled, because I always have to find out.

I ask Donna about the names and the links with social work.

"Why do you want to know?"

I explain I want to write it into my project, to discuss suicides in psychiatric hospitals in a general way.

"It's a contemporary issue," I say.

She agrees it would be a suitable thing to do and within our remit, but tells me to go easy with social work.

"They are tensions in there, they're under a lot of stress."

I've not to overstep my mark. She suggests a joint meeting with Bill Simmons. He agrees to meet us and we see him in his room.

"Bill," I say, "I have some people…"

"Here we go again," he says. "Are you OK with this, Donna?"

"We feel it is something useful to explore," she says. "It may help practice."

He appears happy with this reply.

"Right, go ahead."

"I have some names and dates. I'm just wondering if you recognise any of them."

He takes his glasses from his face.

"Right, go on, do it."

I read them out.

"Mary Burns, ward 17, 13th of January 1980. Jimmy Stewart, ward 6. 6th of February 1980. Isobel McGroarty, ward 25, 23rd of March 1980. Isobel McGroarty, I repeat." His face shows interest. "Clients of the social work department I believe."

I turn to catch Donna's eyes drilling into mine.

Simmons takes time to answer.

"I remember Isobel McGroarty. She was one of mine. The others were clients of the other social workers. Where did you, I mean how, the dates?"

"I have a list, I just wanted to ask—"

"How they died?"

"I just have their names. I have no idea what their association is?" I read out some of the other names.

"I know all of them. They are all dead. I hope you're not going to suggest anything about our involvement." He looks towards Donna.

"I can assure you we won't, Bill," she says, looking my way.

A frown arrives on his face, then he's off like a train.

"There were enquiries, suicides—"

"Suicides?"

"Surely you know they killed themselves?"

If I was astounded before, now I am doubly astounded.

"They killed themselves?"

"Yes, over a period of nearly two years. In a variety of ways and in the usual ways."

"Usual ways?"

"Well, you should know, drownings, hangings, the railway, etcetera."

"I have about thirty names here."

"Aye, that would be about right, and Joan and Oliver. What can we do? The hospital is sick, so are the patients. The staff can't watch them twenty-four hours a day, every day."

"Sick, the hospital?"

"It's an ill environment."

Even Donna looks astounded at this remark.

"It's a high number of patients," I say. "Is this common?"

"Every large psychiatric hospital has them, especially long stay wards. We do our best, but institutionalisation, intractable illness, nothing to live for, all takes its toll."

"They are scared," I say.

"Sorry?"

"Scared of the unknown, about leaving here. Something you said last time, long stay patients, scared about being discharged from the hospital." He goes quiet. I appreciate he might be thinking I am being critical. "Sorry, I hope you don't think—"

"You better not, this department soul searches every day. We do what we are expected to do. We're caught in a dilemma. Get them out into a bloody shit hard world or leave them here to deteriorate and die. Now, if you'll excuse me," he says. He's had enough by this time.

"I'm just trying to establish patterns."

"You have no right to establish anything." I know it's time to leave, but he gives me a pattern just the same. "The only commonality is they were all up for discharge in some way," he says. "To homes, half way houses, some soft relative or neighbour. We can only deduce it was too much for them."

"Too much?"

"Well, after spending most of their lives in this place, every need met, safety guaranteed, protected from the big bad world they escaped from."

"Escaped from?" I wonder about the expression, escaping from the world, presumably when most patients were admitted ill, not escaping the world.

"Well, in many cases the bloody harsh world is the reason for their illness."

We both look at him, then Donna talks for him.

"The changing nature of the cruel world," she says, "greater demands, stresses, losses, tragic circumstances."

"Well, like the man Paterson," he says. "The bloody bad luck which led to his admission."

"He lost his family," I say.

The volume of his voice rises close to a shout. "Yes, bad luck. And what does the world offer these people?"

I look to Donna, she looks at Simmons and then me, then back to Simmons. We both know we are on emotive ground with Mr Simmons. We thank him and leave, retreating to our room.

"Jesus, I cannot believe this man," I say to her. "He's confirming a mental hospital is a place of safety against a cruel world. He's as institutionalised as some of the patients."

She gives me a look, then says, "Don't push it, Sean." I nearly engage her, but know I shouldn't *push* it.

Later, I'm in the Horseshoe Bar, reiterating Simmons' thoughts to Jackie.

"Well, you can understand it," she says.

"What?"

"They aren't strong enough to cope with the world perhaps, and collapse into insanity."

"Insanity, mental illness, please?"

"Aye, all right, mental illness, into mental illness, where they find safety and they get used to it. They feel safe, getting everything they need, settle into a regime, a way of life. Then a piggin' social worker comes along and says they have to go to a home, in a poxy scheme, in a poxy place, away from all the folk they've grown to know, back into the... community. Community, is this the right word?"

"I suppose."

"Back into the community that drove them in there in the first place."

"You've got the wrong—"

"Not my impression, Rooney. It's what most folk think. Jesus, community-fucking-care, the community doesn't fucking care."

I sulk into my beer.

A normally passive Jackie becomes quite aggressive after a few. She starts off by talking about boys taking to crime to get out of social deprivation, then later she is condemning them as mindless thugs.

"They need a good kick in the arse," she says.

"What good would that do?"

"It'd make me feel better."

"Aw fuck, Jackie, don't become like them."

"Who?"

"Your fucking colleagues who believe the best punishment is to take them up an alley and kick the shit out of them. You've got to talk to them Jackie, talk to them."

"Talk to them, like a feckin psychologist would? I'm a police officer, a detective inspector."

"Don't be one of the men, Jackie. Don't be a man to get ahead in a man's force."

"It's a fucking police force, men and women, equal."

"Not equal, Jackie you know that."

"I can make it equal. I'll be harder than any of them."

"Just don't change, Jackie, not for them, the job, or your dad."

"I'll no' be a feckin' social worker," she says. "I'll use my head."

We both laugh. I look at her. Her ambition worries me. Having a father who is Chief Constable can't be easy. If she gets there, he helped her; if she doesn't, she'll never be as good as him. A no-win scenario. But she has to win, to be as good as him. Yes, she has to use her head.

"What do you think of the gangsters, Rooney?"

"They have their place."

"They have more power in Glasgow than us."

"They have more money than us, Jackie."

"Organised crime, like the fucking politicians, Rooney. But we can... use them."

I look at her. What is she thinking about?

"It's all fucking power, Jackie."

"I know it corrupts, we know that."

"No more so than the professions, they have power over life and death."

"The lawyers, the doctors, the—"

"Psychologists, social workers?"

"Priests, ministers?"

"Bookmakers, publicans?"

"Polis?"

She looks at me. "And all the great unwashed that they all feed off!"

We chink glasses, finish off and move away to spend the rest of the weekend in Jackie's flat mulling over the respective power centres in Glasgow: the police, the mob, the courts, doctors.

CHAPTER 10

Monday, and it's time to see Alex again, hoping the effects of his medication are starting to kick in and I can work on his delusions. The theory is out on behavioural and psychoanalytical methods reducing delusions, but Alex's consultant is happy when I suggest I should try.

"Won't do any harm," he says.

I set up the interview room to be conducive to therapy: two comfortable chairs set askew so we don't face each other directly, the regular coffee table between us to give a sense of protection, curtains nearly closed, a table lamp; almost a cosy and comfortable environment. Just before he arrives, however, I put on the main light, fearing with his medication he may fall asleep.

I invite him in and sit him down opposite me. He looks unsure at this set up, slightly uneasy, looking around the room. I get into psychoanalyst mode, note pad and pen at the ready, one leg crossed over the other, one hand under my chin with a finger resting on the side of my nose. I start.

"Alex, do you still think you're Cobra?"

"Well, Mr Rooney, who do you think I am?" He reaches over and opens the curtain a bit so he can see outside into the grounds.

I wait the prescribed few seconds to create distance from his question, knowing I should not attempt to answer it: the analyst has to ask the questions.

"Do you still think your mission is to save humanity from this gang, the New World Gang as you described it last time?"

He talks as he peers through the gap between the curtains.

"Aye, if I don't we are all fucked."

I see it's going to take some serious intervention to dent his fixed beliefs.

"Do you think you may be overly exaggerating these… thoughts?"

He turns to face me for the first time.

"No, I know things."

"Like what?"

He moves to the end of his seat to gain a better perspective on me.

"The New World." He looks around. "They're killing people. They're in the schemes, right through Glasgow, and in here too."

I think about writing this on my notepad to show interest, then decide against it thinking it might reinforce his beliefs. I'll ask another question instead.

"Oh aye, and how do you know this?"

"I keep my eyes and ears open. They're out there." He is back at the window again.

"Please sit down, Alex." I try to get him away from the window. Signs are he lacks any insight into his condition. I leave it for the prescribed few seconds before I say, "Between now and the next time we meet would you reflect on what you have said to me and give some serious thought to the fact you might be mistaken, that you may have a condition which makes you think things which aren't exactly true."

He gives me a twisted smile and crosses his arms.

"And I'll leave you with this, Mr Rooney, and maybe some of it will sink into *your* head. Just watch out, because they're out to fuckin' get you too."

And with this he's up and out of the room. Jesus, I need to reflect on my performance as an analyst and my ability to create a rapport with these patients.

CHAPTER 11

It's time to acquaint myself with this place. My friends and I called it Castle Kooky, but most people called it The Castle, in particular the local folk who live at the other side of Hillwood Loch in the scheme. No one really called it its proper name, Hillwood Mental Asylum, or later Hillwood Hospital. It didn't matter what it was called because everyone knew it was for those with a screw loose, one cup short of a tea set, the dafty folk. Then my mother was admitted and I realised it was for people who need help.

There were stories that scared me, like no one ever left, yet I had to believe my mother would come home one day, it would just take time, she would come out of it, leave well, start smiling again and everything would be fine, but that wasn't to be.

What goes on in here? I need to find out. My clinical training arms me with all the information I need about regimes, structures, cultures. But I also know there are dark and hidden corners of this hospital not available to the everyday person. I need to understand the workings of this institution. I want to know what it is like to be a patient of the Castle.

I have to pass the placement, which will be based on Archie and Donna's view and their assessment of my performance as a student psychologist. Hopefully, understanding the patient life in the Castle, how patients view the milieu within which they exist, will assist in this regard.

I discuss this with Archie and Donna. I'll try to reflect on what life is like from a patient's perspective. They agree, saying it would be a good learning experience, one that would also provide information which could improve the quality of life and care for patients in long stay hospital care.

Doctor J says he'll support it. I'll be 'admitted' to ward 28, a long stay male ward. I'm not known there and only Doctor J would know about this. No ward staff or patient will know of my experiment. I take on the persona of a man with simple schizophrenia who had been living rough for years, completely lacking in any skills, with negative symptoms, such as apathy and a lack of motivation, who needs long-term hospital care.

I'm received into ward 28 and assigned a bed in the dormitory and a seat in the square common seating area, where everyone looks upon everyone else from their respective places. I've to avoid talking to anyone. I'm here to observe.

I had read about an experiment in the States, called the 'Stanford Prison experiment', where a group of students took on the role of prisoners and another group as warders. In the experiment, the prisoners grew increasingly compliant and institutionalised, while the warders became increasingly controlling and aggressive. Although not directly comparable, I need to know about the dynamics between staff and patients, both of whom I know could become equally institutionalised.

Very quickly I observe the power dynamics and gulf between patients and staff existing in institutions. Any patient stepping out of line or even raising their voice are told to sit down and shut up. I'm sitting between a man completely mute and motionless and a man completely the opposite: high, garrulous, constantly on the move, disinhibited. Within a minute of sitting down he hits me with a series of questions.

"Who are you? Where do you come from? Are you married? Do you have children? What team do you support?" His questions become more personal. "Are you a homo? Are you a pervert? Do you know any women I could have? Do you have any drugs? Could you give me some money or cigarettes?" I ignore him and eventually he leaves me alone.

During the day, staff presence is omnipotent and bullying is palpable. Older patients are grabbed by the arms and roughly taken to the toilet. Others are strapped into chairs to stop them getting up. Medication is forced into their mouths. But the application of implicit power has to be seen to be believed. When Dr Jamieson arrives in the ward the normal buzz quietens. This is the bi-weekly ward meeting and patients are given the chance to talk to him if they wish. None take up the offer. I view him as a personable man, caring even; but in here he carries great power. I ask the man beyond the mute guy to his left why no one takes up the offer to talk to the consultant. He replies with something interesting.

"You don't talk to Doctor Death, he talks to you, and if he does you're deid."

I'm gobsmacked.

"What?"

He moves closer to me, drawing a look from one of the nurses.

"You either dae yersel' in or you're... murdered."

"Murdered?"

"Aye, murdered."

"Murdered by whom?"

He looks me in the eye."

"Those who walk in the night."

He's clearly 'off it'. I placate him.

"Oh fine, sir," I say, "those who walk in the night."

"Three men in the last year," he says. "Doctor Death."

"Three men, Doctor Death?"

"Aye, last year. Watch yourself, son. This place isn't... right."
With this, he leans back into his seat and closes his eyes.

"Doctor Death," I mutter to myself, "those who walk in the night."

I'm a bit apprehensive about going to bed this night, when staff input is minimal. After a while I get to sleep. Well, that is until the very early hours when my 'friend' from earlier that day tries to get into bed with me. I'm not going to have any of this nonsense and I push him roughly and he lands on the floor. I expect this will stop him, but he persists. I go to the nurses' station and tell the nurse in charge, who is well asleep himself. I wake him and he tells me to ignore the 'annoying bastard' and he'll eventually stop. But he doesn't, and he becomes a pest. I decide to sit up and watch out for him, at the same time observing the place. The ward is noisy, men are talking to themselves, one is screaming, saying mice are crawling over him; another is chanting the Bible all through the night; another man says the ghosts are coming for him and they are going to kill him. I reckon I can only put up with this overnight, not three or four days.

Everything is shadows and shapes in the middle of the night. The only light is from the corridor emanating into the ward and the light from the nurses' station, beacon-like from this lighthouse. It's impossible to sleep. I guess most of the patients get used to it or are on such heavy medication sleep comes easily. I think about asking the nurse for a sleeping tablet, but feel I really need to keep my wits about me. Eventually things quieten down and I slide down into the bed keeping my head square and high on the pillow so if I open my eyes I can see out into the ward.

I'll try to sleep and be half on guard, which will get me through the night. Then, about three in the morning there is an almighty crashing sound. I open my eyes, thinking someone is up at the toilet and had fallen over the tea trolley. Then I see the patient who talked about 'those who walk in the night'. He's over by the fire exit, which is locked, being a fire escape, and he's trying to get out.

"They are there, they are there," he's shouting. "They're coming in." I sit up in bed and see the nurse walking down through the ward.

"Alright, Jimmy, calm down," he says. No one else appears perturbed about this or wakened by it, except me and Jimmy. I'm just about to accept Jimmy is seeing things, such as his illness creates, but I turn and look out into the corridor and there I see two shadowy figures moving away down the corridor. I can't make them out.

"Who are they?" I ask the nurse as he passes my bed.

"Who?"

"There, out there, in the corridor."

He turns and looks through the ward into the corridor.

"There's no one there pal, now go to sleep."

"There was, I saw them."

He comes over to my bed and gets close.

"Listen pal," the nurse says to him, "there's nothing there and if you have seen something it's your head and I'll need to up your meds. Do you want that?"

I smell alcohol on his breath and by his eyes I see he is annoyed. I know to shut up or I'll also be getting a dose of Medazepam in my arse. I pull the sheets up over my head and turn over.

Then the guy who mentioned the ghosts pulls the sheet down.

"The ghosts are there." He whispers in my ear. "I told you."

I turn over and pull the sheet back over my head, wrapping it up tightly in my hands. Nothing else this night will make me extricate myself from my cocoon.

By morning, I've had enough of ward 28. I get up, say I want to go for a walk in the grounds, and run all the way back to the nurses' home. I shower, change my clothes, have breakfast, and try to shrug off the feeling of being an inpatient of the Castle.

I see why patients become institutionalised. I can also see why some people in this environment might take their own life. I had one night in there. Me, a relatively strong and well individual. For a vulnerable person with no control, no rights, spending your life in such a ghastly place, the only other way out in a box to the graveyard might be quite appealing.

I talk to Doctor Jamieson. He laughs when I tell him what he had been called.

"Doctor Death, that's a good one; me, Doctor Death, Doctor Do-Very-Little more like." He laughs. "With the inability to communicate with patients." He laughs again and asks, "What can you tell us about life as an inpatient?"

"Oh, patients are bored, bullied, undervalued, have minimal human rights." I see from his face this is not what he wants to hear.

"And the staff?"

"Bullies, overvalued, have all the power, a complete imbalance."

"I see."

"Sorry."

Why should I be sorry? I should only be sorry for the poor bastards that live in this place.

"You'll say that in your report?"

"Yes."

"If you do, I'd be pilloried for letting you do it. There'd be an enquiry. The patients would be interviewed and would have to substantiate what you say. It would be very uncomfortable for them. It would create serious tensions between the staff and patients."

And the patients would come off worse I think. I look at him. Is he really trying to stop me highlighting the deficiencies of care in the back wards?

"You don't want me to say anything?"

He takes a short while to answer.

"I'd prefer if you didn't," he says. "There are other ways."

I look at him again. Do I acquiesce and do nothing, or do I risk the placement and my career by doing a report which would probably

have me asked to leave the hospital?
    "What are the other ways?"
    "Let's keep our powder dry for now."
    He smiles. I don't smile back.

CHAPTER 12

Psychosis is an interesting thing. They say if after talking to someone with a serious mental illness you feel mentally ill yourself, even although you don't have any signs of it, this confirms they are mentally ill and you are not. That's the way I feel after talking to Alex Barr.

Alex is convinced this gang, the New World, is operating on the streets and in the hospital, and is intent in killing the weak and vulnerable. I start to doubt my own mental health. Is he right? Is there a group in the hospital killing people? Should I join with him, this man who calls himself Cobra? He was diagnosed with manic depression, later to be called bipolar disorder. He's on heavy medication to bring his mania down, to try to get him to become more appropriate. Then they'll get him on Lithium long term as a way of keeping him on the straight and narrow.

I wonder if I'm becoming a bit paranoid? I know my mental health is questionable. I've always been prone to depression and get high sometimes. I use alcohol to feel better, to temper my mood, to ameliorate the stress of the course. I had a difficult childhood, as they say in the text books. My father was an alcoholic and my mother was abused by him. I was determined to raise myself from the environment and life that had been made for me.

"You'll never make anything of yourself," my father would say. "Don't get above yourself, the factory was good enough for me and should be good enough for you."

I was determined to get a profession, to be the best I could be, to get out of the rattrap created for and by people like my father. My mother had been depressed and had been admitted to the Castle and had gone home after ECT and antidepressants. She talked about suicide and I had heard the gas oven was the method of choice for suicidal people. I was fearful of the gas oven in the house, remembering the hissing sound it made before a match or a piece of newspaper lit from the fire 'poofed' the oven into action. I was always relieved to see it had ignited.

My friend Jim had found Mrs McCrae from across the road dead. Her head was in the oven, her body stretched across the linoleum the breadth of the kitchen. Her pinny was still on, her legs and nylons rolled down at her ankles, her slippers still on her feet. He tried to pull her out but her hands gripped the sides of the cooker and she was as stiff as a board. The gas board eventually moved to North Sea gas which reduced the prevalence of deaths from gas ovens, when they replaced coal gas with natural gas which was less toxic.

"But why would the New World gang want to kill people in hospital?" I ask Alex.

"Because they are a drain on resources and end up homeless on the streets." He sounds convincing. "They're a fascist gang determined to kill the alcoholics, the drug addicts, the crazies. To create the new world order, pure of all the unacceptables."

"Why would they be in here?"

"They can kill hundreds in here easily, it'd be more difficult outside, tracking those in humpy beds in underpasses, cardboard box houses, strangling them. Nobody cares, they died in their sleep, no one misses them." He becomes even more convincing as he goes on. "They're everywhere, doctors, nurses, social workers; and they are even patients. They identify those easiest to kill, most likely to be the biggest cost to support, set up in the community, less likely to be missed."

I wonder, is he mentally ill or is it me?

CHAPTER 13

The Castle hides everything, changes everyone, and dominates all who enters it. I'm beginning to believe it is like a monolithic creature that devours people who exist inside until it excretes them as damaged versions of the persons they once were or spews them out into the graveyard.

This place is like a living thing, I'm sure of it. It lives and it feeds on those who move within its walls. It's dark and moody and is seldom pleasing to the sight or touch. It's depressive, angry, and neurotic. It has symptoms like catatonic schizophrenia, a state close to unconsciousness, a trance-like rigid body, no verbal response, no response to stimuli or instruction, holding a posture that fights gravity.

This building is as psychotic as those within.

I move through its corridors, getting deeper into its bowels. Moving farther from the light into the dark, farther from normal into the abnormal, farther from sanity to insanity, farther from help, love, care, sympathy, humanity. Early psychiatric hospitals set up with altruism and care became like prisons, existing to incarcerate. The concept of rehabilitation developed and the belief it was better to change the inmate to conform or, if not possible, to hold and confine.

I had worked in some prisons, such as Perth Prison which was built to house prisoners from the Napoleonic wars. It was no more than brick, stone, metal and wood, and Barlinnie Prison, which had more compassion than the Castle within its walls.

I reach ward 38, the Male Secure Unit, a locked ward in the depths of the male corridor. I note there is no female equivalent of the 'secure unit'.

The psychology department is involved in behavioural work with this group of patients known for violence towards staff and other patients as a way to prevent transfer to the State Hospital. For a forthcoming team meeting, Archie asks me to enquire of the staff how they think this is going. I approach the door, look through the mesh strengthened glass window, and knock. A nurse unlocks the door and I move inside. The sound of shouting, screaming, hysterical laughing is deafening.

"You've to go in there." A nurse lets me in and shows me into the nurses' office, again another locked door from the inside.

He introduces me to the charge nurse and I say why I am there. They look pretty much askance at my questions. Behavioural work is still in its infancy and nurses have not been trained in the techniques.

"I doubt you'll do anything with this lot," the charge nurse says.

He gestures to the window in the office looking down into the ward. I see some patients restrained to beds, staff pinning a patient to the floor, a fight between two patients in the far corner ignored by staff . Other patients are sitting side by side in chairs in a stupor.

"Best just to drug them to the eyeballs," he says, "and tie them to the bed until they calm down."

I had heard about the 'chemical cosh'. I look at him. I'd get nowhere with him, I think.

He smiles at me and says, "Do you want to see where we put them if they get out of order?"

I wonder what he's referring to. I agree and he leads me down through the ward. It's there I see my first example of a straitjacket. I slow down as I pass a man strapped in a long-sleeved garment, white strong linen with leather belts securing the man's arms across his chest. He shows me to a door at the end of the ward and opens it.

"To get the best effect, I need to take you in," he says. "Close your eyes and promise you won't open them until I tell you to."

I had heard of padded cells but have never seen one. I'm interested to see one and agree. I wonder if this is a novel way of introducing it to a student. I'll go along with it. I close my eyes and he leads me inside.

"That's it, in you come and mind the step."

I take two or three steps in and, holding me by the shoulders, he turns me around three times, reminding me not to open my eyes. Then he moves from me and I hear a door closing.

Then I hear his muffled voice.

"You can open your eyes now," he says from outside.

I open my eyes and focus on a padded panel on the wall about six feet high and three feet wide, and then to others on each side of it. I turn around to see an array of panels around the walls. The room has around ten of them, a decagon array. Immediately I feel unsettled. I turn around a couple of times but cannot identify where the door is.

"Can you tell me where the door is?" I ask. There's no response. I raise my voice. "Can you tell me where the door is?"

There's no reply. I get a rubber smell from the padded walls, a plastic cover over some sort of padded material, then a smell of urine from the floor. It's dim from a central light high on the ceiling. There's no natural light. It's stuffy and lacks in oxygen. It's clear the charge nurse is enjoying the fun of this student in his padded cell becoming increasingly exasperated.

"Right, I would like to leave now," I demand.

This is the sternest voice I can muster. Then the light goes off. Shit, this's becoming really scary. Then, just as I'm about ready to start raising the roof, the door opens behind me.

"This way," comes from outside the door.

I'm not happy.

"I didn't need *that* experience," I say, going out.

"No, but you'll remember it," he says, closing the door behind me.

He's right, it's a learning experience, something I'll never forget. I'm still reeling from my experience in ward 28 and maybe I needed to undergo this to understand the extent of what patients have to tolerate sometimes.

I tell the charge nurse I would relay back to my supervisor that behavioural techniques would be favourable to outdated exclusion methods to deal with patients with behavioural problems.

"Oh, difficult and dangerous patients?" he says.

I shake my head and take a mental note to say to Archie we should offer training to the staff to improve practice.

He says he has a patient who may benefit from our new behavioural techniques. He takes me back into the ward and introduces me to John McGlone, a man who had suffered from schizophrenia for many years. He says he's prone to disorganised thoughts, hallucinations with verbal outbursts. He thinks aliens are determined to steal his brain and has a stone on a string around his neck he believes to be a meteor which would protect him. He's an interesting man who had been a pathologist who had attacked a doctor who challenged his status as a physician. The charge nurse says he has been passive for many years, however, ambles around the ward wearing a white coat, taking notes on a clipboard, which is tolerated by the staff. I wonder why he singles this man out.

He reveals he has a dubious and self-interested motive.

"Do us a favour," he says, "get him out of our hair for a while. He's driving us up the wall."

I agree to take him into my care to work with his hallucinations and his disorganised thinking.

CHAPTER 14

Monday, the 1st of March, I get a call from Doctor J. He wants me to meet the Physician Superintendent, presumably to discuss the 'other ways' to respond to the findings of my unpleasant stay in ward 28. I clear this with Donna, saying I'm prepared to reveal my experience to the man in the hospital who could do something about it. She agrees.

I've to meet Jamieson at the Pass. He is there waiting for me. I note Myra isn't in her usual place.

"Hello, Sean. Professor Owen is looking forward to meeting you. I've told him all about you."

"Can I tell him?"

"Tell him?"

"About the back wards, you know ward 28."

"Let me introduce you and listen to what he has to say. Tommy Stephenson, the nurse manager will also be there. He'll ensure any practice issues are addressed."

"Fine," I say, thinking they're not going to silence me.

"Doctor Donald Owen, Professor of Divinity and Biblical Criticism, MA BD PhD DD," he says, leading me up the stairs.

"Right." Should I be impressed?

He leads me through a solid oak door from the reception area and up the stairs. This is a portal into the world of the consultants, where they have their rooms, offices, and where the head doctor, the Physician Superintendent, has his suite. I'm aware this man is the head clinician responsible for the care and treatment of all the patients in the hospital.

He also chairs the management team and holds sway over the Administrator of the hospital and all the other staff groups in the hospital, including the psychology department. Interestingly, he has no power over the social work department. Due to the Social Work (Scotland) Act 1968, social workers are provided by the council and have a separate system and a degree of autonomy from the medical dictate.

We move into Professor Owen's outer office and Doctor J chats with his PA. We sit on a Chesterfield sofa until she takes us into the physician superintendent's room. Owen is there at the other side of the door and welcomes us in. He asks us to take a seat at the opposite side of his desk to him. Doctor Jamieson moves to his right-hand side, Tommy Stephenson to the left-hand side of the desk. I can't help thinking they look like The Father, The Son, and The Holy Ghost.

As I sit down, I turn and see Myra there, sitting on the floor in the corner, a blanket over her shoulders. I can smell her urine in the carpet. I don't ask why she is there. I just assume they feel she's better there than sitting at the Pass, a humanitarian act. She's silent. I smile at her, but she doesn't respond.

I look around the room, bedecked by Victorian furniture and large oil paintings of the hospital and the grounds. I see one of the loch and the old farm, a painting of the old asylum, and above a central fireplace a particularly large striking painting of God looking down through clouds in a benevolent way, presumably to his flock below. I wonder if Owen sees himself as the benevolent God tending his flock of patients, as he would sheep.

I look out of the large windows into the grounds and think fleetingly of the morning I arrived out there to enter this building. This's the centre of power in the hospital, whereas I'd experienced the hidden and despicable crevasses of its inner sanctum.

Owen talks to me first, as is clearly expected.

"I am Professor Donald Owen, Physician Superintendent." As if I didn't know this. "What would you like to do?"

"What do you mean?"

"With your experience, Mr Rooney, in ward 28. Doctor Jamieson said you had a particular experience there."

"Yes," I say, "an unpleasant experience, sir."

"Unpleasant," he repeats. "What do you want to do with the experience? Which I have to say is not shared by others."

Oh, here we go, I think.

"Sorry, I don't—"

"Your... particular experience is not common. It's merely a student psychologist view of the world." He laughs and looks to Stephenson. "We were all there once." Doctor J also laughs.

I can feel anger rising inside me. 'Cool it, Sean,' I say to myself.

"I saw what I saw," I say.

Stephenson gets up and walks around to my side of the desk, almost standing over me.

"Sean, you got a snapshot on a bad day in the ward, not typical. I've talked to the nursing staff, they're stressed you'll understand, it's hard work looking after the ill. Now, can we move on?"

"Sean," Owen says, "we can recommend to Archie you have pointed out some practices which we'll address. You did good, Sean. We'll say this. It'll reflect well on you, your report, your placement. Now, best leave it with us. Thank you."

"I am sorry, sir, but I can't just..."

He walks over to Myra and puts his hand on her head. She doesn't look up.

"Do you want to harm her? If you harm our hospital, you harm her, and you harm everyone in here."

"I am sorry, I don't want to..."

"She's a personal patient of mine." He pulls open a curtain to reveal a door. "In here, I have the files of my personal patients." He reaches in and pulls out Myra's file. It's thick, like a doorstep. "And in here, I have my clinically effective assessment, confirming exactly the most in-depth psychiatric and psychological assessments. If you adhere to our practices, we can allow you to access these. They will further your understanding greatly, leading to an increased insight into the workings of the human mind. I've no doubt they'd lead to the complete success of your placement."

Shit, he's trying to bribe me. I should've got out of there, but he's on a roll. Then the blackmail arrives.

"However, if you raise a case of detriment here regarding the patients, the Mental Welfare Commission will come in here and shut the place. They'll transfer all the long stay patients out into nursing homes in the community. Do you really want that?" He moves back to Myra and strokes her head, like he would a dog. "Do you want to harm her?"

"Do you want to harm her?" Doctor J repeats.

I'm outnumbered, outgunned, and out-of-there. I get up and leave, without saying any more. Doctor J follows me out.

"Sean, wait," he says, as we go down the stairs. I stop. "Please don't get the wrong impression, there are good things happening here too."

"Oh, yeah, and what about the people who are killing themselves?"

This stops him and he takes a few seconds before he responds.

"Well, we have a state-of-the-art Electro Convulsive Therapy here. I'll show you one and you can see. Many of the patients who commit suicide are severely depressed. We're encouraged with the efficacy of ECT in getting people out of depression and thereby reducing the possibility of suicide. So, we're dealing with the issue."

I decline the offer. My mother's treatment goes through my mind. I walk on.

I go back up the corridor still reeling from my experience with the Physician Superintendent. Just then, I'm confronted by a coffin being rolled along on a trolley.

I stop and stand back to let it go by, dropping my head. I know deaths are a common occurrence in this hospital where many older patients reside. Many patients suffer a range of physical illnesses, such as COPD and heart problems, common after years of smoking and an inert lifestyle.

I get back to the psychology department and ask Donna about the death.

"Choked on his food, an awful shame," she says. "He had dementia and took epileptic fits."

"Right."

"We are seeing his daughter. She's an inpatient too, in the admission ward. She'll be upset. Do you want to see her?"

It seems a straightforward case of grief counselling.

"Yes."

"Mairi MacDougall, ward seven. An interesting woman, you'd like her, she's a crime writer, the true kind."

I asked for most of my referrals to come from the long stay wards because I was trying to specialise in behavioural work with patients with intractable illness. Seeing someone with an acute illness might be refreshing and a chance to do some basic psychology.

I arrange to see Mairi in the interview room. She says she would prefer to go for a walk, it'd be good to get off the ward for a bit. Ward 7 is an acute ward, with lots of people coming and going. She was admitted with drug induced psychosis after smoking copious amounts of cannabis over a long period of time. She says she's now clean, but admits to needing some cannabis to get over the death of her father. She'd been seeing him in ward 12, although he didn't really remember her. His dementia was advanced and he was prone to epileptic fits and was frail. He had been referred to the social work department for assessment for long-term nursing home care, and a nursing home had been identified. Mairi complained it was far from his area of origin and he would never settle there, but it was thought he was too far gone in his dementia to know where he was.

She found her dad slumped in his chair in his room. It is unusual to have a single room, but ward 12 is a ward for frail elderly who need to be observed, and due to his epilepsy he was given one.

We talk as we walk.

"I am sorry about your dad," I say.

"Might be a blessing." I don't answer, letting her explain. "He wouldn't have been happy there. I know he wouldn't have. He had a good life before the dementia. Travelled the world in the merchant navy. Had eight kids, myself included being the youngest, and sixteen grandchildren. At eighty-three, it was time to go, but he didn't need to go *that* way."

"Right."

"He was almost blue when I found him and I alerted the ward staff. They discovered food lodged in his windpipe and tried to revive him, unsuccessfully. "

"Not a nice way to die."

"He didn't choke, if that's what they told you."

"That's what I was told."

"He didn't choke. He was smothered with a pillow. I found it under his bed. It was covered in his saliva and some blood."

This stops me in my tracks.

"Did you tell the ward staff?"

"What good would that have done?"

"Eh."

"He was dead, dead in his head for a long time. Someone helped him on his way, a pillow over his head."

"What you say is very serious."

"I know, but it happens in this place. I'm going to find his killer."

I look at her. There's no sentiment, no emotion in her words. No requirement for grief counselling there. She's forthright and determined.

"Are you sure? You're personally… affected."

"You're right, Mr Rooney. I do have a particular reason to think this."

"Sean. I hear you are a crime writer, actual crime."

"There's a lot of it about, Sean. I'm writing it up. It's all about my dad's murder."

"I'm sorry."

"It's alright, I spend my waking time reading and writing organised crime and deadly deeds, but my father's death is different. I know he was murdered. There's no other explanation for it."

I look at her again.

"If there's anything I can do."

"You can help me, I'd appreciate it. Will you see me again?"

"I don't think I need to."

"I know, no reason to. I'm only in here doing cold turkey. But, although I don't regret my father's death, I want to know who did it. You can help me."

"I don't think—"

"But if you raise any concerns about my father's death I'd completely deny it. You got that? I need to operate… covertly."

"Right. Undercover?"

"Something like that."

"I'll… think about it."

"Don't think about it for too long, they discharge me in a few weeks."

"Thanks, Mairi, I'll be in touch."

I'm not sure about this as I leave her in the corridor. She makes her way back to the ward. I walk down the east corridor deep in thought. There's no way I can investigate a killing in the hospital. That is not for me. There are ethics involved here and my placement would be at stake. Donna's report to the uni is everything. My qualification would be at risk if I do anything out of order. But if I do nothing and there really is something going on, where the hospital authorities have no interest in making any inquiry into any of the deaths, how would I live with myself? Were these deaths to pass into history with no clear confirmation of their cause, every death certificate saying death by suicide? The only message left to family and the world in general for their passing is they killed themselves, their obituary to have spent their life in the Castle, then killed themselves, then to be buried in the hospital graveyard. Surely, they deserve better than this, especially if there are some suspicious circumstances surrounding their deaths.

Getting to the end of the corridor, just before I go back to the nurses' home, I conclude people are killing themselves here. Is this their only way out? If so, I can't stand by and do nothing. I should at least help look into their deaths, get some idea why they died. But I cannot do this on my own. To do this I need help and Mairi has already offered. She's in. But there may be other candidates for this role. Joan would have been one of them had she not died, though her notebook is a source of information. Walter and his perspective on the world of the hospital could be a candidate. It might help him to focus on something else rather than his losses. Maybe John McGlone and his forensic scientist brain might be too. Again to give him something of a diversion and something to concentrate on, which would have therapeutic value. I also need Jackie on board. And I'll need to clear this with Donna.

Then, just as I approach the Pass, I hear a voice behind me.

"Hello, Mr Rooney." I know immediately this is Alex Barr. I don't want to talk to him. I'm tired, I want to get back to my room.

"Alex, how are you doing?"

I don't really want to know how Alex is doing.

"Oh OK, just doing my recon of the passageways, looking out for… them."

"Right," I say, feeling bedraggled. "Maybe you need to get back to the ward and settle in for the evening."

"I will, Mr Rooney. But I know something you should know."

"What, Alex?"

"There are people being knocked off in this hospital and you might think I am a nutcase but I have been talking to people and I have been told things. There are people dying in this place, and the only one I can tell is you."

I look at him. Normally there would be a faraway look in his eyes, a wild gaze, but this time there's conviction.

"Right, Alex, I'll see you soon. We'll talk about it."

He smiles and takes off up the corridor. Alex's intervention convinces me. He'll be in the group.

I arrange to meet Jackie in the Horseshoe Bar. I need to talk this through. But first my supervision. Donna and I get around her desk. We discuss my cases. Then…

"Right." Donna has her feet up on the desk. "That's that for your supervision. Now what are you going to do for your placement assignment?"

Jesus, I had forgotten this, the placement assignment.

"A self-help group." I blurt it out without giving it any thought.

"A self-help group, that's good, it fits well with the placement objectives. Do it."

It's Friday evening. I meet Jackie in the Horseshoe. We squeeze around the back of the bar, taking a couple of high stools by the wall under the massive mirrors.

"Jackie, I think patients are being killed at Hillwood Hospital."

"Boredom or the crap food." She sips her white wine.

"Jackie?"

"I hear you. I know what you are saying. Jesus, since you went into that place."

"Jackie can you lift your head out of your arse for a minute. This is important?" I slurp the head of my Guinness.

She looks at me in *that* way, her mouth pursed, her eyes narrowed, her glass pointed at me.

"Rooney, mind we talked about getting hitched but none of us felt able to commit because you were a mental boozebag? Eh, well, you're being fanciful again. Stay reality based, Rooney, you're spending too much time with loonies."

"Mentally ill, Jackie, how many times…"

"Psychotics, is that better?"

"Better, people are killing themselves in there, and some folk think people are being murdered." She drops her head to look over her glasses. "I'm getting a group together, patients, to consider it. Will you come?" I look back to my glass, licking the froth from my top lip.

She reaches over and grabs my arm.

"Rooney, you're drinking too much, getting too involved, and fucking up your chances of becoming a psychologist. Is this what you want?"

"Just leave it."

"Fanciful, arse." She sees my pained look. "Your mother killed herself, you told me." I remember telling her, one night I had been drinking and it came out. "Is this all about her? People committing suicide has more than a professional interest for you."

This goes right through me. I hadn't thought about this but is she right? Is this about my mother's suicide? I go quiet. She knows when I go in on myself, she'd been there many times when this happens. Sometimes it leads to a bout of depression, sometimes a severe bout of alcohol abuse, sometimes—

"No, she didn't fucking kill herself. OK she took the pills, but that place, the Castle killed her."

"What?"

"She was in and out of there like a fucking yoyo, cyclical, got her better for a while, drugs, ECT, then back out. Then she was sent to a long stay ward, to assess her for long-term treatment. Truth being told, they'd run out of ideas, but also my father said he couldn't take it anymore, her depression, nothing to do with the fact his abuse of her and his drinking led to her depression, oh no. He called her a nutcase, that she needed locked up. She attacked him, which was the final straw."

"She attacked him. I like it."

"The police came in and she was huckled and ended up in the Castle once more. I didn't like it. She was to be assessed for long-term hospital care. She spent six months in a long stay ward. It changed her."

"It changed you, Rooney."

"Although she got depressed sometimes, like me, Jackie, she was always her, though a dulled version of her, but after she had been in there for that time, notwithstanding the courses of ECT, she was flat, empty, lost."

"The place changed her."

"Yes, it did."

"And what about you?"

"He would look after me, he said, kick the fucking shit out of me more like."

"Bastard."

"I was terrified she would never come home. She settled a bit in hospital and I kept asking for her to come back. They thought she was now passive, all the aggression had gone. So, they'd try her at home for a wee while. She came home for a few days' pass, but he just got into his drinking even more and he had his punch bag back."

"I would punch him."

"She got depressed again, but she was different because of this place. He said she was calm when she hit him with a garden spade."

"Jesus."

"He went off to get the police, saying he was going to have her locked up for ever. She was terrified of going back to the long stay wards, forever. She told me this."

"Fuck's sake, Rooney."

"She found every tablet she could find in the house and took the lot. I was at school that day and when I came home the ambulance men were putting her into an ambulance."

"Oh no."

"She was out of it. I went with her to the GRI, where she was wheeled in on a trolley. I had to wait outside the ward when they were working on her. That was until this doctor came out and said she was dead, they'd done everything they could."

She reaches over and puts an arm around me.

"I need to do something in there," I say.

She thinks for a minute.

"OK, I'll do it, I'll come along." She doesn't sound too convincing. "If only to make sure you don't fuck yourself and your potential career up." She waits for my response. I know she's in, but it's nothing to do with my career, she wants to watch me. Then she laughs, like she's trying to lighten the toxic atmosphere I had just evoked. "And if only to confirm you and your cohorts are off your fucking trollies."

I smile and put my hand over hers.

"Thanks, I'll be led by your good counsel, I promise."

"Right, and it's unofficial, got it?"

"Got it."

"And you clear it with your supervisor. I don't want to be taken for a… woodentop."

"Right."

I know, with Donna, I would have some persuading to do, to explain why I am bringing my friend, a polis in on this. I'll think of something. I'll tell her, to support me, that'll do—well it's true.

PART TWO

CHAPTER 15

I spend the weekend questioning myself about the purpose of this group. Do I really believe something sinister is happening here? I'm not sure, but if I step out of this place, having got myself in, and something is happening here, could I live with myself?

However, as Donna says, I need to keep the group within the placement objectives and I need to ensure setting up a group in the hospital would have some therapeutic value, helping some patients unburden, to work through their feelings, build their confidence, even dispel some of the superstitions of this place, and give them something of value to do. If truth be told, it may also make this placement more interesting. I'll do it, but in the knowledge I'm taking a risk.

Right, who should be in the group? I know I would have started with Joan. I liked her and her observations would have been essential. I am, however, satisfied her notebook provides good references, and her gift of the elephant ornament offers a symbol of her determination.

I'll start with Mairi. She's a true crime writer with a penchant for the criminal mind and, totally convinced her father has been murdered, is determined to find his killer. She can't do it officially and knows any official investigation will say he choked on his breakfast while having had an epileptic fit.

How can I not have Walter, with his philosophical mind and his acute, albeit skewed, understanding of this hospital and its inhabitants?

John McGlone interests me. He's a man with a brilliant mind. Albeit psychotic, his forensic brain might show through the delusions and produce something.

Alex worries me. His lability and delusional activity could hamper the workings of the group, but sometimes there is an element of truth in paranoid delusions. He believes there is a force operating in the hospital, intent in culling the vulnerable patients. I need to know if there is any semblance of truth in this.

I swither about Jackie. Do I leave her out, keep her out of the picture, which would give me some ability to operate unabated? But, as Miss sensible, her feet on the ground, she'd certainly keep things above board, and someone needs to keep us reality based. But, for more personal reasons, I know I need her in.

Agnes reserves the interview room in the psychology department and enters it in the daily diary for today, from two to four p.m. She pencils in, 'The Special Interest Group'.

Archie asks her what the purpose of the meeting is.

"Oh, it's a self-help group for patients with an interest in murder."

Archie laughs.

"Oh, that's fine, a murder group, I like it." He shakes his head at Agnes's sense of humour.

Alex is first to arrive. He's five minutes early and agitated as usual.

"Am I on time, what are we talking about, who else is coming, will we get our tea?" He paces the floor, looking out of the window. "They're out there. They'll know we are meeting. They've got their informants. They'll try to kill us. We need to kill them first."

Jesus is this a good idea?

"Alex, please sit down." I look out in the corridor to see if a nurse escort is waiting outside, not this time. "Where's your escort, Alex?"

"My consultant thinks I'm OK to go about the hospital without one. But I've no' to leave the grounds. Otherwise, I'll be off to a secure unit and I don't want that." I feel uneasy about Alex being there without a nurse, but he should be given a chance.

John McGlone arrives next.

He enters the room hesitantly, looking around the room like a surveyor valuing a property. I notice the stone around his neck that the nurse says he thinks protects him from aliens who are determined to steal his brain. I know mentioning it would only reinforce it, so I say nothing.

"I only decided to come here on the preceptertense that patientracide is occurring within these walls," he says, "no other reason."

I smile at the neologisms.

"Yes, indeed, John, please sit down, we'll be starting soon."

Mairi is next.

"Hello, Sean." She looks around the room as she lights up. "And everyone else. Do you mind if I—"

"Please Mairi, no cannabis here."

"Aw, don't worry, I'll stay by the window and waft it outside, no one will know anything about it." She offers a smoke to Alex and John. I step in, waving my finger. She withdraws the offer. "OK boss, their loss."

I shake my head. The place will be stinking. What would Archie say about this?

Walter is next. He rolls himself in on his wheelchair. I reach to help him.

"Leave me son," he says. "I'm more than able to manage the door and my chair myself."

He turns his wheel chair around and backs into a corner of the room, taking time to study each of the others carefully.

Alex is uncomfortable at his stare.

"Are you looking at me sir, what do you have on me, do you know anything about me?"

Walter looks at him dispassionately and shakes his head.

"Rooney, are you sure you want to do this?"

John takes a white coat out of his bag.

"Mr Rooney, I need to wear my coat." I nod and he puts it on. He takes out a writing pad, clipboard, and pen. "Thank you, Mr Rooney, I will record the detail of this meeting to consider later." All eyes are on him. "And, of course, I am ready to provide my scientological services in pursuit of the truth."

"Right, thank you, John."

Alex is in his face.

"Aye, they are out there, pal." John steps back. "And a stupid white coat will no' protect you when they come for you. Only the Cobra'll do this, and that's me, the Cobra, got it?"

"I have my meteorite." John clasps the stone around his neck. "This will protect me. They are determined to take my brain you know, just like Einstein. They took his, they're only interested in geniuses."

"Aye fine John," I say, "and Alex, please sit down."

Alex pulls his beret down onto his brow and puts his sunglasses on, making a cross sign with his arms.

I arranged a visitors' pass for Jackie, and she arrives, late as always, striding in.

"I am Detective Inspector Jacqueline Kaminski of Partick Police Station."

Mairi starts to laugh.

"Aye very good. We've a mad scientist, a psychotic vigilante, and now we have a delusional DI. I might write this into my next investigation, good one that."

Jackie gets right close to her and pulls out her ID.

"Listen, missy, I *am* a police officer, see."

Mairi puts her hands up like she is giving in to be arrested.

"OK, pal, got it down the Barras, no doubt."

Walter is looking straight at me. "Mr Rooney, in addition to the mad scientist and the pathological killer, we have a drug addict, and now we have someone who thinks she is a police officer. What have you got me involved with?"

They all look at each other, summing each other up. Mairi takes a large draw of her spliff and points it at Walter.

"And we have Ironsides with an attitude," she says, blowing smoke into the room.

I move to the door and lean my back on it to ensure it is firmly closed. I can't have any of the psychologists, Archie maybe, or Agnes, listening in or smelling the cannabis.

"Thanks Walter and Mairi," I say. "Jackie please sit down." Jackie looks at them and shakes her head, taking a seat nearest the door, as if to make an escape if she needs to. "We all have a common interest in being here," I say. Jackie smirks and appears content to look out of the window. "Something strange is happening in this hospital and we are here to a, establish what is going on and b, decide what we can do about it."

Alex moves to the middle of the room.

"Leave it to me, I'll murder the bastards."

Jackie turns to them, raising her eyes; looking first at Alex and then to me as if to say, 'Is he for real, will I be making an arrest today?'

"Thanks Alex, if you'll let me finish," I say. I move him to nearer the wall and I go to the middle of the room. "I have no idea what is going on, but we all feel there is something." They all look at me as if they understand exactly what I am saying. "Something unusual is going on, people are dy—"

"Look Rooney, if there is criminal activity going on it is for the force to intervene."

"Aye, Jackie, but as you say yourself, there is no confirmed cause to involve the police, no formal reason to involve—"

Walter reverses his wheelchair bumping into the wall to demand attention.

"And what will the police do? What happens in the Castle stays in the Castle. Anyway, no one cares about us, we are powerless, like the trees out there, we can only look on and do nothing."

"We must analyse, study, understand." John is writing furiously on his clipboard. "Then we must design, determine, detect and—"

"Destroy," Alex adds. "You're so right pal."

I bring out Joan's notebook.

"This, my friends, is why we are here." I pat the book between my hands. "In this book, Joan, who died recently, wrote the names and circumstances of a good number of your fellow patients who have died mysteriously, supposedly at their own hands, but of whom we have suspicions."

"They were murdered by the New World, surplus to society's needs," Alex says. "They needed to go."

I'm really wondering why I brought Alex into this. The man's clearly off it. Would he be of value to the group or not? But I'm interested in what he had said in the corridor that night. Something in his eyes, I remind myself. I want to see where Alex will go with this.

I open Joan's notebook and read out the last entry.

"If you are reading this, then I'll have been murdered. I didn't do it. I believe to kill myself is a sin."

I look up slowly for effect.

"That, my friends, is why we're here."

CHAPTER 16

I feel I've covered enough. I close the meeting on Joan's statement. It established a collective interest, the Special Interest group, as Agnes confirmed in the office diary. Best leave it there for the meantime. I'll leave it with them, and I'll leave it with me too, for I too need to be confident about this. But, even then, I know once started I'll have to see this through, whatever the consequence or effect. But also, importantly, I know I need to apply myself to this placement.

I escort Jackie out.

"Fanciful," she says, as we get to the car park. I know she's right. "You need to do what you are here to do, get through this feckin' placement."

I wave her off knowing I'm taking a real chance with this group. I hope to convince Donna and Archie my group has therapeutic value and is completely within the remits of my placement.

Over the next few days, I apply myself to my work. My only thoughts on the group are prompted by Agnes saying to me a few times, "Do you want me to arrange a meeting, Sean?"

"No thanks, Agnes," I answer every time.

I counsel, attend meetings, do my reports, write up my notes, go back to my room, have a few cans, eat rubbish pizzas, and anything which can be warmed in the small oven in my room. I watch rubbish TV too, anything to numb my brain from the day job listening to the troubles of others.

But I'm conflicted. I know I need to make a success of the placement and exist in this place which offers no intellectual escape, and I should leave here to its troubled people, but I need to do the right thing.

I ask Agnes to arrange a meeting.

We have the second group meeting on the 16th of March. Agnes secures the meeting room for two hours in the morning this time. Last time, I asked them to reflect on what I had said and to decide whether they want to be involved or not. I expect them all to back out.

I worry if Walter's mood would not allow him to involve himself in discussion over the death of others.

I wonder if John would have the concentration in his psychotic state to apply himself in any useful way, but I hope his ego and his forensic psyche would keep him involved.

I feel confident in Mairi, however. She has a personal reason to be there and has an acute criminologist's mind, but can she extract herself from her drug-induced stupor to be of any value?

As for Alex, I know he'll continue to bore everyone with his skewed paranoid thoughts, but like lots of paranoia I have to rule out the possible and confirm if there is any truth in anything he is saying. I really worry about having him in the group. This really is unethical and I can't cross that boundary, my future depends on it.

I go to the room dead on two o'clock. They're all there, in the same configuration as the last meeting. People are pretty predictable, I think.

"Agnes let us in," Jackie says.

"Right, good for her." I move to the kettle. I notice they all have a mug of tea and a plate with a scone on it. "I see she really has looked after you." I note I need to thank her. I make myself a cup of tea and take the last scone from the tray. "Thank you for coming." I pull out a seat and take out the notepad. John imitates my move exactly, taking out his own notebook, pencil at the ready. "Let's get started."

John writes, "The group gets started."

"Before you start reading from that," Jackie says. "I need to advise you that anything you say could be subjudice in any resultant court case."

"Right, thank you Jackie. We'll be careful. Right folks?" No one responds.

Then Walter says, "I want to hear what Joan said, Joan saw everything in here."

Alex and John nod, then Alex says, "If only to confirm what I have been telling you."

I smile at him and start.

"I'll paraphrase." More nods. I read from the notebook. "Mary Burns, they want her to go to a home. Jimmy Stewart is to go to a halfway house. Isobel McGroarty, the social workers are to talk to her about a placement." I take my glasses off and put the book in my pocket. "And there are others."

"Oh aye," Alex adds. "So there is."

"We have Joan," I say, "suspicious circumstances."

"My father," Mairi continues. "He *was* murdered."

Walter adds, "And Oliver, suspicious circumstances there I would say,"

John is scribbling 'suspicious circumstances'.

"There was the woman in ward 17 found in the loch," I say, "and the man in ward 30 who swallowed the pills."

Alex moves centre stage.

"I have information they are systematically eliminating the weak, the ill, the vulnerable, those they consider surplus to requirements."

"It's an organic thing," Walter says. "Endemic. They are there, you just need to know where to look."

"I see them too, Ironsides." Mairi giggles. "But only when I have too much blaw."

Walter pushes his wheelchair towards Mairi. I get in the way. Mairi looks slightly uneasy that Walter might want to pin her to the wall.

"I'll say one thing," she says, "the patients know it, the staff know it, and they do nothing about it, and the consultants are part of it."

"They are all but lemmings," Walter says.

"They will get us too, if we don't—"

"Please, Alex," I say, "this is…"

"All in my head," he shouts.

"Calm down, Alex," I say, waiting for Agnes to come in to tell us Alex is being heard next door.

Alex can't be consoled.

"Why is it when I tell the truth no one listens?" he cries. "But they'll listen to this." He reaches inside his jacket and pulls out a wooden knife, a large one. I recognise it from watching old western programmes. It's shaped like a Bowie Hunting Knife.

Jackie grabs Alex from behind, making him drop it.

"Jesus, Rooney, this has gone too far."

I pick up the knife.

"It's wooden, Jackie, wooden, probably made in the wood-working department."

"He could do harm with it, Rooney, that's the point."

"For God's sake, Alex, do you want to go to the secure ward?"

I move to the door to call the ward to have Alex taken back.

Alex drops to his knees.

"Please Mr Rooney, if they put me in there, I'll never get out, you know this." I look at him full in the face. There are tears coming from his eyes. "It made me feel safe, to protect myself. I'm scared. People are being killed in here. And I could have got a real one. You can get anything in here, patients need to arm themselves."

"Don't you dare. Then you will end up in the State Hospital. The wooden one goes in the bin."

"No, Rooney," Jackie says. "I can't let this go, the man is bloody dangerous."

"I'll accept the responsibility, Jackie."

She shakes her head and turns to Alex.

"Listen pal, if you so much as flutter your eyelids aggressively I'll have you in, and it'll be to Barlinnie not to a fancy hospital with all the mod cons." Alex goes back to his seat, his head bowed. Jackie turns to face me. "I want to know what he is talking about, Rooney, weapons in this place. I know organised crime operates in hospitals and prisons, selling drugs, cigs, drink, anything. I need to know what's happening in here."

Alex gets up once more.

"I can help, Ms Kaminski. The New World guys are in here, as well as the Mafia, the Tongs, and Fleeto. I've been trying to tell people they are all around us."

I need to ensure he has an escort next time.

"Right, Alex, sit down." I look to Walter, John, and Mairi, who have said nothing to these events.

"Walter?"

Walter shakes his head. "Seems to me everyone should be given a second chance. He's no worse than most in here."

John is writing in his notebook.

"John?" He looks up. "Are you OK about this?" He returns to his writing. "Alex is an informitanter," he says, writing. "He gives information about secret or criminal activities, cultural, linguistic data."

I shake my head.

"Mairi?"

Mairi wafts her cannabis smoke out of the window and turns to Alex.

"Can you get me some dope, Alex?"

I shake my head again.

"OK, that'll do for today."

"Do for today," John says, as he writes.

The patients leave and I go to Agnes and ask her to check with ward 8 to ensure the staff make sure Alex returns there as expected. I return to the interview room and to Jackie, its sole occupant. I sit down and put my head in my hands.

"Jesus, Jackie, I'm close to despair over this stuff."

She pours tea.

"Sit down, Roon. Here you need this." She hands me a mug. I take it and sink deep into the corner chair. "Didn't go as you planned."

I shake my head and take a large slurp.

"No, you can say that again."

She's about to say it again, but she sees I'm in no mood for satire.

"What'd you expect, hardly a crack group of investigators?" She's right, a group of mentally disordered individuals and me, as delusional as any of them. "So, what happens now, can you cope with stirring up the hornet's nest?"

"I don't want—"

"You maybe don't want, Rooney, but you bloody well will. You drop a pebble into this pond. You know what I am saying?"

A silence ensues, thinking going on, on both counts. I break first.

"Jesus, Jackie, I don't know—"

"If you can do this? Yet you'll have to."

"What?" What is she saying?

"There might just be something going on in here. I'm not sure what it is, organised crime, criminal practices, maybe even murder."

"You are validating this?"

"If we bring a squad in here, whatever is going on goes underground and we find nothing. I know that much. We keep it—"

"Unofficial?"

"Unofficial."

I escort Jackie out. When I return, Agnes is in the interview room clearing up the cups.

"You alright, Sean?"

She's looking straight at me, like she's wanting more of a 'I'm fine, how are you?'

"I'm fine, why are you asking?"

"You just seem a bit… upset." I really don't want to share anything with Agnes, far less my inner-most concerns about the Castle, but she's pushy. "Is it your murder group?"

"My… murder group."

"Aye, you know, the Special Interest Group, the murder group." She says it very coolly, as she clears all the cups onto a tray. "Investigating the strange goings on."

"Jesus, Agnes, who else knows about this?"

"Just me, Sean, so don't worry." She looks into my eyes as if she is trying to convince me she's safe.

"How do you know anything?"

"Nothing happens in this place which I don't know, certainly not in this office, this is my domain."

I should've known this. Agnes has her ear to the ground and, more to the point hears what is happening through the walls of the office.

"And Archie, Donna, anyone else?"

"Only me, they would ask me if they suspected anything."

I realise immediately Agnes has a place in all of this.

"You won't…"

"Don't worry, I'm all behind it." In the way she says it, this is more than a passing interest. "I love the dark side," she says, "one of the reasons I work here. I'm an avid crime reader, anything black, anything… different."

I see Agnes in these words, a bored secretary, typing reports, taking messages, same old, same old, every day, then this guy arrives and does something different.

"Fine, Agnes, we can have an understanding."

Then she gets a bit too close for comfort.

"We can, Sean, my psychosleuth."

Psychosleuth! Although surprised, impressed, flattered even, at her insight into the forensic world, I like the term.

"A psychosleuth," I repeat. "Good word, Agnes."

"Yes, Sean, a combination of psycho, psychologist, an expert in the workings of the mind, and sleuth, a detective, an investigator, psychosleuth."

John would love this word, I think.

"Psychosleuth, I like it Agnes, where did you get this?"

"Yes, I thought you might. I read about it last night. I've got a pile of books on criminology. I'm thinking of doing an Open University course on it."

Jesus, this is all we need, a psychology secretary cum criminologist? But I don't say it, I need her on my side.

"Oh, that's good, Agnes, if I can do anything..."

Then she gets close. Her thick glasses indicate poor vision, but she comes close enough for me to smell her perfume, which is coming at me strongly, along with her.

"And if I can do anything," she says, "anything..." I move back, feeling uncomfortable, time to retreat to my room. "Oh, and Rooney?"

"Yes, Agnes." I move around her as I move towards the door.

"Doctor J wants to see you, tomorrow for lunch, in his office."

The last time I talked to Doctor J was about the deficiencies of care in the back wards and my time spent in ward 28. Then, he said he didn't want me to say anything about the care deficits there, reiterating there are 'other ways' and how we should 'keep our powder dry for now'. He must want to follow this up, to discuss the 'other ways'.

I've go to go to his office in the admin building, which is right in the front of the hospital, where most of the consultants have their offices. I reach the Pass and stop. Myra is there as usual. I stand over her and say hello. She doesn't acknowledge me. I turn and Doctor J is standing there.

"Hi Sean, I've been waiting for you." He has two cartons of soup and two packs of sandwiches. "Lunch," he says.

He's friendly and welcoming. He shows me up the stairs, to his consulting room and to a table at the middle of it. He passes me the carton of soup and sandwiches. There's a pot of tea in the middle of the table and plates. I expect him to talk about my experiences in ward

28 and he does.

"Sean, I wanted to catch up with you. You know, what we talked about, ward 28." I sit back and listen, but then he goes off like a rocket. "Sean, you should know, there are ways in this place which… sustain it." Then he starts to say grace.

"My dear Lord, we ask for God's blessing on the food we are about to receive."

I always knew the Castle wasn't typical, partly why I'm here now. It is so far from being usual from anything I have ever known. Everybody knows it isn't normal.

Jamieson starts to eat, expecting me to start too. I wonder if he'll say the staff are institutionalised and the move to care in the community will change things, that all the patients will eventually be discharged into modern community placed settings.

"Sean," he says, "there are… cultural deficits in this hospital, but the staff and the patients' faith will see them through."

I nearly choke on the soup as he pours tea casually into two China tea cups.

"Doctor Jamieson, this needs to—"

"I know, Sean, you want to report what you found in ward 28, but I believe a better way is to offer greater pastoral instruction to the staff. We need more of God in the wards. I'll talk to the Chaplain. If the staff embrace God, they will embrace God's children, the patients. This'll do it."

I push the sandwiches away, scared I may be sick.

"Doctor Jamieson, did you know some patients believe there are ghosts in the hospital?"

"Sean, the scriptures says when people die, their spirit and soul immediately go to heaven or hell. We do not wander about the earth, or the hospital."

I look at him. He doesn't believe in ghosts and he thinks God will change the lives of the patients in ward 28. I leave him and go down the stairs passing Myra once more. I know I need to engage her but my mind is on other things. The Castle, however, certainly has a ghostly feel to it, with its turrets, long empty corridors, long forgotten empty wards; but actual ghosts? I'm not sure what I think about ghosts. I've long lost my religion and my belief in God, and I kind-of enquired into spiritualism when my mum died, but ghosts,

I'm not sure of. If one came at me and bit me on the face them I might believe in them, but until then...

I work late, doing reports, and then go out across the lawn to the nurses' home with a different type of spirit on my mind. With all the talk about ghosts and *them*, I cannot help but feel uneasy walking in the dark. It's a moonlit night and clear, and the only sounds I hear are from the television sets in the wards and an owl hooting.

I look over towards ward 22 and can just about make out Walter sitting looking out to his trees. I imagine Alex will be doing something similar in ward 8, looking out into the grounds for *them*; Mairi sneaking a quiet smoke out of the toilet window of ward 7; the patient in ward 28 talking about his ghosts.

There's no escaping the eerie atmosphere of the Castle and its grounds. I look over towards the graveyard and think about Joan. The logical part of my mind cautions me about believing in ghosts, although there is something comforting about me being in touch with my mother, in the other world, or whatever world she may inhabit, where mentally ill souls go.

Will mentally ill people have mental illness where they go, or is this a physical attribute? Is mental illness, as someone once said, the price of being human?

CHAPTER 17

Lately, my mind is on the hospital, its history, its underworld, even its supernatural presence, but I've been thinking of the group, prompted by Alex constantly turning up at the department. Walter has also asked for me in the ward, as has John, and I bump into Mairi in the corridor and she's asking too.

I need to reconvene the group. This time, however, I'll have the benefit of the department's overhead projector. I produce a few acetates to help. I hope this will help the group to focus.

Contrary to last time, I'm waiting for them as they filter into the room. They all take familiar seats, falling into a shape around the room I'm growing to know well. Mairi is close to the window to allow the cannabis smoke out. To her left, Walter, in his wheelchair, is backed into the corner. Then to his left is John, at one side of the small sofa, his notepad and pencils at hand. Alex is to his left at the other end of the sofa, much more subdued since the last time, having been warned by me not to repeat any of his antics. Jackie retains her seat next to the door, her safety route should she need to get out of there quickly. Agnes brings in tea, coffee, and plain biscuits on a tray. I thank her as she smiles at me.

Just before the meeting she says she would be happy to act as a minute taker. I wonder if this may be better than John's indiscernible notes and nearly agree; but I worry, given her interest in the group, she may want to become more involved than just taking the record.

"Thank you all for coming," I say. Jackie looks away as if to say the man thinks he is addressing a rotary committee meeting. I clear my throat. "We're here to consider events in the hospital we feel strongly about. They concern the—"

Jackie shakes her head again.

"Rooney, get on with it, we all know why we are here."

I clear my throat again.

"Right, Jackie."

Alex gets to his feet with his hand up.

"Can I ask a question, Mr Rooney?"

"Go on, Alex."

"Will we be—"

"Sit on your arse," Jackie says, "we're here to talk."

Walter chips in.

"I'll have no part in a hospital committee meeting. It's the hospital's responsibility to formally assess these matters. I'll not do their job."

There is a universal nodding of heads. I need to galvanise this group and fast.

"I accept what you are all saying," I say. "We'll, a, find out why people are dying and—"

"People are being fuckin' killed, Mr Rooney," Mairi says. "My father was murdered, he didn't… die."

"Hold on dear," Jackie says. "No one, as yet, has established murder has happened in this place."

"Just don't call me dear, dear."

"Sorry?"

"You heard me, don't call me dear."

Mairi's scorn is apparent, as is the shrill of her voice.

"A woman not to trifle with," Jackie smirks back.

I need to keep matters on track.

"Okay," I say, "until we can be sure we are dealing with murder we will use the term 'being killed'." There are nods of affirmation. "Then, b, we will establish as best we can, who is doing it."

Jackie's determined to ensure this remains on a proper footing.

"And, c, she says, if there's anything to suggest there's something going on here we will pass it on to the proper authorities."

I add, "If anyone is unhappy about this and no longer wishes to be involved, this is the time to leave, no one would think anything of it." No one moves. "Good," I say, "but we need some ground rules."

Mairi takes a big draw.

"I don't like rules."

"But we need them, Mairi, it kind of makes sure it all works properly."

"Moving from the forming to storming," John says, as he writes.

"Tell us, Mr Rooney. I want to get back to my—"

"Trees, Walter?" Mairi says.

"Aye, trees… dear."

"OK, some basic rules," I say. Walter has his clipboard and pencil at the ready. "One, we keep everything discussed between us to here, no talking about it to anyone."

"Aye," Mairi adds. "If the physician superintendent finds out, we're fucked."

"Right, first, total secrecy; two, no acting on any information we have outwith the group; got it, Alex?" Alex nods. "Three, anyone can leave at any time, but they must be held to secrecy, and four—"

"We bring in the polis immediately we find anything incriminating or we get out of our depth," Jackie adds.

"Yes, something like that. All agreed?"

Nods abound. Alex puts his hand up.

"Do we get to stab the bastard who's doing the killings?"

Jackie is now standing over him.

"No, you fucking will not. No violence, got it, from no one." She turns to me. "That's number five, Rooney, get it down."

"There will be no operational arm of the group," John says, writing.

"I think it is understood, Jackie. All agreed?" All nod. "Any abstentions?" Nothing is said. "Okay, carried."

"Right, let's get down to it," Mairi says. "I want to talk about my dad."

"We need to decide on the order of the cases, Mairi," I say. "I was thinking we should talk about Joan first, she was trying to tell us something and did chronicle the events well."

"Then, my dad?"

"Okay."

Mairi smiles.

I step forward to the overhead projector and put the first acetate on the glass.

JOAN TRAINOR – SUICIDE

"Joan had endogenous depression," I say, "and after treatment for a newly discovered thyroid problem, she became much improved in her mood. Then, she was allowed a pass out into the grounds for a walk. However, she made her way, over five miles, that evening to the Dalmarnock Bridge. Her body was found by a man fishing under the bridge the following morning. It was concluded she had jumped off the bridge and committed suicide."

John gets up.

"For a proper analysis we need to confirm the data and arrive at a hypothesis."

"Jesus wept," Jackie says. "I'm an investigative detective, I know how to make a proper analysis."

"Jackie, please, give him a chance?"

"This is just nuts, these guys are just nuts. Why are you... indulging them?"

"I'm not indulging them. I'm trying to address a serious matter here and they can help. They know things."

"Rooney, if there's an issue here, I'd bring in a team. There ain't anything of—"

"If there ain't an issue, we're not causing a problem for anyone. So, can we let John speak?"

Jackie crosses her arms and turns towards the wall.

"Jesus, get on with it."

"John?"

John resumes staccato style.

"Joan was depressed. She gets better. She's ready for discharge. Going to a care home. Goes for a walk. Gets to Dalmarnock Bridge. Five miles away. Throws herself off the bridge into the river. Found by a fisherman."

"And what is your hypothesis, John?" Walter asks.

"He hasn't arrived at one, yet," Jackie interjects. "She couldn't cope with the reality of her situation, having to leave hospital, and she kills herself?"

"What about she was murdered?" Walter says.

"Yes, she was murdered," Alex says, agreeing. "*They* did it."

"A hypotheses, John?" Mairi adds, ignoring Alex. "There's something feckin' funny going on in this nuthouse."

"I agree with that," Jackie says.

"We know Joan kept a notebook," I say. "Why? She was suspicious of something going on, so much so she wanted to record it. She hid it in her hat for it to be found. She wanted to tell people. Why would she want to kill herself? She was getting better and getting out of here."

"There are... inconsistencies," John mumbles. "Mr Rooney."

"Yes?"

"She was overweight," he says. "And she walks five miles?"

"Indeed, John, and to my knowledge, no one has come forward to say they saw her; which, given how busy the route is, is unusual."

"And," Walter says, "they say—"

"Who says?" asks Jackie.

"My trees, Ms Kaminski."

Jackie looks around at others.

"Oh right, your trees, Walter."

"She wasn't wearing a coat, Detective Inspector."

Jackie knows not to contradict this; she knows Walter will be right.

"And why Dalmarnock Bridge?" I say.

"Yes, when she could have put her head on the railway track."

"Thanks Jackie, something of my point. She could have taken her life in an alternative way."

"Makes more sense they killed her," Alex says.

"It doesn't make sense at all, Alex."

A quiet descends in the room. Agnes pops her head around the door.

"More tea, anyone?"

"No thanks Agnes, we're fine," I say.

Walter looks to John.

"We would like a cup of tea, Mr Rooney," John says.

"Thank you, Agnes, we'll have a cup of tea."

"I'll fill the kettle."

"Thank you, Miss," Walter says. "Mr Rooney, I have something to say about Joan."

"Go on, Walter."

"I have something to say too, Mr Rooney," John adds.

"Yes, thanks John. Walter first."

Walter pushes his wheelchair into the middle of the room and turns to face the group.

"I saw Joan leaving the recreation hall at exactly 4.30 p.m.," he says, "as they set it up for dinner that night. Then she went along the corridor and stopped at the social work department. The social work department only has appointments. Later, at six p.m., I saw her walking in the grounds. No coat, no hat, looking distressed. She passed the tree and turned to me. I saw her face. It looked like she had been crying. She turned and walked through the gardens towards the gate. I thought about telling the ward staff, but decided not to. It was not for me to curtail the liberty of a fellow patient."

"Thanks, Walter. John."

"A tentapotheses—"

"Oh go on," Jackie says.

John takes to his feet.

"Joan watches, gets better, gets scared, gets out. Runs, then jumps, or is pushed. The considered balance of likelybilities is she jumped, not being able to cope with the consquencials of having to leave what she considered to be a safe place." He sits down.

They all look at me.

"Is this all we got?" Jackie says.

"I guess this's all we got," I say.

"Right," Mairi says, "can we talk about my dad?"

Jackie is on her feet.

"You obviously know nothing about investigating anything even resembling a murder. A bloody talking shop. Keep this as a true crime interest group and enjoy. That's your level. If you come up with anything, let me know, and I'll take it from there. Me, I'm away."

She moves towards the door, but Mairi blocks her way.

"You listen, dear. I have evidence my father was killed, but I can't raise it with your lot because you'll come stomping in here with your size tens and whoever did it will disappear out of sight. The person or persons who are doing this are *in* this place. They'll drop off the radar and find another way to kill the folk in here. And what will the patients think about a pile of polis coming in here? Most are paranoid enough as it is." She turns to Alex and John. "There would be panic in here and not a few taking to the loch or the railway track. Then, when you find nothing, you lot will get up and walk away as you are doing now."

I move between them.

"She's right, Jackie. At least see where this goes, at least until we can establish if there really is something going on in here."

Jackie looks at me.

"Right, but only as far as that point." She sits back down, but Mairi isn't finished.

"Remember you're held to a promise of secrecy? I'm saying nothing if you're going blab it to your polis pals."

Due to her delay in responding it's clear Jackie is mulling over why she doesn't walk out there and then.

"OK, I'll hear you out, if only to confirm the inconsistencies of your story."

Mairi moves nearer to the overhead projector.

"Right. My father was killed and I can prove it." Jackie looks at the wall. "Look at this?" Mairi pulls out a polaroid photograph. She passes it around. Jackie studies it longer than the rest and passes it to me. "Sean?" I take the photo. I see a face, presumably John MacDougal's. "Describe it please," she says, so we all get the same information.

"Right. We have an elderly man, mouth open, eyes open, pupils dilated."

"Would you say he was dead?"

"Sure looks like it to me."

"What else do you see?"

I look at the photo.

"Not sure..."

"You're not sure. What else about the eyes?"

"They look bloodshot."

"Yes, a sign of suffocation. Now look at the mouth and the nose." I study the photo intently.

"Is that blood on the nose and the mouth?"

"Yes, and the marks, bruising starting to show." I look intently.

"There's writing on it, on the photograph."

"I know, I wrote on it."

"Ten fifty five, Monday, first of March, 1982."

"Yes, first of March, just before eleven o'clock, my dad was dead by that point. He was stiff rigid, right down to his feet. Rigor mortis usually starts three hours after a person dies. The stiffening starts around the head and neck and gradually progresses downward toward the feet and toes. I reckon he died between three and five in the morning and was transferred to his seat in his room where I found him."

"He had a room?" Walter asks.

"He had epilepsy and took fits, they had to watch him."

"Didn't watch him very well."

"He normally goes there about eight a.m. He was dead by that point and would have had to be taken there. And look at this one?" She hands me another polaroid.

"Do you always have a polaroid camera with you, Mairi?"

"Always in my bag. I'm a true crime writer and always on the lookout for a crime scene to capture."

I look at the photo.

"It's a pillow."

"Yes, the pillow which was put over my father's head."

"There's blood on it."

"Yes, my father's, believe me I know it."

"Where—"

"It was under his bed. The bedding had been changed, but I looked under the bed and found the pillow."

John is writing furiously. "Forensics, blood, time and cause of death, rigor mortis."

"Did *you* kill him, Mairi?"

"What?"

"Well, you were in his room," Jackie adds. "You could have done it, put the pillow over his face, put him in his wheelchair and pushed him out to the conservatory."

"I wasn't there when he died, DI. Apart from the fact my father, although not a strong man by any means, would have resisted my puny attempts to kill him."

"A man killed him," John says.

"Well, what do you think?"

"What do I think," John writes and says.

Jackie persists.

"Did a doctor examine him?"

"Yes, of course, an unexpected death," Mairi replies.

"Who?"

"Doctor Jamieson."

"Not an external medical clinician?"

"No."

The group disperse, Mairi towards the west corridor, the men along the east. Jackie and I go to the car park and out with drinking in mind. We leave Jackie's car at her flat and walk down to Byres Road and into Tennent's Bar.

I reach the bar first.

"Pint of Guinness. You, lager?"

Jackie pushes in beside me at the bar.

"And what if I fancied something else?"

"I knew you wouldn't, you've been drinking it for years."

"Well, white wine is coming in and I like it. Anyway, just don't start taking me for granted or making my decisions for me."

"OK, darling."

She pulls a stool in close to the bar and climbs on it.

"The group, Rooney."

I'm waiting for it.

"Aye?"

"I'm worried about it."

I know what's coming, i.e. this group is crazy, crazy idea, crazy people, crazy thing to do.

"I know you don't approve, but let's see where it goes."

"Mairi's off it."

"What?"

"She's believing things which aren't true, her father, the pillow, murder, etcetera."

"She believes it, Jackie."

"Doesn't mean to say it's right."

She takes a sip and looks straight ahead at the gantry.

"I'm worried about you too, Rooney, you."

Shit, I think, it's the mental health thing again.

"I'll be OK, Jackie, I'm not high, low, confused. I know what I'm doing."

"I hope so. You could mess up your career otherwise. Then you are back fixing TVs. You have a chance here to do something you have always wanted to do. I'm not going to argue with this. You got out of the scheme and everything along with it, the drink, drugs, the gangs."

I see a friend at the other side of the bar.

"Just caught sight of an old friend," I say to Jackie.

She doesn't look the friend's way.

"Your old friends are bad news, Rooney."

"Fuck, he's coming over."

"Just ignore him, he'll go away when he sees me, they can smell a bizzie from a mile away."

"Hello, Rooney, how's it goin'?" comes from over my shoulder.

I know this is Stanley Holland, a fully paid-up member of the Maryhill Fleet. I turn around to greet him.

"Oh, hello Stanley, unusual to see you in here."

"Aye, ah know, a wee bit out of my locality, but I'm here now most nights at the weekend, trendy west end, less gangs around, safer for me. You alright?"

"Aye, I'm fine." There's the inevitable pause. "This your wuman?"

Jackie refuses to engage.

"This is Jackie. Jackie this is Stanley." Jackie doesn't move.

"Aye, hello, hen," Stanley says into the back of Jackie's head.

"Aye, hello, son," Jackie says through wine sipping lips.

"Rooney?"

"Aye, Stanley."

"You're up in the nut hoose."

"Aye, Stanley, the psychiatric hospital."

"The nut hoose."

This's not going to go well.

"If you don't mind, Stanley, we're—"

"I know, having a quiet drink. Sorry, I'll no' cramp your style."

"Fine, Stanley, good to see you."

"Rooney?"

"What?"

Stanley whispers in my ear.

"The big guys, the fuckin' mob are going to kill some folk… in the nut hoose."

I take Stanley by the arm away from the bar. This's not something I want Jackie to hear. "Stanley, get a grip." He makes to walk away. "Stanley," I say, to stop him.

"You heard me, Rooney. Just don't fuck about in there. The teams are going to kill people. Something to do with stopping the Health Board discharging folk into the schemes."

"Jesus, Stanley, these are normal folk, no threat to nobody."

"Rooney, I know some of them," he says. "They're psychopaths, paedophiles, crackpots. The normal folk are no' wanting them. The mob do the people's bidding in return for favours. That's how it works. You know that. Just don't get in the way. You'll get hurt."

Jackie hears this last sentence and is up to face Stanley.

"Listen, son," she says, even although there's hardly an age difference. Stanley says nothing. "Nobody's going to get hurt on my watch or you'll have the whole of Partick Polis coming down on you. Got it?"

Stanley gives more grin than smile, then winks at me and moves away.

"Bye, Rooney, mind what I told you."

Jackie looks at me.

"What did he say, was he making a threat against you?"

"No chance," I say, "just the usual shite, not to get above myself."

"Just keep your friends close and your enemies closer, Rooney."

As Jackie talks, I am thinking, Jesus, Nimby, not in the mob's back yard right enough. We go back to the bar and our drinking. I know Stanley's not a man to say such things without reason. We drink until throwing out time and go back to Jackie's flat.

Next day, feeling less than well, I'm back in my room. I'm know I'm vulnerable to mental health problems, depression during school, some episodes of mania, but nothing serious. I spend Sunday pacing the room, continually looking out of the window. The place is getting to me.

I go to the ward meeting on the Monday morning drawing looks from the ward staff and Doctor J.

"You alright, Sean?" Jamieson pulls me over by the window so no one hears him.

"Yeah, I'm fine."

"You just seem a bit… agitated."

"No, I'm fine Doctor—"

"John."

"John, I'm fine."

"Don't mention this to anyone, Sean, but if you need anything, you know to calm down, or sleep, or to get through the day, let me know. I can give you something, just between you and me, you understand?"

I nod, not really knowing what to say. Does he think I am mentally ill or, if not, some sort of a junkie? I would keep his offer in mind, however.

I spend the rest of the day seeing patients, doing my records, notes, reports, but I can't concentrate and my hands are shaking. I really spend most of the day walking up and down the room, going to the window. I can't settle. My mind is racing. Maybe Jamieson is right, maybe I need something to calm me down. I phone him. He comes right away.

"Right, take these." He hands me a small brown bag. I open the bag and pull out a tablet box with blister packs. "Lorazepam 2.5 mg. Twenty-four in there."

"Jesus, Doctor J."

He shushes me and tells me to take one when I need it.

"If you need any more, just ask."

As soon as he leaves, I go to the bathroom and take two tablets. It isn't long before I start feeling their benefit. I feel less agitated, I can concentrate, my hands stop shaking. I complete my records and notes and feel satisfied to go back to my room having put in a good day's work.

I'm last out of the office this day and lock the door as I leave. It's after six p.m. and I notice Myra sitting in her usual place at the Pass. I had encountered her there many times now since I arrived and gradually I made eye contact, and made a point to say hello every time.

This time I stop as I say hello. I've been thinking about her, wondering how I can help her. She just seems to have such a lonely life, yet she chooses there to sit, only the pivotal point in the whole hospital. If she wants to be nondescript, invisible, why would she be sitting there drawing attention to herself? She's wet herself again, I know from the smell. I'll not get into the physiological reasons for this, but I want to connect with her in a practical way. Maybe I can get an understanding of why she sits there. I know by improving a person's self-esteem, improving their self-worth, their mental health will improve also. One way of doing this is to instil a sense of value. By giving Myra a task, I wonder if this will give her a sense of self-worth. I'm aware she had been a statistician and think this may stimulate her. I know something of the demographics of the hospital, numbers of patients, breakdown on sexes, age groups, conditions, but I wonder whether an interesting task for Myra would be to count the number of patients using the corridors. It would be useful to correlate this with the patients in the wards, giving an idea of the proportion of people who get off the ward each day. I've no doubt Myra would be able to discern between patients and staff. I also have an ulterior motive, however.

"Myra?"

She doesn't look up at me. I crouch down to be in line with her.

"Myra, could you do something for me?" Again no response. "Would you count the number of patients who use the corridors each day for me? I know you would be good at this. It would help the psychology department understand where patients go each day. And rough times, genders, etcetera. Anything you find interesting."

She looks up at me for the first time and gestures she would like to write something. I take out a piece of paper and a pen and hand it to her.

"An A4 diary and a pen," she writes.

I smile at her. "Of course, keep the pen and I'll get a desk diary for you."

She smiles back and writes. "And my own chair to get me off this floor?"

"You'll get your own chair."

She writes again. "Mr Rooney?"

I am surprised she knows my name.

"Yes, Myra."

"Is that all you want to know?" she writes. I wonder what she means. "Thank you, that will give me something to do," she adds.

The next day, I deliver the diary to her. She thanks me, saying she'd start tomorrow, Wednesday, the twenty fourth of March.

CHAPTER 18

Friday, 26th of March. It's time to reconvene the group, not really being sure why. Maybe I need the support of them around me. Although they trouble me as individuals and I am perplexed over why I am doing this, it feels safe when nothing is safe, I can wrap myself in the group.

I talk to Agnes and ask her to book the room.

"Leave it with me, I'll sort it. Would you like tea and scones?" I smile at her and she blushes. "Sean."

"What, Agnes?"

Her blush changes to something more intent, more stern.

"Your group?"

"Aye, Agnes."

"I think what you're doing is really good."

I look at her. She avoids my eyes.

"Thanks, Agnes, I appreciate it."

"No problem, Sean. Sean?"

"Aye, Agnes?"

"My son?"

I'm not quite sure where she is coming from. Her son? There's something coming.

"Your son, Agnes?"

She moves around her desk and gets close to me. She sits on the edge of the desk, her legs showing to the thighs, crossed, the right over the left. I must admit, although she is sexy, I haven't noticed her in this way before. She has good legs, a strong body, her breasts pushing through her angora jumper. She's very close to me. I kook around to see if there's anyone else in the office. We are alone and she knows it.

"Sean."

She reaches for my arm. I know nothing about her, but now I realise from her initial blushes she may have a glint in her eye for me, something I haven't noticed before.

"Yes, Agnes."

I put my hand over hers. It might easily be seen as a response, an equal move towards her, to show I like her too, but I'm not sure if I do. Though, I'm not going to throw away the chance of some intimate contact with someone who clearly has a fancy for me.

"My son, Gerald, they call him Gerry, Gerald Connolly, my ex-husbands name. He's in Ward 10, has been for months." I know I have to let her go on. I have to listen. "He's autistic, very clever autistic, with mental health problems, you know anxiety, outbursts. Oh, and he's been known to set fire to things, to draw attention to him you see."

"A good way to get attention."

"I am so worried about him. I think he'll end up in a back ward and be stuck in there for the rest of his life. I would like…"

She stops, but I know where this is going.

"Like me to help him?"

Her face changes. She puts her arms around me and kisses me square on the lips. I'm worried someone may walk in. I look around and remove myself from her embrace.

"Agnes?"

"I am sorry, Sean, I just feel…"

"It's OK." She returns to her side of the desk. "Your son." I have to pursue this, if only to counter the embarrassment we are both feeling. "Gerry, how do you think I can help him?"

She leans across the desk; this time I move back to a healthy distance.

"He is lonely, isolated, finds it difficult talking to people. Your group, Sean, it would help him, I know it would."

"How Agnes, how would it help him?"

"He's really intelligent. He can work anything out. It's his autism. He remembers things, knows things I'll never know, keeps all this information in his head. He's dead bright."

"But the group…"

"The murder group."

Christ, Archie might hear this.

"Agnes?"

"It's OK, Sean, I won't say. I know all about it. I can't help but be interested in what you are doing. I know what's going on."

It's clear Agnes has her ear to the ground, and to the wall!

"The group?"

"It would help him, his self-esteem, as you psychologists say, and I know he'd help you." I look down at the floor, not knowing what to say. "I think he and Alex would get on well. He's dead gifted, loves Bob Dylan, writes songs and poems, to explain what is going on in his head."

Shit, I think, from the murder group to the hippy group, what is this coming to?

She comes back at me from around the desk and puts her arms around me. "I can help you too, Sean. I know everything about this place. I can sort things for you." She puts her hands around my waist and pulls me close, pushing her crotch into me, her breasts too." I want her. I really want to. "Let me, Sean. Please?"

"OK, Agnes, tell him to come to the group next time."

I extricate myself from her, trying to avoid her seeing the swelling in my trousers.

"And you'll let me help?"

"Yes, OK."

I appreciate Agnes can help me, in more ways than one.

"Come to the nurses' home, later, a coffee…"

She smiles softly.

"Yes, I'd like that, thank you."

I know I shouldn't, but I'm also playing safe. I may decide not to once she arrives. I may have second thoughts. I hope so, I can't start an affair with the secretary of the department, another risk to my placement if we're found out, a risk to my relationship with Jackie too. Can I?

Agnes arrives at the nurses' home door.

"Delivering scones from Greggs for Mr Rooney," she laughs, as she offers the Rottweiler one.

I arrive and explain she's helping me with overdue reports and we go to my room. The Rottweiler shakes her head in disbelief. Agnes is dressed to kill, the works: leopard print coat, little black dress, knee high boots, fishnets. I invite her in and take her coat.

"Would you like a drink?"

She nods, smiles through glittering lips, and makes herself

comfortable on my two-person settee, her legs crossed giving a glimpse of the top of her stockings. I know right then I can't do this. I want to, but I'm worried I may let her and myself down and make a real mess of it. And what would I say when I walk into the office in the morning? Jesus, what do I do?

We have a couple of glasses of wine and she puts her glass down and then she moves closer to me. I move as far as I can to my end, but I'm pinned by the side of the settee. She puts her arms around my neck and reaches across me and puts her leg across me. I can, if I try, I think.

We kiss, one of those kisses which lasts for ages and then the tongues start. I find my right hand opening her blouse and reaching inside her bra. Her breast is firm and her nipple stands out like a thimble. This is the point of no return, I have to go on whatever the risk.

But just then the door goes, it's John Scott. I open it just enough to hear him.

"Rooney, I need you in the car park, now."

I don't know whether to thank him or tell him to fuck off.

"What is it, John. I'm… busy."

Agnes returns to her side buttoning her blouse.

"We have a developing situation outside, you need to come."

"Jesus, John, I'm just—"

"Rooney, just come."

I give my apologies to Agnes and hand her another glass of wine, saying I'll be back directly. I see by her face she is not amused. I follow Scott along the floor and downstairs to the front door, although the Rottweiler had it bolted from the inside. She warns John she would phone the police if he didn't manage to deal with what was happening outside.

"Leave it with me," John says, "we don't want the police in here."

He knows full well any police brought in would want to search the rooms for drink and drugs, both of which are well available in the nurses' home.

We move outside as the Rottweiler locks the door behind us. Out there, we are confronted by a group of serious looking men, dressed ominously in long black Crombies, a well-known uniform of many of the teams in the schemes outside the hospital grounds. I have no doubt deep in the coats there could be a range of weapons, including coshes, knives, blades, knuckle dusters, but they are also known to carry swords, hatchets and iron bars. This's a particularly heavy team. John had left his golf clubs on this occasion, not that they would have acted as a deterrent to this group.

Scott starts. "Can I help you guys?"

A big guy moves forward.

"Mr McGinn wants to ensure the protection of the women in here."

I know immediately these guys are working for Davy McGinn a local godfather figure who runs protection rackets throughout the East End of Glasgow, so does John Scott.

"Oh, I get it," Scott says. "We pay you money and you leave the lassies alone. Is that it?"

"Aye," the guy in the middle of the group growls. "Something like that. Mr McGinn knows the local wankers are giving the women hassle."

I recall the regular occurrence of the local neds coming through the woods to bother the nurses.

"And if we give you money on a regular basis they disappear and if they don't…"

"They reappear in greater numbers and nurses are assaulted."

"We could bring in the polis?"

"Oh aye, they set up an incident caravan in the car park and you have them breathing down your neck, then they disappear and the guys reappear."

"Security men?" As he says this, we all know of the stupidity of bringing in a private security firm which would probably be run by the mob anyway.

As they talk I am reminded of what Stanley Holland said to me in Tennent's Bar. 'The big guys, the fuckin' mob are going to kill some folk… in the nut hoose.' I wonder if there is any connection with this lot arriving to extort money from the nurses.

"So the nurses are kept safe."

"Aye, and we'll throw in some bonus material, at discount prices."

I know this is a sweetener. The mob supplying cigs, drink, and drugs is well established. That there is a market in prisons is well known, but less so in long stay hospitals given the impoverished customer group there. The nurses, however, are a different prospect. Spending weeks away from home with unsocial shift patterns, they are a target for suppliers.

"How much?" Scott asks.

"A big wan a week."

Scott does his mental arithmetic. With nurses revolving over a seven-day, twenty-hour shift pattern, matching around half the population of the hospital, a thousand pounds is less than a pound a week for each nurse. On such a scale this is affordable. He also assures himself collecting the money and paying the mob would be an easier task than policing the nurses' home from the droves of neds who turn up there on a regular basis. He agrees.

I'm relieved. I can return to Agnes in one piece. I get back and she's in my bed, naked. No going back now, I get out of my clothes and slip in beside her. She feels great, looks great, smells great, and I know this is going to be a memorable night. I get on top of her and feel her hand on my cock guiding it towards its destination. I reach down myself to assist to find me flaccid. I try, but I can't. It bends and droops, and fails me miserably. We spend the next hour or so trying to get me hard. Her taking me in her mouth, masturbating me, trying to relax me, but nothing works. I pour us two more glasses of wine and we sit up in the bed, me trying to say this hasn't happened before, her saying it must be her. Jesus, I knew this might have happened. My medication, the drink, the commotion outside, my state of mind, it was always going to be possible. I know I shouldn't have done it.

"I am sorry, Agnes. I…"

"Ach, think nothing of it," she says, graciously. "It happens to every man."

I wonder if I should try again, but a second failure would be a total disaster. At least we can come back together at another time and next time I'll hope to be in full working order.

We drink more and I know she will be staying the night and how will I explain this to the Rottweiler. I tell her it'd be best I get a taxi for her and I'd like to see her again. This appears to satisfy her, not as much as full sex would have had, I think, but she seems OK with it. We get our clothes on and I take her out to wait for the taxi. The Rottweiler is in her room watching TV, which is just as well, no explanations would be needed there.

The taxi comes into view and Agnes reaches for me and kisses me square on the lips. I don't know what to say; but: "Thanks for coming and I'll see you at work," comes out.

"You'll let Gerry into the group." She looks into my eyes. How can I refuse her?

"Yes, of course, arrange the next group meeting and invite Gerry."

Jesus, what will Jackie say about another member.

"And I can help?" Jesus, how can I refuse? "And be the administrator of the group? I'll do tea and scones and take minutes, book the room, etcetera, etcetera?"

I don't remember this being discussed, but she has me over a barrel.

"Yes, OK, Agnes, OK."

Fuck, now we have Gerry and Agnes, Jackie will have a fit.

Agnes gets into the taxi and I return to my room to take stock of this night. I've been impotent on all counts: sexually with Agnes, meekly accepting her son into the group; and, had it come to it, with the thugs, because no doubt I would have backed out physically to stand up to them with John Scott. A total useless man. I open a bottle of whisky.

CHAPTER 19

Saturday morning, I go in to the office to catch up on my notes and records. It's the weekend, so Agnes won't be there. Around noon, I walk down to see Myra. This time I take some of the scones Agnes brought to me, a real treat for someone who only eats out of the hospital kitchen. She eats the three of them as I stand over her.

I see the diary on her lap, the pen stuck in the spine.

"Do you mind if I have a look?"

She nods as she finishes off the third scone.

I lift the diary and open it. Inside as a title she had written PASSING THE PASS, this pivotal spot just outside the dining room, which also acts as a recreation hall and where occasional concerts are held.

I leaf through the pages, most are empty, until I arrive at Twenty-fourth of March. This was her first entry. As discussed with her, I expect to see numbers of patients. There are thirty-three between 2 and 3 p.m. She added, Of the thirty-three, three are doctors, sixteen are inmates (inmates, I think, not patients), ten are women and six are men, roughly in their 60s, sixteen are from east corridor, and seventeen are from the west corridor. I read on, thirty-three crossed the Pass, twenty-nine returned. I deduce four people left the building or stayed in the admin block outwith the next hour and Myra had counted them as 'not returned'.

I notice over the next couple of days, entries Twenty-fifth and Twenty-sixth of March, her records become more graphic, more meticulous. She draws matchstick men and women. The female patients have triangles for skirts; the males two rectangles for trousers, almost like culottes; doctors are in coats; nurses in a kind of a smock; nondescript individuals are portrayed as a circle with four limbs sticking out.

Although she knew some of the people passing by, she gave nicknames and drawings for some people who passed by, such as 'Betty

Boop', for a plump nurse, and 'God the Father,' for a nondescript male in a robe, longer and thinner than the other male drawings. I wonder why she doesn't put names to the shapes.

"Anything unusual in your diary." I move to the last page with text. "Today, Friday, the twenty-sixth of March."

She doesn't answer but I look to the page to see a woman patient figure, crossed out with two thick lines, with the God the Father figure close to her, like he's holding her hand.

"This is today, Myra?"

She nods. Once more I have to question myself for doubting her sanity, but it occurs to me I have unwittingly enlisted Myra to be my eyes, in the way Joan was before she died, on the human traffic moving through the hospital.

I return to the nurses' home to see John Scott collecting a bunch of pound notes from a nurse at the entrance of the nurses' floor, obviously their protection payments.

I go to my room. Tomorrow, Sunday, I'll stay in bed all day and, with a mix of my medication, both prescribed and non-prescribed, and a bottle of whisky, I'll be ready for work on Monday. I wonder what I'll say to Agnes.

Doctor J's Lorazepam ameliorates my pained head. I double the 2.5 mg doze and fall asleep. The next thing I know the door is going again. Oh no, I think, John Scott wants me outside to fight the mob, but this time it's the Rottweiler.

"There was a phone call for you, it was Archie, you're late for the meeting," she says, through the crack in the door.

Jesus, I think, grabbing and thrusting my face into the clock.

"It's only ten o' clock on Sunday."

"Sunday, Sean? It is Monday, not Sunday."

I've lost a day. I jump up and climb into my clothes and shoes, wash my face and brush my hair, to be running across the grounds towards the hospital within minutes. I dash into the meeting. All the psychologists are there, Donna stares at me coldly. Agnes smiles coyly as she prepares to take the minutes.

"You're late," Archie snaps.

"I am sorry," I say, squeezing in beside Donna on the sofa.

"Were you drinking?" she asks, quietly in my ear.

"No, sleeping tablets," I reply. "I've trouble sleeping."

Archie raises his voice.

"OK, no more referrals, we should talk about our main item."

It's clear all the referrals had been allocated and I've missed them. I hoped to pick up two or three to show I am keen, but Archie had allocated all of them without keeping any for me.

This was an admission, a statement from him, I'm not a team player, not a team member. I'm determined to prove myself, however. Stupidly, I mention the group.

"I have set up a group, it has therapeutic value to some serious—"

"Seriously ill patients don't get better talking about... death, Sean," Archie says.

I look to Agnes, she has a blank look on her face. It's clear Archie knows something about the nature of the group, but hopefully not the full extent or its purpose.

"It seems to... benefit them," I say. Agnes smiles.

Archie asks, "And why do you talk about dead patients?"

Jesus, I think, he knows something right enough. How does he know this? Has Agnes being relaying what she heard from reception? Or has Archie, his room the next door down to the meeting room, where I meet with the group, heard something coming through the wall? I doubt it though, if he had heard everything he would have closed us down, nothing surer.

"We, they, need to talk about the deaths of some of their peer group," I say, like I am discussing a group of soldiers returning from active duty. I see the psychologists passing looks from one to another like a Mexican wave around the room. "There are people dying you know."

The shrill rise in my tone only reduces further my credibility within the group.

Archie gets up and says the meeting is over, the psychologists and Agnes follow him out. Donna and I stay behind.

"Sean," she starts.

I know she's going to say my placement there is at risk, and with it my getting through the course. My dreams of being a psychologist are totally at risk.

"I get it, Donna, I really do." But do I?

"I hope so, Sean. I've your report to do at the end of the month and it needs to be positive." I know this as an ultimatum. "You need to show some indication your... therapeutic input is having an effect, a good effect, on the patients in your care."

How can I do this? I know I am helping Walter by letting him express himself. I think I am helping Myra by giving her something useful to do. I feel I'm giving Mairi a way of exploring her father's death, emotionally and practically. But I doubt if I'm helping John or Alex in their psychotic states, or even the new candidate Agnes's son Gerry. If anything I may have reinforced, even entrenched, their delusions.

"Please don't get drawn into what is happening in this hospital."

"What is happening, Donna?"

She gives me a look, like a teacher would give an unruly pupil.

"You know what, Sean, the other one."

"What... other one?"

Her look of annoyance changes to one of incredulity.

"You haven't heard?"

"What?"

It becomes clear immediately she's talking about another death. Myra's drawing means 'another one'.

"Jesus, who?"

"Elsie Murdoch, a sixty-three-year-old ex-nurse of the hospital, who herself was admitted to spend years in ward 23. She was found yesterday, but they reckon she'd walked into the loch on Friday afternoon, shortly after she'd left the ward. Her body was found floating in the loch, a few yards away from her shoes which were found on the bank. There was no suggestion of foul play, she had been depressed for many years and had voiced suicidal thoughts."

Jesus, I wonder if Myra's drawing on Friday afternoon was saying something. Who was the woman patient figure crossed out with two black lines in her diary?

Was this Elsie?

CHAPTER 20

Monday, 29th of March, and it's been snowing. I decide to go to the loch to see for myself. I walk through the trees, crunching through muddy and icy ground. I approach the loch on the route it was thought she had taken, where her body was seen by a jogger on his Sunday run lying face down in the shallows of the loch. A police tape had been strung around a couple of yards between two stanchions hammered into the soft bank a few feet from the loch's edge where her body had been retrieved from the water. It says, *Police Incident Scene, Do Not Enter.* I stop at it, wondering if it'll stop people being curious, a macabre scene to ease the boredom of living in the hospital. I needn't worry, there's no one there. I decide not to go under the tape but skirt it to the left to look to the bank where there is a clear sign of a number of footmarks and skid marks, possibly caused by the nurses or porters who pulled the body up out of the water and away to the morgue, after the police had given the OK.

"No suspicious circumstances," Donna had said to me earlier. "A clear suicide."

The tape they put up was no more than a way of keeping the nosey patients and locals from coming to the scene. I try to imagine Elsie walking down here, stopping at the edge, taking off her shoes and walking fully clothed into the water until she was submerged. I presume she walked directly on a line from the hospital straight into the water, but I decide to explore the bank to the left a few yards, where there were no signs of disturbance to the undergrowth and then to the right. I pull back some bushes and notice some indentations in the mud made by feet, not two, however, I see there are two sets of footprints.

Elsie had been taken to the mortuary. I go there thinking I'd have to explain to whoever's supervising the area why I want to see Elsie. On the way up the east corridor I call into ward 7 to see Mairi. I ask her if I could borrow her polaroid camera for an hour. She agrees, not asking why, but when I tell her, she demands to accompany me in my task.

We go to the mortuary to find no one there. Mairi says when her dad was there she was told there has never been a need to have the room locked or supervised. We go in. Immediately, in the middle of the room, we see a figure on a trolley covered by a grey sheet. I presume it is Elsie and control the urge to lift the sheet to look at her face. On a metal under-shelf there is a black bag, which I presume will be holding her clothes. On the top of the bag lies her shoes. I lift the shoes to observe the mud from the bank of the loch, a brown grainy type I found there. I place them sole up and Mairi takes a photo then returns them onto the bag underneath. As she's doing this I notice Elsie's fingers peeping out from beneath the sheet. I turn the sheet slightly to reveal her hand. It's white, almost translucent from the lack of blood flowing through it. I touch it to feel the waxy coldness I've grown to know in my personal and professional life. I didn't know her but I put my hand over hers and gently grasp it in mine. It seems the right thing to do, to show some comfort to a dead person, to give some respect to her life. I feel sorry for her, to be confined to a place such as the Castle, to end her life in the cold water of the loch, minutes from the hospital where she served as a nurse.

Then Mairi says, "I am sorry for your death, Elsie, but not sorry for your life, for you touched the lives of others. God bless you." Mairi gives me the photo as we go back down the corridor. "I hope it helps," she says.

"We'll see, now we need to go to the loch."

"Hope you're not going to push me in, Rooney?"

I smile nervously, wondering if she's worried I may.

We go to the loch where Elsie was found. I take out the photograph of Elsie's shoes and compare them with the footprints I found to the side of the loch.

"Bingo," I say. They match, naturally, because Elsie had been there, but the other set of footprints don't, they were from an unknown wearer. Mairi takes a photograph of the other set of footprints.

The day after, the Tuesday, sanctioned by Donna and agreed by Archie, I've to see Elsie's sister who lives in Easterhouse. Elsie and her sister Mary had lived together for many years and had both been nurses in the hospital, Mary retiring, a few years ago, shortly after Elsie had succumbed to depression. She had visited her sister on Thursday, the day before she took her life.

Mary welcomes me into her living room and brings through a tray of tea and shortbread. She has the funeral to arrange and has just returned after registering the death.

"Was there a death certificate?" I wonder whether it would be an unexplained death requiring a report to be sent to the procurator fiscal.

"Oh yes, Doctor Jamieson signed it. Suicide, it said, by drowning, although not of sound mind. Why couldn't it have just said something else, like accidental drowning or something. Did it really need to say suicide? Why couldn't they have watched over her better? Bloody hospital, her life was over the day she got a job in there."

She is angry and believes the hospital is responsible for her sister's death. She'll be demanding an investigation into why she was allowed to get off the ward. She says her sister had said she wanted to kill herself to her when she visited her on the ward the day before. She had reported this to the charge nurse who had reported this to Doctor Jamieson. She knows ward 23 is identified as a rehabilitation ward with the patients ready to be decanted to other wards, including Elsie who had been viewed as having intractable depression, but due to her good physical state she could be nursed in another setting.

I explain to Mary I am available to give her support. She says she would be OK. She has a good support system at her local church and would rely on that. She shows me to the door and thanks me for coming to see her. Then, by way of a final remark, she says, "Mary was feart of him."

Although I had heard her I want to confirm what she had said.

"Could you say that again, Mary, please?"

"I said she was feart of him."

"Feart of whom, Mary?"

"The doctor, of course, Jamieson." With this, she closes the door; she's said enough.

We need to meet to discuss Elsie's suicide. It has all the suspicious antecedents found in other deaths: they'll expect it. I am, however, worried about using the meeting room of the psychology department, fearing Archie may overhear some of our talk. I have to be squeaky clean for the next few weeks, at least until Donna does my report.

Where though? Agnes is friendly with an occupational therapist, Sheila Thompson, who offers us a room at the back of the department. It's full of OT equipment, materials to help people rehab.

"You won't be disturbed there," she says to Agnes.

We agree to take it and meet there. Agnes says she'll keep up the tea and scones, and bring them to us. She says Gerry will be there, which is a further component I hadn't factored for and also she wants to sit in on the meetings. We say nothing about the other night, but I'm sure it'll rear its head again, sometime soon. She says she has become bored by typing reports, taking calls, and this would be a refreshing alternative. I wonder if she's to be a mole, that Archie or Donna have talked her into getting involved, to keep an eye on what was going on here. I satisfy myself with the knowledge she's keenly interested and we have... unfinished business.

We meet on Wednesday. The OT room is small and cramped, but we all manage to squeeze in. John and Alex on a bench, Walter in his wheelchair, Mairi, Jackie, and now Agnes and Gerry, on separate chairs. I push the door tight shut and place my chair up tight to it. It feels safe and private, not like the psychology department room.

Gerry is talking to himself and is nervously shifting around in his seat. I introduce him to the group. He springs to his feet, like he thinks he's expected to give an introductory speech.

"Thank you, sir, my name is—"

"Sit, down, Gerald," Agnes orders. "Wait for Mr Rooney, he'll tell you what you need to do."

Agnes gives a smile though glossed lips. I look back at her nervously, wondering if it's a good idea to have them both here.

"It's OK, Agnes, if Gerald—"

"Gerry," he says.

"Sorry, Gerry, if you want to say something, just say it. We have no formality here." I look around the room, they all seem happy to receive the young man, to hear what he has to say, like there's a camaraderie. Gerry says he would like to recite a poem. I look around the room once more, to see less interested faces now looking back at me, but Walter, a liker of poetry, nods at me.

"Yes, a poem; yes, please carry on." I sit down to listen.

Gerry clears his throat.

"Too many die, even less live, ask yourself why, yourself you give. In this damn place, there is no light, only hatred, greed, death and plight." He looks around as if expecting an applause. I do too. There are no dissenters to his words here.

"Go'on yourself, pal," Alex says. "I like it."

Gerry clears his throat once more.

"There is one, my friend, who hopes it will never end. Because profit in healing there is no bread, but profit in killing, the dying and dead." He takes a pause. More to come, I think, and there is. "Doctor Death is he who lives by death, to prolong suffering until his last breath, but do not worry, his time will come, by an assassin's bullet, it will take only one."

I look to Agnes, she is impassionate, like she had heard these words before; then I look around, no one appears perturbed by his words.

Alex has a big smile on his face.

"Aye, an assassin's bullet, that'll do it," he says.

Only Jackie is askance. I have no doubt she'll be saying something soon, to get them to control themselves, but for then all she does is shake her head and frowns.

Gerry continues.

"They call him Doctor Death, him and his factory of pain. They call him Doctor Death, him and his murder campaign."

Alex gets to his feet and starts clapping. Gerry starts to blush but quickly regains his composure. Agnes looks at me as if to say, 'Is this OK?' I look to Jackie, she isn't happy. Then the rest. Walter, then John, then Mairi join in with Alex with a muffled clap. Gerry appears embarrassed. It appears the best way to be accepted by the group is to reveal yourself, your vulnerabilities. I'm impressed, but not so much by his choice of subject matter and the reference to Doctor Death. It takes me back to the patient in ward 28, the night I was there, who referred to Doctor Jamieson as Doctor Death.

We get back on track, talking about Elsie and her death. I explain how Myra had indicated another would die, a woman. I say how I had found another set of foot imprints at the side of the loch, where she died and had taken some photographs, and what Mary, her sister, said about Dr Jamieson, how she was scared of him. Was all of this relevant?

Certainly Mairi thought so. "Another poor fucker fucked, how many is it now, thirty, forty?"

Jackie's not so sure. "Come on, she killed herself, no suspicious circumstances."

John flexes his analytical muscle. "Check Jamieson's shoes, mud from the loch means he's been there."

This isn't such a bad idea.

Walter is more realistic. "If he had killed her, he would have washed his shoes, no doubt."

Walter's right, but John's determined. "You would have confirmed Elsie's foot prints."

"Yes," I say.

"And there was another set of footprints?"

"Yes." I know what's coming.

"Well, compare them with Dr Jamieson's shoes and see if they match."

"Oh for God's sake," bemoans Jackie. "How the hell are you going to get a consultant psychiatrist's shoes?"

"I know," says Agnes.

We all look at her.

"You do, Agnes. How?" I ask.

"He enjoys a game of golf on Wednesdays and Saturday afternoons. He'll wear golf shoes and leave his own shoes in the locker room." I guess Agnes will have a role in the group after all. "He plays with Professor Owen."

"Right. We'll work as a team." This stirs interest. I see it in their faces, but not Jackie's. "We'll sit on a bench just in sight of the locker room, but just out of sight of Dr Jamieson when he arrives to change into his golf shoes." A group of patients, with me and Jackie turning up would raise his suspicions. "When they leave to start their round of golf, we'll nip in and check his shoes."

"On Saturday afternoon?" Walter asks.

"Aye, out there." Agnes points out of the window.

CHAPTER 21

Friday night, as usual, Jackie and I are in the Horseshoe Bar. There's a more sombre atmosphere between us than usual. Jackie's head is down looking into her drink, a gin and tonic, unusual for a lager drinker, which she sucks from a straw. Her eyes are down on the drink watching it vanish up the straw and into her mouth. Clearly, she's in no mood to embark on our usual Friday night banter, politics, policing in Partick, the state of Glasgow's pavements, the state of the world. I know it's coming.

"You're way out of order, Rooney."

I drop my head parallel with hers and I too look down into my drink, now a third of a pint of Guinness in the glass. I know what she means: the group.

"I'm only doing my best to find out what is going on in there Jackie."

She turns her head to face me for the first time this night.

"Are you fuck, Rooney, you are doing it for you."

I know this'll be her line. I know she's unhappy at what I'm doing there, and also how her main reason for being in the group is to watch me, monitor what I'm up to. What I'm not sure of is whether this is to do with her being worried about me or the damage I could do. I'm beginning to believe it's the latter.

"Why don't you drop out, Jackie? If you're unhappy at what I'm doing."

"Will I fuck, Rooney," she snaps, "someone needs to ensure you don't fuck up. You are even starting to identify a suspect. Fuck's sake, Doctor Death, Doctor Jamieson? Correct?"

This convinces me it's the latter.

"It's helping them, Jackie. They all believe there's something going on, they want to do something to make it stop."

"It's helping you, you mean."

I know where this is going, i.e. my own needs.

"I can't deny it makes me feel good to help them. They are powerless. Patients in there have no power. If someone is killing them, they can do it with impunity, they have no way of stopping it, and any of the guys in the group could be next."

"Calm down, Rooney, you're becoming irrational." She sits back in her seat now, her drink in her hand, the straw in her mouth. "Tell me, Rooney, why do you want to be a psychologist?"

"Oh, come on Jackie, you know why."

"Because you are fucked in the head, perhaps?" She sucks through the straw like she's taking a breath, then points it at me. "There are things in your past, Rooney, you can't deal with."

"Oh aye, what's that?"

"Your father and your mother for starters."

"Oh, who is the psychologist now?" I go off for more drinks, I see they'll be needed. I come back with a renewed pint of Guinness, a double whisky and a gin and tonic for her. She looks at the unequal round of drinks.

"Well, maybe I need it more than you," I say.

She takes her drink and adds the remnants of her current glass, topping it up with the tonic.

"I've been there when you have cried out in your sleep. I know there have been things that have happened to you. Maybe why you drink so much."

Again, I know where this is going. I'll nurse my drink until it passes.

"You want to be a psychologist because you want to know what goes on in people's heads. You aren't able to try to understand what is going on in yours, so it's best to try to see what is going on in others, how they deal with the things you are not dealing with in yours. I know there is a psychological term for it, which I am sure you know, but what I don't think you know is why you are doing it. Why you want to be a bloody shrink."

"I am not doing… projection."

"That's the word, putting your feelings on others to avoid confronting them, yourself, that's it." A superior smirk arrives on her face. "I don't think you know you're doing it, Rooney. I also don't understand how you got onto the course in the first place." She says this for effect, and to add to the emphasis she gets up and rounds the table to look over me on her way to the toilet. "Don't they vet psychological cripples to ensure they don't inflict damage on the poor bastards they are foisted upon?"

Ouch, that hurt. I watch her push her way around the bar through the bodies which are formed liked a wall between the bar and the mirrored lined wall. I sit and think for a while. Is she right, am I doing this for me and not for them? If I am, it isn't right. If I am, Donna will see through it and my placement will be a failure, my course a failure, me a failure. Maybe I need a psychologist, maybe I am projecting my needs onto them. Me, displacing my feelings onto these vulnerable people, attributing my own unacceptable urges onto others, like Jackie says, maybe in a vicarious way, trying to understand my own battles with myself. Trying to get their approval of me, where I could never get the approval of my father, trying to get them to love me, for what I am doing for them, when I couldn't get my father to love me. I drop my head into my hands as if to talk into them. Am I trying to deal with my being—

"Oh, for God's sake, Rooney, get your head on, people will think you are a loser." She's back and standing over me.

I look up.

"I'm thinking about what you said to me. Of course I need to think about it. You may be right."

"Aye, I might be right and that is what worries me." She sits down, picks up her glass and directs it at me. "I don't want you fucking up your career."

"I don't want to harm others."

"I hope you don't."

We go silent for a bit. I allow the chatter in the place to invade my sorry mind. The bar is a potpourri, not in the pleasant-smelling sense but in the mix, of all sorts, all laughing, blethering as they say, talking. Not like us, engrossed in what is happening in my head. I suppose alcohol helps you get into yourself, partly why I use it, but not always the best purpose for it.

"And you're drinking too much," she says, as if she's reading my mind.

"I like it," I say, lamely.

"Too fucking much, Rooney, too fucking much."

"I need it."

"And Agnes, what about her, do you want her?"

"What?"

"Agnes. I'm not stupid and neither was anyone in the room the other day."

"I don't know what you are talking about."

"I could see the way she was looking at you. You don't need to be a woman to see there is something going on with her. She couldn't take her eyes off you. Are you fucking her?"

This is heavy. I don't want to get into it. I get up and go for more. When I get back, she's gone. I don't follow her. I just accept she's had enough, enough of me, enough to drink, enough of drink, enough of being there. I'll drink her gin and tonic too, no point in it going to waste.

I study my drink and think about my father. I always do when the drink starts to reach those parts of my brain which hold the thoughts of him, almost to anaesthetise the pain which comes when I think of him, a pain killer to attenuate his words which spill out. "You'll never come to anything, you're a weak snivelling wean, you're an embarrassment to me."

But there's an area in my psyche that even the alcohol doesn't dull, and that is Father Healey. But I'll keep the lid on that box firmly closed until I'm ready to deal with it.

I divert my mind to the group. I know I have a dilemma. Do I keep the group together, pursue what they all think to be true, which is there's a killer in there, a doctor death, or settle with the belief the group is helping them, giving them purpose? Or do I concentrate in getting through the placement, getting a good report, getting through the course, getting a decent job? Do I agree with Jackie that I'm meeting my own needs through theirs? Something will come out sometime, and that'll be that, dream over, no more Mr Psychologist. Maybe I should settle for being Mr Joe Normal, to go and get a shrink myself, get sorted out properly, stop trying to work it out through others more vulnerable than myself.

I take out the blister pack John Jamieson gave me, pop out a tablet and swallow it, oblivious to anyone watching me. But the barman has a keen eye for drugs. He comes over and lifts my glass, a couple of swallows still in it.

"Time you were going home pal," he says.

I stagger out of there onto Drury Street and then round onto Gordon Street to get a train at the Central. It's been snowing and the noise of traffic is quietened by it. It's slushy, splashing gushes of wet snow onto the folks waiting at the rank for taxis home. I wonder about getting a taxi to Jackie's, but I know that wouldn't be right. I think about calling Agnes, I could go to her place, she'll talk to me, and maybe I'll end up in her bed. I also know this wouldn't be right. Anyway, I'd probably fuck up again.

I go back to my room.

CHAPTER 22

Saturday afternoon, we gather at the Pass and go off to the hospital golf course, minutes away at the back of the hospital. Jamieson and Owen are already on the course. We see them on the fourth hole. We wait until they take their shot and they move off up the course.

"Right, the shoes," I say, as we move towards the locker room, leaving Walter in his wheelchair on the path as a lookout. We find his locker. Dr J on the door, but we have to be sure. It's locked with a small padlock. That's it, as far as we can go. Not so for Agnes, however, she's come prepared.

"I thought these might come in handy." She pulls out a set of bolt cutters.

"Where did you get them?"

"From home, from my ex-husband's shed."

"Your husband was well equipped," laughs Mairi.

Agnes laughs too, looking my way.

"Right, give them here," I say.

Jackie takes a step forward.

"You break into his locker and you commit a criminal offence, you understand? I'm a police officer."

"Give them here." Mairi takes the cutters.

Although the padlock is small it resists her attempts to cut the shackle. Alex takes it from her and in a second squeezes the blades of the cutter around the padlock shackle. It holds. He squeezes again and the shackle snaps. He stands back in triumph. I free the padlock from the locker door and open it. Sure enough this is John Jamieson's locker. His white coat is hanging in there. I recognise it and the array of pens he has clipped in his chest pocket. John takes the coat from the locker and puts it on.

"I am Doctor Death," Alex shrieks, as John walks up and down the locker room. It takes some persuasion to get John to remove it and put it back. I pick up his shoes and study the soles.

"Well, are they the same as in the photo?" Mairi asks.

I turn over the shoes and look inside.

"No," I say.

"What, they're different?"

"Aye, they're different."

"But you haven't compared them with your photograph, you didn't look at the photographs."

"No," I say. "They're not the shoes."

Mairi persists. "But how do you know if you didn't compare them with the photos?"

"Because these are brand new." I hand them to her. "Look inside?"

Jackie takes the shoes from Mairi. "Let me see." She turns them over and studies them, smells them. "Absolutely, they smell like new shoes, the label intact inside, hardly worn, the insole is brand new, sole clean, hardly marked."

"So he bought a new pair of shoes," says Mairi. "Why'd he do that?"

"Maybe because the old ones were done," says Jackie. "What do you think?"

I take them from her and put them back.

"Well, that is that then, nothing to suggest he was there at the loch. Let's get out of here."

"And how do we explain breaking into the man's locker?" Jackie asks.

"Easy." Alex sets about other lockers and padlocks. "We make it look like a break in, looking for drugs, there'll be nothing for him to think it was anything to do with him."

Within minutes he has a few other lockers open, including Professor Owen's. John becomes mightily interested in the white coats now revealed.

"Control yourself, John," I say.

Alex opens the end locker. "There's a pair of shoes in here."

I go to the locker and lift out an old pair of brogues and turn them over. Sure enough, there is caked mud, similar to at the loch. I compare them with the new shoes and see they are a similar size, although with no markings it's hard to be sure they were definitely the same size. I take out the photograph from my inside pocket; again it's hard to say they are the same shoes which made the indentations in the mud. I put them back.

"Take a sample of the mud from a shoe," John says, "have it analysed in the lab, compare it with the mud from the loch, if it is the same, bingo." Jackie looks at him with curious interest.

I scrape off some mud and put it in an envelope.

"OK, it's worth a go, not that it'll give us anything definitive." I seal it and pass it to Jackie.

"If it's the same," Mairi says, "then someone who wore those shoes was at the scene of Elsie's death, murder."

"Steady," Jackie says, "there's nothing to suggest murder. Get real."

"Doctor Death," Gerry says, "is he who lives by death, to prolong suffering until his last breath."

"Aye, aw right," Jackie says, "enough Dylan Thomas."

Jackie has just given Gerry a nickname.

"Dylan, I like it," Gerry says. "Bob Dylan."

"He's an authority on Bob Dylan songs," Agnes says.

"But do not worry," Gerry prevails, "his time will come..."

"By an assassin's bullet, it will take only one," adds Alex.

"Fuck's sake you crazies, get a grip," Jackie says.

I can't resist having a look in Doctor Jamieson's pockets.

"Rooney, you're going too far," Jackie says.

There's nothing in the coat pockets apart from a couple of opened packets of Werther's Originals, Butter Candy. He ate them all the time. I am tempted to hand them out as a gift for our efforts, but resist this and put them back.

"Right, let's get out of here," I say.

We leave the place in disarray like it had been assaulted by a gang looking for drugs. We go over to the bench on the path across from the shed.

Walter asks how we got on.

"Nothing definitive," I say.

"I got something," Mairi says.

"Oh," I say.

She pulls out a gold sweetie paper.

"Werther's Original, I went down to the loch and I found it where Elsie went in." We all look at her and at the sweetie paper. "He was there."

"That is it," Jackie says. "I'm out of here. A sweetie paper and a pair of auld muddy shoes gives you crazies a murder suspect. A death which most likely was a suicide. You lot enjoy your game of Cluedo, it'll keep you occupied, but I've real policing to do, fucking live in the real world for a change."

I am about to follow her out, but I see their faces.

"Jackie, mind get it analysed, compare it with mud at the loch?"

"Jes-sus. What have I got myself into? A bunch of crackpots playing at cops, pursuing a factitious killer of nonsuspicious deaths. Whatever floats your boat?"

We go back to the OT room for a while. Agnes appears with fresh tea and scones. Jackie's words have had an effect. Heads are down and no one is saying anything. But then Mairi gets to her feet.

"Right you lot." They look up. "Don't fucking listen to anyone, *we* know something is going on. *We* know people are being killed and we know somebody is doing it. Right? And we're going to find him. Right?"

They look at her. The interest is back in their eyes, these people who had nothing to be positive about, their lives devoid of something tangible to do. This's the one thing that's demanding for them.

"Mairi is right," I say. "We're going to find him and we're going to stop this. Right?"

Nods and smiles confirm this activity is giving them purpose. They need this and I'm not going to take it away from them.

I go back to my room and spend the rest of the afternoon having a few drams looking out into the grounds, where the snow has mixed with rain, covering the ground with slush. I look into the trees and think about the guys John Scott and I scared away that night, and the shapes we saw in the woods at Joan's burial, and Walter's obsession with trees. Trees seem to surround the Castle in a cloak of safety but also insecurity, like they are part of the structure of the place, as much as the walls of the hospital.

I need to know more about these protection guys taking money from the nurses, wondering if there is any connection between the mob and the patients' deaths, as Alex suggests? Stanley says he is in Tennent's most weekend nights. I need to talk to him about the mob appearing at the hospital, hoping he could do something, get them to back off, leave the women alone, but I want to know more about what he said about them killing folk, the patients. The weather has deteriorated. I call a taxi.

I get out of the taxi onto Byres Road just by the crossing on Highburgh Road. It's snowing heavily and the ground is slippery. I stand for a minute to get my balance, the snow gives me a white hat. I look up into it as it covers my face. It feels good, refreshing, I lick it. I stand incongruously as it covers my coat, long enough for it to make me look like a snowman. Maybe, having had a few whiskies, I think I should stay this way. It feels good, safe. I feel as if I have a place, maybe a child will try to stick a carrot on my face for a nose. It doesn't feel cold and I wonder if this comfort is like those men on a mountain when succumbing to hypothermia, starting to feel warm when they were really dying. Am I dying, I wonder.

I'm grabbed by the arm.

"Fuck's sake, Rooney, get yourself inside, you'll perish out here." It's Stanley. He saw me from inside, through the big windows, as I got out of the taxi. He takes me inside and pushes me into a corner seat and drags me out of my coat. He ruffles my hair, shaking the snow out of it. "Want a drink?"

I nod. I start to shiver, then to feel warm, like the blood is starting to flow again through me, my hands. Coming back from the bar, he puts a whisky in front of me.

"Here." He pushes in beside me.

I grip the glass, first finger extended, and drink it down in one.

"Wow, steady son."

I hand him the empty glass. He goes to the bar and comes back with another but keeps it out of reach.

"Take a few minutes, Rooney, get warm." He passes me the whisky. "Nurse it."

I sit for a minute and look around the bar. It's mobbed, mainly with men, a few women. I turn back to face Stanley, looking at him longer than necessary, only to confirm I'm pissed.

"The guys were at the hospital. You said they were going to kill the patients." He looks at me strangely. "Well, are they?"

"What?"

"Killing folk?"

"Well, that's what I heard."

"So, you don't really know?"

"It came from a reliable source."

I look at him through bleary eyes, trying to keep a grasp on all of this. Stanley hears the mob are going to kill folk in the hospital, then they turn up looking for protection money.

"I need to know, Stanley."

He looks at me, longer this time. A few years back I had helped him. I had some redundancy money from a job that had been taken away from me. He was stuck, skint, a new wife and a baby on the way. I gave him two hundred pounds. I never asked for it to be repaid. I see in his eyes he's thinking about it.

"You helped me once, Rooney." I don't answer, I didn't need to. "If I set it up for you with the boss, you won't fuck it up, will you?"

I know he's talking about Albert Timpson, aka Alby, the boss of bosses, a Godfather figure in Glasgow, leader of the most prominent gang in the city. If anyone knows what is going on with the guys arriving in the hospital, he will. He may also be responsible for it. He may also be behind the threat of killing patients in the hospital. But I don't think Stanley would expose me to someone with the wherewithal to kill folk in the hospital. Not that he would have worried about what have happened to me, he wouldn't have been stupid enough to put himself at risk from the boss's wrath. He goes outside to have a smoke and to call someone. He comes back a few minutes later.

"He'll see you, Rooney."

"That is great, when?"

"Ten o'clock tonight, at the Blackhill Bar."

Tonight, concerns me. The Blackhill Bar, even more, tomorrow or next week would be better. In a coffee shop on the Byres Road, even better; men die in the Blackhill Bar. I feel I would have a better chance of survival when I sober up.

"Jesus, Stanley, not tonight."

"Take it or leave it Rooney, it's the only chance you'll get, and you don't miss an appointment offered by the big man."

I think about it for a minute. I have a couple of hours to sober up.

"We'll have some coffee and we'll go there, you'll—"

"No' me, Rooney, you do this yourself." I realise immediately Stanley isn't going to risk fucking up in front of the boss. "But you keep it circumspect, you know what I am saying. Don't mention my name, OK?"

"Right," I say, feeling I had shot my mouth off too much for then.

I should have left. Why did I need to go there, to talk to Stanley? Do I have a death wish?

"You ask about the protection stuff and talk about the hospital in general," he says. "You don't ask him outright if there's a contract on the patients. If he wants to tell you he will. If he doesn't, or he knows nothing about it, he won't. Got it?" I nod meekly.

What have I got myself into?

I go to a café, a short way up Byres Road from Tennent's, order a double black coffee and sit, then I have another. At nine thirty I start up to the taxi rank and I get in the first taxi.

"Blackhill, the Blackhill Bar."

"Jesus, pal, do you know where you are going?" the driver asks.

"Aye, just take me there."

Timpson owns the Blackhill Bar and holds court there. The coffee has worked a bit, but the shock of going there has sobered me up even more.

We travel from the West End along the Great Western Road, onto the M8 and off at the Stepps Road, now in the East End, and turn into Blackhill, a notoriously violent area of Glasgow. We turn and pass Timpson's house and after only a few hundred yards we turn a corner and arrive at the Blackhill Bar. Jesus, what was I thinking of? Get your fucking head on, I tell myself.

I get out of the cab and pay the man. He takes ten pounds and doesn't give me any change. He won't need it where he is going, he would have thought. I open the door of the bar. It's mobbed.

Some men at the door look at me and ask:

"Can we help you, pal?"

"I've to see Alby."

"Mr Timpson, Albert, to you, you plamph."

I nod. I see they also get a nod from someone somewhere at the bar and they point over to a table in the corner of the bar.

"Over there," one of them says, pointing.

I see the table is well placed in the corner, strategically placed where all of the pub could be observed. I see Timpson, instantly identifiable, his back to the wall, suit, collar and tie, surrounded by a group of heavy made guys, also suited, collars and ties. I go over to the table and push through a solid wall of men, the first line of defence should anyone try to get at Timpson. I can hear the guys at the table, making a lot of chatter above the din of the pub. I hear them talking about a battle. One says "I kicked the fuck out of him," and another "I stabbed the bastard." Christ, I think, I have just fallen into a lion's den and the lions are on crack cocaine.

"Mr Timpson." My voice is shaking as I reach the table. He looks bigger in the seat, and though he isn't so big in stature he has massive broad shoulders. He seems to tower over the rest. I wonder if he may have been sitting on a cushion or something. He looks at me and doesn't say anything at first.

"Stanley Holland said I could see you. You said it was—"

"It's OK, Rooney. Stanley told me." I feel relieved I don't need to explain any more. "Sit down there." He orders a guy to his right to vacate his seat. "And call me Alby."

I squeeze through the crowd and sit down. I expected to sit at the other side of a large mahogany table like those in the Godfather films, like he would be holding court to other gang bosses or local dignitaries or someone from the local community asking for a favour, asking for someone to be whacked Mafia style. No, this is a bit too close for comfort. He holds his hand out, this hand which had crushed a few bones, battered a few faces, shot a few… Oh, Jesus, what am I doing here? I shake it. It feels warm, soft, not hard, not cold, nor crushing.

"I don't know you Rooney, but I know Stanley thinks a lot of you, that's why I agreed to see you."

In a funny way I feel honoured he had agreed to see me, maybe Stanley had more sway with him than I might have thought. I relax a bit and open my coat. I notice a few men looking more intently me as I do, perhaps thinking I am carrying something, a weapon perhaps. I put my hands on the table well in sight. They relax.

"OK, what do you want?" His face is quite close to me, and I smell whisky from him. I see scars, one in particular from the right side of his mouth across his cheek towards his neck. His eyes are big, but his eyebrows are bigger, bushy and full. He has blue eyes, lively and intent, they draw me in.

"I don't really want anything in particular, Alby. I just want to ask you something."

"You don't want anything," he says. "He doesn't want anything," he shares with the others around the table. "Everybody wants some-thing and he wants nothing." They all laugh with him and stop as soon as he does. "Alright, Rooney what do you want to ask, you've got a minute, no more?"

I smile, nervously.

"I work at the hospital," I say, faintly. "At Hillwood."

"The Castle, I know it, Rooney. The crazy farm."

"Aye, the crazy farm," I repeat. "I'm a psychologist there."

"You're a shrink at the nuthoose, Rooney. Jesus, I could use you here." He laughs again; they all do. "Right, I said a minute."

I decide to blurt it out. The worst scenario is he could pull a gun and shoot me there, or the best scenario he could burst my nose and have me thrown out onto the street where his men would kick the fuck out of me.

"I hear you want to kill the patients at the hospital."

Fuck, did I say that? I was supposed to ask about the protection racket, maybe call upon his generosity, his sense of responsibility towards the angels, to call off his guys. He could afford losing a measly grand every month. He pushes himself back in his seat. Here it comes, I think, prepare for it, a bullet or a blow, take your pick.

He takes a few seconds before he talks and when he does it is softly delivered.

"Listen Rooney, I understand where you are coming from. No one wants to hurt the poor bastards in there, many of them have come from the East End. I know a lot of them. Sure, we are worried about the pedos harming oor weans and the nutters who have killed folk, like the fucker who took a machete to the auld folks in the shopping centre. They'd hurt the folks oot here where they are going to send them, but the general punters, naw, we wouldn't touch them."

I give him some more time. I know there is more to come.

"Aye, and OK, there's an element of why here, why are they being discharged here? Why no' the West End, where the rich bastards live? We get dumped on all the time. We get the asylum seekers, the drug-gies, the homeless alkies, the mentally ill." I am heartened to hear him say mentally ill, maybe I had misjudged him. "We're making it known we are not happy about it, maybe why Holland inferred it to you."

I take a mental note to tell Stanley I didn't mention he had told me about the mob threat to kill patients.

"Easy mistake to make, not to say we wouldn't take action to protect our folk at risk from any nutter who they send here."

The 'take action' is self-explanatory, i.e. do not send out any paedophiles or psychotic murderers, or anyone who will threaten the local community. The 'take action' would lead to them being found in the loch. I think about Elsie, she wasn't a threat to anyone, and Mary, her sister, a member of the local community.

"Something is happening to the patients," I say.

His look becomes stern and he gets close again.

"Well, it's no' us, Rooney."

I know not to push it. Accept what he says or go flying shoulder high out onto the cold, slushy road outside. Best not.

"OK, Alby, I understand."

He sits back a bit.

"You've got balls, Rooney, I'll tell you that."

Jesus, he's giving me a compliment.

"Thanks, Alby."

Then a voice in my head says: don't say any more, just thank him for his time, shake his hand and leave... alive.

"Alby?"

Oh, please don't say it, the voice inside my head adds.

"Whit." He's more irritable this time.

I'm really pushing it, the voice is telling me. Jesus, why do I do this? Part of my death wish. I resign myself to my fate.

"They are taking money from the lassies. A big one a month, to stop them being hassled, raped. They are just—"

"Enough, Rooney, I said you had balls, not ball bearings in your heid." He leans over and talks to the guy to his left then says to me, "I'll take care of it, Rooney. They're no' mine. No one takes money in my patch without my say so, the bastards won't dae it again, you can be assured of it."

I realise I may be responsible for the hit and possibly the death of a bunch of guys taking protection money in the hospital. Strangely, I don't feel sorry for them. They know the score. The hospital is in Alby Timpson's patch and no one does anything like protection without his say so. I get up, thank him, and leave without shaking his hand. He never looks my way again after talking to his right-hand-man and goes back to talking organised crime with the rest of his cronies. My minute is up and I am on borrowed time. No more to say. Just show respect by getting up, nodding respectfully and leave, as you would the Pope, or the Queen, or the Boss.

I find a pub close by, not too close to the Blackhill Bar, but I need to recover. I don't really remember how I get home, taxi maybe, but home I get and to bed I go, half drunk, half elated for having survived Alby Timpson, half relieved for getting back to my bed in one piece. Sorry that is three halves, but you know what I mean. It's Sunday morning, and I sleep late. That is until Scott batters on my door once more. Oh, fuck, I think, not the guys arriving in the car park again.

"I thought you paid the bastards," I call through the door from underneath my humpy. I look at the clock, it's nearly twelve.

"That's just what I want to tell you, Rooney. We don't have to pay no more."

"Right."

"Aye, a note left with the Rottweiler. I've got it here. It says, 'We have decided to suspend the arrangement on moral grounds, no payment will therefore be necessary from now on. The nurses in the hospital will from this day be safe.'"

"Alby Timpson," I mutter from under my bedclothes.

"Sorry. What did you say?"

"Nothing, which is good."

"And there's another thing, a sealed envelope, it's for you."

"Right."

"I'll slip it under the door."

I lift my head from beyond the covers and see the envelope reveal itself from under the door.

"Thanks." I get up and don my robe and slippers. I read the front of the envelope, it says, 'Only for Sean Rooney'. I open the envelope and then the note inside. It says, 'Rooney, you owe me, and when I ask you will repay without question, AT.' I know immediately Alby Timpson has me exactly where and when he wants.

I wonder if I can rule out the mob from any list of suspects, which I hadn't really compiled anyway, but Timpson did say he would kill paedophiles and psychotic killers in his words being dumped into the local community, and others depending on their threat. Has he already exercised *his* threat?

I spend the rest of the weekend in reflection. Jesus, what have

I got myself involved with? My focus should be totally on getting through this bloody placement, this bloody course, nothing else.

By Monday, I'm determined to extricate myself from the deaths, the group and the stress of it all. But then, just as I'm getting ready for work...

"It's Bella, I've an envelope for you," she says through the door. "It was left at the front desk, and before you ask I don't know who left it. It was there when I came in."

She passes it under my door. Envelopes arriving under my door however are significant. I pick it up and sit on my bed and look at it. Timpson calling in his favour, I wonder. Does he want me to do a contract killing?

I open the envelope and what's there before me shakes me even more than doing a control killing on behalf of a Godfather:

YOU ARE INVOLVED IN SOMETHING YOU HAVE NO RIGHT TO BE INVOLVED WITH. PLEASE STOP NOW OR YOU WILL BE KILLED.

This's an ultimatum. I've to stop what I'm doing, presumably enquiring into the deaths in the Castle. Is this confirming the patients are indeed being killed or something else is going on; for example, the mob? The warning seems clear enough, though. I'm being warned off, but by whom and for why?

I go to the phone in the corridor and call Jackie.

"Could mean anything, Rooney. It could also mean someone is just warning you, not threatening you, and they want to stop you from being harmed?"

"It could also mean someone will kill me if I don't back off."

"Do you want me to organise some protection for you?"

"No thanks, two big plainclothes polis following me around the hospital would not go down well."

"Might increase your street cred."

"Aye, so it would."

"Rooney?"

"What?"

"The mud from the shoes matches mud from the bank of the loch."

"I knew it, Elsie's killer."

"Rooney, whoever wore the shoes was there at the loch at some point, whoever put them in this locker. It identifies nobody, let alone a murderer."

CHAPTER 23

I take Monday off to attend a university meeting, but more to try to think things through. On Tuesday, I arrive in the department to receive two notes of a different sort.

Agnes passes both to me as I arrive.

"The top one is from Gerald. He wants you to have it."

"Thanks."

"The other one. All it says on the envelope is Confidential for Sean Rooney's eyes only, so I didn't open it."

"Thanks, Agnes."

I'm just about to go back to my room when she reaches out and grabs my arm.

"Sean."

I kind of knew she would say something after our encounter in my room in the nurses' home. I have been waiting for it.

"Sean, you haven't mentioned it, but we must… try again. Practice makes perfect." As she says this she has a serious look in her eye. I know she intends we should get back into the sack and have another go.

"R-right, Agnes, we can think about it."

"Aye, right, Sean, but don't think about it for too long, let's keep the kettle boiling, if you get my meaning?"

"Yeah, I get your meaning, Agnes."

"Rooney, we need each other."

I smile and pull free from her grasp to go to the safety of my room, picking up the rest of my mail from my tray on the way. The referral meeting is in half an hour, not time to look at them all.

I get to my desk and lay out the mail. I open the one from Gerry. I think about reading it out loud but know Donna is in the room. Though, I did not think Gerry would say anything she would be concerned about. In fact she had made it clear she likes the out-of-the-ordinary and might even enjoy it.

"It's another poem from Gerry, Agnes's son," I say.

"From Dylan."

I forgot I had told her about Jackie giving him a nickname.

"Aye, Dylan."

"Go on then."

I read it out.

"Born of care in the community, in a rundown hostel in the old East End. The Health Board said, we're doing our best, you had to come out, you passed the test. You're better out here than being in there. Get them out, keep them out, throw them out, lock them out, just stay put. Stuck in a nursing home where no one cared, of who you are or what you are, and all the things that made you scared. You're better in here than being in there. Keep them in, hold them in, drug them up, lock them up, just stay put."

"It's very good." Donna lifts her head out of her notes. "Agnes must be very proud of him, and his talent."

"Don't you think he's saying something... important?"

"What do you mean?"

"You're better in here than being in a nursing home. Donna this is a desperate situation for these patients."

She shakes her head and drops it back into reading her notes, not particularly interested.

I open the other envelope. The one saying 'Confidential, for Sean Rooney's eyes only'. I see it's a memo in hand writing from Bill Simmons. It reads:

'Sean, I have to tell you I am seriously disturbed about your behaviour. I have heard you are delving into some of the deaths that have occurred in the hospital in recent days. Natural deaths and suicides in this hospital are NOT murder, Sean, NOT murder.

'We, in this department, take this very seriously that the vulnerable patients in this hospital could become alarmed by your activity. Especially those who may be considered suitable for discharge to a community-based placement. This paranoia could harm the discharge programme. Please desist. At this stage I have not spoken to Archie or Donna, but I will do so if you do not stop this behaviour. Please consider your placement and concentrate on getting through it without embarking on risky activity. Please destroy this memo after you read it. We don't want anyone to know I raised this with you. Suffice to say you'll heed my words.

'Yours, Bill.'

Jesus, this man is threatening me. I wonder if I should march in there and demand an explanation but decide against this. He obviously knows about the group. This's another indication I need to be more careful.

I think about telling Donna, but decide against it. I tear up the memo and drop the pieces in the waste paper bin. As I do, my eyes automatically move up to Joan's elephant, which now adorns the shelf above my desk. Would she want me to give in, I wonder? I sit back on my chair and gaze upon it.

I know the elephant is a symbol of power, wisdom, and strength, not only physical but also mental and spiritual. In Hindu tradition, elephants call up the image of Ganesha, the symbol of knowledge. Its strength allows whoever invokes the power of the elephant to realise his heart's desires. When one wishes to begin an important endeavour, the elephant is invoked as God of knowledge and destroyer of obstacles, under the appearance of Ganesha.

I think about the warning note: 'YOU ARE INVOLVED IN SOMETHING YOU HAVE NO RIGHT TO BE INVOLVED WITH. PLEASE STOP NOW OR YOU WILL BE KILLED,' and far from scaring me, this emboldens me. Add the memo from Bill Simmons, makes me more determined. How fucking dare he and whoever they are?

The elephant needs to be a symbol of my resolve. I can't allow Joan's death to go down in the annals of the hospital records as a suicide, especially if she had indeed been murdered. For her, with her elephant as a symbol of my determination, I need to get to the bottom of this.

I have to be wary of Simmons, however. He can not only derail my plans but he can also threaten my placement. This is why I should not tell Donna. I need to deal with this on my own.

I look up to the elephant. I take it from the shelf and open the top to peer inside, looking for something, anything to help me. It's an empty vessel, just like me. It symbolises me, empty. I can't see anything at first; but then, squeezed into the bottom, there's something. I can't quite make it out. The bottom is around two inches square and I can make something out. I put it under the light and can just about see something there. It looks like paper. I take a letter opener and feed it into the inside of the elephant. Maybe it's just paper to line the bottom of it. I press the point of the letter opener into the paper to see if it's anything. It feels soft but it presses in about an inch into the bottom. It's clearly a piece of folded paper. I try to prise it up to open it. It remains intact. It takes me a few minutes and then it dislodges from the bottom. It stays intact though and doesn't break apart. I see it's complete, two inches square, and sellotaped. Now free from being locked in the bottom, I turn the elephant upside down and the paper square drops out onto my desk.

"Right, Sean, team meeting," Donna says, getting up.

I pop the note back into the elephant and follow her out.

CHAPTER 24

'Generalised anxiety in the patient group,' is top of the agenda for the team meeting.

Archie starts. "From the HMT the physician superintendent raised this matter," he says. I see around the room people are perplexed.

"He said there is a heightened anxiety around the hospital. The normally non anxious are showing symptoms of free-floating anxiety, sleeping problems, outbursts, etcetera, the anxious are becoming more anxious, the seriously anxious are becoming hysterical, behavioural problems and management issues abound. It appears to be more prevalent in the long stay population."

No one says anything, but I see they're thinking about it. Keeping a settled and content long stay population is essential. A few patients suffering anxiety symptoms is easily managed, a few hundred is a different ball game.

"Yes, the times are a changing," Donna says, looking my way, no doubt referring to Gerry's poem.

Alex Boyd, senior psychologist, nods his head.

"You can feel it, people are edgy, wary, fractious," he says, "and it applies to the staff too, there's something in the air."

"I said we'd be more available to ward staff to assist," Archie says. "Referrals of the most seriously affected, relaxation groups, some tapes for the wards, etcetera."

I am tempted to get into the discussion, like mentioning the patients are scared, the suicides, some saying there is something sinister going on, but think it wiser to say nothing.

"This place contributes to it," Paul Masson, psychologist says.

"Explain, Paul," Archie says.

"Well, it's over a hundred years old, full of ghosts, dark, scary. You've all walked those corridors in the dark. The place contributes to the mental health of the occupants. They even say there is a ghost which stalks the corridors, a demon, looking for souls to devour."

There is a wave of titters around the room.

It chimes with my understanding, having heard from some patients, like the guy in ward 28. I say nothing. I'd only be viewed as irrational, naïve, unprofessional.

"Very profound, Paul, and not lacking in your usual hyperbole," Archie says, pausing sufficiently to move on from the supernatural. "We all know this place is well past its sell by date. Plans are afoot to close the place, transfer the patients groups to modern, state of the art establishments."

"That's it," I say. They all look at me. I don't want to say people are worried about being killed, so I say, "Everyone knows change is in the air, care in the community, nothing is permanent any more. It's unsettling for those who view this place as their home. What does a nursing home offer these people? They are scared…"

There's a deathly silence, then Paul persists. It's clear he finds this entertaining.

"The Gorbals Vampire," he says.

"Eh?"

"Sixty odd years ago, a strange figure was spotted flitting through the gravestones of the Southern Necropolis. It certainly spooked a community, who believed it to be the Gorbals Vampire, a seven-foot-tall monster with iron teeth. Rumours were it had killed and eaten two young boys swept through the neighbourhood like wildfire. Gangs of hysterical youngsters, armed with stakes and knives and accompanied by angry dogs, pitched up at the south side cemetery in the hope of catching the strange creature."

Archie is getting exasperated. "Paul, there are no ghosts, demons, or creatures devouring patients at Hillwood Hospital."

"Sorry, mass hysteria, Archie, just saying we know it happens, in schools, for example."

"Mass psychogenic illness, collective hysteria, group hysteria, or collective obsessional behaviour, I am aware of this, Paul. But there's no suggestion we've such a problem here."

Then he turns to me and says, "And any activity promoted by *this* department needs to be positive, you got it, Sean?" All of their eyes are trained on me. Archie is making a serious statement he's uneasy about the group. "Positive, Sean, therapeutic, change is good, healthy, the raison d'être of this department."

We all go for lunch. Donna and I go to the dining room, the others to the local pub. I am tempted to go too, but I may not stop. I nod to Myra at the Pass. After lunch, as we leave the dining room, I say to Donna I want to talk to Myra. She looks at me over her glasses, as if to say 'keep it therapeutic, Sean, therapeutic'.

I smile and move to where Myra sits. She sees me coming and holds out her diary.

"Passing the Pass," I say, taking it.

Myra is expressionless. I lean my back against the corridor wall. I check today, the sixth of April, and yesterday, the fifth of April pages and the days before. I count roughly 150 people crossing the Pass. There are more matchstick men and women, patients, male and female, doctors, nurses, others. Betty Boop is there coming and going, and this God the Father like figure who appears to be more active after hours, and one she calls the Almoner, the same. Then I see a figure I had missed the last time. I leaf back to the first pages and right enough I had missed this. This is a small hooded figure with no face, just a cloak over its head and body, its arms and feet sticking out.

I ask her, "Myra, who is this?"

She looks at me questioningly, as if to say: 'you don't know?'

I give the diary back and walk up the corridor in quiet contemplation. A hooded figure. I had never seen a hooded figure in the hospital.

Given some of Myra's mysterious figures appear to be around after hours, I decide to work on. I also want to look at the note inside Joan's elephant to see what is says.

I place the elephant on my desk and open it, then turn it over to dislodge the paper. It's taped solid and it takes me a couple of minutes with small scissors to cut it open and release it to its full A5 size. I press it flat and there right in the middle there's a lock of hair. It's dark brown and tied in a piece of string. I put it aside and turn to the sheet. It's hard to read it because it is in rough handwriting, Joan's I presume.

I read it slowly. "Like Mary Magdalene, the reason we stand and weep and listen for Jesus is because we, like Mary, are bearers of resurrection, we are made new. On the third day, Jesus rose again, and we do not need to be afraid. To sing to God amidst sorrow is to defiantly proclaim, like Mary Magdalene did to the apostles, that death is not the final word. To defiantly say, once again, a light shines in the darkness and the darkness cannot, will not, shall not overcome it. In my Bible is my life and my death." I think about this for a few minutes wondering why Joan wanted to put this note here.

Around eight, just as I am about to go for a walk about, Agnes appears.

"Hello, Sean, you're working late. I was up seeing Gerald and I noticed your light on."

"Oh, hi Agnes," I say, hesitantly. I hadn't expected to see her there after hours and I'm lost for words.

"If you had told me, I could have worked on too, to help you with your reports." She closes the door behind her and comes closer than comfortable, sitting on the edge of my desk. Again, the legs are crossed showing a large amount of thigh.

I try to show I am locked in my work and continue to write on my A4 pad.

"Just got a deadline, a court report on a patient in the secure ward needs to be in by the weekend."

"Don't worry, Sean. I'll hammer it out tomorrow and have it on your desk by lunchtime, no problem." She takes her coat off and drops it over the desk. "We have—"

"Unfinished business, Agnes?"

She gets very close to me, pulling her towards me. I think about having her on my desk, and she's making it clear there would be no resistance to this on her part. But again, the old dilemma appears in my mind. What do I do, be unfaithful to Jackie, take a risk, hope it'll work this time, just go for it?

She comes around me and puts her arms around my neck. I smell her perfume. It's fresh and new, I wonder if she's been shopping. She kisses me on the head and pushes her breasts into the back of my head. I have to act. I get up and even at this moment I haven't decided to go for it or escape from it. There's an interplay going on in my head between lust, need, pride, fear, letting it happen, or stopping it in its tracks; from doing the right thing and doing the right thing. I do the right thing, although I question this wondering if this really is the right thing to do, something I'll look back on and regret.

"I am sorry, Agnes, I just…"

"I know Sean, you are dedicated to your work, so much so to deny your needs. I get it." She reaches for her coat and dons it. "But there will be a time and a place, believe me. I can wait. It'll happen between us. It's inevitable."

She leaves with a smile. I give her a minute then lock the door from the inside; not that it would keep her out, she is the main key holder for the whole department. I wait a few minutes to ensure she's gone and I leave the department, cautiously looking left and right into the corridor as I do

I go down the corridor and approach the Pass. Unusually, Myra isn't there. Her seat is though, as is her diary and her pen in the spine. I wonder if she's gone back to the ward or into the dining room. I've no doubt she'll be back in no time at all.

I decide to have a look up the west corridor. I wonder if Myra is back in ward 29, her ward, something I know she feels unhappy with, or maybe she had found another place in the corridor to sit.

I pass a few wards and see, far from hysterical patients, most appear settled, sitting around rooms watching TV. Maybe Midazolam has been administered. I look onto the deepest recess of the corridor and see the Chapel. I remember being there when Joan was laid out. I open the door and go in. The Chapel is dimly lit with low lights and a single candle near the alter. It's empty and it is strangely warm and comforting. I walk up to the end of the rows of pews. It's designed to hold adequate numbers for a service. I look to the stained-glass windows depicting figures of the four cardinal virtues: prudence, temperance, fortitude, justice.

I turn to make my way back out to the corridor to be confronted by the Chaplain, I recognise him from Joan's burial. I nearly walk into him, he is that close.

"Hello, sir." I didn't notice him much at the funeral, looking to the grave and Joan's coffin. But, in the dim light I see he is a small man, thin, but fit looking. He is dressed normally, not like a normal minster or priest, wearing a tweed jacket and grey trousers, with the obligatory dog collar and a Bible in his hands.

"Hello. I'm Sean Rooney, from the psychology department. I hope you don't min—"

"No, I recognise you from Joan's funeral. You're welcome here, anytime. I'm the Reverend James Gordon, Chaplain here. Call me Reverend Jimmy." He laughs and shakes my hand. "Please sit, if there is anything…"

I nearly engage him in the respective roles of psychology and the church, where there's clearly overlap in the comfort and support of patients, but I leave this to another time.

"No, I'm fine, thank you. There's one thing, however. Could you look at this? It was from Joan." I pull out Joan's note and hand it to him. "She wrote it before she died."

He looks at the paper with questioning eyes. He takes it to the light of the window and squints to make out the words.

"I don't really understand it." He mumbles some of it, then slowly and out loud reads it. "Like Mary Magdalene did to the apostles, that death is not the final word. To defiantly say, once again, that a light shines in the darkness and the darkness cannot, will not, shall not overcome it. In my Bible is my life and my death."

"Do you think she's trying to say something?"

"I'm not sure my friend, people say a lot of things before they are about to meet their maker." He looks at the paper once more. "The mention of Mary Magdalene," he says. "Many women refer to Mary Magdalene as a fallen women in some way, wrongly of course, referring to their own past, perhaps misdemeanours, which make them feel guilty, in a sense comparing themselves with Magdalene in a hope of redemption from God."

I feel like saying I don't believe in all this twaddle, but I resist the temptation. Then he says something interesting.

"Foundations are important, they are the bedrock of this place. Magdalene lives on in here."

I watch as he prepares some flowers by the windows and I turn to leave. There, however, before me standing in the doorway is a figure silhouetted by the lights outside in the corridor. The hood indicates this could easily be a monk, but as I walk towards it I see it's a nun, the same nun who was at Joan's funeral and when I put the Bible in her coffin.

"Hello, sir," she says, as she walks by. I can see a Church of Scotland Chaplain working closely with a Roman Catholic Nun, offering a blended ecumenical service.

"Hi," I reply, moving around her. "Lovely and warm in here," I say. She bows her head. "I'm Sean Rooney, from psychology."

"Sister Lilias," she says, smiling. "The Good Shepherds."

"Pleased to meet you," I say, smiling back.

She moves into the Chapel. I go out, close the door and move out into the corridor.

I go down the east corridor and into the hallway of the admin block. Then, as I pass the door to the stair leading to the consulting rooms and the physician superintendent's office, it opens and Myra is coming out. I'm startled to see her there. It's unusual for any consultant to see patients in their consulting rooms after hours.

"Oh, hello, Myra," I say, but in her customary way she avoids my eyes and goes to the Pass where she resumes her normal position, sitting under the directions sign.

I go up to her.

"It's late, Myra. You should be going back to the ward."

She looks at me and shakes her head.

CHAPTER 25

It's the 7th of April and I look at Joan's note again. It's for me, so I believe she wants to tell me something. I voice the last line. I memorise it.

"In my Bible is my life and my death." I repeat it. "In my Bible is my life." I stop and read the final phrase. "And my death." In her Bible is her death.

I decide to share this thought with the group, though not with Jackie. She's becoming increasingly worried about where I am going with them. I invite John, Alex, Gerry, Walter, Agnes and Mairi. We meet in the dining room. I tell them about the note and the Bible.

"You need to get the Bible," Alex says.

"Don't be daft, it's in Joan's coffin."

"Dig it up."

"Don't be daft," Walter says, "that's illegal."

"It's desecriminal," John says.

"We need the Bible," Mairi says. "It may say something about her death, and maybe her killer."

"It's in her grave."

"Dig it, dig it, dig it," Gerry sings, to the tune of 'Dig It' by the Beatles. "Like the FBI, the CIA, Doris Day. Dig it, dig it, dig it."

Agnes stops him. "Gerry!"

"He's right," Walter says. "You need to dig it up, get the Bible and see what it says."

"How the hell do we dig up a coffin?" I realise how absurd it sounds.

"The gardeners have the tools," Agnes says. "They dug the grave. I'll get the tools. Leave it with me."

"When?" I can't believe I am asking this.

"In the dead of night," Alex says. "It's the best time of day. I sneak out sometimes. There's no one around then, no one... except the ghosts."

Alex's delusions really are revealing themselves, contrary to the ghosts.

Far from the coffin, I see I have opened a box that once opened will refuse to be resealed.

"Sean, it needs doing," Walter says. "I can't help, but I'll keep watch."

"For the ghosts?" Alex laughs.

Walter and I pass looks.

"No, for the security men," Walter says.

I am aware after two months Joan's nails and teeth will have fallen out and her body will be starting to liquefy. I need to be prepared for this.

There follows a quiet group contemplation.

"OK, we have agreed," I say. "Now we have to do it."

Next day, we head out to the hospital graveyard like Burke and Hare looking for a cadaver to dig up and sell. It's three in the morning. Through a well-structured memo by Agnes to the nurse manager of MacFarlane House I secured their release from the wards on the pretence of an overnight stay. The house is the halfway accommodation in the grounds, used to acquaint patients with being off the ward and eventually prepare them for moving to a community-based setting. I demand they're dressed in warm clothes. Agnes provides the wellies. Walter and I visit the Grounds Department after Agnes persuades the gardeners that Walter and some of his fellow patients want to plant oak trees. We equip ourselves with good sized torches, spades, ropes, a claw hammer and a screwdriver.

I hope we won't need the ropes to drag the coffin out of the grave. Although I was at Joan's funeral I couldn't remember if her coffin was screwed down from the top or had those fasteners which can be turned and the top opened. I hope I'll be able to remove the lid to access the inside of the coffin and retrieve the Bible. I'm aware there are two coffins in each grave but I know Joan's coffin had been placed above, not directly on, another woman who had died a few days before. A nurse who had lost contact with her highland home and wanted buried in the graveyard alongside the patients and other members of staff who had also been buried there.

I want to find Joan's Bible, leave her body completely untouched, and her coffin and grave exactly as we find it. To be discovered entering a grave would be the end of everything, the group and our mission, my career, and my reputation. I am uncomfortable about desecrating her grave, but feel she would have been OK about this given the purpose.

Alex, John, and Gerry agree to help me practically in my task. Walter will stay on the path as lookout. Mairi will supervise the process.

We get to the site. The graves are unmarked and there's been a few internments there over the last few weeks, but the single flowers and wreath, albeit withered and decaying, mark Joan's grave, the tag on the wreath making it clear this is her grave.

Mairi and John hold the torches, while Alex and I start to dig. Gerry says he'll help, but I don't think he will. It'll be for Alex and me to do the digging. The ground is hard at first, but then the soil seems to give way more and within an hour or so we're well into the grave.

Occasionally, I look over to Walter, who remains impassive on the path, albeit nervously looking deep into the trees. No one is coming our way, we may pull this off after all. It's hard work but I'm impressed by Alex's tenacity. He goes at it with a passion. I get out of the hole and let him get on with it. Within a short time I hear a thud, Alex's spade had hit wood. The coffin no doubt. It's about five feet down. I get in carefully, knowing our weight could damage the coffin. Alex gets out. I dig to the side of the coffin around where I know the upper part of the body would be, until I've cleared enough room by the side to get my feet down and stand. I clear the soil from the top of the coffin all the way around. Then I discover her hat. I clear the earth from it and put it aside. I am relieved to see there are six plastic plume screws around the coffin lid to remove it.

It's been more than two months since her death and I don a mask and glasses and a nose clip, knowing gasses would escape the coffin and there would be a putrid smell. I unscrew the plume screws and the lid opens easily. I push it over on its side revealing the inside of the coffin. I avoid looking at what is left of Joan's face and concentrate on finding the Bible by her side. I quickly remove it and replace the coffin lid and reapply the plume screws. I've no intention of dallying there any longer than is necessary and I get out, and with the help of Alex start to infill the grave.

"I'm sorry for disturbing you, Joan." I place her hat back where it was. I hope she'll forgive me, I believe she will, especially if she had intended I read her Bible.

In no time we cover the coffin and eventually fill in the grave. Due to being disturbed the ground leaves a bit of a mound and we move some of the displaced earth to behind some trees, then we put the flowers and wreath back where they were.

We all stand around like we're repeating the burial. Not saying anything until Gerry starts singing.

"Oh Danny Boy, the pipes the pipes are calling…"

Walter calls from the path, "Shushed."

"Gerry."

"Yes, sir. I've to stay quiet."

"I heard he sang this at his father's funeral." Mairi tells me something I didn't know, but maybe should've, given I was counselling him.

Walter starts waving his arms. I go over to him.

"Rooney, look."

I look over to the hospital and see some lights starting to flicker on.

"We need to get out of here."

"No, there," Walter says, pointing into the trees. I look and see some shapes standing in the trees. My first thoughts are the guys from the scheme are back. "They're there."

"I know, I'll deal with it." I take a mental note to call Alby Timpson as per our agreement. Following the threat on my life, delivered in the recent note, 'stop now or you will be killed,' I am also worried whoever wrote it is around to make good his threat.

"You don't understand me, Rooney, *they* are there."

I look at him in the face, which has drained of blood. Me, I'm getting shivers down my spine.

It's time to get out of there. We gather our tools and retreat back to my office where Agnes makes tea. I'm shaking. We're all shaking. Jesus, I think, if digging up bodies isn't bad for the mental health, what is? And yet they seem OK, calm, resolved, as if they enjoyed it. Walter is whispering to Alex, while John, Gerry and Mairi are in conversation over their *desecriminal* act.

I make sure they all return to MacFarlane House, where Walter convinces the nurse in charge there they were out exploring some nocturnal birds, a local barn owl in particular.

I go back to my room at around five thirty a.m. and have a large drink to calm my nerves. I must admit to looking out into the woods from the window wondering if *they* are still there.

CHAPTER 26

The Bill Simmons memo worries me and I need to do something about it. Why did he write it? Why didn't he approach me directly? Why didn't he talk to Archie or Donna and raise his concerns there? I need to find out more about Bill Simmons. I ask Donna about him in a general way so as not to raise any suspicion over why I want to know. She had known him for a few years and explains he'd been a social worker in the community, in a tough social work team in Maryhill. As Stanley Holland is a member of the Maryhill Fleet gang, I wonder if he has any knowledge of Bill Simmons. Where would I find Stanley? Tennent's bar on a Friday evening, of course.

I see Stanley as soon as I enter Tennent's. He's regaling a couple of women near the ladies toilet. I guess this is his place where he can get maximum contact with women coming and going to and from the toilet. I wait until the women extricate themselves from Stanley and make their way back to their seat.

"Hi Stanley." I approach him from behind.

"I saw you, Rooney. In my business you need to have eyes in the back of your head."

"Rubbish, Stanley." I nod to the large wall mirror. "A good way of keeping an eye on pub without being like a lighthouse scanning the place looking for an adversary from any of the other gang members who like to drink here."

"You got it, Rooney, just why you got a college education and I got my education from the streets." I smile knowing we both understand I could have very easily fallen into the ranks of gangland Glasgow, my getting to university was my way out. "You have a good hearing with Alby?"

I raise my pint to him. "Aye, very helpful, sorted out some things at the hospital, thanks for your help."

"Aye, no problem." He makes sure he whispers in my ear. "Just watch Alby, he plays with both hands."

"Ambidextrous, Stanley." I know we both understand Alby Timpson's duplicitous ways.

"What do you want, Rooney?"

We don't normally meet in a social way. Our paths split a long time ago in our teens. I recall going to the dancing with Stanley when we were teenagers, but I got into too many fights than were good for my ambition to survive.

"Bill Simmons, the senior social worker at the hospital, do you know him?"

Stanley smiles.

"Aye, I know him. He was notorious in Maryhill. I had him as my probation officer for a while after my sentence."

I recall Stanley serving time after taking a blade to a rival gang member. He nearly cut his throat and was lucky to have survived. Stanley was lucky not to have been serving life for murder.

"A tough bastard. He didn't think twice about giving you a punch if you didn't comply with his orders. If you missed an appointment he came after you. I heard he gave a guy a kicking rather than referring back to the Sheriff to breach his probation. The guy was grateful for it, though didn't like his nose being broken. Aye, a right rough bastard."

"A rough bastard," I repeat. "Anything else?"

Stanley looks around and another whisper comes my way.

"He's as much a psychopath as many of your friends up there, Rooney."

"Oh?"

"Aye, and there's a rumour some of his probationers disappeared."

"They could have scarpered to Costa Crime, Stanley."

"Aye, they could have, but most stay in touch or come back eventually. These guys disappeared, this is all I am saying."

"Fuck's sake, you are talking about a social worker here, a council employee. Jesus, disappearing clients. What shite will you come up with next?"

This animates Stanley, a man who had drawn a blade across a face for less than this kind of slight. I find myself pressed up against the wall.

"Rooney, don't push our friendship. I am only telling you what

I know, accept it or not, it's up to you. Now, get to fuck and let me enjoy my pint."

It's time to leave, no doubt. I get out of there saying I'll see him.

"Not if I see you first, Rooney," he replies in his customary way. I get the last bus back. On the way I wonder if Stanley is winding me up. He obviously doesn't like Simmons, but to suggest he is a murderer is way over the top.

Sunday, I hear the musical chime of an ice cream van. This doesn't concern me. Ice cream vans were popular in the grounds of the hospital, just where the bus stops, though the hospital shop complained patients had been spending all their weekly pocket money on them. They sold soft drinks, sweets, and cigarettes mainly. Ice cream was invariably not available as it takes time to prepare. There had been competition from the local rival scheme ice cream vendors. The hospital is a ready target and it has been known there had been wars between rival vendors for the hospital market. Recently, however, there has been stability.

Alby Timpson has arrived.

I know about this, Stanley Holland told me one night in Tennent's. I talked to Archie about it. He in turn talked to the management team in the hospital who agreed the vans created a welcome resource for the patients, and given Timpson was now ensuring stability and order, the vans arriving at regular times each day, the hospital team allowed their entry into the hospital grounds.

In the schemes, however, there was less stability. Baseball bats, knives, guns, and axes were used by gangs to defend their territory as petty vandalism turned into all-out violent conflict. The vendors and families, including Timpson, who ran them started peddling in illegal items, bootleg cigarettes, and drugs, and heroin was particularly profitable.

Friday, in Tennent's, I am confronted by Timpson. Tennent's is well out of his safety zone, but he arrives prepared with four bodyguards. My hope he is there for a social drink is dispelled when I am called over to his table.

"Sean, I need that favour. It's time to call it in."

I realise this is why he is in the hospital grounds. His sorting out of the guys who tried to raise a thousand pounds a month from the nurses in the nurses' home is now to be repaid by me. What the hell can it be?

"The ice cream business is doing well in the hospital, Rooney. We need to move to stage two."

"Eh, Alby?" I know what's coming: drugs and cigs. "Sorry, Alby, I have no—"

"You need to use your influence with the hospital managers."

"Jesus, Alby, I am a trainee, I don't have—"

"You did the last time. Your boss talked to the management team."

"Drugs, Alby. No way they would accept it."

"Just tell them they'll get their share?"

"Fuck's sake, Alby, they're professionals."

"Oh, Rooney, come on, most of them are using it. They live in Denniston and the West End and are into coke and grass and all that shite. I know who they are and they are in charge up there."

"Who are they?"

"Your Doctor Jamieson, for one."

"Jamieson, he's a top doc there."

"He has a fucking habit. Talk to him, Rooney, he'll agree, I know he will. Tell him we'll shop his habit to the police if doesn't and he'll get some extra stuff if he does. That'll do it."

I accept there's no way out of this. I have to do it. But first I have to confirm something, after what I saw in the trees when we were in the graveyard that night.

"Alby, the guys are back."

"What, Rooney?"

"The guys were in the hospital grounds, in the trees. This is outwith our agreement." There is an uncomfortable pause. "Alby?"

There's an even more uncomfortable couple of minutes, then the volume gets turned up.

"Rooney," he blasts. "I sent out word no one sets foot in the hospital grounds except my guys and I can assure you they were not there last night. They do their business in normal time. That's the way it is. So, go fuck yourself, and give me peace. Fuck sake, maybe you should see a shrink yourself."

"Alby, there's been a threat, on my life."

He gives me *that* look. "Rooney, I don't make threats, I carry them out." And with that he is gone, he has better things to do than pamper to a neurotic student psychologist.

I ruled out the guys from the scheme in the trees that night, so who or what the hell were they? I need to know a bit more about the Castle, its provenance, its history, and in particular its supernatural element. On Saturday, I go to the Mitchell Library to delve into the records there. I love the Mitchell, where I do most of the research for my course. It has this enabling atmosphere, quiet and comfortable, and the most amazing records on Glasgow history. I get into the Mitchell's computer and search 'Hillwood Hospital'.

I find out some paranormal journalists had investigated stories of strange goings on in the grounds and in some deserted back wards. Having both a sceptical and inquiring mind, a good basis for a psychologist, I researched the newspaper reports of the sixties where strange noises were noted to have come from ward 49, a locked back ward in the west corridor, the women's corridor. Due to better care and treatments in the community, as the hospital population contracted, long stay patients reduced in numbers and, as admissions to long stay reduced. the hospital authorities closed wards. Starting from the very farthest of wards along the long corridors.

At the ends of each corridor, some long stay wards were closed, starting with wards 49, then 47, then 45, and 43, and 41, then 39, all in the women's corridor; and in the men's corridor, ward 50, then 48, then 46, 44 and 42, and then ward 40. It left both corridors in their darkest deepest extent closed as no go areas.

But, according to the reports I am reading, it was in ward 49, before it was closed and emptied, that strange events were noticed. Women patients claimed to hear screams, laughter, footsteps, and big bangs in there; in addition to seeing full-bodied apparitions at the end of the corridor adjacent to the closed off wards. This was no surprise to the security guards who reported seeing people in the windows and hearing the Chapel bell, directly adjacent to these wards at the end of the corridors, ring for no reason. No explanation could be found for these events which kept the patients awake, unsettling delusional patients who feared the devil was out to possess them. Media attention brought the Glasgow Herald into the scene and a reporter, Alex Brown, ran a story on it attracting interest from across the country.

Glasgow ghost hunter, Professor James Boothroyd became involved and an exorcism of the ward was carried out by Prof Rev. John Cairns, a Professor of Practical Theology at Strathclyde University and the Strathclyde University Chaplain Rev. David McAndrew, then for many years things settled down in the old ward.

But now similar activity has re-emerged.

CHAPTER 27

I have to experience ward 49 for myself, challenge the supernatural element, stay overnight there, establish there's no more than physical threats going on in the hospital. Then, any activity, potentially paranormal, troubling the patients, would be no more than mass hysteria which was discussed in the team meeting.

I explain to the porters and security men part of my research is to try to understand how patients in days gone by lived in the hospital. As ward 49 has been locked off for some years, intact with all the old Victorian iron beds and furniture still in place, this is an ideal place to get an impression of how patients lived in there. I clear it with Archie and Donna. Agnes says she would be happy to keep me company if I so wish. I decline, saying I had to experience this on my own.

Mick, the porter, hesitates before he hands me the key.

"You do know the ward is haunted, don't you?"

I shake my head, lying, as I take the key.

"Really, how exciting."

He smiles and shakes his head.

"On your head be it pal. You wouldn't catch me in there overnight."

I smile back.

"The radiators are still connected. But they're turned off, so turn them on to get some heat in there."

I nod. "Thanks."

Later this night, with my sleeping bag, a pack of sandwiches, a flask of tea, and a torch in my bag, I head along the west corridor towards ward 49. As I pass the last occupied ward, ward 37, with its sounds of patient chatter, the corridor becomes quiet as a church, which was very relative as the Chapel is directly adjacent to these old closed off wards. I pass ward 39, then ward 41, 43, then 45 and 47, and there before me is ward 49. I look beyond the ward along the corridor and see the locked door to the outside, which was only to be opened by the workmen or porters taking coffins out to go to the graveyard, or in times of fire or emergency.

I move to the door of ward 49. The paint is peeling and cobwebs cover the corners up to the ceiling of the outer hall. I put the key into the lock, turn it, and push the door, which opens easily, breaking the cobwebs. I brush the cobwebs aside and move inside, switching on my torch. The porter had explained I had to open the box behind the door to reveal the ward's light switches.

"There's a switch marked Master," he said, "but be careful, ancient wiring is everywhere. It needed rewiring, but they closed the ward off completely, a bloody fire risk."

I push the switch down and the lights flicker on through the ward. I switch off my torch and return it to my bag.

Immediately, I'm confronted by a time capsule. The ward was closed in the sixties, but had remained unchanged for over fifty years before. The dormitory set up is apparent, though the old iron beds have no sheets or pillows, only thin striped single mattresses. I walk along passing the beds, similar to Stephenson in ward 22 the night he found Oliver Turnbull's body.

There had been a few removed from this ward as well, however, after patients died by natural means and there had been a few suicides in the forties and fifties. A couple by hangings in the toilets, and others by wrists opened by razor blades, and one woman who had gouged out an imaginary or maybe a delusional baby with a garden trowel. There is no surprise it's known as the Haunted Ward.

Apart from the cobwebs and the paint peeling off the walls and fading garish ancient wallpaper, the ward is surprisingly tidy. The furniture had been covered by sheets. The coal fires and grates are clean and the heavy curtains are closed over thin laced liners. There's nothing to suggest the ward had been occupied for over sixty years with innumerable amounts of patients staying twenty, thirty, forty or even more years, to die there and to be replaced by others staying the same timescales. I wonder if the spirits of the patients are here, whether imaginary or real. I like to think my imagination is governed by my intelligence. I don't believe in ghosts, but it does feel creepy.

I pull off a sheet to find a large comfortable sofa. I sit down and try to imagine a Victorian ward full of patients wearing stock gowns, being looked after by white bibbed nurses with hair clipped up under caps. Some wards had been identified as fee paying, where relatives paid for an improved quality of care and surroundings, some had called this the profligate asylums, other wards were for pauper lunatics.

Women had been admitted with conditions described as morally defective, after having children outwith marriage, infidelity, moral insanity, insanity caused by childbirth or overwork. A father or husband could persuade two doctors to sign certificates of insanity to put away embarrassing relatives in a madhouse. Women with lower social status, and usually less power and money, were vulnerable.

I pull out my flask and sandwiches and make myself comfortable. It's going to be a long night, but I've no intention of falling asleep. I leave the light on. I want to be able to see the whole of the ward. I try to imagine being here when the ward was full, hearing the soft breathing from the sleeping patients, snores, talking in their sleep. After a while, the quiet of the ward soothes and settles me. Maybe this won't be as bad as I think it might be. A couple of hours go by without anything of interest. Then, as I start to doze, I hear an ill-defined noise. At first I thought it may be a mouse or a rat coming from the top corner of the ward. I shine my torch in that direction. There's nothing to see. I look at my watch, it's 11.25 p.m. I satisfy myself it's not the witching hour which I am dreading a bit.

Then the whispering starts, from the same corner. I keep my torch on the corner although I can see into it clearly. I can make it out. It's muffled and sounds like a few people in conversation. It doesn't sound particularly scary. Then I see a shape silhouetted by the outside lights. I'm not sure it's inside or outside the window, but it's the shape of a person right enough. I think about calling out, but decline, thinking of how stupid it would be if it's the security men walking the grounds.

Then the murmuring from the corner increases in volume.

"Who's there?" I say.

The sound abates for a few minutes then starts again.

It's clearer now. I hear it. "He's a man, he shouldn't be here, he'll wake the weans."

I might have been wrong, but this's how it sounds. I know I need to leave.

Until, "Sean, it's your mammy," comes from a shape in the corner. I can't see it clearly but I know the voice. "It's your mammy, son."

"No please, I don't…"

"You need to leave here son, it's no' safe."

Jesus, my mental health is really getting worse. I had heard my mother's voice in the past in a previous relapse, but not for a while.

"Mammy?"

"Aye, son, it's no safe, go."

The 'go' was strong. I have heard this timbre before in her voice. When she would tell me for the last time at night to get to bed before my father came in from the pub, "Go to bed, now!"

I need to get out of there. I get up and gather my bag, flask, and stuff, and head off down the ward. There are noises of footsteps behind me. I hear metal beds being moved across the floor. I try not to panic as I hurry through the ward. I reach the ward door, open it, and move through, intent in pulling it closed and locking it behind me. I have no intention of putting the lights off and plunging the ward into darkness. But then, just as I move through, the door slams shut behind me, knocking me off my feet and sending me headfirst into the corridor.

Then a voice from behind the door calls:

"Get out, and don't come back."

Shit, it's real enough. I'm not going back in there.

I stand in the corridor looking down towards the Pass. The outside door would have been locked by the security men and I have no intention of getting them out of their warm bothy in the gatehouse of the hospital to let me out. They would have chided me for being stupid enough to stay in the ward after being warned by them. But where do I go? The Chapel is adjacent to the ward and it's warm. I'll go in there.

I'm shaking as I go into the Chapel and I feel heartened there's a singular light over the Alter. I close the door behind me. I'm not religious but it gives me a sense of safety. I pull out my sleeping bag and coory in behind the alter on the carpet. It feels warm and safe as I position myself in the corner giving me a good view of the whole of the Chapel. I open my bag and retrieve a half bottle of Grouse whisky I had put in there earlier. I drink from the bottle and pull myself into my sleeping bag. I finish it and fall asleep. In my drunken state I won't hear any more from ward 49 this night.

Then I awake to the sound of someone singing. It's the nun and she's singing a hymn. I remember it from my days in St Mary's, my mother used to sing it.

"Faith of my fathers, holy faith, we will be true to you till death." She gets up and walks out of the door. I can hear her as she makes her way out and down the corridor. "Our Fathers, chained in prisons dark, were still in heart and conscience free. How sweet would be their children's fate? If they, like them, could die for thee."

I pull my head into my sleeping bag. I would have gone back to my room in the nurses' home had I been able to get the security man to let me out, but I know I have to remain there. I fall asleep. The next thing I know the Chaplain is waking me.

"Are you OK my friend, is it not time you were in your bed?"

I look at my watch; it's 8.46 a.m. I had slept the night on the floor of the Chapel. I thank him and gather my stuff into my bag.

"Why?" he asks me,

"For research," I reply.

He shakes his head and helps me to my feet. I thank him and head out into the corridor. I avoid even looking at the door of ward 49 and make my way down the corridor.

I approach the Pass and already there are many patients coming out of the dining room after breakfast. I look for Myra and she's not there. Interestingly, the nun is, cleaning the floor where Myra normally sits. Whilst knowing her urine has to be cleaned daily after she has been there, I'm not sure why a nun has to do it.

I pop my head into the psychology department and tell Agnes I would not be in today, I hadn't slept very well.

"I knew you wouldn't have," she says. "You should've let me stay there with you. I would've kept you warm."

I smile rather than engage and head back to the nurses' home.

I get back. I am cold, tired, and not a little shaken by the whole experience. I have a shower and make myself toast and a pot of tea. I put my two bar electric heater on, not that the old iron radiators don't throw off heat, but for some strange reason, whether they turn the boiler off when the nurses are either sleeping or on shift, they turn the heating down. I wrap myself up in my old house coat and coory into my inviting old chesterfield chair, one I got from the Barras. I drink my tea and my eyes naturally fall upon Joan's Bible. For two reasons:

one, it might give me some spiritual comfort after my experiences in ward 49, though I doubt it, and two, I had entered Joan's coffin to retrieve it, putting the group at risk, after reading her note, where she wrote: 'In my Bible is my life and my death.' In her Bible is her death and I need to know what she meant.

"Right, let's see what her Bible says about her death," I say to myself. In my initial look at her Bible I had noticed some pages marked by turned over corners.

I open the Bible and go to a few of these pages to see she had underlined certain phrases.in pencil.

"Right, let's see."

I go to Deuteronomy 32:39, where she has underlined, 'There is no God besides me. I put to death and I bring to life,' then Samuel 2:6, where she has underlined, 'The Lord brings death and makes alive; he brings down to the grave and raises up,' then, Kings 5:7, 'Am I God, to kill and to make alive,' and Exodus 20:13, where she has written into the margin, 'he decision of when to die is God's alone,' and 'to kill oneself is a sin'.

I pour myself another cup of tea and vocalise a summary.

"There is no God besides me. I put to death and I bring to life. The Lord brings death and makes alive. He brings down to the grave and raises up. Am I God, to kill and to make alive." Then, "The decision of when to die is God's alone. To kill oneself is a sin."

I sit thinking about these phrases, and there is certainly a theme. I paraphrase, "God can put to death and bring to life," and given she was thought to have committed suicide, where in the final entry of her note, she said, 'If you are reading this, then I'll have been murdered. I didn't do it. I believe to kill myself is a sin', she is saying, 'God kills, but you can't kill yourself.'

I repeat this out loud. "God kills, but you can't kill yourself."

In her Bible is certainly her life and her death. That she lived her life based on her Bible, and that she died, at the hands of God.

I need something stronger and pour myself a stiff one. It works. I don't feel so shaken, I am warmer, though not any less confused about what is happening in this place, nor what had happened to Joan.

I fall asleep on the chair, where I sleep for the rest of the day.

CHAPTER 28

Wednesday, the weather has worsened. The wind is up, gale force, around seventy-five mph, according to the news. I don't go in and I spend the day in bed. My experience has unsettled me and I'm questioning myself. Had I really heard voices in ward 49? Maybe they came from another ward or outside? Did I just get into a panic and scare myself into getting out of there? Did I really see shapes in the trees that night in the graveyard? All of this, and the stuff I had read in the Mitchell library about spooks in the hospital, is getting to me.

I have to get out of the hospital grounds for a while.

I'll pick up a bus outside the hospital grounds and head into Glasgow. I wrap myself up and leave the nurses' home and go out into the grounds. It's dark and I look over to the hospital. The wind is whistling through the trees, giving a whooshing sound. I imagine Walter will be observing his trees and twigs falling onto the grounds from his vantage point in the conservatory of ward 22.

All looks quiet and settled, but I feel apprehensive about the whole thing, after being in ward 49, and my whole experience of the place. Maybe I can get out and get a decent job and put it all behind me. I try to avoid looking into the trees as I walk along the roadway towards the gate. Through the sound of the whistling in the trees, I think I hear something behind me, but comfort myself with Timpson's words: 'Rooney, I sent out word no one sets foot in the hospital grounds except my guys' and he had assured me he isn't out to kill me, as indicated in the death threat I received.

I don't want to look around, reminding myself of how my imagination can get the better of me, but I can't stop myself.

I turn around and look into the trees, and there they are, three of them walking towards me. I resist thinking these are ghostly figures as Walter suggests or guys from the scheme, ruled out by Timpson. I accelerate towards the gatehouse and the security men. Then I realise it may even be the security men themselves taking a short cut across the grounds.

"Hello," I call. "Is it you guys?"

There's no answer and the figures appear to disappear, gone deeper into the trees, perhaps. I walk on trying to believe it's indeed the security men.

Then I feel an almighty whack on my back and I'm plunging down towards the road. I try to bring my hands up but I can't stop my head hitting the tarmac. I never knew a material could be so rock hard. I must have been knocked out momentarily and when I open my eyes my head is on one side, my eyes parallel with the road. Immediately I wonder whether my head has been caved in. I really do see stars and lose my vision momentarily, just before the trauma arrives with the pain in my head, which thankfully becomes more of a tingling, numbed sensation. Whatever hit me on my back was heavy and solid. I try to get up but it's impossible, my arms don't respond, presumably from the thump on my back. I'm barely conscious as I feel the tarmac on my face and my brow. It's wet and cold and I hope it's not from blood. Immediately, I wonder if my back is broken. Even at this point I'm trying to hold on to my reason.

I try to call out to the gatehouse but nothing of any good comes out.

"Help," I mumble, so meekly no one could possibly hear me.

Then I hear whispering, almost like the sound I heard in the ward. There's nothing distinct, like: Is he OK or shall we kill him? Just whispers. They're close, standing over me. I seriously think they're going to cave my head from behind and that will be me. I see myself lying on the road, almost like an out of body experience. Maybe it is, I wonder. There, I'm stretched out on the road, like a forensic sketch.

A lifeless figure on the road. Stupidly, I wonder if I'd be missed by anyone. I wonder if I'll hear my mother's voice telling me to come home. I dispute it all and wonder if my mind is playing tricks on me. I cannot move and begin to accept I may die there.

Then I hear another set of voices. I move my eyes up to see a security man coming out of the gatehouse.

"Help," I say, faintly.

There's no way he'll hear me, and I can't hear the murmur behind me anymore. Surely if he walks along the road he'll come across me. I'm worried I might get another whack which would end me before he arrives. Then, I hear another set of voices from behind. Maybe his colleague security men are heading back from the hospital having locked up for the night.

"You all right, son," from behind me confirms this.

The man from the gatehouse is also now standing over me.

"Maybe he's been hit by a car, in the dark, a hit and run," he says to the men behind me.

Oh, aye, I think, how would this account from the whack on my back which flattened me onto the road?

"Please help me."

I feel their hands on me trying to get me to my feet.

"Please don't," I say, knowing if my back's broken I could be left paralysed by their efforts.

They get the message and put me back on the road. One takes off his jacket and puts it under my head, and another puts his over me, while the other rushes to the gatehouse presumably to call an ambulance. It feels like an age before I hear the klaxon of the ambulance coming through the gate and up the road toward me. For the first time, I think I may survive. If they can get me to hospital, specialist services would do everything to keep me alive. I'm worried I may be disabled for the rest of my life, however.

I'm wheeled in a stretcher trolley into Glasgow Royal Infirmary at speed. I've been here many times and recognise the glazed tiled walls. My mother had been brought here after her overdose, me hanging onto the side of the hospital trolley bed. No one is hanging onto my trolley, only the ambulance men. They get me into A and E and the medics carefully secure my head and neck before meticulously transferring me to an emergency bed. As they connect me to all the paraphernalia, from their mutterings, I know I'm in a serious condition. I get another out-of-body experience, me looking down on my sorry state, around half a dozen medics and nurses going about their business, presumably trying to save my life, then nothing, I lose consciousness.

I regain consciousness. It's Saturday, the twenty-fourth of April and I've been transferred to a surgical ward, presumably to enter my head should I be bleeding inside. They want to observe me, to monitor my reaction, and establish any damage I may have. I'm heartened to be able to feel and lift my arms and move my legs and feet. I raise my hand and feel my head which is covered in bandages. My head feels both bloody sore on the outside and as if it's going explode on the inside. I need pain relief.

"Nurse, nurse."

I'm relieved she is there in seconds.

"Well, hello, Mr Rooney, I see you're back with us."

"I didn't know I had been away."

"That's what I want to hear, cheek, a good sign."

"I'm pleased to entertain you. I need something for—"

"We are giving you a hefty dose of pain relief, but I'll get some more."

"Thank you."

She returns, sits me up in bed, and pops some tablets in my mouth.

"How am I?"

She tidies my bed.

"You're doing good," she says, in a nursey way. "The doctor will be round later and he'll talk to you. You've no fractures to your skull, just bruising which will heal, and there's no bleeding inside, and so far no sign of brain damage, but time will tell on this front. You've been concussed and we think you have been seeing things, calling out in your sleep, saying you are seeing things in the trees, calling out for your mother, who you were saying was at your side."

"I saw them in the trees. They did it."

"Well, you really got some knock to your back. It's badly bruised, but nothing's broken."

"Did they…"

"The police have been investigating and your friend Jackie's been at your side a lot until you got out of danger. She'll be in at visiting time, no doubt. Now rest up and let me know if the tablets help. I can't give you any more other than those prescribed as required, but the doctor will advise on this."

Later, Jackie arrives.

"You really like to do things to get attention, Rooney."

"Yeah, I know, a proper entertainer me."

She sorts my bedclothes like a nurse and pinches my nose in a playful way.

"You really got me worried, you fucker."

"Sorry about it, I need to stop being a fool. Have you any information about what happened to me? What're your lot saying?"

"There's nothing to follow up. No signs of attack. They found a massive branch on the road behind where you were found."

"So, that's what they hit me with?"

"They're not sure, Rooney."

"What do you mean, it was the weapon they used on me?"

"It may have come from one of the trees which hang over the road, the winds brought the branch down onto you."

"It was them, I saw them, in the trees."

"We're not sure, they can't find anything to suggest you were attacked."

"I'm telling you I was attacked, is that not good enough?"

"Rooney…"

"Oh shut up." I go into a sulk. She pulls out a newspaper and starts reading.

Then I see *them*. They're standing in the corner of the ward, three of them. They're staring right at me, I hear them murmuring.

"He's not dead. He's still alive. He's going to live."

At first I'm not sure. They look strange though, strangely dressed, Victorian clothes, two with caps and one in the middle with a top hat. That one is pointing a walking stick in my direction.

"Get him," he says. It's as plain as day. "Get him."

The two men by his side are approaching me.

"No, please. Please go away," I say, muffled at first. Then, "Get away," I shout, as I try to get up, pulling the line out of my arm.

The nurse and Jackie are now holding me down and another nurse is strapping my arms to the bedsides. Then I get a jag in my backside, heavy sedation no doubt. I am asleep again.

On Monday, I wake up in ward 8, Hillwood Hospital, the Castle. I've been sectioned after hitting out at one of the nurses who was trying to restrain me. It'd been established my head injury was not requiring further medical intervention, but my behaviour could not be managed in a medical facility. I needed to be managed in a psychiatric setting. I was sedated and transferred here.

I'm now sitting in one of those highbacked chairs looking out into the ward. I'm clothed and the bandages have been taken from my head. I look around, dazed, wondering how the hell I got there. Seeing I'm awake, this rather plump nurse comes to me and crouches down beside me.

"You alright, Mr?"

Right away, I see a Betty Boop figure Myra indicated in her diary.

"Never better."

"You still seeing anything?" This's the kind of thing a mental health nurse would say. I look around to see a lot of sad bastards in a psychiatric ward, bored stupid and having no life. "I need to ask, it's part of the assessment."

"Right, Betty." I'll preserve my right to anonymity. "So, what're the docs saying?"

She looks at me curiously. "Betty?"

"Boop."

"You've had a psychotic episode and you've to have treatment."

"Psychotic episode, I nearly got my head caved in."

"Did you ever see or hear things before that?"

I know what she's getting at, a pre-existing mental illness, perhaps?

"No." I'm lying. "When will I get out of here?"

"You're on a section and antipsychotic medication, we'll need to see."

I spend the next few days at in the ward completely drugged to the gunnels, the chemical cosh had been administered liberally in my case. I continue to see 'the bastards,' as I call them, those who had been in the trees that night. I consistently call out: "The bastards." I ally myself with Alex, saying I'll destroy *them*, those who were out to destroy me.

This's a locked ward, preventing me from escaping into the grounds. Alex and Gerry are constant companions, and Walter and Mairi visit, and Jackie is there most visiting times, and Agnes, when Jackie isn't around.

My placement has been suspended in the hope I'll recover sufficiently to recontinue it and get through my psychotic episode, as described by the nurses. Donna calls regularly, as a friend I thought at first, but then the questions become more pointed, more clinical.

"Your hallucinations, Sean, do you still see them? Your delusions, do you still believe they want to kill you and you want to kill them?"

"Yes, because they are there. I know they are, and I will, I need to. If I don't, they'll kill me and others in this hospital. They need to be stopped."

After a while, a week or so. I don't see them as much. Jackie says the antipsychotic medication is starting to work. I'm not so sure. I feel calmer though. So much so, I start to get passes out of the ward. I wander down to the Pass hoping to see Myra who's nowhere to be seen. I'm worried about her.

I've to talk to Doctor J. The attack on me was serious and I'm scared it'll happen again if I don't. Alby says I've to get Jamieson's approval for the sale of drugs from the ice cream vans in the hospital grounds. I now believe this is a good thing. However, I'm caught between the devil and the deep blue sea. I've to facilitate the sale of drugs through the ice cream vans and I could be responsible for the patients becoming an exploitable market, but more concerning it could lead to them developing habits, with all the resulting damaging effects, such as becoming psychotic due to mixing prescribed managed drugs with class A illegal and unregulated narcotics. This's a potential firebomb.

What do I do? Do I talk to Jackie and bring in the law, knowing the law doesn't really exist here in the hospital or in the schemes? If Timpson doesn't get his way the guys will be back in the grounds and the nurses will be targeted once more, and at least the patients would be supervised; whereas, before, it's known they can get drugs by going into the local scheme, and the nursing staff are well able to deal with the effects of patients using drugs.

This is about management, I assure myself. Maybe I can convince Timpson to go easy on the supply in the knowledge that too much is volatile, and it'll lead to crisis and the end of his market, whereas just enough is sustainable and over time more profitable. I settle with pursuing the latter.

Meanwhile, Donna says it's OK for me to visit the psychology department and take part in some self-help groups to get my confidence back. My head continues to hurt and, although I still see *them*, I have the wherewithal to say I don't.

I ask to see Doctor J and he comes to the ward. He says he's pleased I am recovering, that I am helping the patients, and I'll be discharged soon. I ask if we could go for a walk in the grounds and he agrees. We go outside and find a bench. I don't want to be overheard.

"You what, Sean, you want me to sanction the selling of drugs in the hospital grounds?" He sounds aghast at first, but then calms down.

I explain the situation to him: it's better to control the supply of drugs, rather than have an unmanaged market in the grounds, and Timpson would keep the patients and the nurses safe in the grounds. He still isn't convinced.

Then, when I say he will get his share, his face and his attitude change.

"When you think about it, Sean, let's be honest, drugs are drugs, there's the licensed prescribed ones that we use and there are the others, the unlicensed ones freely available to people in general in the schemes. Should we be denying the people of our establishment the rights others have outside?" I just look at him as he takes a pause. "Of course not, and if it allows me some way of overseeing their sale, making sure only the soft stuff gets to the patients, then…"

He'll do it. He's found a way of reconciling it with himself, notwithstanding getting a steady access to his drug of choice at the same time.

CHAPTER 29

All is fine for a while, and on the twenty-fourth of May my short-term detention is rescinded. After staying in Jackie's flat for a while, I return to my room in the nurses' home. Donna and Archie agree with the Uni to extend my placement to allow me to recover properly. I argue it's discriminatory not to allow me, a person with mental health problems, to return to the course. She'll supervise me carefully, however, and report to the uni. It's clear I have to keep my nose clean and get through the placement.

In the meantime, Alex has become a regular user of the vans, and he learns very quickly there's a link between the vendors and organised crime, which quickly melds with his delusions they are in the hospital to kill the patients. He makes threats to the vendors. Alby Timpson gets in touch with me and tells me to sort it. I ask the ward staff to be careful of Alex and his contact with the vendors.

But one day it all blows up.

Alex manages to get off the ward and attacks a van with a hammer he steals from the hospital mechanics. He drags the vendor out of the van and sets about him, kicking and punching him, then he ransacks the inside of the van. The patients benefit greatly from this as boxes of crisps, bottles of Coke and Iron Brew are thrown out onto the grass, and sweets and cigarettes are strewn across the hospital lawns. He's grabbed by four nurses and sedated and stuck in a separate room to be calmed. The security men find drugs in the van.

"Ask Mr Rooney, he knows all about it," Alex says, as he's taken back to the ward.

Donna and Archie call me in and they tell me plainly if this is true then this is the end of my placement, potentially my course, and potentially my career as a clinical psychologist.

Jackie finds out about the drugs. She goes mental, which is what she says I am. She brings in a team. The vans are stopped and arrests are made. She stops short at me, believing my mental illness is behind

175

it. She has no idea of Doctor J's place in this, and I am not going to tell her. He is keeping his head down. I expect Timpson will be in touch.

Friday evening, I'm back with Jackie in Tennent's.

"You really have lost it this time, Rooney. Completely out of your box, a delusional nutjob trapped in a belief system involved with the mob supplying drugs to psychiatric patients. Aye, very good, that."

I keep my head down into my beer.

"This's the end of your dreams and our relationship. Rooney, I can't support you anymore. I can't condone what you're doing." She leaves.

I won't be joining Jackie in her flat this evening.

Thankfully, no charges are brought on me. Everyone knows Alex is delusional about the mob. The attack is his making and nothing is attributed to me.

I'm off the hook.

I feel better. I've to stay on the medication. I get a diagnosis of manic depression. 'Manic depression,' where did this come from? I don't know, but they think I may have had it before I hit the road. Apart from hearing my mother, saying: 'You'll be alright son,' which I'm sure is just me remembering her in the way she would soothe me after my father hit me. No further episodes occur. I don't say I still see *them,* but I know I need to present a 'normal me', and I need to get back to my placement.

I need to talk to Timpson. I did what he asked of me. Doctor J agreed to his drugs on the hospital grounds, but Alex attacking his guy put the end to that. He'll be after me for sure, but I need to know if it was his guys who attacked me that night. I call Stanley and ask him to contact Timpson—you don't contact Timpson directly—and ask if I can see him. He gets right back.

"He'll see you," Stanley says. "His house two o'clock, on Sunday."

Sunday, dead on time, I approach his house, more like a mansion, in the Blackhill housing scheme. I press the intercom at his gate.

"Hello, Sean Rooney for Mr Timpson."

A curt voice replies.

"Wait there."

I look around. Timpson lives in a two adjoined five apartment house, ex-council, both bought in the seventies under Thatcher's housing reforms. They look nothing like council houses though. Cladding covers the walls making it look like a south side villa, a five-foot perimeter wall with a metal spiked fence on top, an iron wrought gate, with controlled access and security cameras. This is more a fortress than a residence.

"Hello?"

"Hello," I reply.

"The gate'll open and you'll come to the door, you'll wait there."

The gate opens and my feet crunch through the pebble stone driveway to the house. I get to the door and look at another camera and security access. The door opens.

"Come in," comes from inside. I go in.

There are two heavies waiting for me and I'm taken through the hall and into the front room overlooking the front garden. Timpson is there at his desk, his back to me, on the phone. I see a movement in the sofa to the right of the desk. It's a woman, a very thin young woman. He swings his chair around and gestures me to sit on the seat at the other side of his desk. It's clear he wants me to hear what he has to say.

"Aye, aye, aye, keep talking your shite." He leans over his desk resting his elbows on it as his tone changes. "Well, John…" He puts his hand on the receiver. "John Patterson, the enforcer," he says to me. I know who he's talking to. John Patterson is a well-known East End thug, famed for extorting money from people referred to him by loan sharks and gangsters like Timpson, also known for extreme brutality. I don't react. But Timpson wants me to hear what he has to say. "Listen, John, and get this into your thick head, he doesn't pay up you take his hand, he doesn't pay up after that you take his fucking head, and you get my money to me in a week or I'll take your fucking balls." He slams the phone down and he turns to me.

"Hello, Sean, want a drink? Laura, get Mr Rooney a drink."

Laura moves to a trolley with glasses and a decanter. I see now how thin she really is. I had worked with women with eating disorders in Glasgow. I know the signs.

"No thanks, too early for me."

"Not for me, a large one for me, hen."

Laura gives him his drink. I think about going straight into it, but this is not the protocol with this man, he always leads the discussion.

"Unfortunate circumstances, Sean. My man was badly injured by the crazy guy attacking him in the nuthoose. He could've shot the bastard. He was carrying, but it's as well he didn't, it would have been big shite." I wonder if he knows Alex is linked to me through the group and as his counsellor. I keep quiet. "The thing now is the game is up and the law knows we're in there. Fucks everything up." I nod, hoping this would be the end of the drugs sale in the hospital. "So we need to agree how we are going to recoup my losses. We were doing very well in there. We can't lose the market." No way is he going to give up on the Castle. "You are my man in there, Sean, and Doctor Drugs is our partner." Doctor Drugs. Jesus, I think, Jamieson has another name, from Doctor J to Doctor Death, now Doctor Drugs. "You'll sort it out and when you do you let me know, soon." His eyes are drilling into mine. This's an ultimatum. "That's it, Rooney, on your way." He swings the chair back around to the window.

"Mr Timpson?" He totally ignores me. "Alby?"

"Whit," he snaps from the back of the chair.

"I was attacked. Were you angry at me?"

He spins around once more.

"Listen son." He's pointing at me this time. "If I attacked you, you wouldn't be sitting there, you'd be deid. It wisnae me."

"Somebody did. Do you think it was McGinn's crew?"

I need to know if he thinks the McGinn guys are back in the hospital and they're angry at me talking to him about them extorting money from the nurses.

"He widnae dare, son. He might've attacked you, but he widnae be there to take money from the lassies." His voice gets louder and more gravelly. "He'll no touch ma man in the nuthoose, especially when ah'm doing business in there. OK, you happy wi' that?" I nod. "Just get us back up and running, son. That's your job now. I want a plan, so fucking get to it."

So, I'm no longer a psychology student, I'm now a mobster's lacky.

I get a taxi back. It's getting dark and I'm not walking through the grounds again on my own, in the dark, with *them* around, whoever *they* are. I spend the whole time going back on the bus wondering how the hell I'm going to get out of this, and if I can't, how I'm going to accede to Timpson's orders and save my skin.

CHAPTER 30

Monday morning, the 31st of May, I arrive early at the department.

I'm pleased Archie allows me to take a referral at the meeting, though he wants me to carefully resume my practice and take less serious cases, to get me back into the way of things.

He allocates me a woman in ward 27 with alcohol related brain damage, Korsakoff's, as it's called. She has little short-term memory, forgetting things minutes previously but remembering most things from way back. She's been referred for psychological intervention, which could have been anything, but it's about helping her as best as I can. She has the long-term effects of alcohol abuse, so much so it damaged her brain. I'm not sure what I can do to help her, but agree to assess her with a mind to long-term rehab and a residential placement in the community.

I avoid talking to the group, even although they had all individually turned up at the department and talked to Agnes, asking to see me. Alex is in the secure ward, being assessed for a court appearance on attacking the guy in the ice cream van. It's possible he'll be transferred to the State Hospital.

Agnes pleads with me to see them, saying they're desperate to have a group meeting. I placate them to concentrate on my new patients and getting through the placement. It doesn't rest easily on me, however. I feel bad for having raised their hopes and giving them something tangible to focus on.

Myra hasn't been seen for weeks and everyone is concerned. Over the next couple of weeks I concentrate on the new referrals.

Helga Shultz has a small shop in Parkhead, but got into serious financial difficulty due to forgetting to pay bills. The social work department assessed her and it was likely she would be transferred to a residential resource in the East End. I'll assist in preparing her for discharge, which I know will be difficult because she is determined to go home. I meet with Dr J, her consultant, and Bill Simmons, who's been allocated to do the transfer.

The meeting is fraught. Simmons says she'll do well at the placement, Dr Jamieson says she'll die within a year, which was the norm for most patients who are sent there.

"The disruption blows their mind," Jamieson says. "After being settled in hospital for years they are dragged out against their will and stuck in that place."

Simmons says it is a matter of right to be returned to the community.

Jamieson disagrees and says here is their home. Without his approval, however, she'll be going nowhere, but he is over a barrel. He can't resist the pressure to discharge a woman into the community if her needs can be met there, such is the philosophy of care in the community. He's developing a name for being intransigent and old fashioned in his views. I wonder if he knows he's developing a reputation in the patient fraternity for other things too, like killing patients, for example. I can't resist looking at his shoes and wonder what he thinks of his locker being broken into. He pulls out a packet of Werther's Originals and offers us one. Simmons and I decline. My reason is obvious, but it's clear there is tension between Simmons and Jamieson, a clear tension between the social work department's philosophy of care in the community and the old school psychiatrist's paternalism.

Helga has a couple of trial visits and two overnight stays in the nursing home. A date of Thursday the 10th of June is set for her discharge there. I see her a few times and she appears positive about going. I agree to go with her on the morning of her transfer, to support her.

The 10th of June is a wet and miserable day. I'll ensure Helga is well clothed against the weather.

"I'm here to escort Helga to the home," I say, going into the nurses' office.

"She's dead," the charge nurse says, calmly. "She was very agitated last night and she was found this morning in her bed, dead."

"Dead, in her bed," I repeat, stupidly.

"The docs think her heart gave out, she was overweight, elderly, and maybe the discharge was just too much for her."

"Jesus," I say, "not Helga now."

I return to the department and go into a deep dark mood. Donna tells me to take the day off and go to the nurses' home. I open a bottle of whisky, drink it, and curl up on my sofa. I resign myself with getting out of this. The voices come back, they're in the corner of the room this time.

They stay put this time, however, just there whispering at me. "He's drinking. He's a nut job. He's getting out. Can't do it. Not good enough."

My mother too. "This place is too much for you, Sean. It'll get you, like it got me."

Then I hear my dad. "You're no' good enough son. Not clever enough to be a professional. Get yourself a proper job in the factory."

"Get out of my head," I shout at him. "And you too," to them, throwing a glass at the wall.

This brings John Scott to the door.

"You alright in there, Rooney," he says, from outside.

"I'm fine."

"Let me in."

I let him in and go back to the sofa and cover myself with my blanket.

"Turn on your TV, wait until you see this."

I turn on the TV and see scenes of the hospital and police cars and news teams in the grounds.

"What is happening?"

"A body's been found in the old concert hall, upstairs. Although, while they have to be sure, they think it's Myra Higgins."

"Fuck, Myra disappeared weeks ago."

I can't believe it. First Helga, now Myra, or first Myra, than Helga. I pull the blanket over my head.

"Do you want to hear how she was found?"

"Not really," I say, from under my blanket.

He takes a seat close to me so I can hear him clearly.

"OK, I'll tell you then. She was found when the electricians went to check the wiring and found her body in the corner, or what was left of it. The room had been locked from outside. They think she died of heart failure having hid up there and couldn't get out, she might even had starved to death. She was mute."

"I know. I also know she was terrified of being on her own."

"She was unable to call for help and starved. Strange thing, before she died, she removed her clothes, folded them, and placed them neatly beside her."

"Jesus, Myra."

"By the time she was found, she had decayed so much the substances leaking from her body left a stain on the floor."

"Oh don't, for fuck's sake."

"Still there today, the stain is definitely in the shape of a human figure."

"Just enough, John."

I show him out and return to my bed, where I sob myself to sleep. The voices continue for a bit.

"You killed her," they say. "You, who was supposed to help her."

"You killed her, I say, "the Castle killed her."

A week goes by. I can't go to Myra's funeral. She's buried in the graveyard. I go there when it is quiet. It's a clear summer morning. I won't go at dark. I stand at her grave and look onto the burial mound on the ground. I begin to sob as I think of her, her sitting there at the Pass, her fears about being on the ward that drove her into the corridor to sit for hours each day. Her high drawn eyebrows, her lovely face, always with makeup.

"Her poor, despicable life," I say, sobbing.

Then I feel a hand on my shoulder.

"Every step of the way we walk the line, your days are numbered and so are mine."

"Hello, Gerry," I say, without turning around.

"Time is pilin' up, we struggle and we scrape, we're all boxed in, there's nowhere to escape."

"Aye, very good, Gerry, Bob Dylan's Mississippi." I lift my head and see Walter in his wheelchair over by the bench next to the path, and next to him is John. He's waving, and Mairi, she's there, waving too.

We go over to them and take a seat on the bench. I sit and look around. I avoid looking into the trees.

They move around me.

"We're sorry about Myra," Mairi says.

"It is in the inexplictofutility of it," John adds.

"Thanks, I get it."

"We've missed you," Mairi says.

I smile.

"We thought you'd be taken away from here, after Alex," Walter says, never taking his eyes from the trees.

I smile again.

"It was close," I say. "I have to—"

"I know, keep your nose clean," Mairi says. "You'll be sad about Myra."

We're quiet for a while, all of us. There's a feeling of safety there with them, like a comfort blanket around me. I was worried about going to the grave because *they* might be there. But I was shutting *them* out of my head. I have to.

We move inside and into the corridor. We all look at Myra's place at the Pass. I leave them there.

"We need to meet, Rooney," says Mairi. I look at them, they have been talking about it.

"I don't—"

"Well, we do," Walter says, pointedly. "You started this and we got on board. You can't just drop us. Alex…"

I already feel guilty about Alex. I got the Timpson's vans in here and now Alex is heading for the State Hospital.

"I'll see."

"Aye, you'll see," Mairi says. "Just get it organised, you know you need to. Myra, Joan, my father, the others."

They appear reluctant to move off to their respective corridors and wards, like they feel they need to protect me. I feel insecure when they move away, like they are my family.

I need to see where Myra died.

I call John the porter and we go up the stairway at the Pass towards the first floor and the concert hall. He unlocks the door for me. I move in and look into the dark of the room.

"Over there." I go to the opposite corner of the room where he points, and there before me is the shape of a figure on the floor. It's not clear. I ask him to put the lights on.

"They don't work, never have for years."

The Concert Hall had been shut off since the sixties. There used to be concerts and film shows in here, but when they got television in the wards the shows stopped and the room was never used.

I look up to the ornate grand ceiling and the walls and tried to imagine the happy voices in here, chattering, singing and clapping to the shows. The room is freezing even though it's the middle of June. He hands me a torch. I switch it on and point it to the floor, and there clearly I see the shape, almost like one of those chalked shapes seen at the scene of a murder, the body would have been on its side, the legs pulled up and tucked up. The shape indicates the arms stretching out towards the door, possibly appealing to someone, anyone, to let her out. My ulterior motive for being there, as well as trying to ascertain how she found herself locked in there, is to find her diary; maybe the diary would have an entry, a last entry.

"Was there anything found with her? You know, any possessions?"

"Not to my knowledge. They bundled everything into a bag. What was left of her, that is."

I turn the torch into the corner, trying to imagine what it was like for her in the final days before she died, huddled in this corner. She had pulled some old curtains into the corner to give herself some warmth. I slide the curtains back with my foot and feel something solid. I pull the folds apart, and there's the diary, tucked away in the folds.

"Did you find something?" John is leaning over me.

I keep my body between him and my find, until I stuff it into my jacket.

"No, nothing, just some old curtains, her last bed, I think."

"Poor bugger. Imagine her lying there, hoping someone would come to save her."

I don't answer him. I'm too upset to say anything. 'This place is a monster,' I say inside, 'a monster that devours people.' I regret ever coming through the door that first day.

John lets me out and locks the door behind.

"It's to remain locked. The Physician Superintendent is determined nothing will ever happen like this again."

"How do you think it happened?" I ask. "How did she get locked inside?"

"Oh, who knows, wandered up the stairs, into the room, went

into the corner and fell asleep. Maybe security came up and saw the door open and locked it with the master key."

"Well, did they?"

"I don't know, I'm only—"

"Making an assumption."

"Aye, something like that. The enquiry will find out I suppose."

"Aye, the enquiries that always find out nothing."

I put the diary inside my jacket out of sight of John and we leave the room. We don't talk as we go down the stair into the reception area.

As we leave, we run into the Physician Superintendent.

"Oh, hello, Mr Rooney," Owen says. "You been in to have a look? Terrible thing, poor woman."

I remember the time I saw her in his room. I nearly ask him if he saw her before she had gone missing, but I say nothing. I am sickened by what I saw. I head back to the Psychology Department.

Agnes is curious, as always.

"Hi Sean, terrible what happened to Myra."

"Aye, terrible, Agnes." I just want to get past her and into my room.

"If you need any company, you know, if you want to talk about it, I'm here for you."

"Aye, thanks Agnes."

I gather my mail from my in-tray and head into the room. I lock the door behind me. Luckily, Donna is off today, giving me exclusive access to the room and some privacy. I take my jacket off and pull out the diary from inside. I hope John or Agnes don't see it sticking out; although an A4 desk diary is something some professionals carry about with them.

I look at the diary, Passing the Pass, after the spot Myra occupied most of her time. I open it on my desk and immediately get the feel of Myra's entries. She was quite an amateur artist, and meticulous in counting people coming and going, and her drawings had become more proficient the more she did. The matchstick men and women became more detailed, as were her descriptions. There were the matchstick drawings of men and woman, identified by rough skirts for the woman and trousers for the men, some crossed out like they were now not present, or alive. The nurses with their triangle-like tunics, and doctors their coats. One figure was larger than the rest, this robed figure, arms outstretched. She clearly wanted to emphasise this figure.

I have to know if she made a last entry, and turn the pages to find it on Tuesday, the 20th of April. I remember the day as the day after the night I spent in ward 49 or the Chapel most like, and the nun singing Faith of our Fathers. There on the page she had drawn a small figure with 'ME' above it. It's crossed out like the others she had drawn earlier, presumably to indicate the figure was dead. Had she known she was dying? And underneath the last drawing there is text, almost like a child's composition. The handwriting is difficult to read, it is poorly written. It must have been written in the gloom of the room, which during the day would have been almost dark, and at night totally dark.

I read the first three words and close the diary. I find it too upsetting to read it all just now. The first three words are:

"God save me..."

CHAPTER 31

I'm conflicted, sweet Jesus will I ever be free? I ask you, would you want my head or to be in my head? I don't think so. People are trying to kill me. I'm seeing and hearing people that aren't there. They're saying I am a mobster's man. In this place that is killing people. I need to find out why or what or who. I need to get through my placement.

I need to meet with the group. They want to meet, they expect it and they expect me to arrange it, and lead it. Expectations from them, expectations from Donna and Archie, expectations from Jackie, expectations from Timpson, expectations for myself!

They want to talk about Myra and the others. But it needs to be safe. If Archie finds out? I'll get Agnes to arrange the OT department again, and maybe even tea and scones, then I'll keep my head down.

Whether I can cope with it or not, I must read Myra's diary in full.

I go to the text in the last entry, the last page she entered the drawings, the 23rd of April. I move the diary to under my reading light. The handwriting is hard to read, but I start to identify the words.

I read them out. "I am Myra Higgins and I am his woman in his mad woman's room."

I think about Charlotte Bronte's Jane Eyre. Rochester's secret wife, Bertha Mason, a mad woman locked away in a mad woman's room. I had read Jane Eyre for my English Higher. Mrs Rochester, or indeed his supposed mad woman, lived in an era where mental illnesses were not recognised as conditions, but simply saw those afflicted with them considered as idiots to be locked away.

"He comes to me at night. He brings nothing to sustain me. He promises fine food, clean clothes, a happy life in a fine house, a new life. He takes from me. I give to him. He is rough. He hits me. He holds me down like an animal. It hurts. He tells me no one will find me here. I will die here in the dark, with those who are here with me. I am weak. I am lost."

Then, "God save me," she repeats, finally.

And then I see before this, some weeks before, there are other images. One, the hooded figure, small, with the hood reaching down to its feet, two small stick arms coming out and the hands clasped together like it's praying. And another, a man with a cross around his neck.

And there are others, scattered through the diary at various pages, going back to the date I gave her the diary. They're in the corners of the pages, in each corner as if they were in the corners of the room. At first, I think they're triangles but they're rounded off at the top. They don't have hands or legs, but in the middle near the apex of the top are two eyes. Then it occurs to me these could be drawings of ghosts.

The significance of ghosts on the page doesn't make sense to me unless she's referring in a subjective sense to the patients who had died, or had been killed; or maybe she was not alone.

Now I know, I too need to talk about Myra.

CHAPTER 32

We meet the next day, Friday 18ᵗʰ of June. It's a sombre affair. As a group they appear annoyed with me. I think they detect my reluctance to do this anymore. I look to Jackie. She isn't very happy about coming. I think she has had enough as well. She's clearly not talking to me. I agree to Agnes's request for her to be there, to support Gerry. After the Alex incident, she is worried he may relapse.

"Right, you wanted to meet. Who wants to start?"

I stay in my chair by the door, no standing this time, no orchestrating the meeting. There's a pause, a quiet before the storm.

Mairi is the first to have a go. "My fucking father is dead, Rooney, and you promised to help."

"My friend, Alex Barr is in trouble, sir," Gerry says. "Trouble in the water, trouble in the air, go to the other side of the world, you'll find trouble there."

"Please Gerald," Agnes says. "Talk normally."

"He likes trees," Walter says.

"Who?" I ask.

"Bob Dylan, of course."

Jackie has had enough.

"Oh for fuck's sake, you lot."

"It's time for blue sky thinking," John says, as clear as a bell, no neologisms, no contorted syntax, no delusional material. "We need to think clearly." Everyone looks at him. "We need to conduct ourselves in an organised fashion."

"He's right," Mairi says, "we need to get it together. There's too much at stake."

"I'm scared," Gerry says. Agnes moves to his side.

"So you should be," Mairi says. "People are being killed."

"I was attacked," I say.

Jackie shakes her head.

"You don't know this, Rooney."

"I was."

"I told you they were there, Mr Rooney," Walter says, "in the trees."

"Strategic thinking," John says. "What do we have?"

Everyone looks at John. He is asserting himself. There is no doubt of his intellect, but his ability to pull this together to take the lead, to take over from this feeble, disordered, mixed up me?

"We have nothing," Jackie says.

"We have everything," John says to her.

"We have no evidence of anything, no murders, no suspects, no basis for anything, for any action, no right to be here."

"She's right," I say.

Then John's words cut through the silence that follows.

"We believe," he says.

"I believe," says Mairi.

"I believe," Gerry says.

"And I believe," says Agnes.

"And so do I," says Walter.

"And me too, I believe too," says John.

"And of course, I have to as well. I believe," I say.

"Well, I fucking don't," Jackie says. "Of course, you saw them, Rooney, sure you did, just like you, Walter." She takes a big sigh and looks out of the window.

"I saw them."

"He saw them, Jackie," they all say one after the other, starting with John.

I realise then I'm part of the group. I'm not the leader of the group, I'm a member of the group. It feels good. The responsibility for the group, for them, is off my shoulders. During my absence from them, they have become a viable self-help group with no need for facilitation. I can defend my reason for being involved with them to Archie and Donna. I'm not leading them, they're leading me. It's self-sufficient. I'm no longer responsible or accountable for them.

The next forty minutes of so, I sit back and watch them, listen to them. I'm proud of them. I see from Jackie's eyes she is too, and she's listening too, forensically. I see her eyes tighten like they do when I know she's getting into something. She's writing too, like a police officer, in her notebook. I know she's getting it. She's starting to believe too.

As a team, we unpick, sift, prioritise everything we have. We conclude finally that someone, something, is killing people here. On the dry board on the wall, John lists the people we believe to have been killed, starting with Oliver, John, Mairi's father, Joan, Myra, Helga, Elsie, and the others. The 'others' are listed under this term, all the men and women in Joan's notebook, and other patients in the hospital she had talked about.

John's holding court, walking around the room, putting points on the flipchart.

"Suspects," he says, putting it up.

"Doctor Death," Mairi says first.

"The mob," says Gerry.

"Them," says Walter.

"God the Father, the Almoner, the Chaplain, the nun," John says. "They all feature." We all look at him. "It's in Myra's drawings. She believed and we need to too."

"I don't think we can view the Chaplain or the nun as suspects, John."

"Mr Rooney, they are in her drawings, as is the Godly figure."

"And them," Walter repeats.

"The ones that tried to kill me."

"Or so you believe," Jackie says.

"And the Castle," I add. "The Castle kills people."

They stop, as if I had said something fundamental, something in their heads.

John writes 'The Castle'. Then he writes 'Motive'. That also stops them. Then he writes 'Why?'.

"To stop them leaving," Walter says.

They all look at him, like he's opened a door in their mind.

Gerry gets up.

"Spirit on the water, darkness on the face of the deep, keep thinkin' about you baby and I can't hardly sleep."

Agnes moves to his side.

"Enough for today, son."

"The Almoner," Walter says. "The social worker."

"The social worker," Gerry says. "He's a thief. He steals the patients from here."

"Right, back to the ward for you," Agnes says, taking him by the arm and guiding him towards the door.

"No wait," John says. "Gerry?"

"There must be some way out of here, said the joker to the thief."

"Who's the joker and who's the thief, Gerry?" I ask, recognising the line from Dylan's *All Along The Watchtower*.

"I'm the joker, he's the thief," Gerry says.

Jackie turns to me, like he had hit her over the head with the words.

"Rooney, he's a social worker, get a grip?"

"Put it up, John," I say.

'It's time to stop. Enough,' I say in my head, but I don't say this out loud.

John says it.

"It's time, we have covered enough for one day." All agree, including me

Agnes takes Gerry out, saying, "I'd like to talk, Sean, later?" I nod and smile.

John takes the handles of Walter's wheelchair and pushes him out, followed by Mairi.

"I suppose there's a lot to talk about, Sean," Jackie says.

"Friday night, Horseshoe Bar, your patterns of a lifetime." I know she's referring to Agnes.

"No alcohol for me, though. I don't know what it would do to me."

She smirks, as if to say, 'heard it.'

"I'll be outside in the car," she says.

This evening, we park in Glasgow and go to the Horseshoe Bar. Jackie orders a large wine, showing she intends leaving the car there. In previous sessions, she had received parking tickets for leaving the car outwith out of hours times, but always, as a police officer, never paid them. She had been on 'police duties' in the city centre at the time.

She rests her elbows on the bar.

"And?"

"Coke," I say. I have my sensible head on for a change. "I'm still getting headaches after my injury."

"And you're worried about prompting a bleed in your head,

hypo-fuckin-chondriac."

She pushes my coke toward me. We stay quiet for a bit.

"Myra's diary," I slurp, "the Almoner, a social worker?"

She sips, not slurps.

"She died of her own making, Rooney. She was mute and got locked in, otherwise we would have a murder investigation."

"And what about the drawings?"

"She liked to draw figures, doesn't mean anything."

"Rochester's wife, the mad woman in the mad woman's room, Jane Eyre, Bronte."

"People see things in there, she was ill. What about you, Rooney, are you?"

"I'm fine."

"You? You fuck about with Alby Timpson? What about your career? Come to think about it, what about my fucking career, we all get tarred by the same brush. Fuck's sake, Rooney." I stare at my drink. "And what about Agnes?"

"I have you, Jackie, I don't need Agnes."

She puts her glass down with a thump on the bar.

"You don't have me, Rooney. I have me."

I chink her glass with mine as a gesture of resigned defeat. We sit quietly for a while looking around the pub, as if to seek a way of restarting the conversation. She orders another and gets right back to talking about Alby Timpson.

"Rooney, he'll fuck up your career and mine at the same time."

I know she's right, though I don't confirm it, there's danger here. Will she find out about my pact with him, that he sees me as his 'man in the nuthoose'?

"Are you his man?"

What does she know?

"Eh?"

"I know, Rooney."

"What?"

"Do you think I am stupid? I know you were caught between the devil, Timpson, and the deep blue sea, the going-ons at the Castle. We've been watching things. It was inevitable it would blow up."

I look at her. She knows, of course. She would know. I had told her about the guys turning up at the nurses' home. She knew about

Timpson getting drugs into Barlinnie Prison, the ice cream vans in the schemes, the gang warfare. It was inevitable he would get into the hospital, a ready market.

She also knows in no way is it sustainable, even with his Man in Havana. I didn't mention Doctor Jamieson, which is for me to deal with, but I wouldn't be surprised if she knows about his habit too.

"You still on the tablets, Rooney?"

"Eh?"

"Doctor Jamieson gave you tablets, unprescribed." I had forgotten I had told her. What else had I told her? "You still on them?"

"Only as required." I might as well tell her, she'll find out eventually. "I got some pain killers recently from him. For my head."

"Oh, for your head?" I say nothing. "You fancy the other side?"

"Eh?"

"You like being a mobster, a criminal, living in the underworld; refreshing as opposed to doing the right thing, being a do-gooder?"

Strangely, I remember how my father used to called me a 'so called no-gooder'.

"And you, Jackie, still trying to break through, be the son your father never had, a successful police officer, just like him." I guess that hurts, but I want to take the focus away from me.

Again, the glass gets banged down on the bar. The barman is taking notice.

"You fucker, he doesn't make it easy, that's for sure, gives me all the shitty cases, prostitution, drugs, extortion, you know the stuff *you* are into."

Ouch, touché! We sit quietly.

"So what about us, Jackie?"

"What *us*, Rooney?" I need to shut up, let her get it out. "While you and Agnes are getting it together."

I leave it hanging like a string of sausages hanging from a butcher's counter just out of reach from the hungry dog.

"The Almoner, Bill Simmons. Is he on your radar?"

"Just a weird fuck working in a weird place, doesn't make him a killer."

"Gerry says he's a thief." It doesn't connect. "He sent me a memo, 're I have to tell you I am seriously disturbed about your behaviour. Yours, Bill'."

"Sounds a bit right to me."

"He had a reputation for being a rough bastard with his probationers, a bit of a psychopath even, there's a rumour some of his probationers disappeared."

"They could have gone to Costa Crime, Rooney."

"I know, that's what I said." We stop for a bit, she's looking at her watch. "And there's the God guy."

"God's not a killer, Rooney?"

"The Bible says God killed multitudes of people."

"It also said thou shall not kill, Rooney."

"Appears alright for God. What about our Godlike figure at the Castle?"

"I think you are away on one of your flights of fantasy again, pal." I look into my glass. "Keep me informed, Rooney. I'm away for a drink, up the West End. This's no feckin' fun."

With this, she's off through the pub and out. I'd normally be upset she'd go off drinking without me, but not tonight.

I get a taxi back to the hospital. As I do, I see Agnes getting into her car. I stop the taxi in the car park.

"You alright, Agnes?"

"Sean, I was thinking about you. I phoned you. I went to your room. Bella says you didn't come back. I presumed you were away with... her."

"I presume you mean Jackie, yes, she's gone... home."

"Fancy a coffee. My place?"

I nod and get into her car.

PART THREE

CHAPTER 33

It's Saturday morning, the 19th of June. I climb out of Agnes's bed, just as she arrives back from the kitchen with two mugs of coffee.

"Could you drop me off at the nurses' home?" I say, raking my hair with my fingers at her dressing table mirror.

"You worried about walking through the grounds?"

I smile. "Thanks for the coffee."

"Are you worried we might be seen?"

"People talk," I say, pulling my trousers on. "You know how rumours go in there." I put on my shirt, then my socks and shoes.

"Let them talk, Sean. Saves them from—"

"Talking about someone else?"

She pauses.

"It was very nice, Sean."

"Yes, it was."

We drive into the hospital grounds. I sink down into the seat and pull my bunnet down over my eyes. We don't say anything. I turn to look at her. She's wearing a thick pair of glasses. I try to be funny.

"You must have great eyesight to see through them, Agnes."

"Aye, I need them for driving, I need others for work, and I need another pair to see through people. Are you using me, Sean?"

I look at her again. Am I, or is she using me?

"Jackie," she says. "Is she your wuman, you know your proper woman?" I don't answer, I didn't think I need to. "I can do anything she can do, Sean. I'm sure you appreciate this from last night. Does she do what I do for you?"

I know not to go into this territory. Her face changes to one I hadn't noticed before, serious, demanding, determined. She stops the car and leans over toward me.

"Sean, I'm not a jealous type," she says, which says she is. "But it's not very nice knowing you can come to me when you want and go to her when you want."

I didn't know it was a competition.

"She is, of course, rich, intelligent and lovely. Me, I'm just... here, with no conditions." Which means there are. "I'm vulnerable, Sean, after the breakdown of my marriage. Just don't use me. Like my ex-husband, you'll see I'm not to be used."

Agnes's not a woman to be crossed. I get out of the car just short of the nurses' home car park and close the door. She reaches over and winds down the passenger window.

"Donna is drafting your report."

I lean into the window.

"She is. How do you know?"

"I am typing it, so I'm reading it."

"Oh, what does it say?"

"I don't know if it would be right to tell you. It's confidential."

I nearly say, fuck the confidentiality, but she pulls away before I get the chance.

I spend Sunday in my room, in thought, wondering if they are indeed my thoughts, or am I hearing things? The voices sound much the same. It's a lovely day and I feel able to go for a walk. After my attack, I still feel somewhat worried about going anywhere in the grounds which is quiet or secluded; somewhere I could be attacked again. I'm not going to take the chance.

I go to the bench near to the hospital, the one close to the locker room, the one we broke in to. I sit and look towards the golf course. Then I hear it.

"You'll sort it out, and when you do you let me know, soon."

It's Timpson's words, but they sound like they're outside my head, not that there is anyone there, but it's like I hear them for real, that it isn't in my head, like a thought. I turn around to see if anyone is there. Then I hear it again.

"Let me know, soon." It's as clear as day. I sit back down and question myself. "Is this what it is like to hear things?" I ask myself, surprisingly out loud, as psychotic patients I had known here.

"You alright, Sean?"

"Christ, no' again."

However, I turn and there's Walter in his wheelchair.

"Thank God," I say. "I thought I was hearing things."

"Maybe you were, lots of people do in this place."

"You out to see the trees? It's a lovely day."

"Aye, June is a beautiful month. I love seeing the oak leaves on the ground just now. They're like wee hands reaching out for you."

"The leaves are falling?"

"Live oaks naturally shed leaves in summer, so as long as the leaves are green and healthy, there's no need to worry." I hear the voice again and I spin back to where I think it's coming from. "But if the fallen leaves are discoloured or look unhealthy; it can mean a pest or disease."

"Right," I say, distracted.

"You hearing things, Sean?"

"No' me."

"Aye, that's what we all say. What are they saying to you? I'll help you. I know lots about voices. I hear them too. You can control them if you try. Just takes willpower. I see things as well. You?" I shake my head and look into the trees. "I bet you do."

Jesus, I'm being counselled by a man with a mental illness.

"I'm fine, thanks."

"How's your head?" I look at him. "I mean your injury. You got quite a thump when your head hit the road."

"I heard things before that."

"There you go."

"I mean when I was in ward 49."

"The haunted ward. I would've told you not to go in there, if you had asked."

It's as if he understands, and he is talking to me too, which is good, he doesn't normally talk to anyone. It's like he knows what I've been going through.

"I saw them, in the trees, that night."

"I told you they are there."

"Who are *they*, Walter?"

"If I told you, you wouldn't believe me. You'd think I am mad." I look at him and I see the beginning of a smile; heartening from a man clinically depressed for a long time. "You've got a lot on your mind, Sean." What, he really is counselling me.

"I know, this place."

"Aye, this place."

We both sit for a while looking up over the golf course and at the two figures on the third hole, Doctor Jamieson and Professor Owen.

"Doctor Death and God," he says, "an unholy, deadly mix."

"I can't accept that, Walter, I can't accept any doctor would kill a patient. It's this fucking place which kills people, the environment, the culture, the regime, it's no surprise people top themselves."

"You have him on your short list."

"Jesus, it's only for the group. She got locked in and starved. The Castle's latest casualty."

"He appeared lots, in her book."

"Yes, he did."

We talk like old friends. I think about asking him about his family, the car crash, but chicken out.

"Do you not want to leave this place, Walter?"

"Ah, what do I have outside, Sean? My family are dead, I can't walk, I can't look after myself. In here, I'm looked after. I've my friends, my trees."

"Are you depressed, Walter?"

He looks at me.

"Depressed, Sean? Well, Doctor Death thinks I am, and that's enough to keep me here; stops me being referred to the social workers. No nursing home for me, thank you very much."

He leaves me there, but not before saying, "Watch yourself, Rooney, you don't want to get trapped in this place. It becomes comfortable after a while." He wheels away down the path.

My mind drifts to getting through this placement, then the voice comes back as clear as 'last orders at the bar.' "Sort it out and when you do, you let me know, soon."

I look into the trees, I'm still not convinced it's in my head. Timpson wants me to come up with a plan, to renew his market in the hospital, get his drugs back in.

I drop my head into my hands.

Jesus, a Catch 22. All I need to do is get through the placement, make sure Donna writes a positive report, stop folk dying in this place, and get Timpson back his market. So easy, where do I start?

I go to work on Monday, deep in thought, picking up my mail on the way to my room. Agnes smiles at me, like she's sending me a message. I go to my room and settle at my desk.

"I've done your report, Sean," Donna says, waving a bunch of A4 sheets.

I look up from my notes and push my glasses up the bridge of my nose.

"Oh, that's great, thanks."

I'm hoping she'll give me an indication of whether it is positive or whether I should start thinking of a different career.

"This is the final draft. I've changed it a few times over the last couple of weeks for obvious reasons."

"Obvious reasons?"

"You know." We both know. "I've signed it and Agnes will send it off and do you a copy. I would prefer not to share it with you until it's gone to the Uni. I don't want to change it again."

"Right, thanks."

She walks past me and heads to the front office. And that's that. My placement depends on her report, my course depends on this placement, my whole life depends on whether I pass or not.

Later, Agnes hands me a copy of the report. I go straight to the final page, the placement recommendation. My eyes focus right on the final line: "I recommend a pass, Donna Watling, placement supervisor."

Just then Donna passes by heading out of the office.

"Thanks, Donna, I appreciate it."

"Thanks? I thought you would have been unhappy about it."

"No, it's fine, thanks."

"Oh, OK." She looks at me as if she's expecting me to challenge her on it. "It's up to the uni now, I hope they make some allowances."

"Allowances?"

"For your mental health, Rooney, and your drinking, and your…"

She stops short. I am pleased she does.

"Yes, I hope so."

Is there more in the report than I've read? Something I've missed. I take it to my room and read it again. It certainly says something about my 'problems', which 'at times blunts my decision making', however, 'allows me some empathy with my patient groups,' but nothing damning. Like she says, 'it's up to the uni now'.

Tom O. Keenan

I leave it at that.

I know the university has to round up my whole course, the academic input, the previous placements, my assignments, etcetera. Of course, I still have a few weeks of my placement to go, to continue my work with the patients referred to me and I've my final placement assignment on the group to do. However, having Donna recommending a pass of my placement is a weight off my shoulders. Now this is in maybe I can have a bit more liberty and space to get on with the other things.

Then, just as I am about to head back to my room, as I pass Agnes, I expect her to say, 'Want to come over tonight,' but no, she says:

"I did it for you, Sean, and us."

"Excuse me?"

"Us, Sean."

She looks around to make sure she isn't overheard.

"Us, Agnes?"

"Yes, you'll pass your placement, become a clinical psychologist, and then we can be together."

"I can't remember this being discussed, Agnes."

"It doesn't need to be discussed, Sean. It's the way I understand it, the way it's meant to be."

"Meant to be?"

She looks around again.

"We're in love, Sean. It's a natural next step we would want to be together."

"But I..."

She comes close.

"Just go with it, Sean. It'll work out."

"Will it fuck, Agnes. They'll find out and my placement will be fucked." Jesus, I think, I'll fail and I'll be a failure.

"No one needs to know anything, Sean, it's completely between us."

Fuck, it gets worse, I think, or at least I need to think. Jesus, do I need to think? If Donna and Archie find out about this, I am fucked, my placement is fucked. I go to my bench. It's sunny and warm. I take my jacket off and hang it over the back of the bench. I look around, no Walter, no one on the golf course, no one in the trees.

"What do I do?" I ask myself, aloud as if to prove to myself the words are coming out of my mouth and not from my head. "I need to save the people." Although, more importantly, I need to save my placement, save my skin, get Timpson back in, and save my relationship with Jackie. "Jesus." I hold my head.

I need to draw on learning I had done. If I am rational, clever, methodical, I'll get through this.

To assist, I fall on Maslow's hierarchy of needs, the five levels. First, physiological. All my needs are met in the Castle: food, water, a place to stay. Second, security, I need protection from danger, to ensure my health and safety. I need someone to look after me. Timpson is my life insurance. I'm his man. Third, for my mental health I need relationships, partners, friends, co-workers. I can get all of these in the Castle. Fourth, I need my self-esteem, achieved through academic accomplishment and professional recognition, but more than anything I need some power. I'm fed up of being weak against abuse, my father in mind. I have to be in control. Then, there, at the top of the hierarchy is self-actualization. I need to fulfil my potential, become a good psychologist, but even more I need to be a tough, manipulative bastard to get what I want: power, recognition… revenge.

I'm angry, I need to get the people who are harming folk in this place, but I want to get the place even more because it killed my mother. Sure, I can bring Timpson in and disappear some people or at least scare them so much they'd stop what they are doing. But I'd be thrown out of here. A failed placement and a failed course, and a failed me. I need to use my head. I can't use the group, even though they may want to get involved in getting *them*. But they'd end up being sectioned or jailed. They have no power, no control, and no safeguards should they be unsuccessful. I need to be their operational arm. I need to be clever. I need to assume a pretence of the altruistic trainee out to help, change things for the better for the patients, but behind the pretence I'll get them and I'll get the place at the same time, and I'll do it for Myra, Joan, Helga, and more than anyone for my mother.

I need a plan for Timpson, he'll do me in otherwise, and I need his help. I'll be his man if he'll be mine. I'll talk to Dr J, get the vans back in, make sure it's soft drugs, stolen cigs, the staff'll be happy, they'll have a source, the patients too, those who can afford it. £10 a gram for decent quality weed, once a week after receiving their pocket money, lots of patients would be able to afford it.

I'll write a brilliant placement report. I'll use Goffman's *Asylums*, everybody knows the old Victorian system is crumbling. Here, in the Castle, it's affecting patient mood, their wellbeing, they're scared though of the unknown, the discharge into the uncaring community. They're topping themselves. I'll find a way of dealing with their fears and offer them hope. I'll use my guile and Timpson's muscle.

But first, I need to protect the members of the group. Having Alex sectioned is one thing, but if others take the law into their own hands they'll be in trouble and I won't be able to help them. Although the group experience is building their confidence, and they are really getting their teeth into it, individually they are weak and vulnerable. I really need to protect them.

CHAPTER 34

Wednesday, 23rd of June, I meet the group.

"It's the Castle, everything else is delusional." They all look at me. "Come on, I mean doctors killing people, the mob killing people, social workers killing people. For God's sake, no-one's killing anyone but the patients killing themselves. If you want to blame anything, blame this place." I see them looking at each other. "Blame the ghosts if you like, it's all part of the delusions, which I too suffer with. Blame the place, this place is a living organism, which exists to subjugate everything inside itself. Over a hundred or so years, it has organically evolved to protect itself. And now it is under threat, so it's fighting back, tossing off the parasites which feed on it."

They really are looking at each other now.

"Who are the parasites, Rooney?" Mairi asks.

"We are all parasites," I say, "the patients, the nurses, the doctors, the social workers, the psychologists; everyone and everything who feeds off this monster."

"And how do you suggest we stop feeding off this monster?" she asks.

"And how do we stop people dying here, Sean?" Walter asks.

"You have to change it from within," I say.

"And how do we do that," John asks, "when we have no power?"

"We need a revolution. The place is detrimental to the health and welfare of the people who live here. Like Russia, before 1917, we need to challenge the oligarchy from within, shift the balance of power away from those who profit from it, all the overpaid professionals, administrators, patient services."

"And what about the patients?"

"We give them a sense of pride, a massive exercise in self dependence, which raises self-confidence, self-esteem. The patients are dependent on this place, the authorities need them to be dependent, unable, disabled. I know all about it. It's in Goffman's *Asylums*."

"I've read that," John says. "He's right, this place thrives on having a dependent population."

"And how do we do this revolution?"

I don't reply to Mairi, but it's all part of my plan. I've the placement assignment to do, to get through my placement. I had already talked to Donna about it, it would be on the group, a self-help group, and she agreed it.

"I've been thinking about it," I say. "How do I reflect what's going on in the group, the real reason we're meeting?"

I am aware this's no longer a self-help group, it's something else. I need an alternative, something significant which concentrates on improving the lot of the patients in the hospital.

"We'll call it Patient Involvement, Hillwood Hospital," I say.

I'll put the assignment plan together, have it approved under the auspices of improving the quality of life of patients, to make recommendations to empower the patients, give them a say in the running of this place.

"What we will do, however, is shift the balance of power."

"Like Animal Farm, power corrupts?"

"Not quite, Walter, we know all about that, but we set up a Patient Council and we give patients a voice and we make changes. How does that sound?"

"And how do we stop people being killed?" Mairi asks. "My father was killed, Rooney."

Could I say to her I didn't think her father was murdered?

"Well, I—"

"Well, I fucking do, Rooney, and I thought you were with us."

Am I?

"I thought this was about patientracide," says John.

"And I thought we are about getting *them*," says Walter.

"We'll get them in a different way," I say. "Just give me a chance to show you I can change things here."

"Oh, aye, and what about Joan, and Oliver, my father, Helga, Myra, and all the rest? You going to forget them?"

"There are other ways—"

"To skin a cat?"

"Aye, Walter, to skin a cat."

I'll start by writing up the assignment. It'll flow from me like a river into the sea. I'll use a recorder and talk into it day and night for as long as it takes.

I start:

"The hospital is over one hundred years old. It was set up as an act of altruism by the Victorian Fathers of Glasgow, with a treatment value base rather than containment, but it became a place to separate the insane from the sane, somewhere to put people the community of the time wouldn't or couldn't tolerate, or to keep them safe."

I take a pause, then continue.

"It progressively became an institutionalised setting, a place to subdue, to control, where patients lost skills and became disabled due to being in a disabling environment."

I cite Goffman's *Asylums* as a key text, mentioning the 'total institution' continued to exist in the back wards of Hillwood Hospital. I draw on his later work, *The Insanity of Place*, where the place was 'ill', pathological, rather than the person, the patient.

Five days later, Monday the 28th of June, it's finished, just in time for work.

"It must be close to ten thousand words," I say, as I pass it to Agnes to type.

"Good for you, Sean," she says with a smile. "We'll get you through this."

I feel good at what I have done, maybe my life as a trainee psychologist might be of some use after all. That my mother, who had suffered because of mental illness, and died because of it, would be proud I had done something to improve the lives of sufferers.

Now for the second half of my plan: Alby Timpson.

I arrive at exactly two p.m. He said I should not be late. I didn't want to be early either. I'm shown in by his heavies. Again, his swivel chair has him feet up on his wrought iron radiator facing out of the window into his garden.

"Yes, Lord Provost, we will cooperate fully," he's saying. "We too have an interest in stability on the streets of Glasgow. Yes, we will. Thank you. All the best to you too." He spins around in his seat. "Hi Rooney, you got me a plan?"

I take a few seconds before I speak.

"Yes, to control the market in the Castle, you need to control the Castle."

"Aye, very profound." He smiles, his eyes crinkling at the sides. "Listen, son, we have a few hundred customers in there. The Castle is profitable, but it's a volatile and fragile market, as your man attacking my guy in the van confirmed. We can't have this again." He leans over his desk. "You got that son? How can you ensure I can do business in there, with no threats, supported, maintained? What can you do for me, Rooney, you owe me, mind?"

He's calling in his favour.

"The place isn't safe, Alby." I rub my head. "People are being killed, taking their own lives, patients don't feel safe. You need stability in there. The patients need to use the vans without the staff interfering. They use the stuff themselves. I need your... support." He smiles. "I need you to protect my market, son, the customers."

"And how do I do this?"

"Well, first." I am trying to stop my voice and my knees shaking at the same time. "We need to make sure your supply is sustainable, no dangerous drugs, no drugs which cause people to go off it, recreational cannabis, good quality. Stolen cigs and sweets are fine, but keep the drugs soft. No more than £10 a bag, which is all they get in their pocket money each week."

"I can give them credit." It's clear he intends loan sharking, drugs on tick, crazy interest, people taking too much, becoming dependent. He'll have the patients in his pocket, same as the folks in the schemes.

"No, no credit."

He frowns and pauses.

"OK, no credit and I agree a sustainable market."

"And your support, some practices need to stop?"

"You want some folk threatened, frightened or killed?"

I don't react, but I know he takes it I may.

"You'll be my lieutenant?"

I think about the word lieutenant, how this is a position much like a caporegime in mafia crime families. He's offering me an honour normally bestowed on a long-term loyal soldier. I nod again.

He reaches across the desk seeking my hand with his, this hand which had killed others, no doubt. It may even kill me, I know this. This plan fails, my life is in danger; it works, and I protect patients and I protect me. Timpson gets his market and his man. He releases my hand. I find a small poly bag in it. I look at it.

"It'll help your heid, Rooney. There's more of it if you do what you're told."

"A done deal, Alby."

CHAPTER 35

My assignment has been accepted by Donna and Archie. Archie presents it to the HMT, on Wednesday, the 30th June. My first recommendation, a Patient Council, with a patient chair on the management group, is accepted. The massive cultural change will occur 'developmentally', they say.

On Wednesday, 7th of July, I'm invited to the management group to discuss the Patient Council. The boardroom is on the first floor, next to Owen's room, in the administration block. I wait outside until I'm invited in by Professor Owen's PA. I go in and they're all seated around a mahogany table, in leatherback chairs. I'm offered coffee and a plate of biscuits is put in front of me.

"We are interested in your plans, Sean," Owen says. "But before we start, James could you give our meeting its customary blessing?" The Chaplain, James Gordon, takes to his feet.

"Father, bless us as we gather today for this meeting. Guide our minds and hearts so we will work for the good of our community, and help all your children in this hospital. Teach us to be courageous in the face of difficulty, and wise in our decisions. Amen."

I'm astounded, never before in a business meeting had we started with a prayer. I look around the table. Jamieson has his head bowed, looking at me through steepled fingers. I don't know all of them, but Tommy Stephenson, the nurse manager, is there, as is Bill Simmons, as senior social worker, and Linda Ball, the patients affairs manager, and Sheila Thompson, the OT manager. At the far end of the table I see Donna and Archie, also looking at me.

"Thank you James," Owen says. "Sean, we think the Patient Council is a good idea."

"Thank you sir."

"We see it as a way of responding to patient concerns."

To placate them, I think.

"There are real concerns there is a culture of control in the hospital, sir."

"We're not so sure about that, Sean, but we're prepared to accept a more balanced approach."

Balanced approach, means preserving the status quo, I think.

"How to you suggest we set up the Patient Council?" Jamieson asks.

"Your group, Sean?" Owen says.

Jesus, are we rumbled? Is this the end of the group, of me?

"Yes, sir?"

"Archie is saying it's a murder group?"

That's it, I'm finished.

"A murder group, a great idea," Owen laughs.

I nearly say, 'Mairi, the crime writer, Walter, the philosopher, and John, the scientist'; do you still think it is a great idea?

"A true crime interest group, it sounds fun," he says, looking Stephenson's way. "I hear it's bringing them on, raising their confidence, bringing them out of their shells."

"Yes sir," Stephenson says, "it gives them focus, also some insights into their experience. Also, it gets them off the ward."

Don't push it, I say to myself.

Then I hear it, the voice, It's Timpson. "The plan, Rooney, do it." I don't turn towards it though, being with mental health professionals. They'll see immediately I'm hearing things, hallucinating.

"The vans." It just comes out. They all look at each other. "The patients have a right to—"

"Of course they do." Jamieson looks at Owen when he says this. "There's benefit in the vans, as long as it is managed."

Owen agrees. "I don't see any problem getting them back. Tommy, talk to the police, say we have the van situation under control."

Christ, they are sanctioning the return of the vans, they bloody well want it.

"The patient representative," I say.

"I'm amazed at how well John is doing," Stephenson says. "If you didn't know him you really would think he was a doctor, talking up for the patients, giving them advice on all sorts of things."

"Yes, he is becoming a star."

"The group is a ready-made Patient Council," Owen says.

Shit, I never thought of that. I can only smile and nod.

"And it has ready-made secretarial input," Archie says. "Agnes, our secretary, supports the group."

"Great, it's decided." Owen looks around the table to enthusiastic smiles. "Sean will chair the group until he leaves. By then, we'll identify a proper patient." He laughs again. "Sorry, Sean, I don't mean to say you weren't a proper patient when you were admitted recently, but I mean a long-term patient who can represent the full range of patients in the hospital."

"Sean has been a mole in some of our less salubrious wards," Jamieson says. "Wards 28 and 38."

"And our famous haunted ward," the Chaplain adds.

"Ah yes, 49," Owen says. "You're a brave man, Sean."

"Thank you."

"We'll find a way of funnelling patient issues to the group and to ensure the patient voice is represented in the group. Best of luck, Sean, your assignment and your group are proving very helpful."

I say nothing about breaking into lockers, graves, conspiring to find those they think to be killing patients. I know I'm pushing it, but I decide to push it even more.

"Can I ask a favour, in a professional sense, you understand?"

"Yes, Sean, go ahead," Owen says.

"Alex Barr, ward—"

"We know Alex, Sean."

"Yes, of course, he—"

"Go on Sean."

"He was sectioned after the ice cream van incident."

"He was violent," Stephenson says.

"He thought he was protecting the patients, from the mob. Which in a sense he was. It was appropriate."

"We're assessing him for the Sheriff," Owen says. "He may need secure care."

"It would kill him to be sent to the State Hospital," I say. "He's not a risk to others, not any others."

"Just the mob," laughs Stephenson, turning to Jamieson.

"Allow Mr Rooney to work with him," Reverend Jimmy says, "behaviour modification."

Owen and Jamieson look at each other.

"OK, under Doctor Jamieson's supervision," Owen says.

"And nursing escorts wherever he goes," Stephenson adds.

"The assessment needs to continue," Owen says. "The Sheriff has ordered it."

"He can attend the group?"

"Yes, as long as you report every week to Doctor Jamieson."

It's agreed.

CHAPTER 36

Friday night and Jackie's words cut through the hubbub in Tennent's.

"What the fuck, Rooney?"

"The vans are coming back, Jackie. It was agreed at the HMT and Stephenson has talked to the local polis."

"I know, my father told me. What are you playing at? The lunatics taking over the asylum perhaps? I guess ice cream and coke now have a different meaning, Rooney."

"They're only doing weed, ten pounds a bag. The place will be like happy valley rather than miserableville."

Her eyes widen like saucers. "You're fucking off it, Rooney. You need help."

"I'm going to change the place." I don't add, then I'll destroy it and anyone else who gets in my way.

"How's your head, Rooney, still getting headaches?" I shake my head. "How's the voices, still hearing them?" I shake my head again. "Still walking the floor, high as a kite?" I shake my head once more. "Grandiose delusions, going to take over the asylum?" I don't shake my head. "You are fucking off it, Rooney, you need fuckin' sectioned. Where can I find a mental health officer in this place. Any MHOs?" she calls out. "Nutter here needs to be locked up."

"Shush, Jackie." I pull her close. "Jackie, this is a social worker pub, there are MHOs in here." I look around waiting for the huckle team to come through the door.

"Get fucking pissed, Rooney, I prefer a drunk to a nutter any day." She goes to the bar and brings back two double doubles. I drink mine down in one and we get increasingly and steadily pissed.

I meet Stanley Holland on the way to the toilet.

"Tell Alby, it's done. The vans are back."

"Jeas, Rooney, you are something else," he says.

"I know, I'm unique, omnipotent."

"Eh?"

"All powerful."

"Just don't go too far, Rooney, that's all I'm saying, and don't cross him."

"Don't fucking cross me," comes from behind him. I look around him.

He turns around to see what I am looking at, which is of course no one and nothing.

"Are you alright, Rooney?"

I'm eight whiskies to the better by this point. I go to the toilet. I open the small plastic bag Timpson gave me and snort the powder into my nose. I sit for a few minutes as it permeates into the deepest recesses of my brain. It feels so good, the pain in my head is gone. It's happy valley time. Normally it's busy in there, but not this time, as if he's waiting for this opportunity. I go to the sink and wash the powder off my hands and splash my face. I need to look normal to Jackie after being in here, but there he is, in the mirror, my father.

"You killed her son, not me, not the hospital," he growls. "She took the pills because she couldn't bear being away from you. You whined and pined so much when she was away, when she came back she was riddled with guilt about you. She couldn't handle it. If you had just shut your face she would have been alright. It was you, son, you."

I see his contorted face, the veins sticking out of his brow, the bleary eyes full of hate. I can almost feel his spit coming at me with his words. His hands reach out of the mirror, his nicotine fingers splayed like eagle claws grabbing for a fish.

I move back and gasp: "No don't, please."

"You alright pal," comes from a guy using the other sink. I turn to look at him. "Fuck's sake, Rooney, you look as if you've seen a ghost." He looks like Stanley, but not like him at the same time. I look back to the mirror, then back to the guy and both of them have gone. Did I see him, them?

I leave the toilet, keeping a look out for MHOs. I would prefer not to be sectioned this night.

I go back to the bar. Jackie is in full flow scolding a couple of young girls for looking like tarts, all sexed up, on the town.

"You don't know what kind of men are in here," she says, "and out there, but I do. I pick up the pieces of girls like you, when they run into the wrong guys, so get fucking real."

The girls throw their heads back with the shots, laugh and walk away.

"Fuck's sake," she says, "they don't know the nutters out there."

I'm standing close to her and I can't get a word out, like my tongue is stuck to the bottom of my mouth.

She looks at me.

"You're like a corpse waiting for a casket, Rooney." I guess she's talking about my pallor. "Keep it up, pal, haven't been to a good wake for a while."

CHAPTER 37

Monday morning, the 12th of July, and Archie allocates me a man in ward 24 with Post Traumatic Stress Disorder (PTSD) having just been transferred from Two Para, after being in the Falklands War.

"His name is Peter Galloway," Archie says. "He was at Goose Green on the 28th of May and suffers flashbacks and nightmares." He tells me he's been referred for psychological intervention after being sent back to the UK following an attempted suicide.

I see Peter in Ward 8 later that afternoon.

He's a large man, not quite in height at around five ten, but strong, fit, solid shoulders, wearing a combat jacket. I warm to him; he's a quiet but extremely personable man. Alex, inevitably, takes to him and they become friends, being military men; well, Peter anyway, although Alex would like to be so. We agree to see each other weekly for six weeks. It would be no more than talking therapy, to try to help him put to bed some of his bad experiences, help him to learn ways to cope with the symptoms, and to watch out for other things like, depression, anxiety, or misuse of alcohol or drugs. He has always had a heavy alcohol problem, partly why he was admitted, and given he cannot go back to the forces, the social work department needs to find him somewhere to stay. I give him some advice as to how to deal with the flashbacks and the nightmares. He's been prescribed heavy medication to help him sleep. He explains he'd shot a young Argentinian soldier, who could only have been fifteen. He left his body on Goose Green. This pains him greatly. I know he needs long-term therapeutic intervention, but my placement would not allow me to do this. I'll go back to Archie to have him transferred to a full-time psychologist.

Later, I meet the group. I need to bring them up to speed with developments.

Mairi arrives first and whispers in my ear as she comes in. "I guess they are over Alex attacking the guy in the ice cream van." She gets even closer. "I got a bag of grass this morning for ten quid. Happy days." She passes by me to take her seat by the window.

John wheels Walter in.

"Other ways to skin cats, Rooney," Walter says. "I hope it's good."

"Is this the taxidermist group," John laughs. His mood and lucidity is improving, I think. He'll be put up for discharge soon, I worry.

Gerry and Agnes arrive.

Gerry has his hand in a V peace and love sign. "You don't need a weatherman to know which way the wind is blowing,"

"Aye right, Gerry," I say

"Hello, sweetheart," Agnes says to me.

I look out to see if Jackie is heading in. "Please, Agnes."

"Don't worry, darling, when she comes in I'll keep it quiet."

Jackie arrives.

"Hello, troublemakers." She ignores me as she takes her customary seat at the door.

Then Alex appears at the door, his nurse escort with him.

"And here is the biggest troublemaker," Jackie says.

"I'll take him from here," I say to the nurse escort.

"Call the ward when he is ready to go back. I'll come for him," he says.

I nod and take Alex in. He's subdued, obviously from the heavy-handedness of the nursing staff and medication.

I ask, "You alright, Alex?"

He doesn't say anything. Gerry approaches him and puts his arm around him.

"You alright, pal," he says, sitting him down.

"Don't think twice, it's alright," Alex says, with a smile. Gerry smiles too.

"Right," I say, taking my seat. "We have a Patient Council."

"To skin a cat?" Walter adds.

"To skin a cat," I repeat. "We're to be it."

"What?" Jackie says. "This bunch of whackos is to be the Patient Council, saints preserve us."

"What a great idea," Mairi says. "We'll turn this place upside down and out will drop the perpetrators, the killers. We'll flush them out."

"John will be the patients rep on the HMT."

"Oh, Christ," Jackie says.

John pushes his chest out. "I'm to be an important person." He takes his clipboard out, and says and writes: 'John McGlone, the Patient's Reprobate on the management team.'

"Representative, John."

"Aye," laughs Jackie, "a reprobate representative."

John says and writes: "Reprosentative."

"We'll take patients' issues to the group then into the HMT."

"Right, first issue," Walter says.

"Yes, Walter?" John says, his pen hovering over his clipboard.

"Stop killing the patients," Walter says.

"Remember, cat skinning," I say.

"Aye," Mairi laughs, "get the murdering taxidermists."

"They're here, in the grounds, they're waiting, and they'll take more," Gerry says, his quiet words reflecting a more passive presentation.

"Empowerment, my friends will change things here," I say. "Give the patients power."

"Arm the patients," Alex says.

"Steady, Alex, you've to be on your best behaviour, I spoke for you."

Although I sanction him, his words reiterate in my mind, 'arm the patients'. Is this the answer, to let them protect themselves, help them topple this oligarchy.

"Aye, fucking great," Jackie says, "and the lunatics really do take over the asylum, very good that." She gets to her feet and stands over Alex. "Listen, son, any weapons come in here and I'll bring in an armed team. It won't be the comfy state hospital; those patients who support that way of thinking will see themselves in prison long term; from long-term patients to long-term prisoners, that's what will happen. And anyone who raises a gun in these grounds will be taken down. Do you understand what I am saying, son?"

Alex says no more and sinks further into the sofa. But his pal Gerry does. "You fasten all the triggers, for the others to fire, then you set back and watch, when the death count gets higher."

"Please, Gerry."

"He's talking peace, Rooney," Agnes says.

"He's talking pish, Rooney," Jackie says.

"And you don't, sister?"

"OK," John says, "sisters and brothers together, empowerment, togetherness, strength."

I couldn't say it better myself. Agnes does what she does best and makes the tea and brings through a tray of scones, butter, and jam.

I sit beside Walter, a cloud of stability in a troubled sky.

"Do you really think it'll work, Rooney?"

"What, Walter?"

"This group, this approach, do you really think it'll change things, stop people dying?" I can't answer him, because my plans to destroy this place don't really involve the group. It's a front. I'll work my own plan to bring this place down. He leans into me.

"Rooney, there are people in this room who could act. Do you know what I mean?"

I do, but I can't believe anyone, other than Alex that is, would act aggressively towards anyone in this hospital.

I do a couple of interviews in the acute wards, then head back to my room, crossing the grounds while it is still light.

I talk to myself as I walk.

"I know what Walter is saying. I have no doubt, Alex for one, Mairi for two, and possibly Gerry too, if prompted would do it. But if they did, it would scupper my plans for sure. The Castle will close ranks and protect itself, aided by Jackie no doubt. I need to be so—"

"Careful, Rooney?" The voice comes at me from behind. I spin around.

"Where are you?" I say into the bushes. "I heard you. Where are you?"

I see no one. Again, it's in my head. This voice is becoming more familiar, however, like it is me, it sounds like me, but it trumps my thoughts.

"What do you want me to do?"

There's no answer for a bit, like it's thinking about what to say to me or is going to pick it's time, like it does. Then, just as I pass the Rottweiler heading into the nurses' home, it says, "Get them, Rooney, for you, for your mother, kill them, destroy them, it, before it, they, destroy you."

"Please leave me alone."

"You leave me alone and I'll do the same, Rooney," the Rottweiler says, not taking her eyes out of the crossword.

"Sorry, I wasn't meaning…"

"No, I didn't think you were. Your… friend is in your room. I let her in. She says she's your secretary. Says she'll be helping you with your reports."

"Oh, right.. thanks."

"Rooney?" I'm waiting for it. "You know the rules in the home."

"I know, Bella," I say, giving her some respect, "not to fraternise with the opposite sex."

"You got it pal, make sure she's out of there by nine, or I'll be coming knocking at your door."

"I have no doubt you will."

I get to my room and open the door to find Agnes already in my bed.

"Oh, hello, Agnes." I make sure the curtains are firmly closed. "I didn't expect—"

"No, Sean, I thought I would surprise you. Given you had a stressful meeting today, thought you would need some R and R."

"Aw right, th..thanks, Agnes, do you mind if I pour myself a short one." I see she's already poured herself one.

"Please do, I don't like to drink alone."

"You should be careful, not good to drink and drive, Agnes."

"Oh that's OK, I'll not be going home tonight."

"Well, if the Rottweiler has her way, you'll be shown the door before nine."

"Oh, I don't think so, I have some juicy information on that one, about why she was transferred from the wards. Sister Cock, they called her, due to her love of—"

"Thanks Agnes, I get the picture."

"All good, now pop off the light, get out of your clothes. I'll take off my glasses and we can pretend we met in the dark."

There's no getting out of this one.

I do what she says and climb in besides her. Just as the voice says, "Give her what she wants, Sean, she is gagging for it. Show her your power. Be a man. Get in there."

I don't answer it this time, but I try my best to do what it says, not easy with a voice in your head constantly telling me to "give it to her".

Next day, Jackie calls me as I am getting ready for work. Agnes got out early, before Bella came on shift.

"I called you last night three times. Were you pished again?"

I remember hearing the phone go and assumed it would have been Jackie. There's no way I could've answered her with Agnes in my bed.

"Aye, I guess I was."

"I'm worried about you and I'm worried about what's happening in there. These are dangerous times."

"I know, but everything is under control."

"Aye, so you think. In your mental state you'll think that, but I'm telling you your house of cards is in danger of collapsing. Corruption is rife in there, the mob is back and the nutters are looking to take over the place. Oh aye, everything is hunky-dory."

"And how are you, Jackie?"

As if she didn't expect me to ask, she says, "I'm keeping my neck above the swamp, Rooney, my father is on my back about the Castle, my male colleagues continually chide me saying I'm just a woman, not strong enough to match the bad boys, Timpson in particular. I could bring the whole lot down, pal, but this would destroy you, no doubt. If I didn't fucking care for you, I would do it. Just get through your fucking placement and get out of there before the whole place falls in on itself with you in it."

"Yes, Jackie."

"Don't placate me, arse, and Rooney?"

"What, dear?"

"Fuck about with Agnes and you and I are finished, dear."

"I don't—"

"Well, I do, Rooney, your friend is both liberal with her body and her tongue. Just don't fuck us up."

Tuesday, the team meeting is at nine thirty. I leave my room in the home just before nine.

Bella is at her station.

"A good night, Sean?" I ignore her. "There's a package for you," she says, "handed in ten minutes ago. The guy asked if you'd gone to work yet. I said no, and he left this for you." She hands me a small package. I tuck it into my jacket.

At the team meeting Archie asks me to report on the Patient Council, having reported earlier to the HMT.

"We met yesterday," I say. "John McGlone is the patient rep, he'll gather issues by going around the wards, feed them through the Council and into the HMT. It's all about empowerment."

"Any ideas as to the issues that'll be put forward?" Donna asks.

"Oh, to change the culture of this place," I say.

"To do with the patients, not to do to," says Donna.

"Something like that."

There's general agreement, even a commendation from Archie.

"Keep up the good work, Sean," he says.

This assures me my placement assignment and the placement are heading in the right direction.

After the meeting I head back to my office and, as I take my jacket off, I feel the package. I take it out. It's a small bubble pack envelope, well sellotaped. I take a pair of scissors and cut across the top, taking out a small envelope, which I open. There before me in my hand are two small polybags with white powder. I've no doubt they're cocaine. There's a note. "One for you, Sean and one for Doctor Jamieson, a small gratitude from me for sorting things out at the hospital."

It's not identified, no signature, but it's clearly Timpson. I tear up and bin the note and put the polybags in my pocket.

I meet Jamieson over lunch.

"Our first weekly." He's referring to the requirement the HMT applied to Alex being allowed out of security. But more, I know this's much more about monitoring me, ensuring I'm in step with their aspirations.

I give feedback on the group meeting and on Alex acting appropriately.

"That's good, Sean, we want stability here."

I'll bet you do, I think, plenty of ten pound bags to go around, making the night shifts more palatable. Stability is the vans coming in, keeping the patients happy and quiet, the staff happy.

"I have something for you," I say.

"Ah, yes, I thought you may." It's as if he's expecting it. I put the polybag into his hand, being careful no one sees me doing it.

"Thank you, Sean, and how are you?"

I know he's referring to more than just my mental health. Another double bind, creating conflict in the mind. Getting through the course, pleasing Donna and Archie, acquiescing to Jamieson, the hospital managers, and Timpson of course, while at the same time protecting the patients, nurses, and me.

"I am fine." I fear the voice will tell me I'm not, *they* appearing in the staff canteen to watch me, chide me for eating with a consultant psychiatrist.

"Are you hearing anything, seeing anything?"

'He suspects I am,' I say to myself.

"Are you OK for... tablets?"

I know he is referring to more than my prescription. My tablets include the twenty-four Lorazepams I am halfway through.

"I'm OK for now."

"That's good."

He leaves me there and I leave the room, passing Myra's spot, the Pass, where I stop. I lean my back on the wall and look to where she used to sit. I can't let them away with this, I think. I can't let the Castle triumph.

"Don't let it, Sean, it killed me," comes at me from behind. I turn to face the window. It's my mother's voice, strong and clear as can be. I see her face through the window.

Then I see him, my father. "You killed her, son, you, accept it." His eyes are full of bile. "You're not up to what you're doing. You can't be a professional. Get a job, a life."

I turn away and head up the corridor to the office.

CHAPTER 38

Friday morning, I meet the group again. John's been around the wards and gathered some issues on behalf of the patients.

They all attend. Alex and Jackie aren't there. Jackie says she's under pressure from her father and colleagues to extricate herself from what's going on in the hospital, the links with the mob and Timpson. She's caught between two fires.

I call the ward to enquire about Alex.

"He's gone missing," the charge nurse says. "We've informed the police."

I tell the group. A hush descends. Then John moves centre stage at the flip chart.

"I have five main pointing issues," he says.

"Thanks John."

"One, he writes, more money, the pocket money for long stay patients is inadequate."

"Good one, John," Mairi says.

"Two, more recreational opportunities."

"Another good one," Walter says.

"Three, a patient café."

"I like it," Gerry says, "we'll get a juke box."

"Four, a patient bus."

"Great, trips to the seaside," says Agnes.

"Five, stop the discharge programme until proper facilities, not nursing homes or mini-Castles; normal houses, that the place is shit and we all get our own houses."

"The place should be shut —"

"No, the place is shit and we want our own places."

I'm thinking, two or three of these wishes may be possible, but a home for every patient is a tall order.

"Well done, John, we'll take them to the HMT and we'll see what happens."

Walter's voice carries through the room.

"What about six, stop the killings in the Castle, John?"

"Yes, Walter, this was said," John says, "but Mr Rooney said I shouldn't ask for this."

"Is this true, Rooney?" Walter asks.

"Yes," I say, "this is not within our remit."

"Get me out of here." Walter bashes his wheelchair against the door. "I'm out of here, this group is going to do nothing about what's really happening in this place."

Mairi opens it and Walter leaves.

"I'm sorry, Walter."

"What about Alex?" Gerry asks. "We need to find him."

"I'm worried about him," Mairi says.

"We'll just have to wait until he turns up," I say.

"He'll be in the woods," Gerry says. "That's where he hid out before. He showed me."

"Can you take us there?"

"Aye, let's go," Gerry says.

"I'm coming," Agnes demands.

Mairi says, "I'm coming too."

"And me," John says.

It's mid-morning as we head out and into the grounds. Gerry leads. We snake through the trees, the sun is high as we follow him, not following any of the normal paths. This's clearly deeper and farther into the woods than I have ever been. I'm apprehensive about being in these woods, where I've seen figures, and I know the guys have been operating here.

After walking around fifteen minutes or more, "Stop," Gerry says.

He reminds me of a US captain leading his troops into the bush in Vietnam. We all stop and look around. We see nothing now other than trees.

"Listen," he demands.

We all stop talking and listen. We can hear something, almost like a chant up ahead. Gerry leads his troops along the path, me at the back. Farther along the path the chant is becoming louder. It certainly doesn't sound like Alex.

Gerry is beginning to chant now.

"The path is ever winding, the stars they never age, the morning light is blinding, all the world's a stage." I don't recognise Gerry's poem, but I'm sure this is another Dylan verse. The chant up ahead is becoming stronger, we can hear it more clearly.

"We stocked our ships full of British beer and bullets…"

"I know the voice," I say.

"Shush," Mairi says.

It's stronger now.

"We mobilised the navy and we called up the marines." This is Peter Galloway's voice. "We sailed two weeks 'til we reached the Falkland Islands, so we could teach a lesson to those bloody Argentines."

We reach him, Peter, the soldier who had recently been in the Falklands war. He's sitting on the ground, his back against a tree, looking blankly into the far woods. He continues to sing. I recognise the tune of the *Battle of New Orleans*. "We fired our guns and the British came a coming, off the coast of Argentine our Islands came to be, with eighteen hundred people and a half a million sheep."

We gather around him. I'm both worried and disappointed. One, Peter should not be out here on his own and two, there's no sign of Alex.

Gerry moves to Peter's side.

"Soldier Peter." He obviously knows him from the ward. "Are you alright?"

Peter continues to chant.

"The day they were invaded everybody learned the name, a barren little colony had got a bit of fame."

I crouch down before him.

"Peter, are you OK?" He doesn't look my way, continuing his chant.

Mairi asks him, "Have you seen Alex?"

He stops and looks up at me.

"Mr Rooney, Alex is there." He turns around to point towards a mound of broken earth.

Gerry moves quickly and clears some of the earth where Peter points.

"Oh my God, Mr Rooney, sir."

I move to where Gerry is kneeling to see Alex's face peering through the cleared earth, his dead staring eyes. "Jesus," I gasp. I get up as Mairi and Agnes move closer. "Please don't, it's Alex, he's dead."

"No," they both yell in unison.

I move back to Peter. He continues to sing.

"We stocked our ships full of British beer and bullets, we mobilised the navy and we called up the marines. We sailed two weeks 'til we reached the Falkland Islands, so we could teach a lesson to those bloody Argentines."

"Peter?"

He looks up.

"Mr Rooney?"

"Alex?"

"I found him," he says.

"Where?" I ask him.

"There." Peter points to a cut rope hanging from the branch of a tree. "I cut him down and buried him." He calls out. "He was only a boy, he didn't need to die."

I wonder if he's referring to the young Argentinian soldier he killed in the Falklands.

Gerry clears the earth away from Alex. "Alex, let's get you out of here," he says.

"He's gone, Gerry." John moves to his side.

Agnes and Mairi take Gerry by the arm and sit him on a fallen tree.

"What will we do with him, Mr Rooney?" John asks.

"We have to tell the ward, John, the police will be informed, an investigation no doubt."

"Aye, forensagation, no doubt."

"Yes, John."

"He killed himself," Agnes says.

"Maybe someone killed him," Mairi says. "He would've been on the hit list."

"He came to the department."

I turn to face Agnes.

"Agnes, what are you saying?"

"Yesterday. I meant to tell you. I didn't think it was important. I didn't think he would…"

"What did he say?"

"He wanted to see you, Sean."

"You should have told me."

"I didn't…"

"Did he say anything?"

"Aye."

"What?"

"He said he was going off and wouldn't be back and wouldn't need his things."

"He said what?"

"I didn't think anything of it. He said many things before, that the mob were out to get him, etcetera, that *they* would get him. He was delusional, you said it yourself. I thought he was being supervised."

"What did he leave?"

"His watch, his wallet, and an envelope, they're all in the office."

We take Peter back to the ward. I explain to Tommy Stephenson that we found Alex and the circumstances. I'm aware the police are brought in when someone dies unexpectedly, the law says there must be an investigation to find out what has happened.

I can't leave this with the group and tell them to come to the department in an hour's time. We need to debrief, talk Alex's death through. Agnes and I go into the office to retrieve Alex's things. She hands me the envelope he left with her.

I open it. It's headed, 'To whom it may concern.'

I read it out.

"To whom it may concern. I must leave this place because they want to send me there." I assume he is either talking about the State Hospital or to a resource in the community. I know Alex was unhappy about the halfway house he had been identified for, but more than this, after his attack on the van driver he knew there was a chance he may be sent to the State Hospital.

I read on.

"I have been trying to tell people they want to kill me. I can't let them get me. I thank Mr Rooney and the group for helping me. There is no other way out. Cobra."

"Jesus Agnes, he came to the department, leaves his watch, his wallet, and this note and you don't tell me?"

"Sean, I didn't think. As you know, he was always turning up at the department asking to see you. I know you are busy. He was a bit of a nuisance. I was just trying to—"

"A bit of a nuisance, Agnes. A bit of a nuisance. Jesus, Alex walks into your office leaves a suicide note and you ignore it. Fuck's sake, madam."

She fixes me with a cold stare.

"I was trying to… protect you. I know how stressed you are with all of this. I need to look after you."

I leave her there and go to my room to call Jackie. Though, inevitably, she'll be in touch when Stephenson calls in the local police. I give her all the information I have on Alex's death.

"Alex, I am so sorry," she says.

"There needs to be a full and detailed investigation, Jackie. We need to be sure."

"He killed himself, Rooney, hanged himself from a tree, left a suicide note, what more do you need to know?"

"I need to know why, Jackie, why he took his own life, if indeed he did. It needs to be established."

"We'll do it, but where are the extenuating circumstances?"

"What about Timpson getting back after he attacked their man, certain forces we know exist in this hospital, and previous suspicious deaths?"

"Don't get paranoid, Rooney. He was an ill man, delusional, posing risk to others and obviously himself, being assessed for secure care, couldn't cope with the thought, then kills himself."

I go back to the department. Walter, Gerry, John, and Mairi are waiting for me. I take them into the meeting room. Agnes follows them in.

"No, Agnes," I say. "I need to see them on my own."

She looks at me and her face changes. I have seen this face before.

"Don't push me out me, Rooney, I'm part of this, part of us, you know that. Don't you do this to me, to us."

I see her eyes, they concern me, a woman scorned, I need to be careful with Agnes.

"Gerald, you cannot go in without me."

Gerry looks at her.

"Trust yourself, Gerald," he says to himself. "Do the things only you know best. Trust yourself to do what's right and not be second guessed."

"I'll talk to you later." Agnes storms back into the office.

We go in and Walter is first to talk.

"We're scared, Sean. Any one of us could be next. First it was Oliver."

"Then it was my father," Mairi says.

"Then Elsie, and then Joan," John says.

"Then Myra," Walter adds.

"And now Alex, my friend," Gerry says.

I look at them and hear their voices. They're clearly scared, but they're angry too. They have their say and I need to understand their concerns. We spend an hour or so talking it through. By the time they leave I feel content they will cope with the shock and loss of Alex, though they appear more angry, resolved to find out more about his death, than shocked.

I go into the office. Agnes gets up and looks around to see if anyone is there before she speaks, before she starts putting her arms around me. I also look around.

"Anyone could come in, Agnes. Archie, Donna, or any of the other psychologists."

"Please hold me. I need you."

"Please." I pull away from her.

"Rooney, you know I'm not a woman to be used."

"I do, Agnes?"

She sits on the desk and crosses her legs, showing an ample amount of thigh.

"Yes, Sean, I've made this clear."

"Oh?"

"I have put myself out for you, to ensure your future, our relationship. I've lied for you, done things for you." She gets off the desk and moves close to me again. "Don't slight me, Sean."

Just at this point, Donna walks in carrying a report. She stops and looks. She sees Agnes closer to me than would be normal.

"Oh, hi, Rooney." She's looking at Agnes. "Hi Agnes." Agnes moves to her side of the desk. "I hope I wasn't—"

"No," I say, "you weren't."

She passes Agnes the papers and asks her to make amendments to her report. I escape to my work room, knowing it's best not to be there. Donna follows me into the room.

"Sean?"

"I know Donna, it didn't look good."

"We really are at a crucial point in your placement, please—"

"I know, don't fuck it up."

"Well, not quite on those terms, Sean. Don't have Archie putting pressure on me. After the deterioration of your mental health, I've to monitor you, and your behaviour. Things are at a very decisive point. What I saw may indicate disinhibition, symptomatic of your illness."

I know what she is saying, everything is at stake here.

I need to talk to Agnes.

"What is it, Sean?" I ask myself, a fling, a relationship, me taking advantage of her after marital breakdown? I ask her to my room this evening, clearing it with Bella. She has no problem with this. I guess Agnes had said something about her... reputation.

Later, Agnes arrives and pushes past me into my room in the nurses' home.

"I'm not happy, Sean, Gerald isn't talking to me. Donna says I've to leave you alone or she'll talk to Archie. And you've stopped me going into the group. I've lied for you, risked my job for you, and you're showing me, us, no respect, showing me up in front of the group like that. Also, suggesting I did something wrong with Alex's death. I'm not going to accept this, Sean." She pulls out a packet of cigarettes and takes of her coat revealing a skimpy black number.

"Sorry, Agnes, you can't—"

"I fucking can." She lights up. "Right, what's it to be, Sean? Is it us, our future, your career, or Jackie and failure?" I stay schtum and let her get it out. "Do you know." She's pointing her cigarette at me. "I could bring you down."

"Are you threatening me, Agnes?"

"Call it what you like." She stubs her cigarette out in my sink and lights up another. "I'm getting you through this placement. I redacted your report. Is this what the academics say? I changed it and sent it off. You were failing buddy, failing, I got you through. Me."

"What, Agnes?"

She's marching up and down the room now, not there's much room to do that.

"You don't know what you have, Sean. I'm the full package. I can do things your friend Jackie could only think about. I can give you what you need."

I let her rant and she appears to quieten. She sits on my bed, kicks her shoes off, and opens her legs, just enough to be provocative.

"Come here, Rooney," she orders. I sit on the bed close to her. She opens her bag and takes out a pair of panties, I see they are torn at the side. "Remember these, Sean, remember ripping them from me? I'm not wearing any now." She lies back on the bed.

"I don't Agnes." I really couldn't.

"No, you don't remember much when you are pissed do you."

"No, I don't," I say to myself.

Then, he's there, in the corner.

"Go on, son, give it to her. Show her you're a man."

"Shut up," I say.

"That's it, Sean, get rough, you know this's the way I like it."

"I didn't mean you."

"Oh, and who else is here, Sean, a ghost?"

She pulls me on top of her.

"Agnes, please." I try to get off her but she is holding me tight. "Please, Agnes."

"Mind not to cross me, Rooney," she whispers in my ear. And then she erupts. "No, Sean, don't please," she screams. She's ripping at her dress with both of her hands, tearing it from the top at the zip, breaking the zip open, then ripping at her bra, revealing one of her breasts. Then she starts on her head, punching it wildly, slapping her face, leaving red marks. I get up and look at her. She reminds me of Regan in the Exorcist, writhing all over the bed. She's shouting at the top of her voice, "Get off me, don't, please don't hit me." She's screaming, "He's trying to rape me." She throws herself back against the wall, the back of her head shattering the mirror. She feels her head, her hand is covered in blood.

Next thing I hear Bella at the door. Almost, as if it was rehearsed.

"You alright in there, Agnes?"

"Get security, Bella, he's trying to rape me, kill me."

Then John Scott arrives.

"You alright, Sean, what's happening?" he says.

I open the door. "Come in," I say.

Just then, Bella rushes into the room almost knocking me over.

"Agnes," she says, rushing to her side. "Are you OK?"

Then Scott asks me, "Rooney, what have you done?"

"I haven't done…"

"He tried to rape me," Agnes says. "Get security."

"I did nothing."

"No, look at me?"

Bella pulls the bedsheet around Agnes, wrapping a towel around her head. She sits up and pulls out her cigarettes. Her face looks like she has been in a fight. She did a good job in creating the bruising, her mascara running down her face, her lipstick all over it. The blood is dripping from the towel.

"John, I did nothing."

"No, Sean, but it doesn't look that way, does it?"

"No," I say, sitting down at my small dining table. Bella calls an ambulance and security.

Security arrives first and one stands over me menacingly. I remember the last time he was standing over me, when I was lying on the road. The other is talking to Agnes.

"Will I call in the police, Agnes?"

She takes time to respond.

"No, I don't want…"

"You don't want to have him arrested, Agnes. You don't want to destroy his career."

She looks at Bella, as if she had expected her to say this.

"I just want to go home."

"You need to go to hospital, you'll need stitches," the other security man says. She puts on her shoes, and he helps her to her feet. She follows him out, like the victim of an assault she intends to portray.

Then, as she passes me, she says, "Sean, you didn't need to do this, you know I love you."

"You bitch," is all I can say.

"Steady son," the other security man says, as he lays a hefty punch on the left side of my face, almost knocking me out. John rushes to my side.

"Right, pal," he says.

"He deserved it, John," he says.

"I'll talk to him," John says. "We'll sort this."

"Aye, we will," the security man says. Then he points at me. "I'll be back to talk to you pal, this won't happen again here, and your bosses will hear about this from me. You understand?" I'm stunned into silence. "Do you understand?"

I nod.

"He understands," John says. "I'll make sure he does." They leave and John makes me a cup of tea. "What were you thinking of Rooney?"

"It was a set-up."

He shakes his head. "Stay there and don't move." He's back in a minute with a fresh bottle of Grouse whisky. He digs out two glasses from my cupboard and pours me a large one.

"I don't think—"

"You need it, take it."

We finish the bottle and Scott leaves me there, but not before he says:

"Biffo Bill, the security man will be back. Give me a shout if he does. He'll not stop at a punch the next time. I let him out and lock my door, barricading it by pulling my sofa behind the door and piling everything heavy I can find on it, such as the colour TV, my big rug from the floor, heavy jackets and clothes, and an upended solid G plan coffee table. I buttress my single bed against the sofa and climb on it, facing towards the door. I reach into my drawer and take out the polybag Timpson gave me and the Lorazepam from my bedside table. I take two tablets, open the bag and snort the lot, then pour myself a large one and wait for Biffo Bill to arrive.

He doesn't arrive this night. Or through the night. I know, because I refuse to fall asleep, even although I could have slept for a week. The drugs and the alcohol are taking effect and I'm close to unconscious, though I'm fighting it.

CHAPTER 39

It's Saturday and it's only a continuation of the same: drink and drugs, drugs and drink. Donna appears at the door at one point to explain that Agnes had admitted to changing her report and had forged her signature. She explains she would have to prepare another one and would have to add the events of last night. The police are called in to investigate Alex's death and Professor Owen is saying the group's activity led to Alex taking his own life. Doctor Jamieson appears at one point to ask how I'm doing and to suggest I come into ward 8 for a while. He also suggests he may section me, that following the Agnes incident I may be posing risk to others. He says he'd give me some time to come in voluntarily before he resorts to the section.

Jackie also comes to the door. I refuse to talk to her.

"I'll have the door put in Rooney," she says from the other side of the door. "I'll have you taken to the cells. I am worried about you, you shithead. What was this about with Agnes? Just confirms for me something is going on between you and her."

I listen without answering, but I'm sure she knows I am listening.

"And what I have been fearing is happening to you Rooney. You're going down, down in your mental health, down in your career, down in your life. Let me help you, you bastard."

I whisper, though she doesn't hear me. "Please go away, Jackie, I have to accept what's coming to me."

"I'll be back, Rooney, and I'll have two polis with me to put the door in, so get your head on." She leaves and I go into myself like never before, and there they are, dark shapes like the ghosts I saw in ward 49.

They're whispering, "He's really done it this time. Now they'll get rid of him. He should have stayed away."

Then there's my father's voice booming out across the room. "Never make anything of yourself, killed your mother; you, a professional?"

Then there's my mother. "Help me, Sean, help me."

Then Father Healey. "Would you like some sweets, Sean?"

Like he did before he touched me.

The figures become more solid, almost like I could touch them, they're all around me now, circling me.

They're saying, "They are taking the children away, you must help us."

It goes on for the rest of the day and the Sunday too, and I can't take it anymore. I reach for a bottle of paracetamol and take the lot, around thirty tablets. Then they're on me, holding me down, then I don't remember anything after this point, not until I wake up in the GRI.

"I'm pleased you've come around, Mr Rooney. I'm a doctor. We were worried about you."

"Right," I say. "Thanks."

"You swallowed a pile of pills, but we got most of them out of your stomach. We need to watch to see if you have damaged your liver; so you'll be with us for another few days. Your psychiatrist asked to be called when you regained consciousness. I'll call him. I suspect he'll want to see you."

I know what this means, emergency section, ward 8, the Castle. I need to get out of here.

"Thank you, doctor," I say.

"Do you still want to kill yourself?"

"No," I say. "Nothing to worry about here. Parasuicide attempt caused by too much drink and drugs. My mind is clear now, stupid thing to do, really. Just want to get back to my job, helping people. That's what my life is all about really. What about you, doctor?"

"Good. You're to be transferred ASAP to Hillwood."

"But, I said I wouldn't…"

"It was the way you said it. In my view you are not in touch with reality. I can't take the chance you'll walk out of here and head for the Clyde."

"All fine, doctor." I reach for my clothes which are in a white bag by my bed. I'll wait until visitors time, head into the toilet and put on my clothes. I'll slip out, past the nurses' station as they are busy talking to relatives. Just then I see the huckle team are heading my way through the ward led by Stephenson, the traitorous bastard. I try to jump out of bed but the doctor and a nurse hold me fast. Then Stephenson is on me, my arms and legs held by his team of thugs.

"You bast…"

"Now, Rooney, there are a lot of sick people in this ward, let's not scare them," Stephenson says. Then Doctor Jamieson appears with Bill Simmons.

"Hello, Sean," Jamieson says.

"Oh Christ, Doctor Death has arrived. And you Simmons, what are you going to do, stick me in a nursing home?"

"I'm a mental health officer. I'm here to consent to your detention."

"You lot, the murder squad, a group of assassins who kill for pleasure." I plead with the GRI doctor. "Don't let them take me back to that place. They'll kill me like they are killing other patients, scores of them. Please?"

"You have to go, Mr Rooney, it's in your best interests."

I scream out into the ward, "They're going to kill me. They're killing patients. Help me. Get the police."

"I am the police," comes from Jackie appearing in the ward. "I'm sorry, Rooney, you are completely off it. I knew you would do something. I triggered this. I'm probably the nearest person you have relative-wise and I contacted them. You need to go in, it's for your own good, and your safety."

"You Jackie, you deceived me. You're working for Timpson. You're all working for Timpson, you fuckers. I'll kill you. I'll kill you all. I will… I will…" That's as much as I manage to get out before I feel the effect of the sedation coursing through my veins after it's injected into my arse.

Two days later, Wednesday, I wake up in ward 8. I have restraints across my bed, across my arms and legs. I am parched.

"Can I have some water, please?" A nurse arrives and puts a beaker to my mouth. I drink all of it and ask for another. "Can you please release my arms and legs?"

"I'll see." Next thing, Stephenson arrives.

"How are you, Sean?"

"Oh hunky-fuckin-dory, you fucking criminal. I want out of these fucking restraints."

"You said you wanted to kill us."

I feel the nip and then the heavy sedation courses through my body, no doubt a large doze of Chlorpromazine.

"You're in the acute phase of a psychotic episode, pal. We need to make sure you're safe until you regain some reality."

"And you're in league with Doctor Death. The devil incarnate. In the pockets of the mob. You're killing people."

"Not the right answer. Just stay warm." He pulls the blanket up roughly to my neck. "We'll look after you."

"Aye, you'll really look after me, you fucking murderer."

Two more days go by. By Friday, I'm so zonked out I don't even try to get out of bed. Then they remove the restraints and sit me on a high back chair in a single room, the observational room. I'm going nowhere because my body is like lead, my legs like stone, my mind just a dull, dark place.

Jackie appears. I refuse to look at her.

"I brought you some Carnations," she says. "I know you like them in July, you always said so."

"Stick them up your arse."

She pulls a chair in close.

"They say you'll be in for a while."

"What does it matter how long I'll be in? I'll never leave this place. I'll be next to go. What does it matter anyway, my placement is fucked, my career is fucked, my life—"

"Is fucked? No, it's not, Rooney. You can pick up your life, once you are well."

"Well, what is well, Jackie?"

"Maybe it's time to think about something else, something more suited to you."

"What, like a fucking TV man, a factory labourer like my father said I should be, a fucking has been, a waste of space."

"You can decide, when you are OK. You just need to…"

"Keep taking the tablets."

"Something like that."

"And wait for the inevitable pillow over the face, the noose around my neck, the push into the loch, the shove over the bridge?"

"Just keep the heid, as they say, there's still the investigation."

241

Jeas, I had forgotten about this, the so-called attack on Agnes.

"I never fucking touched her."

"It's only your word against hers at the moment, but I am talking to her, trying to—"

"What about us, this fucks us up?"

"I guess so, in a sense. I just want to help you, to be a friend. I know you're in a shitty place."

"And then you'll dump me?"

"We'll see, Sean. I'm still your friend, but we'll see what we have left after this."

They put me in the dormitory. I spend the evening listening to the patients' squabbles, the shrieks, the call outs through the night, mother, nurse, sometime names, the snores, the incessant snores, over the whole night. I try to stay awake, but they are out there for sure. Surely they wouldn't try to kill me in here, with other patients watching. They'll bide their time though, wait for the right opportunity, then do it. I wish I had a weapon, something to protect myself with. I'm so dulled by the chemical cosh I wouldn't be able to put up much of a fight. I see the shapes, the ghosts, through the half windows into the corridor, shuffling between the wards, looking for victims.

They come in. I pull my sheet over my head. I hear them talking.

"He's in there, we need to get him. He'll get us if we don't. We'll be back, Mr Rooney," one of them says.

"Don't bother, I'm not in," I whisper, keeping my head under the blankets.

They go away. I leave it an hour or so. I can't hear them anymore. I raise my head above my bed clothes, and there he's standing right in front of me. I thought it was a statue at first, he was so solid. He's tall, his eyes are staring down at me, and there's this look on his face. God the Father, incarnate in Professor Owen? Put a white robe on him, extend his white hair and beard by a few inches…

"You?"

"Hello, Mr Rooney," he says.

I look to the clock on the wall.

"Professor Owen, it's three-feckin'-thirty in the night, sir, and you're here to kill me."

"And why would I do that?"

"Because I know about you, you're a murdering medic. Myra, for example."

"Myra, was my patient, my—"

"Mary Magdalene?"

"Delusions, Mr Rooney, and hallucinations. They'll abate with the medication. He moves towards me. I try to get out of bed, but I can't move, my body is like lead.

"No please." I close my eyes and await the lethal injection, the pillow over my head, the noose linked to the bedframe, me pushed onto the floor, the noose tightening on my neck, my lungs starved of oxygen, me blacking out, me dying, seeing my mother waiting for me, my father telling me to go to her. Then there's nothing. I look up again and there he is, Peter Galloway. I look around. Owen is nowhere to be seen.

"Peter?"

"Don't worry, Mr Rooney, I saw him at your bed. I'm over there." He nods over to his bed adjacent to mine on the other side of the dormitory. "I got up and came over and he buggered off."

"Thanks Peter."

"He's gone for now, but he'll be back. You have to rest."

CHAPTER 40

Friday, Jamieson turns up. He tells me I've to be transferred to ward 10, a sub-acute ward.

"For assessment," he says.

"Oh, aye," I say. "Assessment for a long stay ward, a nursing home, the State Hospital?"

"For alcohol and drugs rehabilitation, Rooney."

"Oh, you're a fine one to talk about drug rehabilitation, you fucking junkie. The only difference between you and them on the streets is you live in a fancy house in the West End and they live in cardboard boxes."

"You need to get on top of your addiction."

"You fucker, you gave me the tablets."

"Your alcohol abuse."

"You're a fuckin' murderer."

"Which is perpetuating your manic depression, your mental illness. Only then will treatment be effective."

Later, I'm transferred to ward 10. The only benefit is this is a quieter ward, no loonies crying out through the night. Sub-acute means you're either going farther into the bowels of the Castle or out the door towards a community-based placement. In my case an alcohol and drug rehab centre. The place is full of brain damage, however, Korsakoff's, to the uninitiated, alcohol-related brain damage, drug-induced psychosis, presenile dementia, a smattering of folk with learning disability with behavioural problems, autistic like Gerry.

I'm just in the ward when he approaches me.

"Hello, sir."

How could I forget the Dylanesque fruitcake.

"How's your mother, Gerry?"

"I'm not talking to her, she didn't tell me about Alex and I heard about you and her."

"I never touched her."

"I believe you, sir. She did the same to my father. She got him the jail."

"What? You need to tell them, Gerry. They need to know. They think I tried to rape her."

"She said she would keep me in here, tell them I can't go home. I'd be stuck."

"She's just like a woman, Gerry."

"Walking along the watchtower, sir. There must be some way out of here—"

"Said the joker to the thief."

"Who's the joker and who's the thief, Gerry?" I kind of expected a half smile, but with his lack of eye contact, his stolid face, the only lightness is in his words. Is he the joker, making me the thief? "Am I the thief, Gerry?"

"There are many here among us who feel life is but a joke."

Jesus, I cannot get my head around the crypticity of this.

"Life is no joke, Gerry."

He walks away, humming *All along the Watchtower*.

I need to get out of here, but I'm so tired. I couldn't walk if I tried to. But it all happens in my head: I'll get into my clothes, wait my time, make a run for it out of the ward, down the corridor, traverse the Pass, out the front door, down the road, out of the gate, down towards the city, and freedom. Truth is I wouldn't get past the door of the ward. I see them watching me.

There's one who sits just inside the door of the ward and all he does is watch. Anyone who walks up to the door, he'll say, "Just go back in pal, watch the telly."

'Watch the telly,' that's all they say, and that's all they have to do, 'watch the telly'. But I know if I don't get out of here they'll kill me, absolutely no doubt about it.

Every night she appears, the nun. She sits there and watches me. God the Father is walking around outside, up and down the corridor. He looks in occasionally and sees the nun. I have no doubt if she wasn't there he'd be in. He'd kill me. She doesn't mind me talking to the figures which visit me also, and my mother and my father.

I get visitors during the day too, Walter, occasionally; we talk about trees. John talks about the issues he picks up for the HMT. He asks about our group, and when we will meet again. Mairi wants to know everything.

"I'm writing a book," she says. "It's called Murders in a Mental Hospital."

"Great. I'm to be a character in a crime novel."

We talk about Alex's funeral, which was last week. I wasn't allowed to go. He was buried in Sighthill graveyard. Gerry went, so did John, Mairi, and Peter. Walter wanted to go but they said he wouldn't be able to manage the paths in the graveyard and the ward couldn't spare a member of staff to help.

"I did a poem," Walter says. "Want to hear it?"

"Go on then."

He reads it out loud.

"Alex was a lively lad, he was never very slow. He met his death on a helpful tree, a friendly way to go. He always dreamed of getting out, he didn't have a clue. He always thought they would get him, there's nothing he could do."

I look at him. "Thanks, Walter, a helpful tree."

I sit wondering if Alex would still be alive if he hadn't met me, Joan, and Myra too. With my guilt, I can feel the black dog approaching. It's saying, I am going to devour you. I see its eyes staring at me from outside in the dark, in the trees.

Monday, the 9th of August, I've been sitting here for two weeks looking vacantly out into the corridor, hoping Jackie would come. In my head, though, I have had many visitors. Stephenson says I've become more depressed, intractable, and I've been placed on a long-term order.

"Doctor Jamieson says he wants to try ECT," he says. I demand to see him. He arrives the following morning.

"I hear you want to see me, Sean?"

"You want to give me ECT."

"Yes, I think it will help you."

"I have manic depression, it's not recommended for psychosis."

"Medication isn't helping your mood much, Sean."

"When?"

"Friday, the 13th of August, the sooner the better."

"Friday the thirteenth, lucky for me, Doctor." He grins. "I'm going to spill the beans on you, Doctor Death, the medic with a habit, supplied with class A drugs from the mob. Your career is over, Doctor J."

"Come on Sean, who is going to believe you? Anyway, the ECT will help the thoughts, the memory."

"Aye, eradicate them in your best interests. Anyway, I don't give my consent."

"We don't need your consent. Professor Owen gives a second opinion. He agrees with me the treatment is necessary for your health and safety, and for the safety of other people."

"Aye, a fucking stitch-up. Am I getting one?"

"We're thinking of around four a day until we see some benefit."

"Fuck, you're out to fry my brain."

"We're very careful over the amount of current to use. You'll have a controlled seizure and it'll be over in a few seconds."

I get to call Jackie on the ward phone.

"They're going to kill me, Jackie."

"Wait a minute, how, who, Rooney?"

"You know who, I know how."

"How?"

"By ECT."

"ECT is not deadly."

"It'll be for me, believe me."

"Jesus, calm doon, it's a treatment, it'll help you."

"You need to help me."

"Rooney, you're under a section. I can't help you."

It's Friday the 19th and they come for me. I try to struggle but I've no strength against them. Two of them get my arms. They manhandle me into the treatment room and lift me onto the bed. Then they go about their business like a well-oiled machine. Two of them hold my arms, two hold my legs. One puts this gel on both sides of my head. The other one injects my arm, presumably with the muscle relaxant to prevent me breaking bones and the anaesthetic so I don't feel it. Then this rubber thing is put in my mouth, and I feel these prongs being applied to each side of my head. I fall asleep. Then...

Stephenson is leaning over me. "Hello, Sean, hello Sean."

My body feels like I've been run over by a bus.

"Where am I?"

"In your bed in the dormitory."

"We aren't allowed in the dormitory during the day."

"We made an exception."

"Has it been done?"

"Yes, an hour ago, but we had… problems."

"Problems, what problems?"

"Your heart stopped, we had to do CPR."

"My heart stopped?"

"And you stopped breathing. All very unusual, not sure why, whether you have heart problems due to your alcohol abuse or something else. Anyway, you're fine."

"Until the next time."

"We're going to leave the next one until next week, until the doctor has a chance to check you over."

"You're going to give me another one?"

"Oh, yes, there's no need to change the treatment plan."

Later, I feel a bit better. I phone Jackie.

"Jackie, nothing surer, they're definitely trying to kill me."

"Paranoia, Rooney, very common, you'll be fine."

"Jackie, Jackie." I hear the phone going down.

I talk to Gerry.

"They're trying to kill me, Gerry."

"Where d'you want this killin' done?"

"Fuck's sake, Gerry, out on Highway 61, what do you think?"

Next thing Walter, Mairi, and John are there too.

"They are trying to murder you, Rooney?" Walter says.

"Aye." I explain my experience with the ECT. "Next time, they might succeed. They will eventually. I've to get multiple sessions."

"I'm so sorry," Mairi says, almost like my demise is inevitable.

"No need, Mairi. I'm going to stay out of your book if I can."

"I know you're at risk, Rooney. You could die here and if you do I'll make sure the world knows about it."

I'm not sure if I should thank her. I just look at her.

She takes out her notebook. "I need to know everything."

Stephenson arrives and moves them out, saying Doctor Jamieson wants to see me.

"Right, great," I say. "Doctor Mengele, the angel of death to interview his next experiment."

Jamieson arrives.

"I'm sorry you had a bad experience with the treatment, Sean. We'll be watching you for sure." He takes out a stethoscope and puts it to my chest. "You sound OK, but maybe there's something going on in there, your heart."

"So, you'll stop until I get a specialist assessment, cardiology?"

"Professor Owen thinks you need the treatment. In his opinion, the benefits outweigh the risks. He's the physician superintendent."

"You think I need it, not him. You want me to die. You want to kill me."

"We'll look after you, so don't worry. We have to balance the therapeutic benefits of the treatment against any risk to your... health."

I call Jackie.

"They really are trying to kill me, Jackie. You have to come."

Saturday morning I spend trying to convince the staff and ultimately Stephenson I'm OK, I don't need the ECT. I help around the ward, I'm civil to staff. I talk to the other patients and relatives when they come in. At the same time there's a war going on in my head. My voices rather than talking to me are battling with each other.

My father to my mother, "You know nothing, you were in there yourself, a hideout for those who can't cope with their lives, weak, inadequates, just like you, a waste of space, be best to do away with them or hope they do away with themselves, just like you."

My mother to my father, "You drove me to it, not him, not there, men are his problem, men, like you, who have harmed him."

They've no names or faces, only shapes of people, men and woman.

To my mother and father, "He's damned, he'll be dead soon, like us. He'll come to us, when it's his time. It'll get him, like it got us. He has no chance."

I go into a corner and whisper to them, "Shut up you infernal bastards, leave me alone."

But the nursing staff see me and tell Stephenson.

Stephenson asks, "You still hearing things, Sean?"

"No, Tommy, not a thing, perfectly fine, thank you very much."

That afternoon, Jackie comes in.

"You still think they're trying to kill you Rooney?"

"Aye, my next ECT is next Friday, it'll happen then. You have to help me."

"I'm not doing anything, pal, it's all in your mind. You need the treatment. It'll help you get better and get out of here."

"You have to arrest him, he's the killer, and I am next."

"I can do nothing in here. After Agnes, my father wanted to see me, to talk about you."

"Oh aye."

"They're talking to her, getting evidence, going to press charges. I've to dump you."

"Right."

"You're threatening my career."

"Here we go. Mad rapist boyfriend and aspiring DCI, daughter of the Chief Constable. He has to go."

"He's right, Rooney. "

"What, mad rapist boyfriend?"

"No, you are a threat to me, my career. I can't keep up with you, Rooney. Your links with Timpson, your drinking, the violence. You're unpredictable. I need stability. I need to concentrate—"

"On getting through the glass ceiling, be one of, better than, the boys."

She sorts her bag likes she does when she has nothing to say.

"I need to go."

"Aye, on you go then."

"I've to talk to Timpson."

This doesn't sound good.

"He's not—"

"My father wants me to see him. We have to sort this place."

"And will you?"

"What?"

"Dump me?"

250

She sorts out her bag again.

"Will you?"

"Did you attack her, Rooney?"

The voices turn on me.

"You attacked her, didn't you, didn't you?"

I turn away from her, get up and move to the window.

"There's no one…"

I ask Gerry to help me, to bring in the others.

Monday, Gerry leads the group in. I ask Stephenson if we can have a place to talk. He says to use the treatment room. I'm scared to go in there after the ECT, but he tells me there's nowhere else, he can watch me in there through the half glass door. Mairi pushes Walter in, John follows, then Gerry, then Peter.

"Alex was my friend, Mr Rooney," Peter says. "I want to help."

I smile, probably the first time for a while. He takes a position at the door, his broad shoulders blocking out the room from the ward staff standing outside. I refuse to go anywhere near the treatment bed. The nursing staff have their meetings in there. There's a stack of chairs, which they take as I do and place them round the room.

The voices are in my thoughts, affecting my concentration. I don't know what to say.

"The nutgroup have arrived," they say. "You're one of them, now. Not the leader, not the counsellor, the psycho-psychologist." They all laugh.

"Mr Rooney, we have had a discission."

"And what is it, John?"

"We have decided through discussion, Sean," Mairi says.

"And what's that?"

"We are going to," she looks at the others, "take action."

I think about this for a minute. Thank God, they're going to save me.

"You're going to save me?"

"Well, we hope so."

"You hope so."

Walter pushes his chair next to me.

"We're going to get him."

"Get who?"

He looks out through the half window.

"Doctor Death, Jamieson, of course."

"Thank God. When? I get my next ECT on Friday. He'll kill me then."

"We need to plan, Rooney," Mairi says. "It's not easy for a patient, a group of patients, to kidnap a consultant psychiatrist."

Hearing this nearly makes me laugh alongside the guffaws happening in my head.

"Kidnap him, then kill him?"

Mairi steps forward.

"No, Rooney, we can't kill him, no matter how good it would be in my book, but it wouldn't work and we'd all end up in big shit. We want to be free of him and free of this place, not incarcerated in the State Hospital for the rest of our lives."

"It wouldn't work, Mr Rooney," John agrees. "I've written it down."

"We kidnap him," Walter says. "Get him to confess, record it, pass him and the recording over to the authorities, and that's it. He's out of here and people are safe, you're safe, we're all safe."

"For the loser now," Gerry says, "will be later to win, for the times they are a changin'."

"I can help," I say.

They look at each other, as if to say, he'll help us kidnap a doctor, but he's off his head.

"OK, tell us," Mairi says.

Tuesday morning, Jackie phones. I take the phone into the treatment room.

"We've interviewed Agnes, Rooney."

"Right."

"She's pressing charges."

"Right."

"We've gone over the incident. She says you were drunk, hearing things which were telling you to attack her. We've no reason to disbelieve her."

"She's a liar, Jackie. I did nothing to her."

"She had stitches in the back of her head, Rooney."

"She did it herself."

"It'll go to court, Rooney."

"There's no evidence."

"There's enough, you were, are ill. You'll have your defence in court, however. I'm getting you a lawyer and we're sending a couple of DIs to charge you."

"Not doing it yourself, to be involved in my downward spiral?"

"I'm too close to you, Rooney."

"You're not close to me at all, Jackie."

"She talked to Donna and Archie."

"Oh, here we go."

"She says you've been stalking her, wanted her, seduced her, made her believe you would be together, demanded she falsify your report."

"And what about you now, policewoman Kaminski, climbing the greasy pole?"

"I've to concentrate on Timpson and his activities in the hospital."

"Give him my regards."

"I will."

"Jackie…" The phone goes dead. I bash it against the wall bringing in Stephenson and two nurses.

"Right, you, out," he orders. The two nurses get me by the arms and shove me in a seat in the sitting room. "Any more of it and you're off to the secure ward, you got it?"

I nod and slide down in my seat.

Tuesday afternoon, Stephenson allows me ten minutes with the group. We use the treatment room. I talk at them with my back to the door.

"As you know, he plays golf on Wednesday and Saturdays. You'll need to do it tomorrow. And you need to be successful because I have my next ECT on Friday. He'll kill me then if you fail. And don't be seen. Pull him into the woods from the path before he gets to the course where he meets Professor Owen. Tie him up using rope and plastic cable ties for his hands, tie them at the back. Use gaffer tape round his mouth, keep his nose free for air."

"Aye, we don't want to kill him," Gerry says.

"Walter will keep watch. You, Peter, Gerry helping, will grab him, Mairi and John will tie him up and muzzle him."

"I'll make sure he's good and tight and can't shout out," Mairi says.

"Use a patient wheelchair, stick him in it," I say. "Put a balaclava on him, a ward blanket around him, stick Walter's bunnet on his head. So, from the hospital, it'll look like you are pushing Walter."

"And where will we take him?" Mairi asks.

"Somewhere he won't be discovered, where you can look after him, get the confession."

"I know a place," Peter says.

"Where?"

"Best you don't know, Mr Rooney." I realise immediately I could blab it out in my drug induced stupor.

"What if he doesn't talk?" says Mairi.

"I'll make sure he does," Peter says, quietly.

No one doubts Peter's ability to do this.

Wednesday morning and two DI's arrive and charge me. They would have remanded me they say, had I not been already detained.

Wednesday afternoon, the lawyer, Shirley Ferguson, arrives. I'm pacing the ward looking out of the window, wondering how the kidnapping is going. She thinks it best if I admit the charge. She'll recommend a hospital order, and following assessments and another hearing I'll stay in hospital rather than end up in prison. I tell her to fuck off and do her job. I would be denying the charge.

She shakes her head and leaves, saying she would be back in touch when she got a date of the court hearing.

I call after her.

"Be too late, I'll be dead by then."

Thursday, Jackie arrives. We sit in the sitting room. She kneels by my chair and passes me some grapes and orange juice.

"What, no flowers, Jackie?"

"Don't push it, Rooney, this is not a romantic encounter."

"Oh, you're here to arrest me, take me to Barlinnie, Court, Carstairs?"

"I need to talk to you."

"And what've you to say to me I would want to hear?"

"Only Dad's taking a tough line on drugs and has heard of the dealing in the grounds of the hospital. He told me to stop the vans coming in here."

"Jackie, the hospital agreed it."

"Who agreed it, Rooney? I will find out if you had anything to do with it. You're in big enough shit as it is." I stay schtum. "I've interviewed Timpson. He says his resources in the hospital have been neutralised. What did he mean?"

"No drugs today, the ice cream van has gone away," I sing, mimicking Herman's Hermits, *No Milk Today*.

"I know there are people in here facilitating the sale of drugs to the patients. Who is it, Rooney?"

"Ah Jackie, you'd like to know."

"Rooney, there's illegal activity going on in here, the place's corrupt, and you're implicated in it. You're in big enough trouble."

"What else did the Godfather say?"

"Nothing, but we know he's in here."

I look around.

"Don't see any gang bosses in here, Jackie."

"You know what I mean."

"Is this all you want to say to me?"

"No, something which may concern you."

"And what is that?"

"Doctor Jamieson has disappeared."

I smile into my hands.

"Right."

"Yes, he went out for a game of golf yesterday and didn't come back. The hospital managers are very concerned. Completely out of character. He had meetings later that day. He never misses his meetings, apparently. His car is in the car park and his jacket and house keys in his locker."

"Apparently."

"Do you know anything, Rooney?"

The voices are whispering to me now. "Do you know anything, Rooney?"

"Only he's a murdering bastard and he intends to kill me."

"Well, he won't be killing you now, Rooney."

I hope not, I think. I imagine Jamieson tied to a chair in an outhouse or somewhere in the grounds. Peter's interrogating him, in the way the Paras did to captured Argentinian soldiers. I hope Jackie will soon be saying they've received a tape with Jamieson's confession, to have him arrested and me vindicated. Everything'll fall into place for me then. I'll be a hero for saving the patients of Hillwood Hospital. There'll be a lot of media attention. I'll be famous.

"You'll never be famous," arrives in my head. I'm not sure if it's my father or one of the others. "You're a nutter with delusions of grandeur. You're going nowhere except in a box out of this place."

"I asked Timpson about it," she says. "I'm convinced it has something to do with him, them." I smile. "We're bringing in a team, we need to find him."

She leaves and I'm sitting with a glaikit smile on my face.

Stephenson comes over.

"You seem happy with yourself today, Rooney."

"Aye, you could say that."

"Just to say, Dr Jamieson's on holiday and Professor Owen says you've to get your second ECT tomorrow, Friday. That'll take the smile off your face." He walks away with a smile on his.

I'm not too concerned now Doctor Death is off the scene. I'll be OK, he'll not be killing me tomorrow.

Gerry comes over and sits beside me.

"We did it, sir."

"I heard Gerry. Doctor J is… on holiday. How'd it go?"

Gerry looks around to ensure he isn't overheard.

"Peter managed to get some chloroform which helped. Grabbed him, chloroform cloth to his mouth, gaffer tape, into the chair, wrapped up, balaclava and blanket like you said, and off to…"

"Where, Gerry?"

"I've not to tell you, sir," he whispers. "In case…"

"I know, in case I blab in my sleep or when I'm drugged up, or when I'm under tomorrow when I'm getting my treatment."

"They're still giving you it?"

"Aye, 'fraid so."

"We're working on him, sir. Peter's good at it. He's sure he'll talk soon."

"Waterboarding, 240 volts applied to his testes, sleep deprivation, no doubt."

"Sir?"

"Nothing, just don't kill him."

"Said the joker to the thief, sir."

"Is Simmons not the thief, Gerry?"

"I've to be discharged soon, to a halfway house."

His twitching eyes indicate this's troubling him.

"Look after yourself, Gerry." I am worried at the way others had gone after being referred to the thief. My concerns are less now, however, now given Doctor Death is out of the way. Patients are safer now, surely.

CHAPTER 41

Friday, 20th of August, and I go passively, almost happily, to the treatment room for the ECT. I've slept well and feel good. Doctor J isn't around, so they'll not be killing me today.

They administer the anaesthetic and I slip into a deep sleep, pleasantly expecting to wake up in my bed in the dormitory, it all being over. It might even have some therapeutic effect. I have known some patients with intractable depression where it helped. It may help me too.

Then, I am looking down on my body. I'm up there, floating around with them.

"You are dead, Rooney," they are saying. "Look…"

I look down to a bizarre scene. I'm lying flat out on the treatment bed.

"Tommy, he's no' breathing," this fat nurse is saying.

"You are dead, son." I turn towards my father, his face before me. "You are done for. We all go the same way." He is laughing.

"Don't worry son," my mother is saying, "we'll be together now."

"He'll be fine." Stephenson clearly has no intention of saving me.

"Help me," I shout at them, not they can hear me.

"We need to get an ambulance," Betty Boop is shouting. "We need to help him. He's going."

"I'm no' going anywhere, Mammy, I don't want to go." I'm the wee boy she's taking by the hand, out of the toy department of Stirling Stevens department store off Argyle Street. "No, Mammy I don't want to…"

"You've got to go," the others are chanting. "You've got to go. Cheerio, cheerio, cheerio."

Boop pushes past Stephenson and starts doing CPR, pressing down on my chest.

I lose my out-of-body consciousness. Then I wake up, but not in my bed, in the ward 10 dormitory. I open my eyes to see the reminiscent paraphernalia of the A and E ward. I'm in the GRI again. I turn my head to see the monitors and the lines into my arms.

A nurse leans over me.

"Hello, Mr Rooney, you're back with us. The first time when you battered your head off the road in Hillwood, the second when we pumped your stomach to get the pills out of it."

"And this time?" I groan.

"This time, fortunately we saved your life again."

"What happened?"

"You died, Mr Rooney, you died."

"I died?"

"For over five minutes. The paramedics got to you in time. You were extremely lucky." "Don't do it again," she scolds me. "You're not a cat," she says, laughing.

Then it's Saturday, and a doctor arrives at my bedside.

"I have the results of the lab reports on your bloods," he says. "You had an extremely high concentration of drugs inside you."

"Prescribed or otherwise?"

"Prescribed."

"So much so to stop my heart?"

"I would say so, we are wondering about dosage."

"Dosage?"

"Either that or the mix."

"Mix?"

"The anaesthesia and the muscle relaxant. We'll be sending a report to your consultant at the hospital. Anyway, you're out of danger, you'll be transferred back today."

"Thank you, very kind of you Doctor."

Saturday afternoon, I find myself back in ward 10.

Gerry comes to my side as soon as I arrive. I can hardly stand and slump down on my chair.

"Are you OK, sir?"

"They tried to kill me again, Gerry. What about Jamieson?"

He shakes his head.

"Said nothing, sir. Peter used all of his tricks. Jamieson says he's not responsible for the deaths in the hospital. What do we do with him? We can't just let him go. He'll talk. We'll be arrested. We'll be sent to the State Hospital. Trouble in the City. Trouble in the… farm."

I think Gerry has just revealed through his Dylanism where they are keeping Jamieson.

"Calm down, Gerry. Let me think about it. Just keep him a bit longer until we can work something out."

Sunday, I convince Stephenson I need some air. He knows I'm in no fit state to run, to get out of the grounds, or to do anything to myself. He attaches Boop, however, to stay with me. We walk slowly through the grounds. The sun feels good on my skin. I have a walking aid and I feel weak. I sit on the bench and raise my face to the sun.

"It's a lovely day, Betty," I say.

"Sean, you know that isn't my name."

"You seem to be around a lot."

"I am, because I care," she says.

I look at her, this is a sensitive, caring face.

"Will you give me some time on my own?"

She looks at me.

"Of course, would you like an ice cream?"

"Yes, I say, it's a great day for an ice cream." I am sure we both know having an ice cream in the Castle has taken on a different meaning for patients since Timpson sent in his vans.

"OK, I'll be back shortly."

I wait until she goes along the path, then I gesture to Gerry who is in the trees.

"I got your note, sir."

Before I left the ward I slipped a note to Gerry to meet me in the grounds by the bench on the path.

"That's good Gerry, now take me."

He guides me off the path and we walk through the woods, to the old farm buildings, now unused and becoming derelict. We go to the old dairy where they used to make butter for the hospital, but also for sale in town.

"We're here, sir," Gerry says.

I look around.

"Not very safe, Jackie's guys would find this place, no problem."

"They tried, sir, but come inside and see."

He helps me inside and shuts the door behind him. "This way." He takes me by the arm through to the back of the dairy, which is empty except for some old wooden butter churns.

"Gerry?"

Next thing, he stamps five times on the wooden floor and pushes back the lino to reveal a hatch. It opens from beneath to reveal a set of wooden stairs, obviously some sort of store room, maybe used in the past for milk to keep it fresh before churning it into butter. I look down to see Peter who obviously released the lock on the trap door.

"Well hello, Mr Rooney," he says up to me. Gerry helps me down the stair.

"This way." Peter takes me to a door behind a large muslin sheet and inside as Gerry reinstates the sheet over the door and pulls it shut, bolting it from the inside.

There before me is Jamieson, his eyes covered in a bandana, his mouth by tape. He's tied to a chair in the middle of the room. There's a light on him, much like you would expect in an interrogation situation. I suddenly feel sorry for him. His head almost rests on his chest and he is breathing very heavily. He groans from behind the tape.

"Take it off," I say.

Peter looks at me. "Are you sure?"

"Aye, and the bandana."

"No, the bandana stays on. I don't want him to identify us later."

"Peter, I know you're a professional in these matters, but I am sure he would've recognised your voice. He'll know you are patients."

He takes the bandana off and the tape from Jamieson's mouth.

"Doctor Jamieson?"

"Sean Rooney," he says. "Are you here to save me?"

"Something like that." I see Peter looking at Gerry.

"They have been holding me here, they say I have been killing people."

"And have you, Doctor Jamieson?"

"Sean, you know I only help people."

"And what about the drugs?"

"I thought they would help the patients, keep them happy, so to speak."

"So to speak."

"You need to tell the hospital authorities, get the police, get me out of here."

"I'll get you out."

"Please, Sean."

"But before I do, I need a promise."

"What is it?"

"I need you to promise you'll say nothing about this."

"I can't do that, these are dangerous patients."

"They were working for me."

His voice increases two tones.

"Working for you, Sean?"

"Yes, I thought you were going to kill me."

"Kill you, and why would I do that?"

"I thought you were a killer."

"Do you still think that?"

I'm beginning to think the ECT has had some effect.

"No, but you need to promise if I'm going to get you out of here."

"Promise what?"

"Promise me you'll say you were taken by the mob. Tell the police they were trying to force you to accept drugs into the hospital."

"What if I don't and tell on these guys?"

"I'll tell the authorities about your links with Timpson, you agreeing to the hospital being supplied by drugs, your own drug addiction. Will that do?"

I see he's thinking about this.

"OK," he says.

"And you'll drop my section?"

He looks at me.

"You still have to go to court, they may recommend a hospital order."

"Let's cross that bridge, Doctor J. I promise I won't harm myself again. And—"

"You are really pushing it Sean. What?"

"No more ECT."

"OK, I'll talk to Professor Owen."

"Release him from his bounds," I tell Peter.

"Sean?"

"Doctor Jamieson?"

"Why did this happen? Why was I questioned on all the deaths in the hospital? Do you really think I was, in some way, responsible?" I don't answer. "Sean?"

"Yes?"

"How did the ECT go?"

I look at him. Is he being facetious or is he genuinely concerned?

"Not so good. I nearly died twice."

"Oh," he says.

Peter helps him out, walks him out of the old farm and onto the road, where he'll make his way back into the hospital.

Gerry and I make our way back. Nurse Boop is waiting for me, having ate both of our ice creams. "Sorry, Sean," she says. "I couldn't help it, they were melting."

We head up the corridor, Gerry to ward 8, me to ward 10.

Stephenson asks why we took so long. I tell him because the weather was so good and the nurse was very kind.

"Just don't push it with me, Sean," he says.

"What happened to me in there?" I ask him, pointing to the treatment room. "I need an explanation."

"Your heart stopped, Rooney, your heart."

"My heart, my arse, what happened? Why didn't you help me?"

"Eh?" He looks at me strangely, like how did I know that?

"What did A and E say?"

He pulls out my file.

"I have a report on your bloods from A and E. It says…"

His pause says there's something he is reluctant to reveal.

I grab it from him. Right inside there's a letter from the doctor who attended me at A and E. My eyes focus immediately on the first paragraph. 'Blood's taken from Mr Rooney indicate an extremely high level of succinylcholine or anaesthesia, suggest enquiry into ECT procedure at Hillwood Hospital.'

"High levels of succinylcholine or anaesthesia, Stephenson. What's this?"

"It's a short acting muscle relaxant, Rooney, it's used on everyone."

"But at what level, enough to stop a heart muscle perhaps?" I read from the report. "It's noted intoxication with the muscle relaxant succinylcholine is associated with severe hyperkalaemia, arrhythmia, and cardiac arrest, can also lead to a potentially lethal respiratory paralysis. Well, Stephenson?"

"Give me the file, Rooney, I'll look into it."

I give him the file.

"Aye, you better well do, pal."

I'm extremely tired and ask if I could be allowed to go to bed. He can hardly refuse me and I sleep for the rest of the day.

By Monday, I feel better, until I get a visit from Stanley.

"Not like you to visit, Stanley?"

"No, I'm no' into visiting these places."

"What do you want?"

"Alby wanted me to talk to you."

"Right."

"He mentioned you still owe him."

"Just tell me what he said, Stanley."

"He says he's seriously disturbed about business at the Castle, the agreement you made with him has failed."

I get very close to him so no one can hear me.

"Stanley, it was the polis."

"He knows that, Rooney, but—"

"What else did he say, Stanley?"

"Your wuman, Jackie."

"I know, she interviewed him about the drugs in hospital and put a stop to the vans."

"Aye, she did."

"And what do you want me to do?"

"Sort her out, Rooney, you've to sort her out."

I look at him.

"Stanley, I don't feckin' own her, she's a fuckin' police officer."

"I'm only telling you what he wants, Rooney. Mind, you owe him."

"Get to fuck, Stanley."

"Rooney?"

"What."

"Just don't fuck with Timpson, it won't end well."

Jamieson arrives in the ward and I see him talking to Stephenson. He leaves, hesitantly casting a glance my way.

Stephenson approaches me. "Doctor Jamieson has discharged your section. Apparently your mental health appears improved, so we reviewed your treatment plan."

"No more ECT?"

"No more ECT, for now."

"I am free to go."

"No, we think you should stay. You're still vulnerable and you still have the offence. You'll be going to Court."

"And what if I just leave?"

"We'll section you again."

Wednesday, I meet the group outside in the grounds, near the bench. The weather is warm and sunny. We sit on the grass. Peter has become a member of the group, not that anyone of us would disagree.

"So, it's not Doctor Jamieson?" I say.

"What if he was lying?" asks Mairi.

"Well, short of removing his toenails, we don't know if he is," Peter says. "He would've talked, I think. I told him I would visit his wife and family in the West End."

"Persuasive argument, Peter," I say.

"So, who is it?" asks Walter.

"The thief," slurs Gerry.

John has his notebook out.

"The thief," he says, as he writes.

"Who is the thief, Gerry?"

"The one who steals the patients," he says. "I've to go to the place on Friday, the thief says. Sir."

I look at the others, I see they're thinking what I'm thinking. Gerry sits down, then drops back on the grass.

"Gerry, are you all right?"

"Jesus, he could be next," Mairi says, "and you too, Rooney."

Gerry is looking skyward, smiling a completely unconnected smile.

"He's out of it," I say.

"He'll be back to get you, Rooney," she adds. "He's not finished with you."

"Who, who is?" Walter asks. "Who are we talking about, if it's not Doctor Death?"

"We up the ante," I say.

"Up the aunty," John writes,

"No, up the ante, John. It's a saying, means we increase the pressure."

"How do we do this, Rooney?" Mairi asks.

"I'll think about it, but we need to be careful and we need to be ready to move when we know."

"Just say the word, Mr Rooney. I'll walk him to the loch and he won't come out."

"Thanks Peter, but when we find him out we have to hand him over to the authorities."

Peter looks disappointed. We break up. I help Gerry to his feet. He's mumbling the thief stuff, but he's completely incomprehensible. Mairi helps me get him back to the ward. I intend talking to Stephenson about him, which I do.

"He's been having panic attacks, Rooney," Stephenson says. "He's het up about going out on Friday. He's anxious. Doctor Jamieson has given him sedation. It'll help him."

"Oh, It'll help him," I say.

This afternoon I call Robin Crawford, a feature editor at the *Evening Times*.

I met Robin when he interviewed men in the Special Unit at Barlinnie last year. Described as the most remarkable press conference in the history of the Scottish prison system, it took place in the Special Unit at Barlinnie, when twenty-five journalists fired questions at four prisoners who had been among the most disruptive in Scotland. Crawford was one of the journalists. I was on a placement visit and he's the man I should talk to now, I think.

I also call Alby Timpson.

"Stanley says I owe you, Alby?"

"Correct, son. What you going to do?"

I explain to him the market at the hospital is out of my hands. Hubert is moving in.

"She's your women, Sean, you need to tell her."

I shake my head.

"Alby, your daughter."

"What about my daughter?"

"She's at risk."

"How?"

"She has an eating disorder."

"Bugger off son, she is thin, but she's always been thin."

"Alby, her hair is thin and brittle, her skin is furry; soft, downy hair on her arms and legs. She is deficient in essential nutrients. Has she been to the doctor?"

"No, why?"

"Because she may be lacking potassium, iron, other essential nutrients. If she doesn't get them she could die. She may need to go to hospital for an IV."

"Don't be daft, Rooney, she just needs a good feed. She eats well."

"Alby, she'll be bringing it up afterwards, it's classic behaviour. She's at serious risk, her heart could give up. You need to get her to a doctor immediately."

There's silence as the phone goes down.

"I'll be giving my story to the *Evening Times*," I tell Stephenson.

"What story?"

"The one about me being nearly killed in here and the other patients who died. The story will be titled, 'How the Castle kills its Children.'"

"Oh, very catchy," he says.

In no time, Jamieson's at my side.

"You can't do it, Sean, we can't have this kind of exposure."

"The world needs to know about this place, Dr J."

He gets close, so no one can hear him.

"You can't tell them about the—"

"Drugs, Doctor J? No, I won't mention the drugs. I just want to talk about how patients have died here, especially those who were identified for discharge."

"I think this is your paranoia showing itself again, Sean. I thought you were getting a bit better. I'll talk to the editor."

"I have a feature writer who's prepared to do the story."

"Won't go anywhere if you are viewed to be ill, Sean."

"I'll take the chance."

He shakes his head and walks away.

I'm on my guard now. I watch everything. No one will walk me to the loch, make me top myself, try to kill me on the ECT bed. But I know they'll try to stop me talking, and Gerry, leaving on Friday, could be next on their list. I go to bed this night, half asleep, half with an eye on anyone coming into the dormitory, also watching out for Gerry. I fall asleep though, and wake with the feeling someone is there. I sit up in bed and there's the nun sitting next to my bed reading her Bible, humming away to herself.

"Yes, sister," I say, "can I help you?"

She just smiles and blesses me. I look over at Gerry's bed. He's not there. I check my watch. It's ten past three in the morning. I get up and put on my clothes. I check the toilet, he isn't there. I see Stephenson at the head of the ward. He's well asleep. I pass him and go out into the corridor. I see the nun disappear down the corridor turning at the Pass to head up the west corridor, presumably heading for the Chapel.

I approach the Pass and notice the door to the upstairs, to Admin, the doctors' rooms, and the Physician Superintendent's chambers, is open.

I think I hear Gerry.

"Gerry, is this you?" I go up the stair as stealthily.

I hear his voice more plainly now.

"Gerry?"

The door to the Professor's office is open slightly. I look through the crack in it. No pushing in here to have security drag me back to the ward.

Then I hear Owen.

"You will not manage son, you are safer here, you'll fail. You'll die if you go there."

"There must be some way out of here," Gerry is saying, quietly.

I whisper to myself, "Said the joker to the thief."

"Yes, there is my friend," Owen says.

"Says the thief to the joker," I add to myself.

Gerry is slurring, "The hour is getting late."

"Yes, son, the hour is late, we can walk together out in the moonlight, where it's quiet, and—"

"And we'll walk down to the loch, Professor Owen," I say, moving into the room. "Or, I'll escort you to a tree in the woods, where I'll help you hang yourself. Like you did Alex."

He turns to face me, looking surprised.

"And why would I have done that to Alex, Sean?"

"Because he was terrified of being transferred to the State Hospital."

Gerry is sitting on a seat facing the desk.

"Are you OK, Gerry?" I say.

He lifts his head and looks at me. "The thief, sir," he slurs.

"You have no right to be here, Sean," Owen says. "I'll call—"

"Security? Oh yes, and how will you explain why you have a patient here at this hour?"

"He came here."

"Oh yeah, and you are about to walk him down to the loch and encourage him to take a swim?" He looks stunned. "Nothing to say, Professor Owen?"

I get Gerry to his feet, out of the room, down the stairs, and back to the ward. Stephenson wakes as we arrive.

"What the hell are you doing out of the ward?" he asks me, not Gerry, as if he knows Gerry was already out of the ward.

"Ask Professor Owen," I say.

Thursday, Robin Crawford arrives for the interview. We go into the grounds to the bench. I recount the events of the last months, the drugs, the corruption, the abuse of the patients, the unexplained deaths, the ghosts, everything. I blurt it all out.

"Hold on, wait a minute," Crawford says. He can't keep up as he tries to get it all down on his notebook. "Sean, one thing at a time, please."

Then security arrives.

"You are not authorised to be here," the big one says.

"I don't need to be authorised," Crawford says.

"I'm authorising you," I say.

"You are a mentally deficient patient," the small one says.

"I am a mentally ill patient," I say.

Crawford is aghast.

"I'll be back once I check this out with my editors," he says. "If we need authorisation, I'll get it."

"And I'll have the whole story of this place ready for you," I call after him.

"You have to go back to the ward," the small one says.

They escort me back. Stephenson is waiting for me.

"Professor Owen says you have to complete your ECT treatment, Sean."

"I nearly died the last time."

"We've gone over your case and checked it against the report from the consultants at A and E. We have to take particular care. We agreed it with the Mental Welfare Commission. So all's well, you'll be fine."

"When?"

"Tomorrow, Friday, as usual."

"Tomorrow, Friday, I'll meet my maker," I say.

I call Jackie and tell her. She says I'll be OK, I've to go along with it. I say to Walter to tell the group. I spend the night writing out my story for the Evening Times, to be passed to Robin Crawford should I die before I see him next.

CHAPTER 42

It's Friday, the 27th of August, and it's ECT day. They take me into the treatment room. I've no doubt I'm going to die this day.

The room is full. They're all here for the execution: Professor Owen, Tommy Stephenson, Doctor Jamieson, the Chaplain, the nun, Betty Boop, and two other nurses.

The nurses tie me to the bed, using the leather restraints this time, tight across my chest, holding my arms, and across my legs. I resign myself to my fate. I see my ghosts in the corner and my mother and father. They're all here to witness my demise.

To zonk me out, Stephenson pops a couple of pills in my mouth, then draws the muscle relaxant and the anaesthesia into a hypodermic as they stick the rubber thing in my mouth.

Owen leans over me. "You're in safe hands, Mr Rooney," he says.

"Oh, I'll be going to a better place."

"Put your faith in God."

"God was never a psychopathic murderer, Professor Owen. Don't worry, though, I've written this all up and when I'm gone it's going to the *Evening Times*."

"What, you referring to this?" Stephenson is holding up my report. "I found it in your locker. Will I dispose of it, Professor Owen?"

"Yes, Tommy, the ravings of a disturbed patient, not fit for sharing with anyone."

"You fucker." I try to get out of the bed, but I'm held tight. I feel the medications, deadly drugs more like, entering my arm to course its way into my brain, to stop my heart. I can't get the words out. "I'll, I'll…."

I hear them though and they are there talking about me. "He'll no longer be a thorn in our side, he'll harm our programme, helping our patients to the better place."

"I'll fuckin' haunt you, you bastards." I slur my words as I drift into unconsciousness.

271

I'm floating up and looking down. I can hear and see everything. They are there too: Myra, Joan, Alex, and a smattering of other female ghosts, including some children. They are moving around the room as if they are floating too.

The Chaplain is blessing me and the nun is singing *Faith of my Fathers*. I'm of no doubt I'll be heading soon to the mortuary.

But just then, as I look down, the door bursts open and there's Peter pushing his way forward knocking all aside. Betty Boop grabs the hypodermic from Stephenson.

John is at Peter's side.

"We have it all recorded, this is patientracide, patientracide," he is shouting.

Mairi pulls out a tape recorder from under the bed. Stephenson tries to grab it as Walter arrives and pins him to the wall with his wheelchair.

"Get in here." Walter is shouting out into the ward. "Help us, they're trying to kill him."

Even Gerry is in the melee.

"Fire, fire," he calls, as the fire alarm goes off all around the hospital.

A porter rushes in.

"Fire in ward 49," he's calling out. "The end of the west corridor is in flames."

"The Castle's on fire?" I groan.

They all rush out.

Nurses arrive from everywhere, and the security men arrive. This's a serious riot. Patients are turning over beds, throwing chairs at the windows, smashing everything. Mairi releases me, and Peter lifts me into a wheelchair. The two security men try to stop him. He lays out one of them.

Then the cavalry arrive. Timpson walks into the ward with a team of guys. One cracks the other security man with a cosh over his head, another floors Stephenson, leaving him sobbing in a corner. Walter reaches down and takes my report from him.

"You alright, Rooney," Timpson says. "Did I get here in time? I did what you said, I took my daughter to the doctor. He whipped her into hospital, said she would have died if he hadn't. I owe you now."

Jackie arrives with a squad.

"OK, guys, I'll take over here," she says to Timpson. He nods and backs off. "Professor Donald Owen, I am arresting you in connection with the deaths of Oliver Turnbull, Myra Higgins, Joan Trainor, and Alex Barr."

"And John MacDougal, my father," Mairi calls.

"Indeed," Jackie says. "And Thomas Stephenson, I am arresting you in connection with the abuse of and the aiding and abetting in the deaths of patients at Hillwood Hospital."

Doctor Jamieson arrives.

"I only tried to—"

"Yes, Doctor Jamieson, you too. Take him," she says.

People are being dragged off. Everyone is out in the corridor, including Donna, Archie, and Agnes from the department, and Simmons from social work.

"Agnes," Jackie says. "I'll be back to you to discuss you perverting the course of justice and making wrongful claims regarding the incident with Mr Rooney."

"This is disgraceful," Simmons has the audacity to say.

Timpson hits him hard, the blow sending him across the corridor into the wall. Then he turns to Jackie.

"Detective Inspector Kaminski, we have information we'll give to you which'll make sure Mr Simmons never works in social work again."

Then I hear the fire brigade sirens as the fire tenders arrive in the car park.

The security men are yelling, "Do not go up the west corridor, it is on fire. Get out, out. Everyone, go up the east corridor, the fire escape door is open."

"I must get to my office," Owen calls.

"No chance," Jackie, says. "You're going to London Road Police station. Take him," she orders the officers.

"Jackie," I say, "we have evidence."

"Not sure, Rooney, all pretty circumstantial, enough maybe to press charges, but doesn't mean it'll stick in court."

Everyone, the patients, the staff are going up the east corridor, but I'm in the wheelchair, aided by Peter and Gerry, heading down the corridor. We want to get to Professor Owen's office before the fire does. As we move through the Pass, the smoke is engulfing the west corridor. Firemen are going about their business, heading up there with hoses, presumably fire tenders are at the other end and outside ward 49 spraying water in the windows.

I get out of the wheelchair and Peter helps me up the stairs, where we enter Owen's office.

"His desk," I say, "check his drawers."

"What am I looking for?"

"Files, evidence."

He can find nothing in them. The smoke is now making its way in. We need to get out fast. Then I recall what the Professor said the day Jamieson introduced me to him. "This is where I keep my personal files," he said at the time.

"Behind the curtain, Peter."

Peter finds the door.

"It's locked."

"Break it open."

Peter lifts a marble pot stand and cracks it against the door which splinters, a second blow bursts the lock and the door opens.

We go in and see shelves of files, his personal files. There are alphabetical letters on each shelf pointing to the files of patients. I go to H and find the file on Myra Higgins, ward 29.

I open it, and there's a covering letter from her father, dated 5th of May 1935.

Dear Physician Superintendent,

Please receive my daughter into your care, she is deranged and needs to be incarcerated. I can no longer look after her. In addition, you must take her bastard child and pass it to whatever adoption agency will take it.

Yours,

John Higgins.

I close it and hand it to Peter and follow the shelves to find files on Joan Trainor, then John MacDougal, Oliver Turnbull, Helga Shultz, and some of the others. I hand them to Peter, then go farther into the room where I find some archivist material from the early days of the hospital. There are some ancient leather-bound volumes and one immediately catches my eye, 'Hillwood Asylum'. I open it and in the introduction my eyes are drawn to the introductory paragraph which I read:

"Hillwood Asylum was built on the site of The Magdalene Institution." I read on. "The Magdalene Institution and the Hillwood Asylum were only possible because of the work of the Good Shepherd Sisters in North East Glasgow. I'll have this," I say, putting it under my arm.

Then as I turn, I see shelf R. "It wouldn't be there would it?" I ask myself. I have to lift off a few to find it, but there it is, Mary Rooney, patient number 17638, 22 May, 1927. This is my mother's file.

I add it to the pile in Peter's arms. Then, just as we leave and by the door, I see it, a black box file 'A Better Place'. A better place, where have I heard this before? We go back into the office to find the curtains ablaze.

Peter is agitated, not usual for a Para. "We need to get out, Rooney, the fire is spreading fast."

"I had to help, sir." Gerry has a can of lighter fuel and a lighter in his hands.

"You, Gerry, ward 49?"

"It's all over now baby blue."

"Aye, burn some more, the arsonist strikes again," I say. "Jesus, let's get out of here."

We get out as the fire takes hold of the rest of the room. Peter drops the weighty files on the wheelchair and covers them with a blanket he found in the room. I wonder if it had been the one Myra had wrapped around her that day I saw her there. I feel sufficiently recovered to walk. We get downstairs and the smoke is now engulfing the Pass. It's impossible to see up the west corridor. Patients and staff are being ushered out of the main door into the car park.

Major Incident Planning has been triggered. Buses arrive to take the patients to community centres in the local area.

"I'm going nowhere," Walter says.

We all head back to my room in the nurses' home, even managing to get Walter and his wheelchair up the stairs. We squeeze in, Walter, Gerry, Peter, Mairi, John, and me.

We pull out the files.

I open the 'A Better Place' box file, and there are individual 'transfer plans' on over a hundred or so patients, numerically in order dated from the early 1960s to the current day. The transfer plan is a one sheet writeup describing their ultimate discharge to a community-based setting, or sending them to 'a better place'.

I read:

"Each sheet is concluded, 'It is my clinical opinion this vulnerable patient would not cope in a community-based setting, the patient's suffering would be inconsistent with the fine values this fine institution and our ethical and religious responsibility. We have no alternative but to ensure the patient goes to God.'"

I pause trying to take this in.

"It's signed," I say, "by Professor Donald Owen, MA BD PhD DD, and dated. And, it's countersigned by the Reverend James Gordon." Jesus, I need to get this to Jackie.

"Is this enough to convict the bastards?" Mairi asks.

"Jamieson, Stephenson, Simmons, etcetera?" Walter adds.

"Instruments and lackies," I say. "Obviously going along with the physician superintendent's determination. Just following orders."

I open my mother's file. It has a similar covering report dated 13 April, 1962. I read the summary, which is similar to the others.

"This vulnerable patient would not cope in a community-based setting." I sit down on my bed. "They killed her," I say.

My father always said I had killed her, saying she took her life because she could not cope with the guilt of not being able to look after me and I was responsible for her suicide. Now I know, the Professor helped her take her own life.

I see a concluding paragraph and read it.

"My clinical advice to Mrs Rooney is, it is best for her husband and son for her to take the medication, then they would be spared the shame and disgrace of her mental breakdown and a failed discharge into the community. She, herself, would be spared the damage caused by another failed return to the circumstances which are predisposing her illness. It is best for all she goes to a better place."

"Fuck," I say. I can't control the emotions arising within me. It's like a tsunami overcoming me, as I realise this led to my mother's death.

"You alright, Rooney." Mairi has seen the blood drain from my face.

I can't reply. She opens her father's file.

"It's the same," she says. "My clinical opinion, no alternative but to ensure the patient goes to God."

Gerry opens Alex's file.

"Same here, sir," he says, then opens his own. "Same letter for me too."

I open the Hillwood Asylum book and read the introduction.

"Hillwood Mental Asylum was built on the site of the original Magdalene Asylum in the rural outskirts of Glasgow, the burgeoning second city of the Empire." I read on. "The Magdalene institution was created for the repression of vice and the reformation of penitent females." It says, "Nearly five thousand young women had resided in the institution since 1859," being, as described, "rescued from a life of shame and restored to society." Enslavement, more like.

Then I read the institution was run by the Nuns of the Order of the Good Shepherd.

In the back of the book I find an old map of the Magdalene Institution which was overlayed with an old map of Hillwood Asylum. I see the Magdalene was previously sited on the left-hand corner of the hospital, where wards 49, 47, 45, 43, 41, and 39 are now.

Then I find a rough map which identifies a graveyard in the grounds of the institution which contains the mass grave of former inmates of its Magdalene Laundry. In the inside cover there's an old newspaper cutting of 1914, stating the remains of more than one hundred babies had been discarded in an area near the hospital grave-yard. Presumably, illegitimate children who had died in the institution's orphanage. My immediate thought is, had this been discovered today, there would have been a massive scandal necessitating a major public investigation.

According to the cutting, however, because the find was in the early days of the First World War, a hush-up was required; as many of the woman, and presumably the dead children from the institution orphanage, were associated with service men from the Gallowgate Barracks. Many of these men would have been heading to the Western Front and the last thing the military would have wanted was a scandal which would affect soldier morale. Also, the fact the dead women and the babies, previously in the care of the Good Shepherd Sisters, were buried in unconsecrated ground, would have also been a major blow to the Order, which nursed wounded soldiers at the front. Hence the mass graveyard with its secrets was hidden away from prying eyes.

"Jesus," I say.

"What?" Mairi asks.

"I'm reading here the Castle was built on the site of an old Magdalene Institution and the mass graves of the women incarcerated there and their babies' remains are in an old graveyard, which according to this map is in the area of the current graveyard."

"Oh really," Walter says, "where?"

I open out the map.

"On the left-hand corner of the hospital, where wards 39 to 49 are now, where the fire started."

"Wow," Mairi says. "I know about these places. They had Magdalene Laundries in Ireland and there was appalling treatment of women and babies. I didn't know these places were in Scotland."

"Not anymore," I say.

Just then John Scott batters on the door.

"Rooney, you have to see this," he says.

We go out into the car park. The hospital is on fire, all of it. The roof is ablaze and flames are licking out of the admin block windows, like they are eyes aflame, like a face, the Castle's face. There is a screeching sound, like a wailing coming from within.

"Did they get everyone out?" I ask him.

"As far as we know, the fire drills worked."

We stand looking on. There is something final in this sight, something has ended there in the Castle, something has gone, something has died, but no more will death be a regular occurrence. In its own death throes it's giving off noises more associated with a person fighting to survive: groaning, moaning, crying.

"Can you hear them?" Walter asks.

"What, Walter?"

"The children, do you hear them?"

I can't hear children, but the old timbers are crackling, squeaking, groaning, as they bend, break, and burn. Roofs and floors are collapsing in.

The flames lick high into the night and smoke billows like a blanket over the sky.

I arrange for Walter, Peter, John, Mairi, and Gerry to stay in the nurses' home for a few nights until I can find them suitable accommodation.

We gather the next day in the grounds and Jackie joins us. We sit on the bench looking at the corpse that was once the hospital. The roof has gone and it now looks more like a destroyed castle, its towers now more acutely reminiscent of 13th-century battlements.

"I need to talk to you, Rooney, alone," Jackie says.

"I want to talk to you too, Jackie," Mairi says. "I want them prosecuted for killing my father."

"Be sure I'll be getting back to you on that, Mairi."

Jackie gestures she wants me to walk with her down the path away from the group.

"I'll be expecting a conviction, Ms Kaminski," Mairi adds.

Jackie and I walk along the path.

"Will you be arresting Reverend Gordon?" I ask her.

"There's no indication he caused harm to anyone."

"He countersigned the bloody letters, Jackie."

"We need more than letters, Rooney, we need actual evidence, such as would stand up in court."

"So, the Castle has gone with all its secrets."

"I guess so, at least whatever was happening in there is no more."

"You arrested them."

"I got a call from Mairi. She said they were about to kill you."

"You have Owen, Jamieson, and Stephenson in custody."

"On suspicion, for interview, seemed the right thing to do. We'll have to release them if we can't pin anything on them."

"The files, the letters?"

"Yes, we will look at them and if there is anything incriminating in them, we'll take them into consideration."

"They tried to kill me, does that not count for anything?"

"We never got the contents of your IV to confirm the contents. We went back in just as the fire took hold and couldn't find it."

"Someone took it. Evidence of massive doses of succinylcholine to stop my heart. If this isn't incriminating what is? And what about the tape recording?"

"All it said was, 'He'll no longer be a thorn in our side, he'll harm our programme, helping our patients to the better place.' What does it say, you have been a pain to the hospital management team and to the discharge programme, of course you were? Are you still paranoid, Rooney?"

"I'm feeling better since the ECTs, not that I would recommend it."

"Still seeing things, hearing things?"

"Not since the ECT."

"What about the placement?"

"Donna and Archie and the team have decanted to the local Health Centre, as have the social work department, Bill Simmons, etcetera."

"I still have to talk to Timpson. The placement?"

"I've to check in with Donna and Archie."

"Give up the course, Rooney, you're not cut out for it."

"No?"

"You're too unpredictable."

"What about us, Jackie?"

"Get yourself sorted, your drinking, drugs; get on your medication and we'll see."

"What about Agnes?"

"Are you two over?"

"We were never anything, Jackie. She was just—"

"A fling, a fuck, an infatuation?"

"A mistake, Jackie."

"Aye, I agree with you there, a massive mistake."

"Shirley Paterson, your lawyer did you a favour there."

"Right?"

"Aye, got Agnes to drop her charges, she said she had fabricated things. She has form, did it before with her husband, said he had raped her to get a divorce, to get custody of Gerry."

"I know, I was trying to tell you it was all shit."

"Not all shit, Rooney, she was in your room on your bed. Anyway, Shirley will explain."

"Agnes also fabricated my report, to say Donna recommended a pass of my placement."

"Well, that's all gone now, Rooney. Like I say, time to get out."

I leave her there and go back to the group.

"We don't have any evidence folks," I say.

"What about all the stuff in the files, the recording, you being nearly killed," Mairi says. "Gerry drugged up, ready to be walked into the loch."

"Another patient heading through Heaven's Gate."

"Very apt, Walter."

"Gerry?"

Gerry looks around at all of us, one by one.

"I had to burn it down," he says.

Mairi pulls out a spliff.

"I need this," she says. "Gerry, a light?"

Gerry pulls out his tin of lighter fuel and his lighter.

"Gerry, fuck's sake, you'll end up in the State."

He looks at me. I snatch the lighter fuel and the lighter from him.

"I won't do it again, sir."

"Aye, no more feckin' burn, baby burn, Gerry?"

"Jesus, Gerry, there'll be an inquiry into the fire."

"Electrical fire, no doubt, Rooney," Walter says. "Old wiring in ward 49. I remember the porter telling me this very thing."

"Aye," Mairi agrees, "auld wiring."

"And what about Owen's office?"

"The fire eventually got to it, Rooney. It was inevitable."

"No one needs to know, Rooney," Peter says.

"No one needs to know," John repeats. "I will conclude in my report to the management team the hospital posed a risk to the patients, a fire risk, an unsafe environment."

They all laugh.

The next couple of days is a good time for the group. We get to know each other in a new, fresh, more healthy way. We eat together, relax together, and feel more settled, as if a great stress has been removed from us.

I've been to see Donna and Archie. All has come out, Agnes falsifying the report. They sympathise with my situation but suggest I should leave the course. I try to explain I would still make a good psychologist, given the chance.

Archie says, cruelly, I think, that since I arrived there, there had been chaos in the hospital, drugs were introduced; and, although nothing was attributable, I had manipulated a vulnerable group of patients, which was unforgivable for a professional. That there has been no evidence of any foul play by Professor Owen, Doctor

Jamieson, or Mr Stephenson.

I'm out on my ear, so to speak, and I've a couple of days to pack up and leave. It's Monday, the 6th of September. I've to leave the home by Wednesday, the 8th of September.

I need to go to the Castle, I have to. However, security have put up fences around the hospital and No Entry signs are everywhere. I go around to the back of the hospital, to the back door of the west corridor. The fence is open to allow removal of anything salvageable inside, which isn't very much, given the fire raged for a whole day. I move carefully through the door and into the corridor.

The walls are blackened and peeling, the windows shattered and gone. Blackened remains of burned wood are everywhere. I go into ward 49, now a burned-out disaster area. It's vacant, not even a ghost. I walk down into the corridor and into the Chapel, which, because it sat between the corridors, is intact, possibly the only place still with a roof in the whole hospital.

I move inside.

Everything is covered in soot and the floor is awash with water from the firemen's hoses.

I kind of expect to see the Chaplain there, so I'm on my guard, but I heard he had been moved to a Mission Hall in the City.

I'm about to leave through the other door into the east corridor when I see her. She's sitting at the end of the pew. It's dark and smoky still but it is her, the nun. I move towards her. I want to thank her. I didn't think she had anything to do with my maltreatment and she always seemed to be there when I needed someone to be there, more often than not singing *Faith of Our Fathers*.

As I stand over her she lifts her head and I see a kind, gentle smile, from an incredibly life worn face.

"Are you alright?"

She nods.

"Are you?"

I also nod and smile. I ask her if she'll regret having to leave the hospital.

"My job is over here."

I need to know more about her.

"Were you here long?"

"For over seventy years."

I realise she must be in her eighties.

"Seventy years would mean you came here as a child." She nods. "You would have seen many things."

"Many things, many people. I am the longest surviving patient here."

What, a patient? She's a patient.

"You're a patient?"

"I came here when I was fifteen."

"Your habit?"

"Something I picked up. I was a nun you know."

"Sister Lilias, from the Good Shepherds." She smiles. "And you were allowed—"

"To go anywhere in the hospital. I didn't cause any problems."

I look at her, I'm not sure whether to believe her or not. People take on a strange persona in this place.

"Oh, right," I say.

"You were next to go, you know."

"What?"

"In the treatment room. I was there."

"I know, I saw you."

"I took this." She holds up a vial. "They were going to put this in your arm."

"Can I have it?"

"You won't say anything?"

I look at her. She looks scared all of a sudden.

"No, don't worry. Where will you go?"

"I can't go anywhere, this is where I live. I've been here all my life."

"But you can't stay here, there's nothing left."

"Then I'll die here."

I can't leave her here with the ghosts.

"You'll come with me."

"No, I won't. I'll stay right here."

She's not going to move for me, but I can't leave her there, in this toxic environment. What do I do? I'll talk to the Rottweiler and John Scott. She'll have a room in the female side of the nurses' home. She'll have it for as long as she needs it.

I see Jackie in The Horseshoe Bar.

I'm staying off the drink, she has a glass of wine. We take up our normal place at the back of the bar. At 104 feet, apparently this grand Victorian bar is the longest in Europe and merits an architectural listing all of its own. I ask Jackie about the vial the nun had given to me. I asked her to have it analysed.

"The stuff was about to go into my vein."

"It's Succinylcholine. How do you know it was going to go into your arm?"

"Because, I saw it."

Her look says, 'not good enough'.

"It's SUX," I say. I researched it. I know the amount required to provide adequate muscle relaxation during ECT is 0.9 mg per kg. How much was in it?"

"100 mg."

"100 mg," I repeat. I read from my notes. "100 mg of SUX will depolarize, as it is described, every muscle in the body of a 70 kg man. That's me, in about 20 seconds. After which a patient would not be able to take another breath for at least five minutes. So without assisted ventilation, I would have been toast."

"Where did you get the vial?"

"From a nun."

She laughs, spraying wine from her mouth.

"From a nun?"

"Right."

"Would she testify she saw this about to be put into your arm?"

"I don't know, it would identify her."

"Rooney, you are talking about a High Court hearing here, with QCs and expert witnesses. If you're thinking of a raising a case against doctors you really need to be able to establish definitively the stuff about to put in your arm was a lethal dose. This is serious legal shit."

"I know."

"I need to talk to her, where is she?"

"In the hospital."

"No one is in the hospital."

"She won't leave. "

"You need to get her out, she'll die in there."

"I know, I've asked Gerry to take her in some food and water. I'm going back in tomorrow to see she's OK."

"I'll go with you."

"The files?"

"All part and parcel of any case that is made. You have to establish intent to cause harm or kill. High Court stuff, Rooney."

"What about Owen, Jamieson, Stephenson?"

"We had to let them go. Truth be told Rooney, I arrested them because I was worried about you more than I was convinced they were trying to kill you. I was playing safe."

"Does the Professor know we got the files from his office?"

"No, not yet. Keep your powder dry, Rooney. Let's see where this goes. And what about you, what now?"

"Well, without any evidence or conviction, I'm just a raving lunatic not fit for a professional role."

She smiles. "As I have said all along, Rooney."

"Bill Simmons. Timpson said he had information to make sure he never works in social work again."

"I talked to him about this."

"Tell me."

"It's confidential, Rooney."

"Thanks, Jackie."

"Aw shut up, Rooney. Again, no evidence of anything. He said Simmons was doing something he shouldn't have been doing. But again, no evidence."

"Thanks, Jackie."

I go back to the nurses' home and the group are still up and sitting in the common room. Mairi says they all have to attend the local health centre for their medication and are not to leave the nurses' home until alternative accommodation can be found.

Walter says Bill Simmons has been in touch and many male patients including himself are to go to the Great Eastern, a massive male homeless persons' hostel in Duke Street. Similar arrangements are to be found for female patients, in female hostels in the East End.

I explain The Three Amigos, as Peter calls them, Owen, Jamieson, and Stephenson, have been released.

"I know," Mairi says, "they're working out of Duke Street Hospital."

"Well that's that then," Walter says. "The Castle is no more, anything the Castle did is no more, anything the Three Amigos did—"

"Is no more," John says.

"Trouble no more," Gerry adds.

"Dylan Bootleg series," Peter says.

"And they fucking get away with everything," Mairi says. "My father, Alex, Joan, Myra, Helga, all the rest."

"We have the files and the letters on everyone," I say.

"The law will protect them," Walter says. "It always does for the powerful. No one protects the weak."

"I'll get the bastards," Peter says.

"And I'll help," Gerry says. "Alex was my friend."

"Look, kidnapping is one thing, but murder will only get you locked up for life."

"Not if it's done right. Alex was my friend too."

I look at this ex-Para. I have no doubt he has the ability to do this very thing.

"No, Peter, it's not the way."

Even though I say this, I doubt my authority to tell him not to do anything.

Jackie and I go to see the nun. She's not in the Chapel, where she was the last time I saw her. We tread carefully down the west corridor and see her coming out of what is left of ward 29.

"Hello, Sister Lilias." She stops and looks at me, then at Jackie. She doesn't say anything. "Can we talk to you?"

She walks past us and heads towards the Chapel. We follow her into the Chapel, she takes her seat at the end of the pew.

I ask her if she is OK. She nods.

"Where did you sleep last night?"

"In ward 29, where I normally sleep."

I'm aware this is where she was a patient, a long stay ward, where Myra was also a patient. I can't imagine where she would have slept in this burnt out ward.

"I have a place for you, in the nurses' home."

She looks up at me.

"I won't have to leave?"

"You won't have to leave."

"It's a small but comfortable room overlooking the grounds."

She looks up, interested.

"My own wee room?"

"Yes."

"My own door, TV, and bed?"

"Right."

"Thank you."

"I'll take you there."

"I have things, in the ward."

"OK, I'll help."

She nods again.

"Can I ask you a few questions?" Jackie says. Lilias looks at me. "Just simple questions, nothing to cause you any trouble."

She nods once more.

Jackie asks her if she knew what was happening in the hospital, Professor Owen and Doctor Jamieson, what had happened to me, the vial with the SUX, etcetera.

She asks if she would have to go to court. Jackie nods.

"I can't leave here," she says.

Jackie looks at me. I know the look says we have nothing to take to court.

We walk Lilias back to ward 29. The door is lying open and the floor still has puddles from the firemen's hoses. The roof is partially destroyed, but a small part still exists. She walks to what would have been her bed. It's in the corner and is intact, albeit singed by the flames and damp from the water hosed over it during the fire. She had been sleeping on it the previous night. She goes to her locker beside her bed and pulls out a black bin bag presumably with her worldly possessions, a change of clothes she would wear under her habit. She also pulls out a small backpack. From her drawer she transfers her toiletries, some old photographs, and a pile of notebooks.

"When did you come here, Lilias?"

"Sister Lilias."

"Sorry, Sister Lilias. When?"

She hands me an old photograph of a child and a young woman.

"In 1911, I was ten years of age. This is my mother. She was here for a short time, in ward 49. She was a Magdalene lassie and was moved into the hospital when it opened, many lassies were. She was pregnant with me. When I was born she sneaked me out, but a lot of the children didn't get out, and they're in the cemetery as well. I was in the Barnhill Poorhouse until I came here too. I was a bad lassie. The Sisters looked after us. I worked in the farm and never left."

"Why not?"

"I was an inadequate, I couldn't cope outside."

I feel so sorry for her. Jackie helps her through the wreckage of the ward. I look down upon her bed, her locker, and think of her staying her for seventy years, a whole lifetime.

Jackie heads off and I walk her over to the nurses' home and the Rottweiler takes her by the arm. Men are not allowed in the female side. I see her walking alongside the Rottweiler along the corridor, the small figure against her bulk. I imagine her as a small child being removed from her mother for whatever reason. I wonder if her mother was a moral defective, as having a child out of wedlock, which was not uncommon in an area of military barracks, was called. She herself said she was a bad lassie.

I think about the hospital being built on the site of the Magdalene Institution providing continuity from one institution to the other, fallen women becoming moral defectives, medicalising their predicament. Where the Magdalene was about reforming them, making them god-fearing members of the community, the hospital treated their 'illness', both institutionalising them and making them unable to survive outwith these places. The children and the mothers were separated, many to die and be buried in the graveyard which transcended the two places, others to be sent to children's homes, some to be left in the hospital, never to leave, like Lilias.

I imagine my own mother walking along the same corridor in the hospital having seen me in the waiting room, taken there by my father.

'She can't look after you now, he said, 'she can't even look after herself. You're the reason she is in here, you know.'

I get back to my room and find her discharge letter. I go to the end of the conclusion.

I read it.

"'We have no alternative but to ensure the patient goes to God,' signed Doctor Donald Owen, thirteenth of April, nineteen sixty two.' This is my tenth birthday," I say. Then "L24."

L24, I wonder.

I go to the old map of the graveyard and follow the lines indicated presumably by the dates of interment. A being the first row, which I establish as female, males being B. A1 is the first female double grave, B, being the male rows, and on. I walk along the rows, spacing the letters out and I pass some indicators. There are few headstones, a couple of crosses, a few plaques on the ground, but mainly no headstones or anything to indicate where anyone was.

I count out "A, C, E, G, L." At L, I stop and look along the row. "L24," I say.

Given there were two women to a grave, I count along. "L1, L2, L3," until I find a single plaque, L14, which gives me a measurement. I walk on. "L16, 17, 18, 19, 20, 21, 22." Then I see a cross with 24 on it, nothing more than 24.

"There she is," I say.

I am standing at my mother's grave. I've no idea who she shares a grave with or whether she is on top or under the other occupant, but she is down there. Now I know where she is. I stand and look to the ground. I'm happy I found her grave, but I don't feel happy.

"I am sorry, Mum," I say, as if I really had something to do with her being there. Maybe I did, maybe he was right she killed herself because of me, the guilt. So, I'm sorry, if this was the case. I will return with some flowers.

I reach into my pocket and pull out the elephant Joan gave me. I want to leave something as a way to remember where she is, but also as a symbol of my determination to put a headstone up one day. The elephant will remain as a symbol of my respect and love for her until I do. I place it on the grave.

Then I move to Joan's grave, the ground still loose from the burial and our intervention. I pull out a trowel, the Bible, and her lock of hair.

I dig a small hole, around ten inches square into the ground, just enough to ensure the Bible is well covered. I open the front of it. I look at the lock of hair, dark and fresh. I think she was telling me she was young once, carefree, happy, until the Castle got her, just like my mother and the others. I place the lock of hair inside the Bible, put it into the hole, and cover it up.

I bow my head and move off.

I get back as Jackie phones. I get in first.

"And don't forget Reverend Jimmy. He knew it was going on, countersigned their deaths, he could have stopped it."

"Rooney, I've just spoken to my dad."

"Oh, aye." I'm waiting for it.

"We have nothing to convict them."

I kind of expected it.

"Oh aye, the establishment looks after its own," I say. "Put the evidence in a context of Lawyers, Doctors, Sheriffs, QCs, and no one will convict Professor Donald Owen, Physician Superintendent since the 60s."

"We have to let it go, Rooney. It's stopped for good."

"Thanks Jackie." I put the phone down.

I need to see Timpson. I see him at his home.

He talks first as always.

"My daughter."

"How is she?"

"Her blood levels are coming up and they are monitoring her heart. The consultant says she is an anorexic."

"She has Anorexia Nervosa."

"Aye, what should I do next?"

He is asking my advice, which is good, but if I give the wrong advice it'll come back on me, no doubt.

"She'll need treatment to deal with her illness."

"Illness?"

"Aye, it's an illness."

"An illness." I see he is thinking.

"She'll need treatment to gain weight and manage it."

"She just needs to eat."

"No, she needs specialist treatment, she can't just eat."

"And where can she get this... specialist treatment."

"Not in Glasgow or even in Scotland."

He thinks about this.

"Why did you want to see me?"

"First, to thank you for your help at the hospital the other day."

"No problem. Peter Galloway called me to say you were going to be topped."

"How'd he get your number?"

"Don't be stupit, Rooney. Anyway, I saw One Flew over the Cuckoo's Nest, I know what they do to people, fry their brains, I didn't want this for you."

"Thanks, what about Simmons? You said to Jackie you had information to make sure he never works in social work again."

"I told your wuman."

"She wouldn't tell me, said it was confidential."

"Oh, that shite."

"Tell me then."

He takes his time.

"He was taking money from the nursing homes, a wee cash bonus from the private nursing home owners for every patient he sent them, a right wee earner."

"She said there was no substantive evidence."

"No? Do you see the car he drives, do you think social work pays for that?"

"What, a Vauxhall Astra?"

"Don't be fucking daft, son. That is what he uses for work. He wouldn't bring in his export Ford Mustang GT to work or to take it into the schemes. It wouldn't last long there. And his Kelvindale pad, not many social workers can afford them."

"Bastard."

"Aye."

"You said you owe me now."

"I am obliged for your help with my daughter. What can I do for you?"

"Professor Owen, I want him… stopped."

"Killed?"

"Brought to justice."

"That's your wuman's job."

"No evidence."

"What about the others?"

"They did Owen's bidding."

"Jamieson did our bidding too."

"I know. I think he should be encouraged to… retire."

"I'll take care of it."

Now for Robin Crawford.

"The story," I say.

"Yes," he says.

"I wrote it up and... lost it."

"Lost it."

"Aye, but it's in my head."

"Things have changed at the hospital, Rooney."

"Sure have, Robin, even bigger story now."

I spend the rest of the afternoon with him recounting my whole experience at the Castle.

I talk to the group.

"I'm going to kill him, Rooney. Professor Owen," Peter says.

"Seems a good idea to me," Mairi says, "we need to get him, he can't get away with it."

"He won't. I'll deal with it," I say.

"You're a psychologist," Walter says.

"He has friends," John says.

I tell the group everything has changed. We can no longer meet. Our raison d'être is gone. The Castle has gone. I'll support them in any way I can in alternative settings.

CHAPTER 43

On the 8th of September, I move in with Jackie and things start to settle down. I feel our relationship is improving, healing. I try to get my head around the events of the last months. There are plans for a new community-based psychiatric hospital and a range of community-based residential resources and homes for ex-psychiatric patients of the hospital. The hospital managers have been included in a cross health social work group for new resources. Owen, Jamieson, and Stephenson are leading on this. They are still in control.

Donna and Archie, while not coming out to say I cannot continue the course and the placement was an abject failure, have asked me to take a break, to consider my future. There would be a meeting at the university to consider whether I can continue.

I start considering what I should do next. One morning over breakfast, Jackie, pouring over the papers, says, "Did you see this, Rooney?"

"What?"

"Mairi MacDougal's debut novel, *The Castle*."

"What?"

"There's a write up in the *Glasgow Herald*."

"Tell me."

She reads, "Mairi MacDougal, debut crime writer in collaboration with Robin Crawford, feature writer at the *Evening Times* has released a true crime drama called *The Castle*. It's bloody dynamite, Rooney. Did you have any part in this?"

"Key advisor. No, I had no part in it. I had no idea."

"It's been serialised in the *Evening Times*. They've repeated the first episode in today's *Herald*."

"Right."

She goes farther into the paper. "Right, it starts: 'My father, John MacDougal, was killed by a regime at a major Glasgow psychiatric hospital called The Castle.' It goes on: 'Over a period of over twenty years a systematic series of murders have occurred in the hospital…'"

"Jesus, how can she?"

"She can say what she likes, Rooney, freedom of…"

"Doesn't mean anyone will believe her. As you say, there's no evidence to convict any of them."

"Right, it continues, 'This is not the only blight on this major institution. Since its inception the Castle has been responsible for a number of scandals. It was built on the site of an old Magdalene institution, where many women and children were incarcerated, and many babies were separated from their mothers at birth and conveniently disappeared, to be found later in a mass grave in the hospital grounds. Evil practices continued in the hospital,' she says, and it goes on."

"I'll read it all, I'll have to."

"There's a note on the author, explaining her fight against mental illness and drug addiction. There's a picture of her, she's looking great."

I take the newspaper.

"She's looking well, true crime writing obviously agrees with her. What's this?"

"What?"

"It says she intends raising a civil case against the managers of the hospital for the unlawful killings of patients, which if successful will amount to many millions of pounds and may see the health board bankrupt. Individual civil cases will follow."

"I wonder who is funding this."

"Alby Timpson, look."

I read out the part which says Albert Timpson is providing financial support for the action, citing the need to bring the managers to book over practices at the hospital.

"Poacher come gamekeeper."

"He is also pouring money into a new specialist centre for eating disorders."

"Wow."

"Wait a minute. Jackie is now pointing into the middle of the introduction. There's a mention of you."

"Shit."

"It's complimentary. Read it."

I do. "'Sean Rooney, trainee psychologist, believed in us, the patients, and did his utmost to challenge the practices at Hillwood Hospital, to the risk of his health and his life.' Wow."

"There's more."

"That's enough, I suppose I should contact Mairi to congratulate her."

"There's a book launch on the twenty-second of September, you should go."

"*We* should go."

CHAPTER 44

Wednesday, 22nd of September, the night of The Castle book launch at John Smith's Bookshop at 57 St. Vincent Street, Glasgow.

I leave it until late to arrive. I want to be at the back, out of sight. I don't want to draw attention to myself. This is Mairi's night. I wait until I hear her speak before I make my way upstairs to the third floor. The place is packed. Robin has done a great job on marketing both the book and the event. I take a place by a pillar at the back, just out of sight of Mairi. She's busy welcoming everyone to the event. Any chance of anonymity, however, is lost when I hear her say:

"Tonight and my book, *The Castle*, would not have been possible without Sean Rooney." I see people looking around to try to see me. It's impossible to stay out of the limelight.

"Sean, if you are here, please take a bow?"

I can't hide, I move out into the middle aisle of the room at the back.

"Mr Sean Rooney." She starts to clap. They all get up and I get a standing ovation.

"Je-sus."

I raise my hand and disappear behind my pillar, but not before I catch sight of Donna and Archie, Robin Crawford, Alby Timpson, Walter in his wheelchair, and Gerry, John, and Peter, all sitting along the front row. I turn to see Jackie and Hubert to the right near the back; and then casting my eye across the room I see a slight figure, no longer in a nun's habit, but in a pretty dark blue suit, with a bright pink perm, Lilias.

"I could have called the book, *The Murder Group*," Mairi says. "The geneses of the book occurred when Sean Rooney formed a group of patients to investigate the suspicious deaths of patients at Hillwood Hospital."

I hope she doesn't say much about the group. I've managed to keep my head down and indeed out of the controversy surrounding the book and the group. But no, she goes for it.

"My father's death brought me into the group, his murder more like." There's a sudden hush, no one dares breathe. "He died, as others did, under suspicious circumstances, which will be explored in my civil case against the hospital management team."

Then, following a well-placed power pause, she says:

"I dedicate the book to my father, John MacDougal, Myra Higgins, Joan Trainor, Alex Barr, Helga Shultz, Oliver Turnbull, Elsie Murdoch, and all the patients, past and present, of Hillwood Hospital, The Castle."

She gets more applause.

"I'd like to give you a short recitation from the book." She takes a big breath. "They stalk the corridors at night, seeking victims, the ill, the vulnerable, the confused. Come to God, the world out there is not for you. It's harsh, cold, evil. You're safe here, but you are next to go, to a place where you will not survive. Come with me. He puts out his hand. I'll take you to the better place, the safer place, a place you will never be threatened with discharge again, where you will be safe in the loving arms of God."

"Are you saying people were murdered in Hillwood, Mairi?"

She looks around for the source of the voice. I see him. He's right at the end of the front row of seats, right at the end.

"Sorry?"

"I'm asking if you think people were murdered at Hillwood, this is a very serious accusation."

She sees him this time.

"Can I please say if people ask a question they identify themselves?"

"William Hood, journalist, BBC Scotland."

Shit, this is going national.

"Thank you," she says. "Yes, I am saying that. This will be explored in my upcoming civil case against the people concerned."

"The people you think are concerned?"

"The people I know it concerns."

"So it is all conjecture, very incriminating and damaging conjecture."

"I believe it to be true and I am confident this will be proved in court."

"And if it isn't, your book will be discredited and you will be open to serious damages."

Her voice drops in volume.

"I understand this."

This intervention has clearly taken the wind out of her sail.

"Until you can prove this, this is merely fiction."

"Aye, fiction; all names are fictionalised, with a basis of fact, which is what I am trying to say in the book."

By this time, people are beginning to get up to move away.

"It happened to me." They all turn to look towards me once more.

"Eh, sorry, Mr Rooney." The hack turns my way.

"They tried to kill me."

"Are you in the book and will you be drawn into the civil case?"

I look to Mairi.

"Yes, he's in the book."

"Fictionalised?"

"Fictionalised."

"And who will fund this court case? It could be a very expensive exercise."

"The book."

"The book, I very much doubt it. Are you expecting it to be a best seller?"

"Aye."

"And if it's not?"

There's a communal holding of breath as everyone waits for a reply.

"Then I will meet the expenses of the court case." Though still in his seat, Alby Timpson's voice cuts right through the quiet of the room. Then he gets up and his shoulders almost shut out the light.

"Why, Mr Timpson?"

"Why?"

"Yes, why, you are a known—"

"Businessman."

"Businessman in the East End. Why would you want to fund a court case which could cost you many thousands of pounds, maybe hundreds of thousands of pounds?"

"Because I don't like East End folk being killed in my patch."

I see from Hood's face this is a gem of a story. East End gang boss funds court case against doctors agedly killing patients in large mental hospital. Wow!

Next day, Thursday 23rd of September, presented by Mary Marquis, Hood's story is chronicled on BBC's Reporting Scotland, and followed up substantively on an Agenda programme, presented by George Reid. On the same day, the Robin Crawford story hits the newsstands. Consequently, The Castle flies off the shelves.

Concurrently, Mairi's civil case against the managers of Hillwood Hospital has its initial hearing in Glasgow High Court. I find a seat in the public gallery. Timpson enlists an eminent QC, Tony Grant, to take the case forward.

The arguments are to be put by Grant, answers by Alexander Glasgow, QC. The High Court judge will decide whether there is a case to answer.

"This is a case," Grant says, "against Greater Glasgow Health Board, alleging it failed to protect vulnerable patients at Hillwood Hospital who subsequently died in suspicious circumstances. I will present the arguments put forward by our honourable friends."

He doesn't get the chance. The judge says, "I have read the initial arguments and answers and have decided there is no case to answer. There is no substantive reason to bring the case before this court."

"What," Mairi says, then asks Grant, "Are they dropping it?"

"My Lord, can I confirm there is no case to answer?"

"I can confirm this, Mr Grant."

"My Lord…"

"You know there needs to be substantive evidence with which to proceed."

"We have—"

"There is nothing substantive, Mr Grant."

The case is about to go south. I turn to Timpson and his face is fit to burst.

Then, "I would like to say something." The voice is weak but it is heard through the court room.

The Judge looks over his glasses to the small figure which has now taken to her feet. It is Lilias, back in her habit.

"Excuse me, madam, all comments have to be made using usual

court protocol and from the witness box. Do you have something important to say you think will have a bearing on this case?"

"Yes, sir."

The judge shakes his head.

"Bring her down."

A court official is sent to the gallery to escort Lilias down into the witness box.

"Now, madam, tell me what you wanted to say. Being mindful it needs to be important enough to halt these very important proceedings."

"I was raped by the Professor, the heid doctor."

The judge takes a breath.

"Madam, this is not a criminal court and this is not a criminal matter. You need to take this up with the police."

"My Lord," she says, as forcibly as her gentle voice can muster. "You need to listen to me, because, like the other cases Miss MacDougal is talking about, I was about to be killed by him too, like he killed Myra Higgins."

"Mrs—"

"Sorry, your honour, he said he was God, he is madder than anyone up there. He killed people saying it would be better for them to be with God. He used the women too, Myra, Joan, me, others, saying we were fallen women, like Magdalene, and by taking us, using us, he would not only put the fear of God, but God himself, into us."

I look at the judge, he is stony faced, and there is a deathly silence throughout the court room.

"And others knew about him, doctors, nurses—"

"Fine, please, Ms—"

"Sister Lilias."

"Sister Lilias."

"And I am one of the nurses," comes from the gallery.

I look up to see Betty Boop, then to the judge who is shaking his head. "Bring her down," he says. Boop squeezes in beside Lilias in the witness box. "Yes, madam, what do you have to say?"

Betty Boop pulls out a hypodermic. "In this, my lord, are the drugs they were about to put into Mr Rooney's arm to kill him."

There's a powerful silence as the judge gathers his thoughts. Then he calls the two QCs to the bench. Then, after a minute or so, he says:

"I believe there is sufficient reason to bring this case to court, but I caution all present that this case, albeit lacking sufficient evidence to pursue criminal proceedings against individuals, i.e. not having the standard of proof, i.e. beyond reasonable doubt, may have the standard of proof necessary in this case judged on the balance of probabilities. That is what this court will determine. That is all."

And with this the initial hearing is over, the nurse and the nun's interventions have saved the day for Mairi's case.

I wait outside for them to leave the court.

"Hello, Lilias."

"Sister Lilias, Mr Rooney."

"Right, Sister Lilias."

"Hello, Betty—"

"Jane Baird, RMN."

"Jane," I say, sheepishly.

I know intuitively their evidence will be discredited, Lilias's based on her being a mentally ill patient, 'incapable,' they'll say; Jane's based on inability to prove the SUX in the hyperdemic was intended for me. Their word against three powerful clinicians: the Three Amigos, aka the Father, the Son, and the Holy Ghost.

I am really worried about Lilias. She is extremely vulnerable, and now, I also believe, extremely at risk.

She explains she's now living in a nursing home in Easterhouse and 'it's very nice'. She introduces me to her carer, Michael, who would take her back in his car. I say I'd like to visit her there. She says she would like this too.

She tells me she'd received a visit from Professor Owen, who said he's still her doctor. He wanted to give her new tablets. She refused and called the care staff who questioned Owen, saying he should go through the care staff to introduce new medicines.

I call Timpson.

Later this day, Professor Owen leaves Duke Street Hospital. He walks along towards where his car is parked in Westercraigs, his usual parking place. A man in a long coat walks towards him, making him step onto the road, just as a motorcyclist slows to within inches of him. He hears two pops and feels two thumps on his chest as the bullets enter his body at close range. He slides down to the pavement.

The men look down on him to determine he is dead before walking away.

The news gets out about Owen. It quickly becomes a cold case. No one has seen anything and the men concerned cannot be identified or found. Mairi drops the civil case and Timpson meets the expenses. Her book continues to sell, however. I meet with the group in the Horseshoe Bar. They have had quite a transformation. Mairi has developed quite a profile as a true crime writer. She has chronicled Timpson's life in a new book, *The East End Godfather*, something Timpson himself likes. Gerry becomes a folk singer singing Dylan covers and sings regular in the Scotia Bar. John has become a forensic adviser, after Jackie gets him a job in a new forensic team at the Police HQ, Pitt Street. He donates his meteorite to the Hunterian Museum. Walter becomes an authority of trees at Glasgow University having a welcome philosophical approach, a big favourite of the students. I have no doubt had Alex survived he would have become an authority on gang culture. Peter becomes a counsellor for Combat Stress for service men suffering from post-traumatic stress disorder and moves to Helensburgh.

The Chaplain has been transferred to Greyfriars Kirk in Edinburgh, where he is re-designated a historian. It transpires he had been a kindly man who was exploited by Professor Owen, almost to defer responsibility to him as God's servant, almost giving him credence for his acts against the hospital patients. Stephenson is struck off the nursing register for abuse against patients in his care and becomes a car salesman in Dumbarton. Bill Simmons is sacked by Strathclyde Regional Council Social Work Department and moves to Costa Crime as an advisor to crime lords there. Alby Timpson develops a persona of doing good while doing bad around the East End, until he is shot in his bar by a rival crime lord. His daughter survives her eating disorder and goes on to work as a social worker in the East End. Doctor Jamieson is investigated by the BMA who finds him too old to practice and he's developing dementia himself. He is forcibly retired and moves to Arran where he dies within months of arriving. Agnes never works for the Health Board again and becomes a supervisor in Marks and Spencer.

Sister Lilias lives her last few years happily in the Easterhouse nursing home, where she becomes something of a celebrity, wandering around the local shopping centre talking to children and blessing people.

Jane Baird, aka Betty Boop, is promoted and eventually becomes nurse manager at the new community-based psychiatric hospital, which replaces Hillwood Hospital.

I meet Jackie in the Horseshoe Bar.

"And what about you, Rooney?" Jackie brings back drinks, Guinness for me, lager for her, to the table I secure for us.

"Well, I've to be given another chance."

I explain the university received a letter from Mairi, John, Walter, Gerry, Peter, and Sister Lilias, explaining I had given them a new life. I had saved them from abuse and possibly death in the toxic environment of Hillwood Hospital. I also receive a commendation from Greater Glasgow Health Board, which secures me a placement at Gartnavel Hospital where I'll see out my studies and become a fully qualified clinical psychologist.

"I know this stuff, Rooney, but are you good?"

"I am, Jackie, and being honest all of the stuff coming out about my mother was a catharsis and my mental health has improved."

"Aided by you embarking on the controlled drinking programme at my advice, Rooney."

I look at my Guinness, the one and only drink I have of an evening.

"Aye, and did this help us, Jackie?"

I don't need an answer. Since we moved in together things are good between us. We have worked through our problems and she had forgiven me for Agnes on the basis of my failed mental health at the time.

"And what about you, Jackie?"

I thought I'd ask, but I know all about her. She had been appointed Detective Chief Inspector following her work with the mob in Glasgow. Timpson assisted her in securing some convictions in the West End of Glasgow, which partly, I suppose led to his untimely death.

"The glass ceiling continues to resist me, Rooney, but one day I'll shatter it and get the big job."

"I hope you do, darling." We chink glasses. "If you need any help in catching villains—"

"I'll keep you in mind, Rooney."

END

The Sean Rooney Psychosleuth series

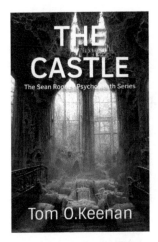

Original paperback £9.99
ISBN 9780857162427
eBook 9780857162434

Original paperback £8.99
ISBN 9780857161956
eBook 9780857161963

Original paperback £8.99
ISBN 9780857161970
Ebook 9780857161987

Original paperback £8.99
ISBN 9780857161994
Ebook 9780857162007

ABOUT THE AUTHOR

Born and raised in Hamilton, Tom O. Keenan now resides in Morar in the North West Highlands of Scotland. His experience as an independent social worker in the mental health field underpins much of his writing.

The Father, the first book written by Tom in his crime thriller series was shortlisted for the ***CWA Debut Dagger Award*** in 2014.

www.tom-odgen-keenan.com